THE HALFADAY CREEK SERIES BY
JAMES B. HENDRYX

*Skullduggery on Halfaday Creek*
*The Saga of Halfaday Creek*
*Badmen on Halfaday Creek*
*Adventures on Halfaday Creek*
*Hell's-a-Poppin' on Halfaday Creek*

Visit www.jamesbhendryx.com for more information on
forthcoming installments in the Halfaday Creek
uniform matching series.

HELL'S-A-POPPIN' ON HALFADAY CREEK

*James B Hendryx*

# HELL'S-A-POPPIN'
# ON HALFADAY
# CREEK

## JAMES B. HENDRYX

ILLUSTRATIONS BY
PETE KUHLHOFF

ALTUS PRESS • 2014

© 2013 Altus Press • First Edition—2014

EDITED AND DESIGNED BY
Matthew Moring

SERIES EXECUTIVE CONSULTANT
Richard Hall

PUBLISHING HISTORY
"Black John Declines a Reward" originally appeared in the April 10, 1943 issue of *Short Stories* magazine (vol. 183, no. 1). Reprinted by arrangement with the Estate of James B. Hendryx.

"Constable Buck Counts Heads" originally appeared in the January 25, 1949 issue of *Short Stories* magazine (vol. 207, no. 2). Reprinted by arrangement with the Estate of James B. Hendryx.

"Left Handed Justice" originally appeared in the January, 1950 issue of *Short Stories* magazine (vol. 209, no. 1). Reprinted by arrangement with the Estate of James B. Hendryx.

"Poison on Halfaday" originally appeared in the November 10, 1931 issue of *Short Stories* magazine (vol. 137, no. 2). Reprinted by arrangement with the Estate of James B. Hendryx.

"The Gambler" originally appeared in the December 10, 1943 issue of *Short Stories* magazine (vol. 185, no. 5). Reprinted by arrangement with the Estate of James B. Hendryx.

"Halfaday Evidence, Package Style" originally appeared in the Februay, 1953 issue of *Short Stories* magazine (vol. 215, no. 2). Reprinted by arrangement with the Estate of James B. Hendryx.

"Target Practice on Halfaday" originally appeared in the July 31, 1955 issue of the *Boston Sunday Globe* magazine. Reprinted by arrangement with the Estate of James B. Hendryx.

"Trial and Error" originally appeared in the January 10, 1934 issue of *Short Stories* magazine (vol. 146, no. 1). Reprinted by arrangement with the Estate of James B. Hendryx.

THANKS TO
Everard P. Digges LaTouche, Robert Loomis, Richard Moore, Rick Ollerman, Cynthia Whyte, & the Leelanau Historical Society

# TABLE OF CONTENTS

# BLACK JOHN
## DECLINES A REWARD

**CORPORAL DOWNEY OF** the Mounted looked up from the papers that littered his desk as Black John Smith sauntered into the room at detachment headquarters in Dawson, dropped into a chair and proceeded to fill his pipe.

"Hello, John! Didn't know you were in town. Fact is, I figured on makin' a trip to Halfaday Crick to sort of look things over."

"You know yere always welcome up there, Downey. But it looks like, if a man wanted to look over a crick, there's a lot of 'em closter than Halfaday."

"Any strangers showed up there lately?"

"'Lately', bein' what you might say a relative term, I jest couldn't say, off hand. Is there some specific individual you've got in mind—er was you jest inquirin' fer the census?"

"There's a bird supposed to be headin' for the Yukon, if he ain't here already, that the American police want plenty bad— robbed an express car back in New York State."

"New York, eh? Cripes, it looks like he run a hell of a ways to get away from what couldn't be deemed no more'n a nominal prank. It would have be'n cheaper to hire a lawyer."

"It would take a lot of lawyers to get him out of this jam. He killed the express messenger and the conductor of the train and wounded a brakeman. The brakeman furnished his description. He's about thirty—tall, smooth face, blond hair, left-handed, and lightning fast with a gun—seems well educated, talks like a gentleman."

"H-u-m. Ignorin' the murder angle, was the venture a success—in a mercenary way?"

"That all depends on the luck he has in getting rid of what he got. This consisted of a shipment from the U. S. printing shop in Washington of a hundred thousand dollars in five, ten, and twenty dollar notes to the Farmers' & Merchants' Bank in Olean, New York. This is a new bank that had never issued any notes before. They were unsigned, of course, and are not legal tender until signed by the president and the cashier of this bank."

"Ondoubtless sech party as you've described would stoop to pass on legal tender if he thought he could git away with it."

"He's managed to pass some of it, all right. Accordin' to our information he's left a trail of them bills that reaches from New York to Seattle. Of course, all banks have been notified, and the notes are spotted the minute they show up—but he passes 'em in stores after signin' 'em himself with whatever names pops into his head."

Black John blew a cloud of smoke from his lungs as he slowly wagged his head. "Don't it beat hell what lengths of dishonesty a man will go to, onct he gits started? It's a sad commentary on the onstability of the human soul. Is this here left-handed gent the only exponent of onrighteousness that's botherin' you at the nonce—as a poet would say when he was goin' good?"

"He's the main one—but there's plenty of others. There's another U. S. robber—took a small town bank somewhere in North Dakota for fifty thousand in small bills they'd got in for the farmers to pay off harvest hands with.

"It seems that he stopped in at the post office and grabbed off a pad of money order blanks, too."

BLACK JOHN grinned. "Sort of a greedy cuss, wasn't he? Them North Dakota folks ort to be glad he left 'em their town."

"He's supposed to have hit for the Yukon, too," Downey said, sourly. "I wish to God some of these U. S. crooks would hit the

other way once in a while! Why the hell can't they try Mexico, or South America? We've got troubles enough of our own."

Black John grinned. "The gold rush has given ondue an' highly erroneous publicity to our neck of the woods. Chechakos is pilin' in on us by the thousands, an' the fact that one chechako looks an' acts about like another gives these here malfeasors a swell chanct to merge their identity with the masses. Besides, Mexico ain't so good. I rec'lect onct when I took up a temporary residence south of the Rio Grande an' my ignorance of Spanish made my identity stick out like a sore thumb."

Downey grinned. "Did they nab you?"

"Who?"

"Why—the Mexican police."

"It ain't no crime, even in Mexico, not to talk Spanish. But to change the subject before it gits technical, did this other malefactor have any particular description? Er was he jest a run of the mill bank robber?"

"We didn't get much of a description of him except that he's tall an' wore a black mask over his face. He shot the cashier of the bank and the only ones that saw him were the postmaster, and a few citizens of the town who heard the shot an' saw him run out of the bank carrying the money in a flour sack, and jump onto his horse an' ride hell for leather out of town."

"H-u-m. He's prob'ly had time to git shet of his horse, by now. An' it might have occurred to him to discard his black mask an' the flour sack, too."

"Chances are, we'll never pick that one up, unless he tries to cash some money orders," Downey said. "We haven't got enough to go on—and he could pass them small bills anywhere. It's the other one I'm interested in. Accordin' to our information he's a damn bad actor—a mighty slick article. His real name is Joseph Allen, but he's got a string of aliases as long as his record of hold-ups and robberies. The rewards for his arrest totals somewheres around twenty thousand dollars.

"Of course, we don't go in for rewards—but there's a nice piece of change in it for anyone that could locate him. What I'm afraid of is that he'll pull off some robbery here in the Yukon. I've notified the bank, and all the saloons an' stores to be on the lookout for them Farmers' an' Merchants' banknotes, in case he'd try to pass any of 'em here. He's a damn slick crook, an' we don't want him operatin' around here."

"The other one's prob'ly slicker," Black John opined. "I'd sooner have fifty thousan' in good passable bills than a hundred thousan' in phoney ones."

"Guess you're right at that," Downey grinned. "But you haven't answered my question—are there any strangers on Halfaday?"

"Not that I know of, but I've be'n away fer a couple of weeks—swung around through the hills to look at a crick where a Siwash claimed he seen some colors. He lied. I'm hittin' back in the mornin', an' if there's any strangers there, an' I deem it necessary, I'll slip you the word. I shore as hell wouldn't like to see Cush stuck with none of them phoney bills—he's got troubles enough makin' both ends meet, as it is."

Downey shot the big man a glance. "Huh—I guess Cush don't need to worry much—what with his bank balance here in Dawson, an' what he's got in that safe of his. What do you mean, he's got trouble makin' both ends meet?"

Black John turned in the doorway and grinned broadly. "So long, Downey. I was referrin' to his rheumatism—he can't bend over to lace his shoes."

## II

EARLY ONE EVENING, some ten days later, Black John stepped into the barroom of Cushing's Fort, the combined trading post and saloon that served the little community of outlawed men that had sprung up on Halfaday Creek, close against the Yukon-Alaska border, crossed the floor, and elevated a foot to the battered brass rail as the somber faced proprietor shoved the square-framed steel spectacles from nose to forehead, deliberately folded the well thumbed copy of the *Police Gazette* and placed it on the back bar from which he lifted a bottle, two glasses and a leather dice box.

Without a word, Black John picked up the box, shook it, and cast the five dice onto the bar. "Three fives," he announced. "I'll leave 'em in one."

Cush gathered the cubes into the box and rolled them out. "Horse on me," he admitted, eyeing the three deuces, and shook again. "An' there's three sixes right back at you."

Black John rolled out four fours, poured his drink, and shoved the bottle toward Cush.

"What I claim," said the somber one, as he filled his glass, "take it with this here Jim Corbett an' Bob Fitzimmons, an' all the rest of them fighters—there ain't a damn one of 'em could lick old John L."

"Corbett done it," Black John reminded.

"Yeah, but you can't tell me it wasn't a put up job. Cripes, didn't Sullivan lick Charlie Mitchell, an' Jake Kilrain, an' all the rest of them real fighters? It don't stand to reason no bank clerk could lick him. Gentleman Jim, they call him! Now, ain't that a hell of a name fer a prize fighter? By God, old John L wasn't no gentleman, any ways you look at him. He was a fighter!"

"Shore he was," Black John agreed. "But you've got to re-member, Cush, John L was an old man, as fighters goes, when Corbett licked him. A man can't keep on fightin' forever."

"I wouldn't give a damn if John L was a hundred, there couldn't no damn gentleman lick him! He come in my saloon one time, down to Cincinnati—an' I know."

"Hell, I've come in your saloon a thousan' times right here on Halfaday, but that ain't sayin' I can lick the world. From what I've be'n able to gather, an' occasional gentleman strung along here an' there wouldn't be no discredit to the prize fightin' profession, at that."

"John L done his fightin' fair an' square, an' most of it bare fisted. What's this here solar complexion, they claim Corbett knocked him out with?"

Black John grinned. "Solar complexion ain't nothin' but sun-tan. It was solar plexus Corbett used—solar bein' derived from the Latin fer sun, an' plexus meanin'—er—a stroke, er some sech matter. But don't try to make me believe you was inter-ested in the prize fighters in that paper. I noticed it was open to a whole page of buxom lookin' gals that run mostly to legs."

"If they print them pitchers a man would be a damn fool not to look at 'em. I was lookin' at Corbett's pitcher, an' turned the page jest before you come in."

"Prob'ly quite a while before—but we'll let that pass. Any news? Any doubtful characters showed up on the crick while I've be'n gone?"

"Couple of fellas drifted in. There ain't nothin' doubtful about 'em. They both claimed their name was John Smith—till I made 'em drag another one out of the name can. One draw'd Jubal Sherman, an' the other one got William T. Early."

"So the John Smiths is comin' in droves now, eh?"

"They didn't come in no drove. They come separate. Fer's I know they ain't even saw one another. One of 'em's in Whiskey Bill's shack, up that feeder, an' the other one's in that there shack where Benedick Hale lived that time."

"Anything distinctive about 'em?"

"I didn't smell nothin'. What difference would it make if they did stink?"

"I was referrin' to physical characteristics—not to an odor," Black John said.

"You mean, what did they look like?"

"Yeah—that's the thought I strove to put acrost the bar."

"If a man would say what he means someone could know what he was talkin' about. One of 'em's what you could say, tall—an' so's the other. One of 'em's left handed an' got light colored hair an' whiskers. The other one's hair is brown-like an' so's his whiskers. Neither one of 'em's pack had no heft of dust in it, an' neither one of 'em deposited no dust er bills in the safe. Both of 'em asked if we wasn't all outlaws, up here, an' how fere is it to the line. The brown whiskered one is a clumsy cuss, but he seems to be the smartest. He asked where was you at, an' I told him you was out in the hills but wouldn't be gone no hell of a while. But if I was you I wouldn't have no truck with him. He's nothin' but a damn crook, er he wouldn't be claimin' his name was John Smith."

"What do you mean!" Black John scowled. "That's my name, ain't it?"

"I never seen it on no birth certificate," Cush replied. "This here brown whiskered one that's up to Whiskey Bill's shack, he claimed he'd be back an' have a talk with you." He paused and glanced toward the doorway, "an' damn if here he ain't, right now!"

A man stepped into the room and advanced to the bar. He was a tall man with clear blue eyes and dark brown hair and beard. The legs of a pair of new overalls were tucked into his pacs, and he wore a red and black checked shirt open at the throat. Black John's brow puckered into a slight frown as his glance centered on the shirt. The man smiled as he elevated his foot to the brass rail, showing well kept teeth behind the dark beard.

"You'd be Black John Smith, eh?" he said.

Black John nodded. "I would."

"According to the name can, I'm Jubal Sherman."

"Glad to know you, Jube."

"Heard about you in White Horse—how you're king of a bunch of outlaws, up here. Drink up an' have one on me. Got quite a set-up here."

"Not bad," Black John replied, swallowing his liquor and refilling his glass.

"I kind of figured, from what I heard in White Horse that Halfaday Crick would be a good place to kind of hole up for a while—give a man a chance to sort of look around a little."

"Help yourself. The sights hereabouts ain't nothin' astoundin'. We're a quiet industrious folk whose tastes runs mostly to solitude. By day we work our claims, an' in the evenin's we're wont to seek surcease from our hum-drum existence with a little stud."

The man grinned and winked. "Just a hard working bunch of miners, eh? Not an outlaw among you, I suppose?"

"Well, I wouldn't go so far as to say that. It might be that somewhere in their past some of the boys might have be'n outlawed here or there. What a man done before he come to Halfaday ain't no one's business but his own. After he gits here, though, he's got his choice of abidin' by our code of ethics which includes refrainin' from committin' all forms of murder, larceny, claim jumpin', an' all other acts that would come under our skullduggery law, sech as cheatin' at cards, an' sellin' hooch to Siwashes—er gittin' hung. Some has chose one way—an' some the other. The ones that chose right can be seen up an' down the crick. Them that chose wrong can only be got at by diggin'. Any crime committed on the crick might fetch in the police, an' that would make it mean fer all of us."

"I see. But that isn't saying you wouldn't welcome a little outside talent?" Drawing a wallet from his pocket the man clumsily drew a bill from it, tossed it onto the bar, and downed his liquor. "Fill 'em up again," he ordered. "Take me—my specialty is banks and express jobs. It got a little hot for me down in the States," he added with a grin, "so I came north to cool off."

"Quite a lot of folks has got cooled off on Halfaday," Black John observed, dryly. "Here comes some of the boys. We'll be startin' a game of stud. If you'd care to set in, yer welcome."

The game progressed with Sherman handling the cards and chips rather clumsily.

After an hour or so Black John laid out a hand and stepped to the bar for a drink, just as a stranger entered, crossed the floor, and ranged himself beside him. "The ticket I draw'd out of the can there says I'm William T. Early," the man grinned. "Good idee—that name can."

The big man replied, noting that the other was a tall man with blond hair and beard. "Yeah, keeps the crick from gittin' all clogged up with John Smiths."

"I s'pose you're this here Black John I've be'n hearin' about?"

"In person."

"What'll you have? I'm buyin' a little drink."

Black John contemplated the row of variously labeled bottles on the back bar. "Guess I'll take whiskey, seem' all them bottles is filled out of the same barrel. What you goin' to have?"

"I was goin' to call fer some of that there coneyac. But if it's all whiskey, I'll take some, too."

Black John poured his drink and shoved the bottle toward the other who grasped with his left hand and deftly filled his glass. He extracted a wallet from the left pocket of his trousers and tossed a bill onto the bar. It was a new bill, and Black John noted that it bore the superscription of the Farmers' & Merchants' Bank, of Olean, New York.

They drank, and the man glanced toward the card table. "Got room fer another player?" he asked.

"Oh, shore. The more the merrier, as the sayin' goes."

As the man took his seat his glance met that of Sherman who was seated opposite him. "Oh—hello! You here, too? Hell, if I'd know'd down to White Horse where you was headin' we could of come up together."

"That's right," the other grinned. "But how in the devil could I know you were heading for Halfaday?"

"That's right. Well, here's hopin' you git that three hundred back I took off'n you shootin' craps in White Horse—but if it's just the same to you, git it off'n these boys—not me."

"Okay," the other grinned. "I don't care where it comes from."

Both strangers lost steadily. The man, Sherman, drank steadily, too. And when the game broke up shortly after midnight both were cleaned out, but good naturedly vowed vengeance. A few drinks were had and Sherman quite drunk, left the saloon with a quart bottle in each coat pocket. At the doorway he turned and grinned tipsily. "You boys took me tonight—but there's plenty more where that come from. I'll be back."

AFTER THE others had departed for their claims, the blond, left-handed man turned to Black John. "I've got the damnedest luck," he said. "I was headin' fer Dawson, but a little ways out of White Horse I goes into the cabin of the steamboat an' there was a kind of a board like hangin' on the wall with papers tacked on it with pitchers and descriptions of different crooks that was wanted here an' there in Canady an' the States. I was kinda lookin' 'em over, like a fella will, an' I seen how one of them there descriptions would fit me to a T. Yes, sir, some guy name of Joseph Allen, with a long string of aliases, and a long string of robberies an' a few murders throw'd in. He was wanted so bad that there was eighteen, twenty thousan' in rewards posted fer him, dead er alive. But mostly fer an express robbery where he knocked off a agent an' a conductor. This guy was even left handed like me. The photograft of him was took smooth-faced. But I seen where it would look jest like me if my whiskers was shaved off. I heard about Halfaday Crick back in White Horse, an' bein' as I didn't dast to go on to Dawson, I got off the boat at Selkirk an' come up here. It would be jest like some cop, er someone to pinch me, er knock me off fer them rewards."

"Too bad, Bill," grinned Black John. "It would be hell to have to pay fer another man's crimes."

"It's tough luck that this damn cuss should look like me."

"That's right. But, at that, it hadn't ort to be so hard fer a man to prove his identity."

"Oh, I could prove it, all right—give me time. But the hell of it is, I don't dast to. You see, I'm wanted myself. I had to shoot a guy, an' they might call it murder."

"Yeah. That's a kind of a habit the police has got. But it looks like you ain't got no hell of a lot of worryin' to do. What difference would it make which job you got hung fer?"

"But hell—I don't intend to git hung at all!"

"That's a good intention—if you can live up to it."

"Sure—that's why I come to Halfaday. I heard how you was all outlaws, up here. Well, so long. I'll be gittin' back to the shack. Be back tomorrow night with a fresh set of money. My luck's due to change."

As the door closed behind the man Old Cush wagged his head. "Don't it beat hell what a jam these damn chechakos kin git into? This here cuss, he's likely to git hung fer somethin' someone else done, an' he don't dast to claim he's him, er he'd prob'ly git hung on his own account."

"Yeah. When a man departs from the ways of rectitude he's got a devious course to steer on an uncharted sea."

"I don't see no call to get off no sermon on me. Not when I know damn well yer figgerin' on slippin' into the bresh the first thing in the mornin' an' layin' there till this bird goes to his cache fer that fresh set of money he was talkin' about."

"Yer wrong, Cush. Fact is, I ain't even, interested in his cache. Why the hell should I lay in the bresh to locate a cache that's full of phoney money?"

"Phoney money! What do you mean—phoney?"

The big man grinned. "How many of them new bills did he pass on you?"

Cush pawed over the cash in the till and selected a small sheaf of the new banknotes. "What with the drinks, an' three, four stacks of chips he bought, they run up to a hundred an' thirty dollars. But what's wrong with them bills?" he asked, holding one of them to the light. "They don't look phoney to me."

"They didn't to quite a few folks strung along from New York to Seattle, either. But when they took 'em to the bank they found out different. Them bank notes was printed by the U. S. Govern-ment in Washington, an' shipped to this bank—but they never got there. This left handed, blond gent grabbed 'em off an express car, after shootin' the agent an' the train conductor. They ain't worth no more'n the paper an' ink till they're signed by the president an' cashier of the bank."

"But these ones is signed," Cush declared, extending a note. "You kin see the names yerself."

"That's right," Black John grinned. "Signed by the bird that passed 'em. It don't take no hell of an expert to see that them two signatures is in the same hand-writin'."

As Cush examined the notes the scowl deepened on his brow. "Guess that's right," he admitted. "But how come you know so much about him?"

"I swung down by Dawson while I was gone, an' Downey told me."

"You mean he's the same guy this paper he seen on the steamboat told about—about the rewards, an' all?"

"Shore he is."

"Why—the damn crook! Lyin' about it bein' some other fella—an' then passin' them phoney bills on me! When he shows up here tomorrow night I'll split a bung-starter over his head if he don't make them bills good! But say, John—ain't that some kind of skullduggery?"

Black John grinned. "If we begun hangin' folks fer lyin' it would establish a bad precedent, besides depopulatin' the crick."

"But how about shovin' phoney bills—by God, that ort to be hangable!"

"Oh shore. We could overlook the lyin' an' hang him fer that, all right."

"By cripes, that's jest what we'll do! An' we kin cash the corpse in fer that reward money! Eighteen, twenty thousan' he claimed the paper said. I kin take my hundred an' thirty dollars out, an' we kin split the balance between us."

Black John's grin widened. "It don't seem ethical, somehow, to hang a man fer a reward."

"But cripes, John—neither it ain't thrifty to leave no eighteen, twenty thousan' dollar corpses lay around in a graveyard!"

"Yeah, a man ort to plug all them economic leaks. We better jest go ahead an' let our conscience be our guide."

"Huh," grunted Cush, "if we done that there ain't no tellin' where we'd end up at."

"How's yer meat holdin' out? Mine's gittin' a might high. Guess I'll jest swing around in the mornin' an' see if I can't knock over a moose. If Bill Early shows up here before I do, lay off him with yer bung-starter till I git back."

## III

**WITH AN AMPLE** lunch in his packsack Black John headed up the creek shortly before daylight the following morning. Dawn was tinting the eastern sky as he paused on the rim of the little valley to glance down on the cabin occupied by Early. As he stood there the door opened and the man stepped out, glanced sharply about him, and walked hurriedly to a gravel dump beside a dilapidated sluice, dropped to his knees, and clawing away the gravel, drew out a compact package and swiftly transferred something to his pocket, after which he covered the package with gravel again, and returned to the cabin.

Black John passed on with a grin. "Figgered on goin' to his cache before anyone else was stirrin'. Too damn bad there ain't nothin' but phoney bills in it. I s'pose he'll sign up a fresh batch fer tonight's game. It's Sherman's cache I'm interested in. He won't be stirrin' around so early, the way he was lit up, last night."

Turning up a small feeder Black John slipped into a niche in the rim rocks that gave a clear view of Whiskey Bill's shack and the workings of the abandoned claim. "Jube's prob'ly dead to the world yet," he muttered. "This might be a wild goose chase, but I've got the hunch that he's this North Dakota lad—an' if he is, it ain't goin' to be amiss to locate that fifty thousan' in small bills."

It was two hours later before Sherman stepped from the cabin, water pail in hand. He stood for several moments eyeing the creek that burbled past. Turning into the cabin he reappeared with a bottle in his hand. Stepping to the creek, he stooped, set the bottle on the ground, dipped the pail into the water, and raising it to his lips, drank copiously. Setting the pail beside the bottle, he stripped off his clothing, and stepping into the creek, lay down and wallowed about in the ice-cold water. Then he stepped out onto the bank, drew the cork from the bottle and took a good long pull at it. For several moments he stood rigid, his lips pressed tightly together.

"By God, it stuck!" Black John grinned, as the man reached for his clothing. "Whatever weaknesses Jube's got shore as hell ain't in his stummick. An' it took a lot of nerve to waller around in that cold water, too."

The man dressed himself and standing there, methodically went through his pockets. Then he stood and carefully scrutinized the little valley, turning this way and that until apparently satisfied. Then he walked to the rim-wall, lifted out a loose rock fragment, and reaching in, drew forth something which he transferred to his pocket. Replacing the fragment, he returned to the cabin, picked up an axe, chopped a few sticks of firewood, and carried them inside.

As smoke issued from the stovepipe, Black John slipped hurriedly down the side of the steep rim-wall after satisfying himself that the single window offered no view of the cache. Hastily removing the rock fragment Black John thrust his arm into the fissure and withdrew a compact packet—of brand new unsigned notes of the Farmers' & Merchants' Bank of Olean, New York! For a matter of seconds he stood there staring in astonishment at the packet. Reaching in, he removed a second similar packet, then hastily returning the packages, he replaced the fragment and returning to the rim, picked up his rifle and packsack, and headed back down the creek.

An hour later, on Halfaday Creek, a mile above the cabin occupied by Early, he shot a cow moose, and a short time later, as he was cutting out chunks of choice meat, he looked up to see Early approaching, rifle in hand.

"Hello, Bill!" he greeted. "Where you headin'?"

"Figgered I'd sort of poke around an' see if I couldn't shoot me some meat, an' heard a shot so I come over to see what it was. There'd ort to be deer er somethin' around here, hadn't there? What the hell's that you've got?"

"A moose. There's no deer in this country. Too fer north."

"A moose! Hell, a moose has got big wide horns. That damn thing looks like a mule."

"Yeah—but it's better eatin'. This is a cow moose. They don't have horns. Git out yer knife an' whittle off what meat you want. I can't get no more'n sixty, seventy pounds in my packsack."

Both men fell to work, and a half hour later Black John stowed his meat in his pack sack, washed his hands in the creek and filled his pipe. "You know, Bill," he said, seating himself on the ground, as the other continued to work at the carcass with his knife, "you was tellin' me an' Cush, last night, about hearin' how we was all outlaws, up here on Halfaday?"

"Sure—that's what they claimed in White Horse."

"I wouldn't go so far's to say all the boys on the crick is outlawed, nor yet I wouldn't deny that possibly some of 'em might be. Take Cush—I don't figger he's outlawed nowheres—onless steerin' clear of three, four assorted wives could outlaw a man. But no matter what a man done before he come to Halfaday, after he gits here he's got to refrain from crime of every description, er git hung. We don't allow no crime on Halfaday."

"Well, that's fair enough."

"Yeah, we deem it a reasonable provision. An' I might p'int out that while lyin' is condoned, passin' queer money is extremely hangable."

The man paused in his work and eyed the speaker sharply. "What do you mean—lyin' an' passin' queer money. What's that got to do with me?"

"Meanin' that providin' Cush would refrain from tunkin' you on the head with a bung-starter, we'll be callin' a miners' meetin' tonight an' hangin' you fer passin' them phoney bills on him."

"Phoney bills! What d'you mean—phoney? By God, them bills ain't phoney! I got 'em fair an' square."

"Yeah? Off'n an express car back in New York, eh?"

"New York—hell! I never even seen New York. I got them

bills right there in White Horse. Won 'em in a crap game off 'n Sherman—him that got soused in the stud game, last night. An' there ain't nothin' phoney about 'em!"

"No? Got any more like 'em? I'll show you."

Reaching into his pocket the man withdrew a thick roll of bills, Black John noting that except for half a dozen new bills on top, the roll consisted of used currency. Selecting a new ten-dollar note, the man handed it to Black John. "There's one of them bills like I give Cush. Now show me what's phoney about it!"

"I happen to know that these notes was lifted off an express car in New York. They was bein' shipped from Washington to this bank—but they never got there. An' they ain't worth a damn till they're signed by the president an' cashier of the bank that was to issue 'em."

"They are signed—look at them names there!"

"Yeah—an' if you'll look closter you'll see that they're signed in the same handwritin'—signed an' passed by the man that lifted 'em off that car."

The man scrutinized the bill, and several similar ones. "By God, that's right!" he exclaimed, his eyes flashing angrily. "Why—that damn crook! Passin' that phoney stuff off on me when I won that three hundred fair an' square. An' me liable to git hung fer it! Honest to God I didn't know them bills was phoney. You can't hang a man fer nothin' he didn't know. It wouldn't be right!"

"It would seem a mite onreasonable, at that," Black John admitted. "But so fer we ain't got nothin' but your word fer it."

"Wait till I git holt of that damn Sherman—an' you'll have more'n my word! By God, he'll make them bills good, er I'll blow his damn head off! Where's he at? I'll show him if he kin damn near git me hung!"

"Sech differences as you two boys has got can ondoubtless be adjusted amicably. He's in Whiskey Bill's old shack. Take the first feeder that runs in from the north, that's the right hand side, goin' up the crick. It's a mile above here, an' foller the feeder up a couple of miles. It's the only shack on the crick, you can't miss it. If I was you I'd slip up an' sort of talk things over."

"I'll talk it over! He'll either fork over three hundred in good bills—er else."

Picking up his rifle, the man headed up the creek, and a few minutes later Black John cached his packsack and climbing to the rim, cut across the hills and took up his position in the niche in the rim rocks from which he had watched Sherman visit his cache. He had not long to wait before Early swung into view and headed straight for the cabin. Sherman, evidently hearing the man coming, stepped from the cabin and stood before the door. Early paused within ten feet of him. From his point of vantage Black John could see, but could not hear what went on in the little valley. Evidently the men were engaged in heated conversation, for he saw Early shake a clenched fist. Then suddenly he jerked the rifle to his shoulder—but before he could fire a pistol shot rang out, and the rifle dropped from the man's hands, his knees buckled under him, and he crashed forward and lay very still.

Black John emitted a long, low whistle. He had heard the report, and had seen the light puff of smoke. But Sherman still stood in the doorway of the cabin—and his hands were empty!

"An' he's the guy we all figgered was clumsy," he murmured. "Downey claimed this express robber was lightnin' fast with a gun—lightnin' fast is right!" Suddenly he smote his thigh with his hand. "The damn cuss is left handed, like Downey claimed. Usin' his right hand to throw folks off, made him clumsy. An' I know, now, what was wrong with his shirt—the buttons is on the left side—like a woman's—so he could slip his left hand in an' grab a belly gun. An' that brown hair prob'ly ain't nothin' but dye. But—two blond men—an' both left handed—that's kind of crowdin' the probabilities."

Hastening back through the hills, Black John descended into

the valley of Halfaday, retrieved his pack, and passed on down to Early's shack. Clawing into the gravel dump, he uncovered a flour sack from which he removed package after package of used bills of small denominations. Hastily he estimated their value. "Right around sixty thousan'. He's that North Dakota robber, all right, an' it looks like he got about ten thousan' more'n they figgered. He got shet of his horse, an' his mask—but he hung onto the flour sack. Oh, well—he won't have no further use fer these bills, an' sech heirs as he's got prob'ly won't never put in no claim fer 'em, so I'll jest take 'em along—no use lettin' 'em lay here an' rot in the gravel."

Removing the meat from the packsack, he placed the money in the bottom, repacked the meat, and heaving the sack to his shoulders, headed down the creek. And within two miles of Cushing's Fort he came face to face with Corporal Downey! He greeted the officer with a smile. "Hi, Downey! What you doin' up here? Come on back to Cush's an' I'll buy a drink."

"The drink will have to wait. I've got some business to attend to first. It's that blond, left handed cuss I was tellin' you about. Cush tells me he's here on the crick—and that he's be'n shovin' that Olean bank money around. He showed me a hundred an' thirty dollars worth the fellow passed last night."

Black John swung the heavy pack from his shoulders and seated himself on a fallen spruce. "Set down an' light yer pipe. I need a breather, anyhow. That packsack of meat's be'n gittin' heavier by the mile. An' you don't need to hurry. That bird's up in Whiskey Bill's old shack, an'—"

"Whiskey Bill's! Cush said he was in that shack up the crick where I arrested that fellow, Benedict Hale, that time."

"Yeah—but he ain't the one yer after, Downey. The fact is, some complications has arose that Cush don't know nothin' about."

The officer frowned. "I'll say there's complications," he growled, as he seated himself and produced pipe and tobacco. "I get a tip from the captain of the *Hannah* that a man answering this fellow's description boarded his boat in White Horse for Dawson, and quit the boat at Selkirk. Then, next day a prospector shows up at Selkirk with a story of being held up and robbed of ten thousand dollars in bills by a tall blond left handed man."

"What," asked Black John skeptically, "would a prospector be doin' with ten thousan' in bills?"

"He had cashed in his dust in Dawson an' was headin' upriver in a canoe, goin' outside. He was camped jest below Selkirk, when this blond fellow came along an' camped alongside him. They got to talkin', an' the damn fool told him about the stake he'd made, so the left handed guy pulled a gun on him an' made him fork it over, then shoved the fellow's canoe out into the river, an' got in his own canoe an' shoved off. The prospector made his way to Selkirk afoot an' reported it. I headed upriver in a canoe, and met no one answering his description coming down—so he must have headed up the White."

"Yeah—he's here, all right. But if you figger on arrestin' him yer a little late. Fact is, Downey that bird is deader'n hell."

"Dead!"

"Yup. He's layin' up in front of Whiskey Bill's door, right now—onless the fella that shot him has drug him off an' hid him."

"Who shot him?"

"Why, the fella that robbed that express car back there in New York an' got all them onsigned bills."

"But this left handed blond man is the one that pulled that job! An' he's the one that passed those bills off on Cush. Cush described him to me."

"Oh shore—he passed 'em, all right. But he done it innocently."

"Innocently!"

"Yup—he didn't know they was phoney till I told him, this mornin'. He won them bills off'n the robber in a crap game in

White Horse, an' he thought they was good. He passed some of 'em on Cush, an' when I showed him how them signatures was signed in the same handwritin' he grabbed up his rifle an' hit out fer Whiskey Bill's place where this guy has holed up. Surmisin' the meetin' might be interestin', I slipped acrost an' hid on the rim so I could see what come off. It didn't take long after he got there. The other bird stood in the doorway, an' they talked fer a couple of minutes. I couldn't hear what they said—but I jedged the argument was kind of heated, because this bird shook his fist in the other one's face, an' then swung his rifle on him—but he never had time to pull the trigger. The other one nailed him in his tracks with a belly gun. An' believe me, Downey—when that description said he was lightnin' fast with a gun, it didn't lie none! It all happened in a second—an' the next second the bird stood there in the door empty-handed! I'm warnin' you—when you arrest him, be shore you've got him covered."

The frown deepened on Downey's face as he slowly pulled at his pipe. "The whole damn business is all muddled up. If this left handed blond cuss ain't the express robber, who in the devil is he?"

"Well—your guess would be as good as mine. He's ondoubt-less a miscreant of some sort, er he wouldn't have held up that prospector."

"But—is the one that shot him blond and left handed, too?"

"His hair an' whiskers is brown—but brown dye's cheap, an' would furnish a reasonable disguise. If he ain't left handed, he's the clumsiest right handed man I ever seen—an' the way he handled that gun wasn't clumsy, by a damn sight. I wasn't very near—but I was watchin' pretty clost, an' it happened so damn fast, I couldn't tell which hand he used. An' here's a tip—the first time I seen him I noticed somethin' funny about his shirt. I couldn't place it, then. But when I seen him shoot I figgered it out—the buttons is on the wrong side—like a woman's. That's so he can reach in quick with his left hand fer his belly gun."

Corporal Downey knocked the dottle from his pipe. "Well, I'll be goin' along. Thanks for the tip. I'll be seeing you at Cush's."

Black John shook his head. "Nope. I'm goin' up there with you. I'll cache my meat here in the bush an' go along—jest in case. That bird's too damn fast. I wouldn't feel right if you went up there alone. This is a case where two guns is better than one."

Downey grinned. "But—I thought you never openly helped the police. What will the boys here on Halfaday think if they find out you did?"

"That ain't worryin' me none. In the first place there ain't one in a dozen of 'em that's got anything to think with, an' them that has will see that I'm doin' this fer their own good. Mind you, Downey—I ain't doin' this to help the police, in no sense of the word. It's only fer the good of the crick. Think what would happen to us if this damn scoundrel should knock you off. Why the police would come in an' scatter us all over hell! You know damn well that me an' Cush has strove to make Halfaday the moralest crick in the Yukon. Cripes—if a thing like that would happen, all that strivin' would be a total loss!"

"An' that would be a damn shame," Downey laughed.

"It shore would. Don't it beat hell how the devil seeps in on a crick in spite of all we can do?"

## IV

**AT THE MOUTH** of the feeder Black John paused. "I'll slip on ahead, an' take up a position in the bush clost enough to his door so I can't miss. There's no window on that side—so he'll have to come to the door. You go on acrost the clearin' an' I'll have him covered—an' the first crooked move out of him, I'll blast him to hell."

"Okay—but don't shoot unless you have to, John. Remember, we're supposed to bring in our prisoners alive."

"It's a good way—when practical," the big man admitted, and disappeared into the bush.

Half an hour later Corporal Downey crossed the little clearing as a man stepped to the doorway of the shack.

"What's this?" he asked abruptly, pointing to the body of a man that lay sprawled before the door.

"Hello, officer!" the man in the doorway exclaimed. "I'm certainly glad you happened along! It has saved me a long trip to Dawson to report this matter. Unfortunately, I was forced to shoot this man in self-defense. He lies just as he fell. I have not disturbed him in the least. In my opinion the police are entitled to all possible cooperation in a case of this kind."

"Yeah," Downey admitted. "We generally need it."

"Exactly! To make a long story short, this man and I, with several others, were engaged in a game of stud, last evening at Cushing's Fort. We both lost and I drank a little too much and as I left the place, I very foolishly called back that there was plenty more money where that came from, and that I would come back for revenge. He knew that I am well supplied with funds because a short time ago he won three hundred dollars from me in a crap game in White Horse—and I have reason to suspect that he used loaded dice. Having lost heavily in the stud game, it undoubtedly occurred to him to recoup his losses through robbery—so he appeared here a few hours ago and demanded my money at the point of a rifle. You can see that his gun is at full cock. I tried to reason with him, but all to no avail—and when he raised the rifle to fire, I shot him. As you can readily see, it was purely a case of self-defense. No one deplores the taking of a human life more than I. But a man has the right to defend himself and his property."

Downey nodded—and the next instant the man's eyes widened as they looked squarely into the muzzle of the officer's service revolver. "Stick up your hands—an' do it quick!" he commanded in a hard voice. "You'd ort to have done yer deplorin' before you knocked off that express agent an' that conductor, back there in New York."

"What do you mean?" the man cried, as his hands shot

upward. A moment later he smiled. "Ah, I see. A mistake, undoubtedly. In White Horse I noticed a poster offering a reward for the purporter of that crime, dead or alive—evidently a notorious outlaw. I hadn't thought of it before, but it occurs to me, now—that this dead man fits that description to a T. He is tall and blond—and he was left-handed, too. You can verify that fact by asking any of the men who sat in that stud game. By George, I believe I'm entitled to that reward! The amount escapes me at the moment—but I recollect that it was a substantial sum. I am a peaceable man, but I see no reason why I should not claim that reward."

Downey grinned. "There's quite a few reasons. You're right handed, I s'pose?"

"Certainly. And my hair and beard are distinctly not blond."

"Not till they get to within half an inch of yer hide, they ain't. An' bein' right handed I s'pose is why your buttons is on the left side of yer shirt. An' bein' a peaceable man is why you're packin' a belly gun. An'—"The sentence was never finished. Like a flash the man's left hand flew downward as he jerked swiftly sidewise to avoid Downey's gun. And in that same instant a rifle roared from the bush, and the man crumpled in the doorway. The next moment Black John stepped into the clearing and stood beside Downey, looking down at the two bodies.

"I didn't dare to take a chanct," he said. "When he ducked sideways, I was afraid you'd miss, an' he wouldn't."

Downey nodded. "It might well have be'n that way, too. I'm sure grateful to you, John."

"Oh, hell, Downey—think nothin' of it. I s'pose there's nothin' left to do but bury these two birds. We can shove 'em in that old shaft of Whiskey Bill's an' toss some gravel on 'em."

"I've got to search 'em first," Downey said, and proceeded to suit the action to the word. The dead outlaw's pockets yielded nothing of importance save a roll of the Olean banknotes which he had not had time to sign. From the blond man's pockets he drew a roll of used bills of small denomination together with a hundred and seventy dollars in the signed banknotes. "That's the balance of the three hundred he won off the other," Downey announced. "He passed a hundred an' thirty on Cush." A moment later, from another pocket he withdrew an object that brought an exclamation to his lips. "Look at this! A pad of money order blanks. By Gosh—that's killin' two birds with one stone! This other one is that North Dakota robber. I rec'lect he robbed the post office, too—an' got away with these blanks."

"Good work, Downey," the big man approved. "I sort of mistrusted these two wouldn't prove no credit to our community."

"You drag 'em over to the shaft, John. I'm goin' to hunt around here an' see if I can locate the rest of them new banknotes."

As Black John finished covering the bodies with gravel, Downey emerged from the cabin. "Have any luck?" the big man asked.

The officer shook his head. "No." He paused and glanced about him. "They're not in the cabin, an' I don't suppose there's much use lookin' any further. There's a thousand places he could have cached 'em."

"Yeah, caches is mostly pretty hard to find. But as long as we ain't in no hurry we might look around a little. If we don't find 'em somewheres along this old sluice er the woodpile, we can look along the rock wall. There's generally some cracks er holes where a man could cache stuff."

Neither the sluice nor the woodpile yielded anything and the two passed slowly along the rock wall, examining each crack and crevice. Presently Black John pointed to a rock fragment that protruded slightly from a crevice. "Look at that sliver of rock wedged in that crack," he said, and pointed upward at the face of rock. "There ain't no way that chunk of rock could fall from the top an' lodge in there—so it must have be'n put there. Jerk it out, Downey—it might be his cache."

Downey removed the fragment and thrusting his arm into the aperture withdrew a thick packet of new unsigned banknotes.

Other packets followed until the cache was emptied. "We'll stop in at Hale's cabin an' hunt fer this other fellow's cache," he said, when he had stowed the packages in his light packsack. "Accordin' to that report we got, there ought to be right around fifty thousan' in small bills in it—besides the ten thousan' he got off that prospector."

"Oh, shore, we can hunt fer it all right," Black John agreed. "But the chances is we won't find it. You've got to remember, Downey, a man ain't got only so much luck. Here you start out after this damn crook, an' you got him—er at least you can rub him off the slate. An' you located his loot—an' on top of that you can account fer another malefactor, an' rub him off. That looks to me like luck enough fer one man in one day. The law of averages says a man can't go on winnin' all the time."

"Guess that's right," Downey agreed. "But we'll hunt for it, anyway. I didn't think we had a chance in the world of locating this cache—but we did."

**REACHING HALE'S** old cabin the two explored each nook and cranny in the rock wall for a considerable distance up and down the creek. They searched around the broken down flume and sluice and Black John even dug into the gravel dump. At the end of two hours Downey gave it up. Seating himself on the old flume he wiped the sweat from his brow with a blue cotton handkerchief. "Guess it's no go," he admitted. "But I would like to have found that cache. That prospector was robbed right here on the Yukon—lost every cent he had in the world. He's back in Dawson, now, workin' fer the Detroit-Yukon outfit. I sure would like to get his money back to him."

"Yeah—he shore had tough luck," Black John agreed. "But mebbe it'll learn him not to go shootin' off his mouth to every stranger he sees along a river."

"It was partly his own fault, all right. But he was a chechako—an' they ain't supposed to have much sense. By the way, John—you're entitled to that reward. It's right around twenty thousan'

dollars. I'll certify to Joseph Allen's death, an' fix up the necessary papers for you."

The big man shook his head. "Not me! Hell's fire—where
would I stand if the boys here on Halfaday heard how I'd gone
in fer rewards? Tell you what you do, Downey. You put in the
claim fer the reward in the name of John Smith, Dawson. If
you leave the 'Black' off, no one will figger it's me—John Smith
bein' a fairly common name—an' Dawson bein' my post office
address."

"Post office address!" Downey grinned.

The big man returned the grin. "Well—it would be if I had
any need of one. An' then when the reward money comes in,
you give it to that damn fool chechako. The pore devil prob'ly
needs it."

"Well—that's damned white of you, John. An' I'll not be
forgettin' that if you hadn't be'n there in the brush with your
rifle, I might be layin' up there in front of Whiskey Bill's door
along with that other fellow."

"Hell—don't mention it, Downey. Like I said, it would make
it mean fer us boys if a policeman was to get knocked off on
Halfaday. An' as fer the reward—cripes, Downey—I wouldn't
think of takin' a reward fer performin' a simple duty. It wouldn't
be ethical. Come on—let's go down to Cush's, an' I'll buy you
that drink. We'll pick up my packsack an' make Cush's klooch
fry us up a big batch of moose steak."

# CONSTABLE BUCK
# COUNTS HEADS

**PADDLING EASILY DOWN** the Yukon, Black John Smith swerved his canoe toward shore and drew it clear of the water beside a clumsy rowboat that was beached on a rocky point, some twenty miles below the mouth of the White River. The two men who were seated, one on either side of a small driftwood fire above which hung a tea pail, eyed him sharply as he stepped toward them. "Hello, men!" he greeted. "Just figurin' on landin' for a noon snack when I seen your smoke. Kind of lonesome eatin' alone, so I swung in."

The smaller of the two, a hard-eyed, tight lipped man, nodded, and glanced across at the other. "Fetch the packsack outa the boat, Jess, an' cut off five, six slices of bacon." He glanced up into the big man's face. "There's tea in the pail, an' we got bacon an' dough-gods. You'll have to furnish yer own eatin' tools—we ain't only got the two outfits."

"I've got my own grub," Black John protested. "I didn't drop in for a hand-out."

"We got plenty," the man replied, "an' it can't be no hell of a ways to Dawson."

"Matter of sixty mile or so," Black John said. As he turned toward the canoe, the man called Jess deposited a packsack on the rocks beside the fire, while from another pack he lifted out a small chunk of bacon from which he cut slices into a frying pan. "You boys strangers here?" he asked, as he returned with his eating utensils, and squatted close beside the unopened pack.

The thin lipped man nodded and glanced sharply at the other, who moved the pack to the opposite side of the fire. "Yeah," he answered, "we're headin' fer Dawson. You acquainted around here?"

"Fairly well acquainted, you might say."

"Know a guy name of Black John Smith?"

"No, I can't say I know him. I never met him, personally. Friend of yours, is he?"

"No, I never seen him, neither. Some guys down around Frisco was tellin' us about him. Runs some kind of an outlaw gang up some crick name of Halfaday, don't he?"

"Yeah, that's the talk. But, cripes, a man can hear most anything."

"I guess it's the straight goods, all right. These guys that was tellin' us about him, they know'd him, personal."

"Friends of his, eh?"

The man grinned, thinly. "If they be, I shore as hell don't want no friends. They're all guys he's run outa the country, fer one reason an' another. They'd all like to come back, but they don't dast to—what with him layin' back to knock 'em off if the police don't. Accordin' to their tell, if a man's outlawed, up here, he hits fer this here Halfaday Crick. If Black John likes him when he gits there, he's all jake. But if he don't like him, he either hangs him er runs him outa the country. Accordin' to what they claim, a man might a damn sight better be picked up by the police than run foul of Black John."

"I've heard he's a tough guy."

"He damn well thinks he is. These boys we was talkin' to has all lived up there on Halfaday Crick, one time er another, an' they know what they're talkin' about. They claim that they's a guy up there, name of Old Cush, that runs the saloon an' tradin' post, an' about a dozen er so more, that Black John could count on. But they's thirty, forty others along the crick. Some of these is guys that hates Black John's guts, an' would throw in with

anyone that could knock him off an' take over. The rest is guys that don't give a damn, one way er another, who runs Halfaday Crick so long as the Law can't grab 'em."

"So you boys figure on slippin' up to Halfaday an' takin' over an' then passin' the word on to them Frisco boys to come on back in, eh?"

"I ain't sayin' we are, er we ain't. Anyways, it don't never hurt a man none to look around a little. All we got is them fella's word fer it, down there in Frisco. It could be they was lyin'. An' besides that, we don't even know where this here Halfaday Crick's at."

"It runs into the White River quite a ways up. That's the river you passed the mouth of about twenty miles back."

"We're headin' fer Dawson, now," the man said. "Accordin' to these boys if we hunt up a guy name of Cuter Malone, he could give us the low-down on this here Black John. He hates Black John's guts."

"Yeah, Cuter, he runs the Klondike Palace. You won't have no trouble locatin' him."

"You hittin' fer Dawson, too?"

"Yup. Goin' down to file a claim. Be'n doin' a little prospec-tin' in the back country."

"How long you goin' to be there?"

"O-h-h, week er ten days, mebbe. Long enough to git caught up on my drinkin' an stud playin'."

"How about gittin' you to guide us up there to Halfaday, if we decide to go?"

"I won't say I will, er I won't. If you make up yer mind to go in a few days, you might hunt me up. You can find me at the Northern Hotel or the Tivoli."

He drank the last of his tea and rose to his feet. "Well, so long, boys. Much obliged fer the grub. I'll be shovin' along, now. See you in Dawson, maybe."

## II

**ARRIVING AT DAWSON,** Black John beached his canoe, stopped in at the Tivoli saloon for a drink or two, and strolled over to detachment headquarters of the Mounted Police. The young constable on duty scowled at him across the flat-top desk.

"What do *you* want?" he asked sourly.

The big man grinned. "Oh, nothin' in particular, Rollo. Just dropped in to chaw the fat with Downey."

"Well, Downey's not here. He left this morning for Forty Mile. Won't be back till Thursday. This is Monday. So, if you haven't got any business here, suppose you clear out. I'm busy."

Black John's grin widened, as he glanced about the room. "I see you've got the spittoon cleaned, an' the place all swep' out nice, an' your shoes shined. Downey'd like that. I s'pose, now, you can put in the rest of the day figurin' how much royalty to charge on another batch of fool's gold." His reference was to one of those Northern episodes that happen once in so often.

Constable Buck's face flushed angrily. "Don't try to kid me!" he growled. "I collected the royalty on that stuff, all right—but I wasn't damn fool enough to pay twenty-five thousand dollars in cash for it—like you did! I got a good laugh when I heard about you paying that woman twenty-five thousand for a hundred pounds of fool's gold. She sure played you for a sucker, all right—and got away with it!"

Black John shook his head slowly. "No, Rollo, she didn't play me for a sucker. The poor woman needed the money so she could catch the boat for the outside, an' I let her have it—so she's satisfied. I made a mighty good profit on the deal—so I'm satisfied. An' you got a good laugh out of it—so you're satisfied. I'm just wonderin' how satisfied Downey was when he found out you'd collected royalty an' issued a receipt on that fool's gold. I'll bet you know."

The flush deepened on the constable's face. "Corporal Downey's always finding fault with what I do," he replied, sulkily.

"Well, so long, Rollo," Black John said. "I'll be trottin' along, now. I'm bettin' that some day you're goin' to blunder onto doin' somethin' right—then Downey can't find no fault."

FOUR DAYS later as he again stepped into detachment head-quarters, Corporal Downey greeted him cordially. "Hello, John! I was thinkin' jest the other day that it's about time you were showin' up."

"Oh, shore—just dropped in for a week or ten days of this an' that. Where's Rollo? When I stopped in a few days ago he was presidin' behind the desk. He claimed you was down to Forty Mile."

"He's off on detail."

"Someone swipe a diaper off'n some woman's clothesline?"

Downey grinned. "If they did they'd still have it, for all Rollo could do about it. That's one of the things I went down to Forty Mile for—to try to talk Sam Steele into takin Rollo off my hands. But Sam jest laughed at me. So seein' I'm stuck with him I sent him up Ladue Crick to count the Siwashes in Sebastian's Village—not that I give a damn how many of'em there is, but I get shet of Rollo fer a while. How's things on Halfaday?"

"Oh, about as usual. We just go ahead mindin' our own business, livin' our uneventful lives as any quiet little community should."

"By the way—there's a guy on the loose that I'd like to get holt of. Bat Eye Cantrill, his name is. Tall, dark hombre—eyes sort of twitch when he talks. Never run accost him, have you?"

"Shore. I used to know Bat Eye. Last time I saw him his eyes had quit twitchin'."

"Is he up on Halfaday?"

"Yeah, he's up there."

"What's he doin'?"

"Nothin' much. Just layin' around."

"I'm goin' up there an' get him."

"Okay. We're through with him. You can have him."

"What do you mean—through with him?"

"We sort of lost interest in him when we buried him."

"You mean he's dead?"

"That's what Cush claimed—an' he's the coroner. If he ain't he's tougher'n hell after bein' hung, an' buried for a month."

"What did you hang him for?"

"Two murders, a couple of robberies, widow-swindlin', general skullduggery, seekin' to join up with a notorious gang of outlaws, et cetry an' so forth. After listenin' to him brag of these here peccadillos for an hour or more, it didn't take the miners' meetin' no time at all to convict him. What's new along the river?"

"Our main headache, right now is a twenty-thousand dollar payroll robbery that was pulled off on the trail to Hunker day before yesterday. I've got Constable Peters on the job. We got a couple of breaks on the case, this time. We know who done it. All Peters has got to do is locate 'em an' bring 'em in. If he don't have any luck in the next week or so, the chances are they've hit for Halfaday, so keep your eyes open when you get back, an' I'll drop around that way myself."

"Howcome you know who done it?"

"Couple of lucky breaks—this Excelsior Development Company's payroll messenger was shot in the head an' left for dead. But the bullet jest glanced off his skull—knocked him out for a while, but he came to, an' gave us a good description of the two robbers.

"Then, last evenin' I happened to be walkin' by the Klondike Palace, an' I noticed a young fella slip out the back door, I happened to know he worked in the Excelsior office. I took a chance, collared him, an' slapped a confession out of the damn young punk. He admitted tippin' the payroll information off to a couple of brothers that jest hit the country. Watson, their name is— Frank an' Jess Watson. Accordin' to this punk, he knew 'em back in Oregon—they knew he'd skipped out on account of some girl he'd got in trouble, an' when they found out he was workin' in the Excelsior office they made him tip off this payroll job, on the threat that they'd slip the Oregon folks the word on where he is.

"When he told me their names, I checked up on a hot dodger we got a short time ago from the Seattle police. These Watsons are bad actors—damn bad. They're wanted in Oregon for a train robbery. Shot a mail clerk an' got away with eighty-six thousan' in unmarked bills. So we've got that description, along with the one the messenger gave us, an' they tally to a T. There's no doubt at all but what these Watson brothers are the birds we want."

"H-u-u-m, eighty-six thousan' in unmarked bills, an' twenty thousan' more," Black John said. "That's a hundred an' six thousan'.

Was these Excelsior payroll bills onmarked, too?"

"They weren't marked—but we've got their numbers. I've put out copies of the list in all the stores an' saloons in town."

"What did you say these birds looked like—just in case they'd show up on Halfaday?"

"I didn't say—but here's all the dope we've got on 'em." Reaching into a filing cabinet, he withdrew a paper and read: "Frank Watson, thirty. Slight, wiry build, five-seven. About one hundred an' fifty pounds. Hard gray eyes. Thin lips. He's the shrewder, dominatin' one of the two brothers. Jess, twenty-seven. Six foot. Blue eyes. About two hundred pounds. Dangerous. Always armed. Quick on the trigger." Downey returned the dodger to the file. "So there you've got it. If they show up on Halfaday, better keep an eye on 'em till I get up there. I'll give Peters a week or so to try to locate 'em along the river first. When you goin' back?"

"Oh, I ain't in no hurry. Got to sort of hang around a week or so to see a couple of fellas about a deal. So long. I'm goin' over to the Tivoli. The boys'll be startin' a stud game."

## III

**CONSTABLE ROLLO BUCK,** spick and span in the uniform of the Northwest Mounted Police, drew his canoe from the water as he reached the collection of log huts and ramshackle hovels known as Sebastian's Village on Ladue Creek, one of the main tributaries of the White River. A dozen gaunt, fly-tortured dogs nosed about among the discarded tin cans and refuse that littered the creek bank. Two Indians paused in their work at a fish net stretched on a nearby frame to stare at him. In the doorway of a cabin a klooch added chips to the smudge pan before the door, and in the rear of another cabin an enormously fat klooch poked and prodded with a stick at the contents of a huge iron kettle hung over a fire.

Constable Buck scowled as the sour odor from the refuse

heap blended with the smudge smoke in his nostrils. "Counting Siwashes," he muttered angrily. "Peters gets a real detail—and I've got to count a lot of stinking Indians!"

He turned to the two at the fish net. "Where's Sebastian?" he demanded.

One of the men pointed toward a cabin slightly apart from the rest, and the officer picked his way amid a litter of fish boxes, overturned sleds, small heaps of firewood, and broken canoes. Rounding a corner of the cabin he encountered an old man seated on a bench beside the open doorway before which the inevitable smudge pan belched forth its smoke. He was a heavy-set man, broad of shoulder and wide of mouth. Kindly dark eyes stared up from beneath a mass of gray hair twisted into a sort of mop on top of his head.

"You Sebastian?" Buck asked gruffly.

The old Indian took the short pipe from his mouth and nodded.

"How many people you got here in the village—all of them, men, women, and children?"

The old man considered the question. Slowly he shook his head. "I ain' know. Mebbe-so t'irty, fo'ty—feefty, mebbe. I ain' know."

"Well, I've got to count 'em. Where do I start?"

The old man's brow creased as he puffed slowly at his pipe. "Start wan, two, t'ree, fo'—"

"Don't try to get funny with me!" Buck snapped. "I mean, is this all there is to the village? Where does it end?"

The oldster pointed upstream. " 'Roun' de ben'—mebbe-so fi', seex more cabin. Got two w'ite mans."

"White men? Who are they?"

"No say de nem. Com' two day ago. Geeve Tom John fi' dolla' for he's cabin—mebbe-so few day. Tom John go in he's tent."

**CONSTABLE BUCK** turned away and headed upstream along,

a well-worn foot trail. Rounding the bend, he came abruptly upon the two white men seated close to the smudge in the doorway of a squat log cabin. Both men leaped to their feet at the sight of the uniform. The smaller of the two, a slight, wiry man, with hard gray eyes and thin lips stepped forward. "Hello, copper," he said. "Lookin' fer someone?"

Buck smiled. "Yes—looking for some Siwashes to count."

"Some—what?"

"Siwashes—Indians. Guess you haven't been in the country very long, eh?"

The man's body seemed to relax slightly. "Not a hell of a while," he replied. "But—what's the idee of countin' Injuns?"

Buck shrugged. "Search me. I'm only a constable. Corporal Downey in command of detachment handed me this detail—so here I am."

The other was quick to note the touch of bitterness in the young officer's tone. The thin lips smiled. "Sort of throws it into you, eh—this Corporal Downey?"

"I'll say he does! Every chance he gets. Someone else always gets the important details, and I get the dirty work."

"Yeah, that's the way it goes, kid," the man replied, a touch of sympathy in his tone. "Sew a stripe er two on a cop's arm, an' if he gits it in fer someone under him he shore shoves him the dirt. Speakin' of important details," he added casually, "is anything of importance goin' on, now?"

"Sure there is. A twenty thousand dollar payroll robbery on the Hunker Crick trail. Peters got that detail. Couple of brothers named Watson pulled off the job. All Peters has got to do is locate them and bring them in, and he'll get the credit."

"Howcome they know who done it?"

"In the first place, they shot the messenger and left him for dead, but the bullet only grazed his skull and he came to and described these men. Then Downey grabbed up a young fellow who worked in the Excelsior office and made him admit that he'd tipped off the Watsons to the job. He claimed he had to because these Watsons recognized him and threatened to turn him in to the Oregon authorities on account of some girl trouble he skipped away from down there. Then, on top of that, Downey compared the description the messenger gave with the description of Frank and Jess Watson in a police dodger from Seattle where the Watsons are wanted for a train robbery. I guess there's no doubt but what the Watsons are guilty, all right. I'd sure like to draw a detail like that. Mostly you've got to figure out who did a job, an' then bring in your man besides."

The other nodded. "Yeah, that's right, kid. An' on the dope this Downey's got, it looks bad fer the Watson boys. But the fact is, the Watsons never had a damn thing to do with it."

Buck stared at the man in surprise. "Why—how do you know?" he asked.

"By God, I'd ort to know! We're the Watsons. I'm Frank, an' he's Jess."

The color slowly drained from Constable Buck's face as he stood facing the men. "But—but—" he stammered, "how about the messenger identifying you—and—and—that fellow in the Excelsior office?"

"That's easy, kid. It's a frame-up. That's what it is. That there young punk in the office—he told Downey the truth, all right, when he said he'd skipped outa Oregon on account of having hit a girl. He done it, an' he knows damn well me an' Jess, here, knows he done it. So, when he seen us there in Dawson, he got scairt we'd turn him in, on account this here girl was the daughter of a friend of ourn. So, when the guy that really pulls off this robbery gits next to this punk to tip him off when the payroll goes out, the punk seen the chanct to throw it into us, an' he give the messenger our description so he could tell the cops we was the ones that done it."

"But how did the messenger know he was going to be robbed?"

Watson laughed "Know it! Why the hell wouldn't he know it? He was in on it—fer a cut."

Buck shook his head, doubtfully. "I don't believe anyone would take a chance on getting shot, no matter how big a cut he was to get."

"Git wise, kid," Watson said. "The shootin' wasn't s'posed to be in the play. The guy that pulled it off, throw's in the shot jest to make shore—an besides, a dead man can't collect no cut. Don't you git it?"

"But—how about that Oregon train robbery?"

"We didn' have no more to do with that job than you did. An' when the time comes we'll prove it right in court—an' believe me, we'll show up the ones that done it. Jest like we'll show up the one that pulled off this here payroll job, when the time comes."

"You mean—you know who pulled that job?"

"We shore do."

"Who was it?"

The man smiled. "Well now, kid, playin' in with the Law ain't exactly in our line. But it could be mebbe we could make a deal."

"What kind of a deal? I won't stand for anything crooked."

"Shore you wouldn't, kid—no more'n what we would. But if we'd agree to sort of string along with you—figger somehow on puttin' this guy on a spot where you could arrest him, we'd be doin' you a good turn, wouldn't we? If you was to fetch him in, an' mebbe the twenty thousan' along with him, it wouldn't hurt yer record none, would it? A stripe er two on them sleeves wouldn't look so bad, eh?"

**ROLLO FROWNED.** "If I'd had a fair chance I'd have had stripes on my sleeves long ago," he said. "Corporal Downey never gives me a break. I get all the routine details and all the chores around detachment to do, and when anything important comes up, Downey either handles the case himself, or details Constable Peters to handle it."

The man grinned. "Oh, shore. That's how all them police captains an' inspectors an' sech as that holds their jobs, handle all the important cases, an' take all the credik. But like now—if you was to fetch in the guy that pulled this hold-up, along with the twenty thousan'—cripes! When the inspector, er captain, er whoever this Downey's boss is, heard about how you handled the case, it's a ten to one bet that he'd up you to anyways a sergeant—might even put you in command there in Dawson instead of Downey."

"But who is this robber? And where is he?"

"Like I says—how about a little deal?"

"What kind of a deal?"

"It's like this—you've heard of Black John Smith, ain't you—him that runs a gang of outlaws up on Halfaday Crick?"

Rollo scowled. "Of course I've heard of him! I know him—and I hate him like poison. He's always trying to get me in bad with Downey—either that or making fun of me, as if I didn't have a brain in my head. I've warned him that when my chance comes, I'll get him! And someday I will!"

"That's the talk, brother!" Frank Watson agreed enthusiastically. "An' it looks from here like yer chanct has came!"

"What do you mean?"

"Well—jest s'pose Black John was to lose his holt, over there on Halfaday Crick, an' someone else was to take over. Me an' Jess, here—we wasn't made in a minute. We got contacts. There's a guy in Dawson name of Cuter Malone that's hep to what goes on in this country. He give me an' Jess the lowdown. Now you might not believe this, kid. Sometimes a man overlooks somethin' that goes on right under his nose. But it's the God's truth—there's a hook up between this here Black John an' Corporal Downey."

Rollo's brow drew into a frown, and he nodded slowly. "I've known, for a long time, that there's some sort of a set-up between those two. Nothing gets by me that I don't see—and I've seen plenty. Corporal Downey is the only policeman that ever goes up to Halfaday—and Black John never comes to Dawson without dropping into headquarters for a pow-wow with Downey."

"You've got the dope right—an' that shows yer smart. Shore there's a set-up between them two. Like you said—Downey's the only copper that dasts to show up on Halfaday, an' when he does he sometimes gits his man. An' when he does, it's allus someone Black John wants him to git—an' not no one elst. You're right there at headquarters where you kin see what goes on—you never seen him fetchin' in none of Black John's pals, did you? Yer damn right you never!"

"But—what's all this got to do with this payroll job?"

"It's got a hell of a lot to do with it! We'll jest s'pose, fer instance, that from now on, it's you that's callin' the turn on Halfaday, instead of Downey."

Rollo shook his head. "That would never work. I just told you that Black John's got it in for me. He thinks I'm dumb."

"He won't be thinkin' yer so damn dumb a week from now. An' even if he does, it won't make no difference to you what he thinks. It's what me an' Jess thinks, from then on—an' we like you. We know damn well yer smart. Hell, you don't think we'd fool away our time tryin' to deal with a dumb cop, do you? You jest string along with us, an' play yer cards right, an' it won't be long till you'll be the one that's handlin' the important cases— an' Downey'll be doin' the chores."

"But—I don't know what you mean?"

"Meanin' that me an' Jess has decided to step in an' take Halfaday Crick over."

"But—what about Black John?"

Frank grinned. "You'll have him locked up in the bird cage there in Dawson—fer that payroll robbery."

"What!"

"That's right. He's the bozo that pulled it off."

"But—the proof! How could I ever prove it?"

"I guess if you was to fetch him in, along with the twenty

thousan' he took that messenger fer, it wouldn't be so hard to prove, would it? Besides that, by the time the trial come off, there'll be witnesses that'll swear they seen the hull play—an' not only you'll be able to git a conviction on Black John, but that office punk, an' the messenger, too. Then, when me an' Jess takes over Halfaday, you'll be the onliest cop that dasts to show up there—an' I'm promisin' you right now, we'll see to it that you git yer man every now an' then—same as Downey does now."

"An' on top of that," Jess cut in, "we'll see to it that you git hold of an important piece of change, now an' then."

"What do you mean by that?" Rollo asked, eyeing the man, sharply.

"Why, meanin' that I never seen a cop yet that would shy off'n a bale of the long green."

Rollo flushed. "You can't bribe me! I won't have a thing to do with it!"

FRANK SCOWLED at his brother, then grinned. "Don't pay no heed to Jess, kid. He was jest kiddin' you—sort of feelin' you out. He wanted to make shore we was dealin' with an honest cop, an' not no grifter we couldn't trust. It's like this—everyone knows them boys over on Halfaday Crick is all outlawed—Black John along with 'em. But as long as they don't pull off nothin' here in the Yukon, Downey don't bother 'em. Then, when someone does pull a job, he hits fer Halfaday, an' Downey knows where to look fer him, an' Black John helps him out—jest like me an' Jess will help you out. Every smart cop has got his contacts with outlaws—that's what makes him smart."

Rollo nodded. "I guess that's right," he agreed. "But how am I going to arrest Black John? And how do you men happen to be here on Ladue Crick."

"It's like this—neither me, nor Jess has ever saw this Black John, personal. But Cuter Malone, he tips us off that Black John is in Dawson, right now—an' that he'll be headin' back fer

Halfaday in jest a few days."

"That's right," Rollo concurred. "He'd been in Dawson for several days before I left there. I see it all, now. He found out about the payroll, and slipped out and grabbed it off!"

"Shore he did," Frank agreed. "An' knowin' that, me an' Jess slips up here to kill time ontil Black John hits fer Halfaday, which, accordin' to Cuter, will be about day after tomorrow. Cuter shore knows what's goin' on. He's got stooges an' stoolies spotted in all the saloons, an' whatever a man says whilst he's drinkin' at the bar, er playin' cards, gits to Cuter in jig time.

"Our idee was to slip down to the White River tomorrow an' lay fer Black John, an' grab him off when he went past on his way back to Halfaday. Then we figgered on takin' him back to Dawson—him an' the twenty thousan'—an' turnin' him in to the cops. We figgered, that even if Downey was a friend of his'n, he wouldn't dast to do nothin' but throw him in the can, an' then me an' Jess would hit fer Halfaday an' take over.

"But you showin' up makes the play all the better on account, Downey, bein' a friend of Black John, might botch things up so he wouldn't git convicted. But with you handlin' the case, an' right there to keep an eye on things there ain't no chanct but what Black John'll git what's comin' to him."

"You bet he will!" Rollo cried. "But—how do we know he'll have the twenty thousand with him. If he hasn't—we wouldn't have a leg to stand on."

"He'll have the swag, all right," Frank said. "He's bound to have it. What the hell would he do with it? He wouldn't dast to deposit it in no bank. He wouldn't dast to throw none of it around Dawson, on account the bills might be marked, er their numbers took."

A worried look crept into Rollo's eyes. "Black John's a dangerous man. Suppose he resists arrest?"

"Let him resist an' be damned. There's three of us an' only one of him, ain't there? I ain't no good with a gun so I don't carry one. I leave the shootin' part to Jess. He's got a gun, an' you've got one. An' besides Black John'll be loaded down with his canoe, an' a pack. It's like this—comin' up here, me an' Jess talked to an old cuss name of Hizer which he lives in an old run-down tradin' post jest above Fish Rapids. He says how Black John allus camps at the foot of the rapids comin' upriver, an' then packs his stuff around the rapids on the foot trail. We'll drop down to the head of the rapids, an' lay fer him there, an' crack down on him whilst he's loaded down with his pack er his canoe—an' we've got him, cold turkey."

"By George, I believe you're right!" Rollo cried. "At last I've got my big chance. And believe me, it is big! Just think of catching Black John, with the goods—single handed! You men have sure done me a good turn—and I won't forget it. But I want it distinctly understood that when you take Halfaday over, there's to be no crime up there. Black John has always boasted that he keeps Halfaday moral—and he's really done it, too."

"Don't you worry none about us, kid. Me an' Jess knows what side our bread's buttered on. From now on Halfaday'll be a damn sight moraler'n what Black John ever kep' it—you kin bet on that!"

## IV

**BLACK JOHN BEACHED** his canoe on the gravel at the foot of the Fish Rapids, stepped ashore, yawned and stretched. He glanced toward the west where the sun hung low over the mountains. "Damn them sourdoughs," he grinned, "keepin' a man up all night, six, eight nights hand-runnin' playin' stud! What with the hotel room bein' so hot in the daytime, if you keep the window shut, an' if you open it, you can't sleep for the hollerin' an' the noise of Cuter Malone's damn piano acrost the street—it shore makes a man yearn for the peace an' quiet of Halfaday. I'll camp here an' get a good night's sleep before I tackle that portage. At that, though," he added, as his grin widened, "Halfaday might not be so damn peaceful an' quiet if them Watson boys has arrived there an' took over, like they figured they might. What with them eighty-six thousan' they fetched with 'em from Oregon, an' that twenty thousan' payroll on top of it, I shore hope they don't get lost somewheres along the trail. If they'd have hired me to guide 'em, like they figured they might, there wouldn't have be'n no question about their gettin' there."

Unloading his blankets and packsack, he built a fire, hung his tea pail above it, and slapped a thick beefsteak into the frying pan. Having eaten his fill, he washed the dishes, and lighted his pipe. "Beefsteak makes a nice change, now an' then, when a man can get it," he said, "but in the long run I'd rather have moose." Again he glanced toward the west, where the afterglow of the long twilight hung above the hills. "Guess I'll slip up an' chaw the fat with old man Hizer for a while. The poor old devil must be kind of lonesome—him an' his tradin' post just rottin' their last days out together."

As he neared the head of the portage trail a gleam of firelight caught his eye. Abandoning the trail he slipped through the bush and wormed his way beneath the low-hung branches of a spruce thicket to a point within half a dozen yards of the three men grouped about the fire. He recognized the two men he had met on the river a few days before, and as his glance rested on the uniformed one he grinned broadly. "It looks like Rollo has stepped in somethin' clean up to his ears," he muttered. "He'd ort to stuck to his Siwash countin', an' left the Watsons for Peters. Or maybe," he added, "they just hired Rollo instead of me to guide 'em to Halfaday."

The thin-lipped, hard eyed man glanced toward the west. He indicated the duffel that littered the ground. "You boys make camp an' git supper goin', an' I'll slip down to the foot of the rapids, an' see if Black John's got there yet. I kin get back afore dark." Picking up one of the packs, he turned toward the bush. "I'm cachin' this pack," he said. "The grub's in the other one."

Noiselessly Black John followed the man back into the bush where, at the foot of a rock wall he crammed the pack into a crevice and tossed a few loose rocks on it. Then he headed down the portage trail.

Five minutes later, Black John tossed the rocks aside, withdrew the pack, and opening it, lifted out a canvas container with the words Excelsior Development Co. stencilled in black letters on the side. "This is the payroll money," he muttered, and laying it aside, he proceeded to remove packet after packet of bank notes. "An' this here is the Oregon money—eighty-six thousan' accordin' to Downey. Don't it beat hell the way them damn thieves carries on!" Picking up the canvas container, he returned it to the packsack. "I shore hate to pass up them twenty thousan'," he muttered. "But after all, if Rollo takes in his men, he's got to have the evidence to convict 'em." Gathering great bunches of caribou moss that grew abundantly at the foot of the ledge, he crammed it in the packsack in place of the packets of bills. Then he returned the pack to the crevice, without, however, tossing any rocks on it.

Re-caching the bills at some distance, he slipped to the trail, and stepped boldly into the little clearing where the two were busy about the fire.

**BOTH WHIRLED** to face him. Jess Watson, recognizing him as the man they had questioned on the river bank, scowled. "What the hell you doin' here?" he demanded truculently.

Rollo's mouth had dropped open, and he was staring, wide-eyed, into the face of the newcomer. "Bla—Black John!" he gasped.

"What—him—Black John!" cried the other. "Oh, my God! Arrest him! Arrest him quick!"

Black John grinned. "Why would Rollo arrest me?" he asked.

"Fer that payroll robbery—that's why!"

"Cripes, it looks to me like he's already got the damn fools that pulled that job. Looks like you shore put one over on Peters this time, Rollo. I'll bet Downey'll be surprised. Yes sir—you got the robbers. An' I'll bet you got 'em with the goods."

There was a quick movement beside the fire, and lurching swiftly aside, Black John's hand flashed from beneath his shirt as two guns roared and Jess slumped sidewise and collapsed beside the fire, a six-gun clutched in his hand.

Rollo's horrified glance strayed from the dead man to the face of Black John. "Where—where's Frank?" he managed to croak.

"Who's Frank?"

"Why, he—he's the other Watson. He went down to the foot of the rapids. Didn't you meet him on the trail?"

Black John nodded. "Oh, that was Frank, eh? Yeah, I met some fella a little ways down. I saw him comin', an' stepped into the bush till he passed. He didn't see me."

"He—he'll be showing up in a minute—hearing those shots," Rollo said.

The big man shook his head. "He'd never hear 'em. What with them rapids roarin' like they do, a man couldn't hear a cannon-shot a hundred yards away. But howcome you'd let him get out of your sight? Hell, man, what's to hinder him from keepin' right on goin'—an' takin' that twenty thousan' along with him?"

"What twenty thousand?"

"What twenty thousan'! Why the twenty thousan' they picked up on that Excelsior payroll robbery, of course."

"But—but—they said you pulled off the robbery! We—we were just waiting here till you came along, and I was going to arrest you."

Black John regarded him seriously. "You can think up more damned mistakes to make than any four men I ever seen. But this time, it looks like you've blundered onto a piece of good luck." He pointed to the two packsacks on the ground. "Listen, Rollo—that pack there would be yours. The other is the grub pack. Ain't there another pack around here somewheres?"

"Why, yes—Frank's pack. He always had it near him. If he set it down, it was always within reach. When he went down the trail he took it with him—said he was going to cache it!"

"Shore, he'd always have it within reach. Don't you know why?"

Rollo shook his head.

"It's because he had that twenty thousan' dollar payroll in it—that's why. He didn't have no pack on him when I met him a little ways down the trail. So he cached it, all right—an' like you said, he don't never get very far away from it, so the chances are he cached it right clost to here. We'll take a look. An' when we find it, I'll bet you a thousan' dollars agin a week's pay, you'll find that payroll in it." The two stepped into the bush. "Now let's see," the big man said, "if I was goin' to cache a pack right clost by, I'd prob'ly hit fer the rock wall yonder. Them rock walls has always got cracks an crevices in 'em where a man could shove somethin'. We'll start here—you go that way, an' I'll go this."

A few minutes later Rollo called excitedly. "Here it is! I found it! It's shoved in a crack in the rocks!"

Black John joined him and stood looking down at the pack. "You're shore that's Frank's pack, are you?" he asked. "If them damn cusses be'n tellin' you it was me pulled that robbery, I don't want Frank claimin' this pack belongs to me, an' not him."

"It's his, all right," Rollo said. "I can swear to that. I've seen it too many times to be fooled."

"Okay. Open it up, then, an' see if them twenty thousan' ain't in it."

Rollo opened the pack and stared into it. Then he began pulling out moss. With quite a heap of it on the ground beside him, he looked up. "There's nothing but moss in here," he said. "Why would anyone be packing around a sack of moss?"

"Keep on. That payroll is prob'ly in the bottom. The moss,

he prob'ly just stuffed that in to fill out the pack. Prob'ly figured it might look kind of funny to be carryin' around a pack with hardly nothin' in it."

A few moments later, Rollo withdrew the canvas container. "Here it is," he cried, "with the company's name printed right on it!"

"That's right," Black John agreed. "Better take the bills out an' count 'em—just to make shore it's all there. I don't want the damn cuss to try to blame me if some of it's missin'.'"

"It's all here," Rollo announced, after counting the money. "And that clears you, all right." He paused and stared into Black John's face. "Do you know," he announced, "that these men had actually planned to take Halfaday Crick over, after you were under arrest? They even promised me that when they took over, and any crooks sought refuge on the crick, I could go up there after 'em, an' they'd turn 'em right over to me. But that was when I thought you were guilty of this robbery."

"Yeah," Black John grinned. "It would have be'n quite an arrangement, at that."

"There's one thing I can't see—and that is, how they expected me to ever convict you, if they had this payroll money."

"That's easy—the damn crooks would have switched the payroll from this pack into mine—an' you'd never known the difference. Take men like them, they're so damn onderhanded in their dealin's they wouldn't stop at nothin'. They'd figure the twenty thousan' was a cheap price to pay for control of Halfaday. Come on, fetch that money along. Frank's liable to show up anytime. When he comes, you better cover him with your gun, an' I'll slip the bracelets on him for you."

**THEY HAD** not long to wait before Frank Watson stepped into the firelight to face the leveled revolver in Constable Buck's hand. "Frank Watson," the officer said, "you are under arrest for the Excelsior payroll robbery, and it is my duty to warn you that anything you say may be used against you."

"What the hell!" cried the man, his hands elevated above his head, as his glance shifted from the revolver in Rollo's hand to the body of his brother, and then to the face of Black John.

"This is Black John Smith," Rollo explained. "The man you told me was guilty of that payroll robbery. But you didn't get away with it, Watson. I found that payroll money in your packsack right where you cached it, there at the foot of the rock wall."

"You—you found the pack?" Watson managed to gasp. "An'—an' the twenty thousan'?"

"That's right."

"An'—an' the rest of the stuff, too?"

"Rest of the stuff," Rollo grinned. "You mean all that moss?"

Slowly Frank Watson's glance travelled from Rollo, to the face of Black John. "Moss, eh?" he muttered. "He said 'moss'."

The big man nodded. "Yeah, Watson. I told Rollo, here, that you prob'ly stuffed in that moss to sort of wad your pack out, so it wouldn't look so little. It jest goes to prove that those old sayin's ain't always right—like 'a rollin' stone gathers no moss'. You're a rollin' stone, Watson, if ever there was one—but you gathered quite a bit of moss." He paused and turned to the officer. "Better toss me the bracelets, Rollo, an' I'll slip 'em on him, before he tries to make a break for the bush."

As the big man slipped the cuffs on his wrists, Frank Watson's lips moved in a venomous whisper: "You win—you skunk! I don't dast to squawk. But you ain't heard the last of me yet. They don't give a man life fer a twenty-thousan' dollar job, when there ain't no murder along with it."

"That's right," the big man returned the whisper. "But for an eighty-six thousan' dollar job, with a murder throw'd in, he'd shore as hell git life—if he didn't get the rope—wouldn't he?"

**BLACK JOHN** camped there that night, and the following morning he accompanied Rollo and his prisoner down the trail. "We'll just trade canoes," he said, "an' save packin' 'em over the trail. You take mine on to Dawson, an' I'll go upriver in yours. Better keep an eye on your prisoner, Rollo," he advised, when they reached the foot of the rapid. "He don't look to me like no one a man could trust. Guess we better tie his feet together, an' leave them cuffs on. I'll help you lift him into the canoe. If I was you I'd hold off the mouth of the river an' flag down the *Sarah*. She's due downriver today. That way you won't be takin' no chances."

Arriving in Dawson on the steamboat, Constable Buck marched his manacled prisoner to headquarters, and proudly laid the payroll money on Corporal Downey's desk.

The old officer glanced from the prisoner to the canvas packet. "Is that all you found on him?" he asked. "An' where's the other one—his brother. Both of 'em was mixed up in that job."

"He's dead. He pulled a gun and Black John shot him at the head of Fish Rapids. That payroll money's all there. I took it right out of his cache. And that's all there was in it—that and a lot of moss."

"Where does Black John come in? You say it was him that shot Jess."

"Why, the Watsons and I were laying for him at the head of Fish Rapids. I ran onto them at Sebastian's Village, and they told me it was Black John who committed that robbery, so we were laying for him. I was going to arrest him when he came up the river. I'll explain it all in my report."

"Was it Black John found this cache—or you?"

"I found it. Black John said it would probably be along the edge of a nearby rock wall—and it was. I found it in no time at all. What made you think it was Black John that found it?"

"Oh, I don't know—jest sort of wondered, that's all. Take it first an' last, Rollo, Black John's gathered a hell of a lot of moss. An' by the way, how many Indians is in Sebastian's Village—er will you have that in yer report, too?"

"Why, I didn't count 'em. I ran onto the Watsons, and figured the arrest of Black John was more important."

Corporal Downey nodded. "Okay, Rollo. We can handle Watson here. You go back to Sebastian's Village an' count them Siwashes."

# LEFT HANDED JUSTICE

**IT WAS EARLY** afternoon as Black John Smith stepped into the barroom of Cushing's Fort, the combined trading post and saloon that served the little band of outlawed men that had sprung up on Halfaday Creek, close against the Yukon-Alaska border. Old Cush, the proprietor, folded the month-old newspaper he had been reading, placed it carfully on the back bar, shoved the square-framed, steel rimmed spectacles from nose to forehead, and set out a bottle, two glasses, and the inevitable leather dice box.

As Black John picked up the box a shadow darkened the doorway and both eyed the man who paused momentarily as his shifty eyes seemed to take in every detail of the room. Advancing to the bar, the stranger swung a pack from his shoulders and addressed the big man who stood dice box in hand:

"This here'd be Cushing's Fort on Halfaday Crick, ain't it? An' I s'pose you'd be Black John Smith, an' him behind the bar there'd be Cush."

The big man nodded. "The supposition, in all its aspects seems eminently tenable."

The man's brow furrowed. "How?"

Setting out another glass, Cush shoved the bottle toward the newcomer. "That's jest John's way of sayin' you done some good guessin'. Fill up. This un's on the house."

The man filled his glass and pushed the bottle along. "I heard about you fellas down to Cuter Malone's in Dawson," he said. "How you was a bunch of outlaws, that hung out up here clost to the line, an' how the police don't dast to show up here on the crick. I hain't afeard of the police, not bein' no outlaw, myself—jest a common prospector. An' the way I figger it, outlaws is jest as good to live amongst as anyone else. As long as a man minds his own business, they'll mind their'n. So I come on up here, figgerin' on stakin' me a location. Accordin' to the tell they's plenty of ground that hain't be'n staked yet, besides quite a few abandoned claims a man could relocate. How about it?"

Black John filled his glass and passed the bottle on to Cush. "W-e-e-l-l," he drawled, as he eyed the little beads that rimmed his glass, "as to us bein' a bunch of outlaws, I couldn't say. Some of the boys might have be'n outlawed somewhere in their past for all I know. But once they locate on Halfaday they've got to refrain from murder, larceny in any form, claim-jumpin', an' any other form of skullduggery, or get hung. Also I'll p'int out that the police are free to come and go as they please. As you said, there's plenty of room for prospectin' along the crick, an' several good claims that were abandoned before they were worked out."

"Why would a man abandon a good claim before it was worked out?"

"Oh, different reasons. Mostly because their morality got to slippin' an' we hung 'em."

The newcomer raised his glass. "Drink up," he said, "an' I'll buy one." When the glasses were refilled he eyed the big man. "My name's John Smith—same as yourn," he announced. "Might's well git acquainted, bein' as I aim to settle down here."

"Not on Halfaday yer name ain't John Smith."

"How come? You ain't took out no patent on the name, have you?"

"No. But we outlawed it. You see, every damn miscreant that hit Halfaday claimed his name was John Smith. It was all right till we run out of distinguishin' parts—like, Long, Short, One Eyed, One Armed, One Legged, Pot Gutted, Black, Red an' so

forth—so me an' Cush invented the name can. We got holt of a history book an' scrambled up the names an' wrote 'em on slips of paper an' put 'em in that tin molasses can that sets there on the end of the bar. Now when anyone comes along with the misinformation that his name is John Smith, we invite him to reach in the can an' pull him out a more fittin' alias. The name he so draws becomes his until such time as he departs from the crick."

The man remained silent for a few moments, the furrows deepening in his brow. "I git you," he said, at length. "Too many guys come along claimin' their name is John Smith, an' you don't want no more John Smiths on the crick, so you make 'em draw a name outa the can, eh?"

"That's the thought I strove to put across."

"How?"

"He means 'yeah'," Cush interpreted.

"It hain't no bad idee, at that," the man agreed, and reaching into the can he withdrew a slip of paper and read the name, "Robert E. Grant. Okay, then. I guess I'm him."

Black John raised his glass. "Here's lookin' at you, Bob," he said. "Drink up, an' I'll buy one."

The glasses were emptied and refilled. The man tossed a little moosehide sack onto the bar. "I better pay fer the one I bought," he said. "Weigh it outa that."

AS CUSH trickled the dust onto the scale Black John glanced at the man. "Be'n doin' some prospectin' eh? What's the matter— did yer claim peter out?"

The man nodded. "Yeah, it wasn't nothin' to brag of to start out with. Upriver, it was—on a little crick that runs into the Pelly. When I found out I couldn't do no better'n wages, I says 'to hell with it'." Picking up his glass he nodded at Black John. "Here's mud in yer eye," he said, and downing the drink, returned the glass to the bar and reached for his pack sack. "I'll shove on up the crick an' look around. If I locate anythin' that suits me I'll be back fer some supplies." Slipping into his pack straps he crossed the floor. In the doorway he paused. "So long," he said. "I'll be seein' you."

When the man had disappeared Cush eyed Black John across the bar. "Don't it beat hell—the kind of riff-raff that drifts in on us? Claimed he ain't no outlaw—jest a common prospector! Cripes, one look into them shifty eyes of his, an' a man would know he's a liar!"

Reaching across the bar Black John lifted the pan from the scale, and holding it to the light, examined the particles of gold.

"He never panned this dust on the Pelly, nor nowhere else upriver," he said. "That's downriver gold—see that red glint to it?"

Peering into the pan Cush nodded. "Shore it is," he agreed. "An' that proves Grant's a damn liar—jest like I said."

"Well, I guess one more liar won't hurt the crick any."

"It ain't his lyin' I give a damn about," Cush opined. "It's what he might do an' then try to lie out of."

A FEW days later, the man Grant reappeared and accosted Black John at the door of the barroom. "Come on in an' I'll buy a drink," he invited. When the glasses were filled, he glanced up. "I found me a location that looks pretty good," he said. "It's on a feeder that runs in from the north, about five mile up the crick. It's be'n abandoned quite a while, looks like. There's a cabin on it an' a couple of shafts that don't go down more'n five, six foot. I panned some nice colors outa one of 'em. The porkypines had messed up the cabin quite a bit, but I made me a spruce broom an' swep' it out. Funny a guy would abandon a location like that. Looks like he might of did all right there."

"That's Whiskey Bill's old cabin," Black John said.

"Why did he abandon his claim?"

"It was quite a while back. I disremember the circumstances."

"It must be pretty clost to the line, up there," Grant observed. "Like if a man would want to quit the country, he would hit out through Alasky, an' not have to go on out upriver."

"It's clost to the line, all right," the big man said, "but no one yet has ever made it out through Alaska. Several have tried it, one time an' another—but none of 'em made it. There's several hundred miles of rough mountains in there—them an' the ornery Siwashes that lives in 'em."

"There ain't nothin' to hinder me locatin' on that claim, is there?"

"Nothin' whatever. You can record it with Cush here—he's an emergency recorder."

"I won't bother to record it yet. They'll be time enough later, if I figger to hold it. I'll git me a load of supplies an' shove on back."

When Cush had filled his order, the man tendered his gold sack and Cush weighed out the dust. "I done pretty good the couple of days I worked that shaft," he said. "I tuk out about seven ounces."

When he had gone, the two examined the dust in the scale. "More red dust," Black John said. "He never shoveled that out of Whiskey Bill's shaft, any more'n he got the dust he claimed he did on the Pelly. Methinks our friend Grant will stand watchin'. A man might lie once, sort of off hand, or inadvertent. But if he persists in lyin', there's a reason."

## II

**ONE AFTERNOON, SOME** two weeks after the departure of Grant for Whiskey Bill's claim, Black John and Cush were whiling away the time playing cribbage in the barroom for ten cents a point. Cush spread his cards on the table. "Fifteen-two, fifteen-four, fifteen-six, an' eight is fourteen."

Black John picked up the deck. "My deal," he said. "Too bad you couldn't have got another point, an' you'd have be'n out. The way it is, I might peg twenty, thirty cents worth."

"Hold on there!" Cush cried. "By God, that jack of spades was nobs! I got fifteen p'ints! The seven of spades was turned!"

"It was the seven of clubs," the big man replied, shuffling the cards.

"It worn't no sech a thing! It was the seven of spades, an' you know damn well it was! An' what's more you ain't got no business grabbin' up the deck till I git through countin' my hand. I win the game, an' you owe me three dollars an' forty cents!"

"I do like hell! You better get them glasses changed, if you can't tell a club from a spade!"

A man in the uniform of the Northwest Mounted Police stepped into the room and approached the table, a broad grin on his face. "What's the war about?" he asked. "Cripes, I could hear you fellas halfways across the clearin'!"

White teeth flashed beneath the heavy black beard as the big man glanced up at the officer. "Well, dog my cats, if it ain't Corporal Downey himself! Let's adjourn to the bar an' Cush'll buy a drink. He just hornswaggled me out of three-forty. He shore ought to buy."

"I did like hell!" Cush retorted. Gathering up board and cards he stepped behind the bar and set out a bottle and three glasses. "I win the game, an' he know'd it. He retch out an' grib up the deck 'fore I got my hand counted—an' then claimed I didn't have no nobs! Take it in a stud game an' John'll toss a hundred dollars in the pot, er a thousan', an' never bat an' eye, but in a cribbage game he'll auger his head off fer a dime! An' like in any kind of a proposition, I'd take his words fer any amount— an' so could any other honest man—an' know damn well he'd make good on it. But shakin' dice fer the drinks, they ain't no onery, low-down trick he wouldn't stoop to. An' let some damn crook show up on the crick, an' John'll take him fer all he's got, an' mebbe call a miners' meetin' an' hang him, to boot. An' if it was some pore man, er some prospector the crook had robbed, he'd git every damn cent of it back. Trouble is, they can't no one figger John out."

"Speakin' of crooks," Downey said, reaching for the bottle, and filling his glass, "we've got a murder on our hands—an' a damn dirty one. It's a downriver case—a prospector got knocked off in his cabin on a feeder about fifty miles up the Porcupine from Rampart House. The Porcupine is in Forty Mile Detachment's territory, an' Sam Steele investigated the case himself. Then he passed it on to me because a man answerin' the description of the suspect was seen headin' upriver. We inquired around an' found out that the man we're lookin' for had be'n seen around Cuter Malone's Klondike Palace a week or so before we got word of the case. We went through Dawson with a fine-toothed comb, but he ain't there. I figure he went on upriver headin' either for the outside, or for here."

"Hum, yer deduction seems reasonable," Black John admitted, toying with his glass. "You say it was a dirty murder, eh?"

"It shore was. This prospector was a young feller that came into the country a couple of years ago. He worked for Jardine, the factor at Rampart House for a year till he got a stake, then hit out for himself. He hit what looks like a pretty fair proposition on this feeder, an' then he married old Ben Hardy's daughter. You rec'lect old Ben—he got killed a few years back when that delayed shot he was investigatin' went off an' blow'd him to pieces down on Forty Mile."

"Shore, I knew old Ben, an' I rec'lect the girl too—'Sis', we used to call her, never did know her right name. Me an' Bettles was winterin' in a cabin about a mile up from old Ben's. Sis, she was about ten, twelve years old then, an' come Chris'mas, she shows up bright an' early in the mornin' with a dish of candy she'd made, an' a whole batch of popcorn. Cripes, it tasted good! We hadn't neither one of us had no popcorn or candy in years."

"Well, she's grow'd up, now—Agalia, her name is."

"Cripes, no wonder they called her Sis!" Cush exclaimed, as he tossed off his drink and refilled his glass.

**DOWNEY IGNORED** the interruption. "She was visitin' Jardine's wife, when this young fella—Joe Brooks—went down to Rampart House for supplies. He met her there, an' hung around a few days courtin' her, an' when Father Judge happened along, damned if they didn't up an' get married. Brooks, he'd throw'd up a shack on his claim, an' they went to work on the location. Couple of months ago she made the trip in a canoe to Rampart House for supplies, an' he stayed on the claim. She made the trip down in two days, an' it took her five days to go back up the river. When she got there she found Brooks dead on the floor with a bullet hole in the side of his head. She found that their cache had be'n robbed, an' she hit hell-bent back to Rampart House. Jardine sent a breed to notify the Forty Mile detachment, and the breed run onto Sam Steele at Circle. Sam was headin' downriver on a trip up the Porcupine to Lapierre House. He hit for Rampart House an' took up the investigation.

"Agalia Brooks was stoppin' there an', accordin' to Sam's report, both her an' Jardine told him that as far as they knew there was only three other white men on the lower Porcupine—a couple of old timers that was pardners in a location about thirty miles above Brooks's, an' a kind of shifty-eyed hombre that hadn't located no claims. He jest worked along the river, snipin' the bars, here an' there, an' proddin' around on the cricks. The girl said he'd stopped in to their place a few times, an' Jardine said he'd show up there now an' then for supplies, payin' for 'em with dust out of a mighty lean sack—never had more'n half a dozen ounces in it. The man claimed his name was Orrin Parker, accordin' to Jardine.

"Sam went on up to Brooks's location, an' found Brooks layin' on the floor of the shack, like the girl said. His rifle laid on the floor beside him. The girl said they kept it on a couple of pegs drove into the wall above the table. Sam figures that when Brooks seen the gun in the man's hand, he turned to reach for his rifle an' the robber shot him in the side of the head. Agalia told Sam where the cache was, an' like she said, he found it empty. She told him they had about four hundred an' fifty ounces left in it after she took out the ten ounces she took down to Rampart House to pay for the supplies.

"Sam found that the bullet had gone through Brooks's head an' was lodged against the skull on the other side. He dug it out, an' figured it to be a thirty-eight calibre, but it's so flattened out it's no good for identification purposes. It was prob'ly fired from a pistol of some kind, because a rifle bullet would have gone on through.

"From there Sam went on up the river an' talked to the two sourdoughs. They claimed that this Orrin Parker had be'n farther up the river prospectin', but had come on back down a couple of weeks back, claimin' he hadn't done no good, up there. They said he borrowed three ounces from 'em to buy grub with. Sam went back to Rampart House an' Jardine told him that Parker hadn't bought any grub lately, an' that he hadn't seen him for more than a month. They all described him as bein' around thirty, or thirty-five, stocky built, with pale blue eyes that kept shiftin' around here an' there when he talked.

"Sam hit back to the big river, an' at Fort Yukon, he found that a man answerin' this description had bought supplies there an' paid for 'em with dust out of a well-filled sack. The trader thought he headed upriver. Sam run onto his trail at Circle City, an' again at Eagle. An' a couple of fellas camped at the mouth of Coal Crick remembered him. He stopped an' et with 'em one noon, then shoved on upriver in his canoe. At Forty Mile Bergman thought he rec'lected servin' a shifty-eyed character a couple of drinks a short time back—but he wouldn't be sure.

"So, Sam sent a copy of his report up to Dawson, an' passed the buck to me. Like I said, we found out he'd hung around Cuter Malone's for a couple of days, an' then disappeared. So I headed upriver. No one at Ogilvie, or Stewart, or Henderson's Crick had seen him, so when I hit the mouth of the White, I headed up here, figurin' he might have hit for Halfaday."

AS THE officer finished his recital Black John downed his liquor and refilled his glass from the bottle. "S'pose you caught up with this Orrin Parker—what you got on him?" he asked.

"Why, he was known to be on the Porcupine, headin' down toward Brooks's location about the time Brooks was murdered. He told these two prospectors he was broke an' borrowed three ounces of dust from 'em to buy grub with. He didn't stop at Rampart House and buy any grub. When he did stop at Fort Yukon for supplies, he paid for 'em out of a well filled sack of dust. An' if I'd find a thirty-eight pistol in his possession I'd have a pretty good case."

The big man smiled and shook his head slowly from side to side. "Not a very good case, Downey—not one that a good defense lawyer couldn't bust wide open without half tryin', what with the law demandin' evidence that's damn near iron-clad an' conclusive. Let's run over it, p'int by p'int. You say Parker was comin' down the Porcupine about the time Brooks was murdered. Anyone might be comin' down any river about the time someone was murdered. He claimed he was broke an' borrowed three ounces of dust off them two prospectors to buy grub with. But he didn't buy any grub from Jardine. There's nothin' in the law that says he had to buy grub there. He could go on the witness stand an' claim he shot a caribou an' didn't need no grub till he got to Fort Yukon."

"Yes," Downey interrupted, "but when he got there he paid for the grub out of a well filled sack of dust."

"Uh-huh. But it don't necessarily follow that he got that dust out of Brooks's cache. Maybe he lied to those prospectors. Maybe he had that poke of dust when he borrowed them three ounces. The most he'd be guilty of would be obtainin' them three ounces under false pretenses—an' that's a hell of a crime to be chasin' a man all over the Yukon for. An' if you do run him down an' find a thirty-eight gun on him, that wouldn't prove nothin'— with the bullet all flattened out, like you claim it is. Cripes, any smart defense lawyer could rustle around you an' find a dozen fellas right around Dawson who owned thirty-eight guns!"

"But if I was to arrest him, I might work a confession out of him."

"You might. But it ain't likely. That's the trouble with the law, Downey—it goes too damn much on evidence. Common sense tells you an' me, an' Sam Steele, an' Jardine, an' Sis Hardy that this here damn Orrin Parker murdered Brooks an' robbed his cache. But common sense don't suit the law. It demands proof— which in the absence of witnesses, you ain't got. Take a miners' meetin', now—we look over the known facts, viewin' 'em in the light of probabilities an' common sense, an' arrive at a verdick. Tried by miners' meetin' this here Orrin wouldn't have a chanct in the world to lie out of that murder. But in a court of law, you ain't got a chance in the world of convictin' him—short of a confession, which is too remote a probability even to consider."

Corporal Downey shrugged. "Oh, I know, the law demands evidence that's sometimes impossible to get. But the police don't make the laws—all we do is try to enforce 'em. Has any hombre answerin' Orrin Parker's description showed up here on Halfaday?"

Black John shook his head. "No, but you can bet your shirt that we'll keep our eyes open. It might be I'll get the chanct to pay Sis Hardy back for that candy an' popcorn she give me an' Bettles, that Chris'mas. You know, Downey, that here on Halfaday we always work hand in glove with the police. You can shove on upriver. You might be lucky enough to locate Orrin at Selkirk, or Whitehorse, or Hootalinqua. If the damn cuss shows up here you'll know about it—I'll promise you that. Drink up, an' have another."

Downey shook his head. "No more for me, thanks. I'll be on my way. It's barely possible I can head him off before he gets outside. So long. Let me know if he shows up here."

When the officer had gone Cush scowled across the bar. "Of all the damn liars I ever heer'd, you take the cake! You know damn well that there Robert E. Grant ain't no one elst but this here Ornery Parker, er whatever his name is! An' you up an' tell Downey he ain't showed up here on the crick."

The big man grinned broadly. "Oh—Bob Grant, eh? Cripes I'd plumb fergot about Bob! Come to think of it, he might fit that description, at that."

"Well, Downey ain't got fer. You kin holler him back."

The big man shook his head. "No, it wouldn't hardly be worth while."

Cush snorted. "Sometimes, John, you talk like a damn fool—

an' act like one too. But then agin, they's be'n times when I figgered you was one when you wasn't. That's why I kep' my mouth shet. I figgered mebbe you had some scheme you was goin' to work—like callin' a miners' meetin' an' hangin' that stinker."

"Certainly not, my good man! Such high-handed procedure would be unethical in the extreme. This murder was committed well outside our jurisdiction."

"You an' yer damn jewishdiction! This here Grant was spendin' downriver gold, wasn't he—right here over this bar?"

"Yeah, but if we was to hang everyone that spent downriver gold we'd run out of rope."

"But he lied about it! He claimed he got it upriver—on the Pelly."

The big man's grin widened. "If we was to hang a man for lyin' it would establish a bad persenent."

"Yeah," growled Cush, "an' you'd be the first one to git hung! Not only you lied to Downey, but you lied to Grant the other day—you telling him they hadn't no one ever got out of here by way of Alasky on account of Siwashes an' mountains. You know damn well a lot of 'em has gone out that way—an' some of 'em got through all right."

"In sizin' up Grant, I found little to admire in his cosmos."

"In his which?"

"His ego."

"What the hell's that? By cripes, when you run out of big words you find little ones to say that don't mean nothin'!"

"All right, then—in *him!* I don't like him. Can you get that through yer skull? Such bein' the case, I opine that it won't be long before he'll overstep the bounds of rectitude somewheres within our jurisdiction, in which case, we can call a miners' meetin' an' strive to correct the idiosyncrasy. But in the meantime I wanted to make sure he wouldn't try to evade justice by slippin' out the back door on us, an' hit out through Alaska.

"As I see it, Cush, our course is to simply bide our time, an' let nature take her course."

Cush shrugged. "All I kin make out of it is, yer goin' to lay low an' hang Grant for somethin' he does here on the crick, instid of what we're really hangin' him fer, so you'll figger around fer some confustification that'll let us do it—an' if yer so hell-bent fer big words, chaw on that one!"

✦

# III

**AFEW DAYS AFTER** Corporal Downey's departure from Half-aday Black John stepped into the saloon to find Grant standing at the bar talking to Cush. Joining him, the big man ordered a round of drinks. When they were disposed of Grant tossed a well filled pouch onto the bar. "We'll fill 'em up agin, Cush," he said. "An' while yer about it you might's well weigh out the dust fer that there grub I ordered."

Black John glanced at the poke. "You must be doin' all right up there on Whiskey Bill's old claim," he observed.

The man nodded. "Yer damn right. She's a good location. What I claim any time a man kin pan out three, four ounces a day he's doin' all right. I kin take that much outa either one of them shafts without breakin' my back doin' it. I can't figger what this here Whiskey Bill ever abandoned a location like that fer."

"Seems like he got mixed up somehow with the law. He went down to Dawson an' got into some kind of a rookus an' hit for the outside. An' speakin' of the law, Corporal Downey stopped in here a few days back."

Grant darted him a swift glance out of the corner of his eye. "What did Downey want?" he asked.

"Oh, nothin' in particular. Just a routine patrol."

"Any news down along the river?"

"Nothin' to speak of. Couple of chechakos got stuck up just above the Caribou Crossin'. They was headin' outside with their dust when some guy pokes a revolver at 'em an' made off with their gold."

"Huh," Cush grunted. "Looks like the two of 'em could of put up a scrap of some kind."

Black John shook his head. "Not with a gun on 'em. They'd be'n damn fools to. You bet, if anyone was to pull a gun on me, like that, I'd shore let 'em get away with whatever I had—no matter how much it was. I wouldn't take a chanct of gettin' shot for all the gold in the Yukon."

"That's where yer smart," Grant agreed heartily. "If folks that was gittin' robbed wouldn't put up no fight they ain't no robber with any sense would shoot 'em. Hell, s'pose somethin' should go wrong an' he'd git ketched! If he ain't shot no one, all the law could do would be to give him a stretch in stir. But if he knocked someone off they'd call it murder an' then he'd git hung. A man would be a damn fool to take a chance of gittin' hung— if he didn't have to."

"That's right," Black John agreed. "I look at it just like you do, Bob. The bird that was gettin' held up would be a fool to put up a scrap in the face of a gun—an' the guy that was holdin' him up would be a fool to shoot him, if he didn't have to."

"Yeah," Cush said, "but s'pose he didn't kill him an' the police should ketch the robber—then the one that got helt up could identify him."

"How the hell could he if the guy was smart enough to wear a mask of some kind over his face?" the big man asked. "All he could tell about the robber would be that he was tall, or short, or fat, or skinny, an' how he was dressed. An' if the robber was to do away with the clothes he was wearin' there's a thousan' men that would fit any one of them descriptions."

"Shore there is," Grant agreed. "They couldn't no one say fer shore it was him, if he kep' his face covered."

Pot Gutted John stepped into the room and tossed a well stuffed poke onto the bar. "Shake out enough fer a round of drinks, Cush, an' stick the rest in the safe an' give me credik fer it."

**AS CUSH** swung the door to the iron safe open, Black John noted that Grant's shifty eyes opened wider at the sight of the tier upon tier of well filled gold sacks.

"By cripes, Cush," Pot Gutted John said, as his poke was added to the hoard, "if you stick much more dust in that old safe she's goin' to git sprung at the corners!"

Black John nodded. "Yeah, there's too much dust on hand. Paper money don't take up half the room. You better weigh out a couple hundred pounds of dust, an' I'll hit out for Dawson with it in the mornin' an' cash it in at the bank for big bills."

"A couple of hundred pounds," Grant exclaimed. "My God, that's better'n fifty thousan' dollars!"

Black John nodded casually. "Oh, shore. You see, most of the boys along the crick banks their dust with Cush instead of cachin' it. Not that we don't trust one another you understand. But just in case some felonious stranger might show up on the crick an' stumble onto a cache. Then, every oncet in so often, I take the dust down to the bank an' fetch the bills back. Let's see—I can make Dawson in ten days, then allowin' for a night of stud playin' with the sourdoughs, will make eleven days, an' I can make it back in twelve—that'll be twenty-three days. This is the third. I ought to be back here by the twenty-sixth with the bills."

After Grant and Pot Gutted John had hit for their claims Cush scowled across the bar at Black John. "By cripes—looks like you ain't got no more sense than a rabbit!"

The big man grinned. "W-e-e-l-l, offhand, I'd say that raises a moot question. I'll be glad to argue the matter."

"I don't know what a moot is, no more'n what you do. An' they ain't no augerin' about it! What I mean—you standin' there an' tellin' jest how long it'll take you to pack that dust down to Dawson an' fetch them big bills back, an' that damn Grant

standin' there pertendin' not to listen—an' his ears jest a twitch-
erin' not to miss a word!"

"Oh, Bob's all right. Looks like we've be'n kind of misjudgin'
him. He's smarter'n he looks. Didn't you notice how he agreed
with everything I said—about how a man ought to act durin'
a hold-up?"

"Huh," Cush grunted. "It ain't him I figger ain't smart—it's
you!"

## IV

**TEN DAYS LATER** Black John stepped into the bank at Dawson
and swung a heavy packsack from his shoulders. After weighing its contents the receiving teller totaled the figures on a slip
of paper. "Thirty-two hundred ounces," he announced. "That's
fifty-one thousand, two hundred dollars. How do you want it?"

"I'll take the two hundred dollars in one dollar bills, an' I'd
be obliged if you'd make 'em up in a neat sealed package an' put
a thousan' dollar bill on top—jest to make the package look
nice. You can give me a deposit slip for the balance—make it
out to Lyme Cushing."

The teller, who had known the big man for years, smiled as
he slipped the package beneath the wicket. "I'd be willing to
bet, John, that someone is due for a slight disappointment when
he opens this," he said.

"You'd ondoubtless win the bet," the big man replied. "But
the disapp'intment will be merely temporary, I can assure you—a
slight annoyance that I've got a hunch will terminate abruptly."

Proceeding toward the Tivoli Saloon he met Corporal
Downey on Front Street. "How'd you make out, upriver?" he
asked. "Did you locate that damn cuss that knocked off Sis
Hardy's husband down there on the Porcupine?"

The officer shook his head. "Not hide nor hair of him. He
didn't show up at Selkirk nor Whitehorse. For all we've found
out he could have evaporated into thin air right here in Dawson.

It's possible he hit out on a prospectin' trip somewheres. Al Scougale says he dimly remembers sellin' a hombre of his description a bill of supplies a while back, but he can't be sure. There's one guy I'd shore like to get my hands on! Not only he murdered Agalia Hardy's husband, but he stole every damn cent she had in the world. Jardine was here a few days ago, an' he says she's gone back to work the claim alone—an' I'm tellin' you that's guts! There's damn few young women that would have done that—after what happened, up there. If there's any such thing as justice in this world, that bird should wind up with a rope around his neck! But it's like you said, up there at Cush's—I'm afraid we haven't got any evidence that a smart defense lawyer couldn't shoot full of holes."

Black John nodded. "Yeah, like I've often told you, Downey, demandin' evidence, like it does, the law always gives a murderer a damn sight more breaks than he's got comin'. But don't let it get you down. I've got a sort of hunch that in this case justice might work out all right."

The officer's eyes lighted. "What do you mean, John? Has that damn cuss showed up on Halfaday?"

"W-e-e-l-l, maybe not exactly on Halfaday. The fact is when I was headin' down the White, four, five days ago with a bunch of dust I was fetchin' to the bank, I met a character headin' up the river that might turn out to be the man yer after."

"What did he have to say?"

"Not much. Asked how far it was to Halfaday Crick. I gave him directions that would take him to Cush's, if he follows 'em."

Downey's brow drew into a thoughtful frown. "If he gets to Halfaday it's a cinch he'll stay there. I'm goin' to slip down to Forty Mile an' have a talk with Sam Steele. We're goin' to need every bit of evidence in this case we can get. Sam's a mighty thorough investigator. He was right there on the ground. There might be some little things that didn't show up in his report—an' sometimes it's the little things—a footprint, a discarded cigarette butt, that cinches a case. How long are you goin' to be here, in Dawson?"

"Oh, it's kind of hard to tell. You know how it is—things get kind of monotonous up there on Halfaday, an' so when I hit here I sometimes horse around with the sourdoughs fer four, five days, or a week. An' that reminds me—it's time to start horsin' around. I'm dry as a bone. Come on to the Tivoli an' I'll buy a drink."

The officer shook his head. "Not right now. I'm hittin' for Forty Mile. I'll be back tomorrow night, or the next day. Then I'll hit for Halfaday. Maybe we can go on uptogether."

"Well—maybe. I don't run on no reg'lar schedule. I might take a notion to pull out sooner than I expected. It's accordin' to how much stud I get played."

At daylight the following morning, after a night of stud, Black John shoved his canoe into the water and headed upriver. As he shoved off he grinned to himself. "Downey won't have no kick comin' if I pull out an' leave him. I told him I don't run on no schedule. I've got a hunch he'll be showin' up at Cush's not more'n a couple of days after I get there."

On the evening of the fifth day thereafter, at the foot of the portage trail around the Fish Rapids on the White River, Black John adjusted his pack, swung the canoe onto his shoulders, and headed up the trail. At the head of the rapid he lowered the canoe to the ground, and divested himself of the pack. As he did so a rough voice greeted him. "Stick 'em up—an' hold 'em high!"

He whirled around, even as he elevated both hands above his head, to be confronted by a stockily built man, his face masked by a handkerchief in which a couple of eye slits showed beneath the low-drawn brim of a battered felt hat.

"Back away from the pack—an' keep reachin'," the man ordered, "'cause if this gun goes off you ain't never goin' to know what hit you."

Black John's gaze centered on the muzzle of the nickel-plated revolver in the man's hand as he backed slowly away. "Don't shoot," he pleaded in a voice that trembled slightly. "Yer wastin' yer time stickin' me up, pardner. There's nothin' in that pack a man would want."

"That's fer enough. Stand right where you be—an' keep 'em high," the other commanded. "I'll tell you in a minute if there's anythin' in here I want." Loosening the straps, he grasped the pack by the bottom with his left hand and dumped the contents onto the ground. Swiftly he reached for the packet of bills. "If they ain't nothin' here a man would want, you won't mind me takin' this here package along," he said, with an audible chuckle. "I got use fer a nice big bundle of thousan' dollar bills."

"Hey—that money ain't mine!" the big man cried, in a voice that sounded shrill with terror. "It belongs to the boys on Halfaday Crick. I was fetchin' it up from the bank for 'em. If I ain't got it when I get there they'll think I stole it on 'em—an' they'll hang me!"

"Well—that'll be your funeral—not mine," the man replied. "I've heer'd about this here Halfaday Crick an' the gang of outlaws that hangs out there—an' I don't want no part of it. I heer'd how they hang folks, up there. An' I'm as clost to it right now as I ever was—er ever want to be. I seen you luggin' that heavy pack to the bank in Dawson t'other day, an' I follered you in an' seen the clerk fork over this here package of big bills fer that dust you fetched in, so I follered you clean up to here. I'm right now hittin' back to Dawson, an' you better not try to foller me, 'cause I'll be layin' fer you along the trail an' I'll blast yer guts clean out through yer backbone."

The twilight had deepened, and as the man talked he backed slowly away and suddenly disappeared in the thicket of young spruce that surrounded the little clearing at the head of the rapid.

When he had gone, Black John lowered his arms, built a little fire, hung his tea pail to boil, returned the scattered articles to his packsack, and placed a thick cut of beefsteak in his frying pan. "I'm shore glad he overlooked this steak," he muttered. "A man gets tired of moose meat, an' it's the last one of the five I fetched from Dawson."

Supper over, he spread his blankets and was soon sound asleep. In the morning he breakfasted on bacon and bannocks, slipped his canoe into the water and headed upriver.

## V

REACHING HALFADAY, A few days later, Black John stepped into the saloon and laid a slip of paper on the bar. Cush set out the bottle and two glasses, and picked up the paper. "What's this?" he asked, as he adjusted his spectacles.

"It's the deposit slip for that dust I took down to the bank."

"Deposit slip! How come you didn't fetch back the bills fer that there dust, like you allus done before? You know damn well the boys likes to have their money in cash right here in the safe where they kin git holt of it—like if they want to git outa the country in a hurry."

"I deemed it more prudent to vary the routine in this instance."

"By God, John, when you ain't deemin' yer mootin', er doin' some other damn thing no one but you ever heard tell of! S'pose one of the boys found out the police was on his trail fer somethin' he done 'fore he hit Halfaday! Instid of comin' here an' pickin' up his bills an' hittin' out with 'em, he's got to go clean down to Dawson an' draw 'em outa the bank, where the police would be shore to pick him up!"

"You will note," Black John retorted, "that the deposit slip is made out in your name. In the event of your suggested contingency—"

"You don't need to go shootin' off no more big words!" Cush interrupted. "I never had no congested intengenty—an' you know it!"

"The idea I intended to convey is that in case any of the boys deemed it prudent to depart in haste, there is plenty of money in the safe for you to pay them the amount they had on deposit here, and credit yourself with it."

"Listen!" Cush exclaimed. "I'm already runnin' a tradin' post, an' a saloon, an' takin' care of the boys' dust fer 'em, without runnin' no branch bank on top of it! An' that ain't all!" he added pointing to the slip of paper on the bar. "You tuk thirty-two hundred ounces down to Dawson, an' that figgers fifty-one thousan' an' two hundred dollars—an' this here slip only calls fer fifty-thousan' even money. Where's them other twelve hundred dollars?"

"Oh—them I used 'em for bait. By the way, Cush, has Bob Grant be'n around lately?"

"Bait? What do you mean—bait? An' what's that got to do with that damn Grant? No, he ain't be'n here sence jest before you hit out fer Dawson with that dust, an' stud here at the bar an' shot off yer mouth about fetchin' back the money in bills. I figgered he'd lay fer you an' stick you up somewheres 'tween here an' Dawson. But at that," Cush added, "it wouldn't done him no good if all he'd of got was this here deposit slip."

The big man grinned. "He overlooked the slip, but he shore as hell grabbed the bait—hook, line an' sinker."

"You mean he helt you up an' grabbed off them twelve hundred dollars!"

"The robber was masked. I couldn't see his face. But someone did—and his build was suspiciously like Bob's."

"Shore it was him. I know'd damn well he'd make a play fer that money. So he got away with them twelve hundred, eh?"

"Only temporarily, Cush. Only temporarily. You rec'lect Bob sat in a stud game an' won about thirty ounces, one night shortly after Downey was up here an' told us about Sis Hardy's husband gettin' murdered down on the Porcupine, an' their cache robbed of four hundred an' fifty ounces. Well, when the game broke up along towards mornin', instead of goin' to bed I slipped up to

Whiskey Bill's, an' sort of laid there on the rim till Bob came along. Like I figured, he went to his cache an' poured them thirty ounces into a sack, an' then went into the cabin. When I figured he'd be asleep, I slipped down to his cache, an' found six of them eighty-ounce sacks of dust. Five of 'em was full of that reddish colored downriver gold. The other one had downriver gold in it, too—without about thirty ounces of our gold on top. I also took occasion to look into those two shafts of Whiskey Bill's—you remember Bob claimed he'd be'n scoopin' gold out of both of 'em. Well, the fact is, he never took an ounce out of either one of 'em—they're both half full of stagnant seepage water. So I know damn well it was Bob that knocked off that young fella on the Porcupine. In all justice he should hang for that murder, but it was pulled off so far from here that I figured Downey might raise hell if we went ahead an' hung him—so I gave him the chance to pull off a hangable crime right here in our vicinity.

"I saw Downey down in Dawson, an' sort of hinted that his man might be on Halfaday, an' Downey admitted he didn't have enough evidence for an iron-clad case. He went down to Forty Mile to see if Sam Steele could give him a little more to go on. Then he's comin' up here an' arrest Bob. But hell, the way the law is—even with that red dust in his possession, it's no cinch a jury wouldn't turn him loose.

"I'm headin' up to Whiskey Bill's now, to interview Bob. You go ahead an' call a miners' meetin' fer this evenin'. If the interview should happen to involve Bob in the Porcupine murder, an' the robbery of them twelve hundred dollars, I have no doubt that the boys will see that justice is done—an' no quibblin' about it, neither." As Black John started for the door, he called back over his shoulder: "An', by the way, Cush—tell Pot Gutted John to have the noose all tied when I get back. We ain't got much time—Downey's hell on the trail, an' if the Law gets holt of Bob first, justice'll shore miscarry."

As he stepped casually into the tiny clearing that surround-

ed Whiskey Bill's cabin, with the barrel of his rifle slung carelessly in the hollow of his arm, the man Grant, who was seated
on the doorstep whittling, greeted him cordially:

"Hello, John! What fetches you up here?"

"Oh, I'm just doin' a little huntin'."

"Huntin', eh? Hold on till I git my rifle an' I'll go 'long. I
could do with a little moose meat, myself."

"Never mind the rifle, Bob. I ain't huntin' moose."

"What the hell you huntin', then?"

"I'm huntin' the damn cuss that robbed me the other night
down at the Fish Rapids!"

"Robbed you?"

"Yup—got away with a good sized package of thousan' dollar
bills. It was the money I got for that dust I took down from
Cush's."

"A big package—of—thousan' dollar bills!"

"Yeah. You wouldn't know nothin' about it, would you, Bob?"

"Who—me? Hell, no!"

"An' while I'm about it, I'd like to locate about four hundred
an' fifty ounces of dust that was stolen out of a cache on the
Porcupine. The man that owned it was murdered while his wife
was down to the tradin' post. You wouldn't know nothin' about
that, either, would you, Bob?"

"What d'you mean—do I know anythin' about it? How the
hell would I know what happened on the Porcupine?"

"This man was shot with a thirty-eight revolver—an' the man
that held me up, done it with a thirty-eight. You wouldn't have
a thirty-eight revolver, would you, Bob?"

"I hain't got no revolver! I never did have none!"

"An' you ain't got them four hundred an' fifty downriver
ounces in yer cache, either, eh?"

"I hain't got no cache! An' I hain't got no dust except what I
dug out of——" He paused abruptly as he noted that Black John
glanced down into one of the water filled shafts. "Except what

I dug up on the Pelly," he said.

"I thought you told me an' Cush you was doin' pretty good in these shafts of Whiskey Bill's, the other day."

The man managed a sickly grin. "Yeah, I—I guess I did say that. But I lied."

The big man nodded. "You've done quite a bit of lyin' since you hit Halfaday, Bob," he said, swinging the rifle muzzle to cover the man. "Better reach yer hands up as high as they'll go an' step out here before you take a notion to go for yer rifle."

When the man had complied, Black John stepped between him and the cabin door, and reaching into his pocket, produced a pair of handcuffs he had taken from the person of a U. S. Marshal, who had once visited Halfaday. "Just slip 'em on, Bob, an' see how they fit. If they're a might too loose, I'll adjust 'em."

"What—what the hell!" cried the man, his eyes wide with terror. "What you goin' to do?"

"That depends, Bob," the big man replied. "If I locate a thirty-eight nickel-plated revolver around here, an' about four hundred an' fifty ounces of red gold, an'—"

"Red gold! Whad'ya mean—red gold?"

"Maybe you don't know it, Bob—but what we call down-river gold—dust taken off the lower river, an' its tributaries, like the Porcupine, has a reddish look to it. Any sourdough can spot it in a minute. You claimed you got your dust on the Pelly. But Cush an' I knew you was lyin' the minute we saw yer dust. As I was sayin', if I find them items, you'll be tried by miners' meetin'. Better show me yer cache, Bob. If you come clean, I'll turn you loose."

"I tell you I hain't got no cache!"

"Maybe not. But you don't mind if I sort of look around a little, do you, Bob?"

"I hain't got no cache—but s'pose someone else had a cache around here—like this here Whiskey Bill, er someone—an' you'd find some red gold in it, an' a thirty-eight—then I'd git blamed fer it."

Black John grinned. "You shore as hell will, Bob—especially if I should find that package of big bills in the cache along with the other stuff. Let's see, now—if I was goin' to cache somethin' around here—where would I do it? Guess I'll start in there at the foot of the rimwall behind the cabin. Go ahead. It's a likely place for a cache."

The man's face was deathly white. "Listen, John—mebbe you an' me kin dicker."

"Dicker?"

"Yeah—make a deal. If I kin show you where you was hornswaggled outa fifty thousan' dollars, will you fergit about this here red gold, an' the thirty-eight?"

"I don't rec'lect ever bein' hornswaggled out of fifty thousan' dollars. The only loss I can remember is that money that I was robbed of the other night."

"An' how much was that?"

"Well, I took thirty-two hundred ounces down to Dawson, an' that figures fifty-one thousan', two hundred. I carried the package of bills out of the bank, an' stuck 'em in my packsack."

"Did you count the money?"

"No, I just took the bank's count."

"Okay. Now if I can show you where you lost fifty thousan' will you fergit about the Porcupine job?"

"You pulled that job, eh?"

The man gulped and nodded. "Yer headin' right fer my cache. You'll find the thirty-eight, an' that red dust, anyhow. Yeah, I pulled it. Now how about dickerin'?"

Black John considered. "Tell you what I'll do, Bob," he said. "If you can show me where I was hornswaggled out of fifty thousan' dollars, I'll turn you loose. If not, it'll be up to the boys at the miners' meetin'."

"It's a deal. Come on, here's the cache. Pull out that rock an' look behind it. All there is in that package is two hundred one dollar bills, an' one lousy thousan' dollar bill on the top! Count it yerself, an' then turn me loose!"

Black John counted the money. "It's all here," he said, "every cent of it." Pocketing the money, together with the six little sacks of dust, and a thirty-eight revolver, he turned to the other. "All right, Bob. We'll be headin' for Cush's now."

"Cush's! Turn me loose, like you 'greed. I hain't a-goin' to Cush's!"

"You might think you ain't—but you are."

"What fer?"

"To get what's comin' to you—that's what. You didn't get the fifty-thousan' the other night when you stuck me up, because I had it in my pocket in the shape of a deposit slip. If ever a damn skunk needed hangin', you do. You've admitted committin' that murder an' robbery on the Porcupine—an' I've got the evidence to prove it in my pocket, an' also the evidence to prove it was you who stuck me up. Get a move on. We're headin' for Cush's to see what the boys have got to say about it."

## VI

**TWO DAYS LATER** Corporal Downey stepped into Cushing's saloon, to find Black John and Cush shaking dice for the drinks.

"Is that damn cuss here on Halfaday?" he asked, as Cush slid a glass toward him.

Black John grinned. "W-e-e-e-l-l, there's quite a few here on the crick that might fit that description. Did you have anyone in particular on yer mind?"

"You know who I mean—Orrin Parker?"

"Oh—him! Yeah, he's around."

"Around—where?"

"Around back. He's about four foot under that there newest slab in the graveyard. The damn cuss stuck me up at the Fish Rapids when I was comin' back from Dawson. We caught him with the goods, called a miners' meetin', an' hung him."

Downey frowned, "He got what was comin' to him, all right. But I'd rather it had be'n accordin' to law—for that Brooks murder."

Black John nodded. "Yeah, that would have be'n all right, too. You know an' I know he knocked young Brooks off an' got away with the dust. But suppose the jury disagreed, or turned him loose. Where would be the justice in that? Up here on Halfaday, we see that a man gets justice—justice with the bark on."

"He was guilty of that murder," the officer agreed, "most likely had the dust cached somewhere. I'd like to have located it. Ben Hardy's girl could have used it."

"I wouldn't know nothin' about the Porcupine job, it bein' outside of our jurisdiction," Black John said. "But speakin' of Ben Hardy—I just happened to remember I owe Ben four hundred an' fifty ounces. I borrowed 'em one time, down on the Forty Mile, an' forgot to pay 'em back." Stepping around behind the bar, he reached into the safe and placed six little moosehide sacks onto the bar. "Here, Downey, you take this dust an' see that Sis Hardy gets it."

The officer picked up the sacks, and weighed them, one by one, on the scale. "There's four hundred an' eighty ounces here," he said.

"Oh, that's all right. Them extra thirty ounces are to pay for that candy an' popcorn Sis fetched up to me an' Bettles that time."

Corporal Downey pocketed the sacks with a grin. "Okay, John—okay. I'll see that Sis gets the dust. An' as I said, justice has be'n done."

The big man returned the grin. "That's right, Downey. Up here on Halfaday we're hell fer justice—even if, sometimes, it is a sort of left-handed justice."

# POISON ON HALFADAY

**AFTER A WELL** directed bullet had ended the career of the notorious Soapy Smith, recognized guiding spirit of the gang of murderers and thugs that ruled Skagway during the early days of the gold rush, certain of his henchmen were warned by an aroused and irate citizenry that should they be found in Skagway twelve hours later, they would perforce tread the old hemp trail to hell.

Among the many who took the warning to heart were Dog Tooth Hardin, and Spread Hook. They had departed Skagway singly, and had come together by accident beyond the Chilkat, where Hardin had surprised Spread squatting fearfully beside a little fire. A born hunter and trapper, he had slipped up almost to within arm's reach before the other was aware of his presence. "Drop that!" he ordered savagely, as the cowering one's pistol was thrust almost into his face.

"Hell, you give me a scare!" whimpered the smaller man. "Another second an' I'd of plugged you. I thought you was one of *them*."

Hardin stepped to the fire, his lips twisting into a sneering grin that exposed the two tusk-like canines that had given him his name. "I thought mebbe you was, too. But I slipped up to make sure before I done no fool shootin'."

"How'd you git so clost? I be'n watchin' the back trail, but I didn't know you was here till—till jest now."

"I didn't mean you should. I wasn't raised in the bush fer

nothin'. I've snuck up that clost on moose an' bear. An' as fer watchin' the back trail—you don't suppose anyone would be damn fool enough to come on you that way after they seen yer smoke, do you?"

"I never thought about the smoke. I never be'n in the bresh before. I was raised in Frisco."

"Where the hell you headin' for?"

"I ain't headin' fer nowheres. All I figgered was gittin' to hell out of Skagway. Now they've knocked Soapy off, them damn vigilantes ain't goin' to give us no break."

"I'll tell a man they ain't! But if you don't know nothin' about the bush, why in the devil didn't you slip onto the boat an' hit fer Vancouver or Seattle?"

The other shook his head wearily. "They'd be someone waitin' fer me," he said. "I don't dast to show up in Vancouver, nor neither Seattle, nor Frisco. An' besides, the damn vigilantes wouldn't of let me took no boat. They was watchin' the dock. They know it was me knifed the Jew fer his roll. They'd string me up, if they ketched me, jest like they shot Soapy."

"There was White Pass, an' the Chilkoot. If you was goin' inside why didn't you hit fer one of them?"

"Them damn red coats is watchin' the passes. They know about the Jew, too. They'd of turned me back."

Hardin nodded. "Yeah, I s'pose they would. Me, too. That's why I come this way. They suspicion I done them two p'izinin's."

Spread chuckled evilly. "Suspicion—hell! They know damn well you done 'em. It kind of looks like me an' you's in the same boat."

"Yeah—an' the paddle's busted. How much grub you got?"

"Around two hundred an' fifty pound. It's cached there in the bresh."

"Two hundred an' fifty pound!" cried the other eyeing the smaller man. "You can't pack no two hundred an' fifty pound— nor the half of it!"

"I packed fifty. An' the Siwash packed the rest."

"What Siwash?" asked Hardin, glancing into the bush.

"Jest a Siwash. I offered him a hundred dollars to pack the two hundred pound. He wouldn't go no further than here fer no money—so I paid him off."

"How long ago?" asked Hardin. "It's damn funny I didn't meet him. I come along the trail till I seen yer smoke."

A grin twisted the thin lips of Spread Hook, as he drew a long, keen knife from its sheath. "I paid him off with this," he said. "It's cheaper. He's back there in the bresh, too."

**DOG TOOTH HARDIN** looked on in fascination as the other drew from his pocket a thin oilstone, smooth as satin, and began affectionately to hone the glittering blade. Involuntarily, he shuddered. The slight gesture seemed to anger Spread.

His lips twisted in a sneer. "It's a damn sight better than p'izinin'," he taunted.

"I seen them two fellers kick out in Soapy's. Seemed like they was a half an hour at it—all twisted up. Take a knife, an' if it's done right, a man ain't put to no misery—an' a lot of 'em's better off dead than alive, anyhow."

"Yeah," admitted Hardin. "But you got to be there—an' with p'izen you don't, if you don't want to. I'm kind hearted, that-a-way. But they ain't no use in us quarrelin' amongst ourselves. Every man to his own way of thinkin', I claim. It's like you said, we're both in the same boat. It looks like we better throw in pardners."

"How much grub you got?" asked Spread shrewdly.

"Forty, fifty pound in my pack there, mebbe. But you got plenty. It's like this! I'm puttin' up what I know—an' kin git with my rifle an' traps—agin' what you've got. Yer gittin' the best of the bargain. I kin live in the bush, indefinite, as long as my ca'tridges holds out. An' I know the country, an' you don't. You've got more grub than you kin pack, an' you wouldn't git nowheres if you could pack it. You'd either git bushed in a week, or else have to hit back to Skagway. An speakin' like we was, about ways of dyin'—chokin' out on the end of a rope's got 'em all beat fer misery. Green hands, like them vigilantes, don't hardly ever break yer neck. I'd ruther die of a disease."

"Where'll we hit fer? An' what'll we do when we git there?"

"That's what I was gittin' at. That's where what I know comes in. If we foller this here Dalton Trail down to the Yukon, the chances is we'd git picked up by the Mounted, pronto, an' took back to Skagway. I know a place up in the White River country where we kin go an' roll us up a shack an' lay low till what's on us is fergot about."

"Hell! The Mounted don't never fergit nothin'!"

"Hold on, Johnny Wise, an' let me tell you a thing er two. What we done, er was claimed to have done, was in Skagway, which it's American territory, an' ain't no business of the Mounted. Of course, while them things is right fresh like now, the Mounted would know about it, an' figger we was ondesirable folks, an' take us back to the line. The Mounted's busier'n hell, right now—but that ain't a patch on what they'll be next year, when every damn fool in the States that kin scrape together an outfit will come stampedin' into the Yukon. They'll be so damn busy then, that they won't pay no 'tention to us."

"Yeah, but how do you figger to live while we're layin' low? Two hundred an' fifty er three hundred pound of grub ain't goin' to last us a year."

"It don't have to. You've got the money you rolled the Jew fer, ain't you?"

THE WELL filled money belt beneath his underclothing seemed suddenly to become a dead weight against the belly of Spread Hook. "Hell, no! I ain't got fifty dollars. Listen—the damn Jew only had six hundred on him. Soapy got half, an' the damn robbers soaked me the rest fer this here grub. How much you got? When we frisked them two that kicked out in Soapy's they didn't have nothin' on 'em, an' they was know'd to have plenty a little while before they went in the back room with you."

"Them that know'd it got it, then," growled Hardin. "They wasn't a hundred on the two of 'em when they rolled off 'n their chairs. But it don't make no difference. We got grub enough to git to Halfaday Crick—that's a feeder on the upper White. It ain't only a couple of mile from the line, an' if the police shows up all we got to do is duck acrost into Alasky till they go back where they come from. They's a feller name of Cushing's got a tradin' post an' saloon there, an' we kin live high."

"On what?"

"Hell, they's plenty of moose! An' we kin trap. We'll stake us a claim, an' git out all the dust we need. A man kin make good wages up there most anywhere he sinks a shaft—an' they's always the chanct of a real strike."

"You mean work?" Spread's tone was a blending of injury and horror.

"Well—the dust ain't goin' to fly up an' hit you. It's got to be dug."

"How many's up this here crick?"

"Oh, mebbe fifty, sixty—mostly boys that's outlawed one way er another. They're a good bunch. I was there, myself, fer quite a spell."

Spread glanced significantly at his knife. "Mebbe," he suggested, "we could kind of—put over a little deal that would save us from workin'. You say some of 'em's made 'em a real strike?"

Dog Tooth Hardin's eyes widened in swift horror. "Not," he cried, "by a damn sight! Git this—they's two men runs that country up there. One of 'em's old Cush, an' 'tother, which he's the real bull of the woods, is Black John Smith—an' believe me, they don't stand fer no one pullin' off nothin'! Halfaday Crick is about the moralest country I ever seen. An' it's all right, too, when you come to think about it. They figger that if they ain't nothin' pulled up there, the police ain't comin' nosin' around an' they kin live in comfort. An' them boys is hell fer their comfort.

They've got a nice shack over on the Alasky side, where they kin go to if the police does show up, but they don't stand fer no doin's that would call the police in. They're damn handy with miners' meetin's up there—an' damn swift in carryin' out the verdick. Hell, I've saw men tried an' hung in half an hour—they was guilty, too. If they ain't guilty they don't try 'em. I'd ruther take a chanct with the reg'lar police than them. A man would have some show of bustin' jail, er gittin' bail, er an appeal, er somethin'—but not on Halfaday! It's jest guilty! Git the rope! An' then drinks is had, an' the corpse buried. All my life I've had a horror of the rope. When we git to Halfaday, you keep yer knife in yer pants."

## II

**AT CUSHING'S FORT** the two purchased a small tent, paying for it with what Spread insisted to Hardin was the last of the money he had taken from the Jew he had murdered one night near the dock at Skagway.

Up the creek they made a temporary camp, and for a month Hardin prospected while Spread cooked the meals and assumed the light camp work. Then, one evening, Hardin returned after an absence of several days. "We'll be packin' up an' movin' tomorrow," he announced, when he had devoured a huge chunk of boiled moose meat.

"Movin' where?" asked Spread sourly.

"Up onto a crick I found that runs into Halfaday way to hell an' gone above."

"What," asked the other, "will we have there that we ain't got here?"

"Gold!" answered Hardin, and Spread noted that his eyes glittered with excitement. "Yes, sir—gold, an' plenty of it. If she keeps on like she'd ort to the deeper we git, we're rich! Take a look at that!" Producing a pouch the man tossed it onto the table, and the other untied the string, and poured the contents onto a paper. "Ten ounces, if there's an ounce," continued Hardin excitedly. "An' I took her out an' pan-washed her in one fifteen-hour day!"

Even Spread, who knew nothing of mining, or of raw gold, felt the excitement creeping into his veins as the two bent over the little pyramid that showed dull yellow on the paper before them. "Nuggets an' dust," continued Hardin, poking at the pile with a forefinger. "An' I didn't go two foot down, nowhere."

"What's it worth?" asked Spread.

"Sixteen dollars an ounce—ten ounces, one sixty."

"An' work like hell fer fifteen hours," sneered the other.

"Yes," answered Dog Tooth, his voice grown suddenly hard. "An' not one day, but every day—one right after another. They's good men workin' like hell all day an' every day fer less'n one tenth of what lays there! An' that's jest the top strippin'. She gits better as she goes down. An' when we git a sluice an' a rocker rigged up, we kin take out two, three times as much. We'd ort to be takin' out a couple hundred apiece, one day with another, when we git strung out."

"Where the hell's the excitement in shovelin' dirt into a pan, er a bucket, er whatever you shovel it in?" asked Spread, but Hardin noticed his eyes remained fixed on the little pile of gold.

"You'll find out, onct you git into it. The gold gits any man."

FOR THE next three weeks, Spread found plenty of good hard work without any compensation in dull yellow gold. After packing the outfit and setting up camp on a spot selected by Hardin, the two set to work in the building of a cabin. "We'll build her right agin' that rock," explained Hardin one evening when the timbers had been cut and laboriously dragged to the spot. "We won't put in no winder, but we'll have loop holes fer the rifles. We ain't so clost to the line here as they be at Cush's, an' if the damn police come nosin' around after us, we kin stand 'em off till hell freezes over. They's a spring comes out from in under the rock, an' we'll have water right in the shack."

"What would the police be wantin' us fer?" queried Spread. "It ain't no crime to dig gold, is it?"

"Well," sneered Hardin, "they might some of 'em remember that Jew."

"Er the two that kicked out with the strychnine fits on Soapy's floor."

"Yeah," said Hardin savagely, "but, from now on, you keep yer mouth shet about them two—d'you git that?"

There was an almost imperceptible movement of Spread's hand toward the knife at his belt as his venomous eyes met Hardin's. "An' that goes fer the Jew, too," he answered. For a long moment their eyes held. Then both turned away.

## III

**THEY HAD LITTLE** enough in common, these two, who toiled together beyond the farthest outpost of civilization. Offscourings, both—the one from the slums of a city, and the other from a vast wilderness, each distrusted, and feared, and hated the other. But, still they toiled on—Hardin because he realized the enormous worth of the gold that lay in the gravel, and Spread because there seemed nothing else he could do. He realized very well that in his ignorance of woodcraft, he would become hopelessly lost after crossing the first ridge. Later, when, as Dog Tooth had pointed out, the chechakos would crowd the valley of the Yukon and the police would have time to forget the bad men of Skagway, then, by the simple process of following down stream, he could reach the big river—and then, the excitement of living once more by his wits, and his good keen blade. There should be rich pickings in Dawson!

With the passing of the days the hoard of nuggets and dust in the cache under the floor grew, and with each addition of gold, the distrust and the hatred grew in the mind of each of the partners. Dog Tooth Hardin gloated, evilly, as between crankings, he leaned upon the windlass and gazed down into the shaft upon the bent back of the smaller man. At the proper time, a dose of strychnin' in a juicy moose steak—and all the gold under the floor would be his. And in the bottom of the shaft Spread Hook gloated and planned, at the proper time— when the police had had time to forget—a swift, silent thrust with the knife at his belt, and he would show up alone on the Yukon with much raw gold to spend at the bars and the layouts of Dawson. But he must be wary—a false thrust and well he knew that the big man would grind him to atoms in his fury. Best catch Dog Tooth asleep, but he was a light sleeper, and smart—witness the fact that Hardin had built his own bunk high up, so close to the ceiling that he could barely squeeze into it at night, a position that absolutely precluded any possibility of a fatal knife thrust being driven home in the darkness.

Hardin returned to the shack one evening from a visit to the carcass of a moose he had killed the day before. Spread noted the glitter of rage in the man's eyes as he seated himself at the rude table and attacked a steak. "What's up?" he ventured. "Did someone pinch yer meat?"

"Wolves," growled Hardin. "I'll learn 'em! I'll give 'em meat— all they want!"

After supper Dog Tooth took the small cylindrical metal box from its place on the shelf by the clock. Rummaging in his pack, he produced a bottle, and, drawing the cork, smeared his hands with a few drops of an evil smelling liquid.

"What's that?" asked Spread.

"Scent," explained Hardin. "So they can't git the man smell." With a butcher knife, he cut pieces of meat, and then Spread Hook watched in fascination as the other scored the meat deeply with the knife and sprinkled white crystals from the metal box into the slashes. "There, damn 'em—that'll curl 'em up!" he said, as the last piece was doctored.

The interest of Spread was not lost upon Hardin, and when the man observed in a tone of studied indifference, "It would curl a man up, too, I s'pose," Hardin slanted him a swift glance.

"Twenty of 'em," he announced, "if they et it all."

When Spread turned his back to put on the dishwater, Hardin scratched a thin hairline with the point of his knife from cover to body of the little poison receptacle. Then, he returned it to its place beside the clock.

Three or four days later Spread stood beside Hardin at the moose kill, and gazed upon the horribly distorted bodies of three wolves sprawled within a few yards of the poisoned bait. As Hardin's gloating laughter floated out on the keen autumn air, Spread Hook turned away with a shudder.

## IV

**WITH THE FIRST** snowfall Hardin made a pronouncement. "I'll go down to Cushing's an' fetch in our winter's grub. You go ahead an' chop wood. They won't be no more sluicin' till spring."

"Hell—we ain't got to lay here all winter doin' nothin', do we?" growled Spread.

"Not by a damn sight, we ain't. We're goin' to winter mine. Chop cordwood, an' burn in, an' throw us up a dump fer sluicin' out in the spring."

"I bet the police has fergot about us by now. Why not winter in Dawson?"

"Like hell they have! Wait till the chechakos comes pilin' in next spring. If we hit the Yukon now, the police would hustle us out to Skagway so quick it would make your head swim. An', believe me, ROPE spells Skagway fer me an' you."

"Mebbe yer right," admitted Spread, with an effort keeping the hate from blazing in his eyes. "But I prob'ly won't git much wood chopped. I got a bad heart."

"You ain't tellin' me no news. But that don't give you no license to let no moss grow on that ax handle."

"How about fetchin' out some licker? We've certainly earnt

us a jamboree."

"So we have," agreed Hardin, as he filled a small pouch from the gold cache beneath the floor. "I'll fetch up a few gallon."

"Go easy on that dust," growled Spread scowling. "What you think yer goin' to do—buy the hull damn saloon?"

"The hell you say!" retorted Dog Tooth. "What you want to do—winter fer nothin'? I got around eighty ounces here, an' there's a good thousan' ounces in the cache. I s'pose you think I kin git a dog outfit, an' licker, an' ca'tridges, an' a winter's grub fer the askin', eh? Well, I can't. Stuff comes high in these camps. I'll fetch out some scales, too. I'm bettin' we got sixteen—eighteen thousan' dollars in that hole." The man paused and grinned a grin that exposed the two hideous canines. "An' it'll be right there when I git back, too, old timer. 'Cause you ain't got sense enough to git nowheres with nothin'—see?"

**WHEN HE** had gone, Spread sat for a long time staring down at the yellow hoard. "Sixteen, eighteen thousan' dollars," he maundered, "an' I can't git away with a damn cent of it!" A wave of self pity swept over him, and a torrent of futile profanity poured from his lips. Then terror, mingled with abysmal hatred for the wolfish man who was his partner, superseded the self pity. "Damn his soul!" he shouted shrilly. "He aims to kill me! I seen it in his eyes! I've know'd it all along. He'll make me work all winter, an' in the spring he'll slip some of his damn p'izen in my grub, an' stand there an' laugh while I'm a-twistin' an' throwin' fits." The paroxysm of terror subsided, and the thin lips writhed as the long fingers gripped the hilt of the keen bladed knife and drew it from its sheath. "It's me that'll spend that gold," he muttered, running a lean finger caressingly along the glittering steel. "He don't hold his licker good. I'll drink him plump out, an' then one good shove an' six inches of this'll slide in under his fifth rib, an' I'll throw the gold on the dog sled, an' foller down the cricks to the Yukon!" The man drew the thin oilstone from his pocket and honed at the keen blade, caressingly. "It's too good a way fer him to go, at that," he muttered. "He won't know nothin' about it. If I only thought I could tie him to hold, I'd whittle him down like the Chinee told me how. But I guess it's every man to his trade—only he'd of made me die horrible." Involuntarily the man's eyes flashed to the clock shelf. The honing ceased, and for long moments he sat staring at the little metal container. "Damn him!" he muttered. "Damn his lousy soul to hell! It would serve him right to give him a dost of his own medicine!"

## V

**TWO WEEKS FROM** the day he left Hardin swung his dogs onto the creek upon the headwaters of which the two had staked their claim. He grinned with satisfaction as he mushed beside the dogs. "We'd ort to put another fifteen, twenty thousan' on the dump by spring," he muttered, "an' then I'll feed him his. But I got to watch my step, an' not git soused. The little crook would knife me if he got the chanct. I seen it in his eyes."

A few miles below the cabin he shot a moose that broke from the cover of a copse. With his sled loaded to capacity he paused only long enough to gut the animal and cut out a liberal chunk of loin. "That'll go good fer dinner," he said. "I'd ort to make camp by noon, an' I'm hungry as a dog."

A mile farther on he halted to jerk a lame dog out of the team, and urged the others on.

Pulling up before the cabin, he pushed the door open and entered. The room was empty. Kindling and split wood were piled beside the stove. On the table, all ready for the pan, lay a choice cut of moose steak. Hardin eyed the meat greedily as he filled the stove and applied a match to the kindling. "He's got some sense, anyway," he growled grudgingly, "leavin' the meat cut an' thawed out." As the fire roared in the stove he took the frying pan from its nail and picked up the steak. Then abruptly he paused, stared at the steak in his hand, and carrying it to the doorway examined it minutely in the better light. Long thin scores and cuts revealed themselves as he worked at the meat with his fingers. Drawing apart the edges of a deep slash, he held it to his lips and gingerly inserted his tongue. The next instant he withdrew the tongue and spat repeatedly to rid his mouth of the bitter taste. Glancing swiftly about he noted a well packed trail that led toward the timber on the opposite ridge. Then he turned once more into the cabin, and returned the meat to the table. For long minutes he stood, silent and grim, staring down at the poisoned meat.

**HE GAVE** way to none of the futile cursing with which Spread had vented his spleen, but stood there with clamped jaw as his brain battled down the surge of insensate hate to form a clear cut plan of vengeance. Deliberately, he stepped to the clock shelf and, taking down the little metal container, carried it to the light. An evil grin twisted his lips as he noted that the cover had been removed and replaced with no thought to matching the hair line he had drawn on it with the point of his knife. Returning the poison to the shelf, he called in the lame dog, and tossing him the meat, watched it disappear down the animal's throat in a half dozen voracious gulps. In grim silence he watched the dog's muscles begin to twitch as he staggered about the room. In five minutes he was in convulsions. In fifteen he was dead. A sudden thought struck Hardin, and dropping to his knees, he hastily raised the puncheon that concealed the gold cache. The gold was there, apparently as he had left it.

"Wouldn't be no use in him movin' it," he muttered. "He thinks I'll be curled up an' dead as that dog a half an hour after I git my dinner et. The damn doublecrosser! An' me workin' like hell a-fetchin' him grub an' whiskey!"

Producing the cut of meat he had taken from the moose, Hardin fried himself a huge steak, wolfing it down with relish, his eyes resting from time to time upon the contorted body of the dog. By the time the meal was finished his plan was formulated. He grinned, and as the excellence of the scheme impressed itself upon him, the grin became audible laughter, and he smote his thigh with his palm. "An' safe!" he roared. "Safe as preachin'. If anyone happened along they wouldn't have nothin' on me—not even the police!" From his chunk of moose meat the man cut a steak as nearly as was possible an exact replica of the poisoned steak he had found on the table. Carefully scoring, and slashing it as the other had been scored and slashed, he placed it in the exact position in which he had found the other. When he had finished he picked up his rifle. "He's prob'ly watchin' from the timber, an' when he thinks the p'izen's got in its work, he'll come sneakin' down." Once again the wolfish grin twisted the man's lips. "But that way, he wouldn't git to see me throwin' no fits—he'd lose half the fun. After all the trouble he's went to, he'd ort to git his money's worth. Guess I'll jest put on a show."

Staggering from the doorway, rifle in hand, Hardin fell into the snow beyond the dog sled and writhed about as though in terrific convulsion. Regaining his feet, he staggered on, and again fell and writhed and twisted about in the snow. Again he regained his feet and staggered about, but always in the direction of a thicket that jutted out into the creek bed at a distance of forty or fifty yards from the cabin. Again and again, he fell, going through horrible contortions until he gained the edge of the thicket. Apparently in the last throes of weakness, he disappeared behind the low-spreading branches of a young spruce.

Then he sat up, removed the snow from his rifle, and worked himself into a position that gave him a view of the opposite timbered ridge and the narrow valley between.

An hour passed before Spread Hook emerged from the edge of the timber. For some moments he stood, staring straight toward the spot where Hardin had disappeared, then moved slowly forward across the open valley. Time after time he stopped, and glanced about him. Once he seemed on the point of going to the cabin, and Hardin grinned as, apparently changing his mind, the man continued to approach the copse. "Didn't dast to, till he was sure I'd croaked," he muttered. "He's cagey. He ain't takin' no chances."

When within twenty-five feet of the copse, Spread paused and drew the knife from its sheath. Hardin could see that his lips were drawn—that every muscle was tensed. Then, with his rifle covering the man's chest, he stepped from behind his spruce. "Drop it," he commanded, in an even voice, "an' step back."

The knife dropped from Spread's nerveless hand and he staggered backward, almost falling to the snow. Abject terror showed in his eyes, and his sagging jaw worked spasmodically before the words came: "What—what the hell?"

Hardin grinned as he stepped forward and picked up the knife. "Nothin'," he answered casually. "I come back. That's all. You was expectin' me to come back, wasn't you."

"But—but—"

"Turn around an' we'll go to the shack," said Hardin. "You must be hungry. You ain't had no proper hot dinner like I have."

Abject horror leaped into the man's eyes as he stared at the larger man. "I—I ain't hungry," he stammered.

"That's all right. You will be," grinned Hardin, genially. "Yump—I'm bettin' you'll be good an' hungry."

**SLOWLY THE** man turned and preceded Hardin to the cabin. In the doorway he recoiled in horror at sight of the dog on the floor. "Go on in," said Hardin, "he won't hurt you. He's dead."

Spread had turned and was regarding the larger man with eyes wide with terror. Hardin stood for a moment gazing at the keen bladed knife in his hand. He shuddered slightly, and hurled the weapon far into the snow. "Hell of a thing to kill a man with," he said. "It gives me the creeps."

"But—the dog—what happened?"

"Oh, don't mind him. I was jest practicin' on him—that's all. I kilt a moose down the crick, an' I don't aim to have the wolves tear him all to hell like them others done. So I fixed 'em up some meat I fetched along. You see, I got soused down to Cush's, an' my head ain't workin' jest right yet, an' I fergot the dost to put in. So I tried it out on the dog. It worked, all right. I thought I know'd—but I wanted to be sure. It tuck him jest fifteen minutes to die. I set there eatin' my dinner, an' timed him by the clock."

"Shut up!" Spread's voice, shrill with horror, rang thin against the cliffs and returned a weird echo.

"Oh, all right—I was jest a-tellin' you. Go on in. You see, I didn't bother the steak you left. So you kin git right to work an' fry it up fer yerself. I fetched some of my own. After you've et we'll start in on our drinkin'. I fetched along the whiskey."

"I ain't hungry, I tell you! I—I took my lunch to the choppin'."

Hardin shrugged. "Suit yerself," he said. "You kin have it fer supper then. Step over there an' set on yer bunk. I got a few chores to do."

The man obeyed, and for half an hour, sat speechless, watching Hardin as he removed the tent, and all of the scanty supply of food to the outside. When he had finished, the steak on the table was the only particle of food in the room. This done, he removed the stout hasp that had been bolted to the inside of the door to hold it in case of an attack, and fastened it to the outside.

"What—what in hell you doin'?" faltered Spread between stiff lips.

"I'll tell you," grinned Hardin from the doorway. "It's a hard thing to say to a pal, but the facts is, I don't trust you no more. I might be wrong, but I got it into my head that you aim to harm me. So I'm goin' to set up the tent back in the timber, an' live in that. You kin have the cabin. I left you a fryin' pan—an' yer steak. When you git hungry, jest fry you up a good dinner. I left some salt there on the table."

The man half rose from the bunk his eyes staring. "I—I tell you I ain't hungry!"

"Set down," commanded Hardin, the rifle swinging into line. "You will be—damn hungry."

"But listen, Dog Tooth! I—after what we be'n through together—I wouldn't harm you! You'd ort to know that!"

"I do know it," replied Hardin grimly, "damn well."

**THE NEXT** moment the door slammed, and in the gloomy interior, Spread Hook heard the heavy hasp grate on its staple. From outside, came Hardin's gruff commands to the dogs, then the sound of the sled runners on the hard snow, and—silence.

For a long time he sat there on the bunk, his head in his hands, racking his brain for a solution of his plight. Well he knew the futility of attacking those log walls with his bare hands. He had helped build them to withstand a siege. If only Hardin had left him his knife! But with diabolical thoroughness, the man had gutted the cabin clean, leaving only a frying pan and—the steak. Spread shuddered at thought of that steak, and despite himself, his eyes strayed to the body of the dog, terribly contorted, that showed dimly on the floor in the gloom. "Damn him!" he cried in a paroxysm of futile rage. "He'll starve me, or p'izen me! The dirty crook!"

The fire died down, and he replenished it from the pile that he himself had ranked along one wall. He thought of burning his way out, but realized that he would be roasted like a rat in a trap before either the wall, or the door would burn through. Kneeling, he drank at the spring that trickled from beneath the rock wall against which the cabin was built. Lifting the puncheon, he stared at the yellow gold in the cache, and reaching down, allowed the heavy particles to trickle through his fingers. "I'd ort to took it an' went!" he said. "Gettin' lost—freezin' on the trail—anything would of be'n better than this!" When darkness came, he slipped between his blankets and slept.

In the morning he heard Hardin at the door. "Have you et yet, pal?" Spread answered nothing, and the man outside laughed. "Must be gettin' hungry if you ain't. Me, I had mine—a good slug of licker, an' then a nice batch of pancakes, with thick moose gravy poured over 'em. They was good, I must of et a couple dozen. How'd you like a nice big shot of licker?"

Spread stepped close to the closed door. "Give me some licker," he begged. "Dog Tooth, will you give me some licker?"

His answer was a mocking laugh. "Sure. Sure thing, I will. After you've et, feller, after you've et. Licker don't set good with some folks on an empty stummick."

Spread Hook heard the sound of retreating footsteps, and from a distance, another peal of mocking laughter.

Twice each day, thereafter, Hardin came to the closed door, and each time he talked of food—of stews and roasts, and of thick, juicy steaks sizzling in the pan; of pancakes, and of good sourdough bread, and of dough gods and jam—of liquor, and its warming glow in the belly. His answer had been silence, and once or twice a spasm of hysterical oaths accompanied by futile volleys of blows on the thick panel of the closed door.

Spread Hook was growing weaker. He drank quantities of water and lay for hours at a time in his bunk. He thought of eating the dead dog, but remembered that Hardin had told him when skinning the wolves, that the flesh of poisoned animals was itself a deadly poison. Visions, it seemed, of every meal he had ever eaten floated before his sunken eyes. If only Hardin left him his knife, he would have killed himself long ago. But no—there was still the chance, an almost hopeless chance, but still a chance, of someone coming along—a hunting or a prospecting party. Three or four such parties had stopped during the summer. But they would have to come soon.

**ON THE** sixth day Spread awoke with a start. He was standing upright beside the table, and he was aware that something had dropped from his hand—something that had thudded dully upon the table. He looked down, and started weakly back, his staring eyes fixed upon the thing that had dropped from his hand—the steak! Cold sweat broke out all over him as he realized that his hands must have carried it almost to his mouth! Once again, his eyes fixed upon the dog, dimly visible on the floor at his feet. Then they rose to the clock shelf—to the little metal box that contained the deadly crystals. He had noted it there the first day of his imprisonment. Apparently, it was the only thing that Hardin had forgotten to remove from the cabin. Upon legs so weak as to barely sustain his weight, he made his way to the shelf, and with fumbling fingers procured the little container and carried it back to the table. With difficulty he removed the lid, and stared at the little white crystals. "If I do eat that damn steak in my sleep, I'll do a good job," he muttered, thickly. "I'll put in a double dost—an' it'll git me in five, six minutes—mebbe quicker. Mebbe even before I wake up." With shaking fingers he strewed the poison deep within the slits, and scores, and slashes in the steak. Then, laughing weakly, insanely he tottered back and threw himself upon the bunk.

## VI

**ON A MORNING** a week after the departure of Dog Tooth Hardin with his sled load of supplies from Cushing's Fort, Black John Smith, dean of the little community of outlawed men who had foregathered on Halfaday Creek, found himself alone in the barroom of the fort with Old Cush.

"Would you care," he asked, thoughtfully drawing designs with the bottom of his glass in a little puddle on the bar, "to partake in a moose hunt, which hunt should account fer a disappearance of about ten days?"

"Fer why," asked Cush, "should I indulge in a ten-day hunt when I kin shoot a moose from my back door every other Thursday, reg'lar?"

"We wouldn't need to kill us no moose till we got back," said Black John.

"An' in the meantime?" queried Cush, filling his glass, and shoving the bottle toward the other.

"In the meantime," imparted Black John, "we wouldn't be overlookin' no bets."

"Meanin'?"

"Meanin' Dog Tooth Hardin an' that there rat-eyed pardner he showed up with last summer."

"I didn't shoot off no fire crackers when Hardin showed up agin," opined Cush. "There's one hombre which Halfaday could git along without. I had hoped when he pulled out a year er so back, that he'd keep on puttin' one foot before the other with ondeviatin' diligence. Instead of which, he shows up last summer with another guy, which if he rated a hangin' he would be gittin' all the best of it—er I ain't no jedge of souls."

"Yeah," agreed Black John, "an' it's told in the hills how they've built 'em a kind of a fort up a crick, which it's got loop holes instead of winders."

"Such a buildin' ain't commendable," said Cush gravely.

"None whatever," agreed the other. "It bein' primo facial a defiance of constituted authority. Meanin', that if the law should show up, they aim to shoot it out instead of hoppin' acrost the line like the other boys does. Such conduct would bring Halfaday into ill repute, an' divert the thoughts of the police to us, instead of mindin' their business down on the Yukon. Now me an' you, bein' as you might say, responsible parties in lookin' after the welfare of Halfaday, we should ort to investigate this here rumor pronto an' thorough."

"Yeah," agreed Cush, somewhat doubtfully, "but you know, John, they ain't no buildin' regulations on Halfaday, at that."

"We could draw us up a set of plans an' make regulations," suggested the other, "but I wouldn't hardly advise goin' so fer as that. Didn't you notice nothin' irreg'lar in the way of them financin' their supplies?"

"Meanin'?"

"Meanin', that when they come through this summer they bought 'em some drinks, an' tobacker, an' a tent, an' the party which Dog Tooth calls Spread, he pays the shot with paper money. Then, when Dog Tooth come down fer supplies a week ago, he come alone, an' he pays in dust—an' he seemed to have a-plenty. His sack was stuffed out fat as a link of bologny. My dooty weighed heavy to find out all I could, so I tried to git him drunk, so's he'd talk. But he drunk canny, an' wouldn't say nothin'. Now you know, an' I know, that such ain't Dog Tooth's nature—and when a braggin' man don't talk, it's a cinch he's a-watchin' hisself fer a reason. An' whatever reason Dog Tooth would have fer anything, it would be an ornery one. The way I look at it—his perfound rettysince, as a lawyer onct said about me on the witness stand, is due to one, er both, of two reasons: either them two's made 'em a strike up that crick, an' not neither one darin' to show up on the Yukon to record, they're keepin' it mum; er else Dog Tooth has murdered his pardner, him not bein' along when Dog Tooth come down fer supplies."

Old Cush nodded thoughtfully. "Sounds reasonable," he admitted.

"It's even reasonabler'n it sounds. An' whichever way the cat jumps, me an' you's dooty is plain. If they've made 'em a strike, we should ort to locate in above, an' below 'em, before some other hombre beats us to it. Am I right, er wrong?"

"Sounds reasonable."

"An'," continued Black John hopefully, "if Dog Tooth has murdered his pardner, he should ort to be brung in an' hung all fair an' reg'lar at a miners' meetin'. Not, you understand, because this here Spread don't need murderin'—any right minded man lookin' at him could see that he does—but, bein' a human bein', the law claims he's felonious fer to kill. Therefore we got to consider this here crime as murder, an' hang Dog Tooth—which gits red of 'em both."

"Sounds reasonable," agreed Cush. "I'll git Joe Smith to look after the fort. Let's git a-goin'."

# VII

IT WAS ON the twelfth day of the imprisonment of Spread
Hook that Dog Tooth Hardin stepped out of the timber where
he had been chopping wood to see two men standing before
the door of the cabin. The door was open, having been secured
by means of a wooden pin driven through the staple, and the
men were staring into the interior. The men turned at the sound
of his approach across the clearing, and instantly Dog Tooth
was covered by two rifles. He advanced, grinning.

"Drop yer rifle!" commanded Black John Smith.

Dog Tooth complied, and continued to advance, still smiling.
"What's the big idear?" he asked.

"Yer pardner's dead," said Black John.

"Starved to death, by the looks of him," added Old Cush.
"Starved to death locked in the cabin."

"Starved to death!" exclaimed Dog Tooth, who had joined
them at the door.

"Yeah. Er starved down so weak he couldn't tend the fire, an'
then froze. It's the same thing."

Hardin pointed to the steak lying on the table. "How in hell
could a man starve to death with all that meat in under his
nose?"

"Why was he locked in the cabin?" asked Black John.

"I'll tell you why," said Dog Tooth, pointing to the spot where
the floor puncheon had been pulled aside exposing the little
pit filled with yellow gold. "We made us a strike, here—an' a
rich one. While I was gone fer supplies that damn skunk packed
up all the dust an' tried to pull out on me. But he ain't no good
on the trail, an' I run him down. He had tried to make it out
through the mountains, an' he was damn near bushed when I
ketched up with him. I hauled him back, an' locked him up,
figgerin' to wait till the dogs got rested up an' fetch him down
to Cushing's fer to try him at a miners' meetin'.

"I moved all my stuff out, an' set up my camp over yonder in the timber, figger'n mebbe he might try to knife me, so's I couldn't take him down to the fort. Well, five, six days ago I run out of meat, an' I figgers on gittin' me a moose. I trails one till plumb dark, an' then figgers to camp on his trail, an' git him next mornin'. But in the night it snowed an' I couldn't foller him no more, an' neither I couldn't find my way back here. I was plumb lost, an' I be'n wanderin' around the hills ever sence, tryin' to locate this here crick."

When Dog Tooth finished his narrative, Black John, whose eyes had been roving about the interior of the cabin, pointed to the body of the dog on the floor.

"That there dog," he said. "It looks like he'd bad luck."

"Yeah, I was a-goin' to tell you about him. He went lame on me, an' wasn't no use fer to feed, so I done some practicin' on him. You see, I kilt a moose a while back, an' the damn wolves chawed him up on me 'fore I got him cut up an' carried back to camp. I figgered on p'izenin' 'em. I'd fetched along some p'izen, but I didn't know how much to use, so I tried it out on the lame dog."

Both men regarded the speaker with disgust. "It looks like you made a good guess with the p'izen," said Black John dryly.

"Yump. Tuck him jest fifteen minutes to croak. I timed him by the clock."

"Yer sure it was wolves you was practicin' fer to kill?"

"Hell, yes! What else would a man be p'izenin'?"

"Well—his pardner, mebbe, fer one. Now, Dog Tooth, you say you b'en wanderin' around the hills fer the last five, six days, you must be awful hungry, ain't you?"

"You bet!" answered the man, with a grin. "I shore could crawl outside of a meal of vittles."

"All right," said Black John, pointing toward the table. "Jest you set down an' eat that steak that yer pardner left. That ort to look damn good to a hungry man."

"It shore does, an' I'm damn glad Spread didn't eat it. I ain't had no luck gittin' meat." He entered the cabin, and reached for the kindling. "Mebbe you'll j'ine me," he invited, with a mocking grin. "Looks like they might be enough fer three."

"We've et," answered Old Cush, eyeing the man narrowly. Black John Smith fingered the lock of his rifle.

Lifting the frying pan from its nail, Dog Tooth sat it on the stove, and when it was hot, picked up the steak and tossed it into the pan, and stood turning the sizzling meat with a sheath knife he drew from his belt. Lifting the pan to the table, he salted the meat, and with the knife, he cut off chunk after chunk which he devoured with evident relish, while in the doorway the two looked on in profound silence. Then, suddenly, Hardin paused and into his face leaped a look of mingled horror and surprise. The knife dropped from his twitching hand, and he essayed to cross to the doorway. But his muscles went out of control so that he staggered jerkily, and then crashed to the floor, where for twenty minutes he thrashed about in horrible convulsions finally coming to rest with his body upon the body of the dog, and his head in the gold cache.

**OLD CUSH** was the first to speak. "He'd give his pardner the choict between starvin' an' p'izen," he said. "But anyway, he was game. He stood there an' et that meat like he didn' know it was p'izen!"

Black John nodded. "He know'd it, all right, seein' he done it hisself. He was game as hell—but I've saw lots of men go out game. The way I figger it, he know'd we had him—an' he know'd it meant the rope. Now take a feller like him, I s'pose he's lived so damn long in fear of the rope, that it had got to lookin' to him like that was the worst way in the world to die, so when it come to a showdown he chose the p'izen—like his pardner chose starvin'."

"Sounds reasonable," said Cush. "But, me, I'd took the rope!"

"Now," said Black John, after a few moments of silence,

"everythin' bein' satisfactory, as the feller says, it's up to us to take care of this here dust so the first son of a gun that comes along don't steal it."

"Yeah," agreed Cush. "It ort to be turned over to the public administrator."

"Jes' so. We want to have everythin' legal, an' reg'lar. They ain't no public administrator be'n app'inted fer this here country, yet—so it's your dooty, as the main property holder on Halfaday, to app'int one. A man can't app'int hisself, without it would excite suspicion that it wasn't on the up an' up. So that leaves me. Now, bein' in charge of these here assets, I got to list 'em. How in hell much dust do you figgers in that hole?"

"Dog Tooth bought him some scales. I'll go to his camp an' git 'em," said Cush.

**WHILE THE** man was gone, Black John searched the bodies, and when Cush returned, he was counting the bills in a leather belt he had taken from about Spread Hook's waist. "Twenty-seven hundred an' forty dollars in paper," he announced. "Put her down, Cush. I deputize you as clerk. Now, I'll weigh the dust."

Half an hour later, he announced the result of the weighing: "Ten hundred an' sixty three' ounces. Figger her up."

"Seventeen thousan' an' eight dollars," announced Cush after a few moments of laborious calculation.

"All right. Now fer the rest of the stuff, dogs, an' outfit, we kin lump it off at a hundred ounces—that's sixteen hundred dollars more. Now what does she figger?"

"Twenty-one thousan', three hundred an' forty-eight," announced Cush, after totaling his notations.

"All right," said Black John. "Divide her by two."

"That's ten thousan', six hundred an' seventy-four."

"Now me, regardin' this here administrator job as a public dooty, I ain't a-goin' to charge no fee. But these boys has got to be buried. As public administrator, I app'int you grave digger.

The ground's damn hard, an' I hereby fix the fee fer such service at ten thousan', six hundred an' seventy-four dollars. Now you app'int me assistant grave digger at the same salary, an' everything's all fair an' reg'lar. Not only that, but they won't be no, what they call, remnants of the estate left over fer the heirs, if any, to squabble over. Here's your half—stick it in yer pack, an' let's git to work. At that price we'd ort to bury 'em all of a foot deep. An' after that, we'll re-locate us a couple of claims."

# THE GAMBLER

**THE SHARP TANG** of autumn was in the air as Brent Cavalier beached his canoe, drew it clear of the water, ascended the bank, and crossed the little flat to the doorway of the low log trading post of Colin Duncan, on the Yukon, a good day's paddling below Forty Mile.

He waved a hand at a couple of Indians who had paused in their work of hanging split fish on the drying rack, to eye with approval the swift long strides and the free swing of his shoulders. Spruce smoke, blue-gray in the sunlight, curled from the stone chimney, and as the odor of it reached his nostrils, he threw back his head and gave tongue to a weird quavering ululation that was the long howl of the timber wolf.

At the drying rack the Indians grinned broadly, and in the doorway of the trading room appeared the figure of a girl. She, too, smiled into the face of the young man whose eyes devoured every line of her well-rounded figure and came to rest on the suntanned face above which the play of the sunlight caught steely purple glints in the high-piled mass of raven hair.

"That was almost perfect," she said, "except that wolves don't howl in broad daylight in front of a trading post. Just the same it gave me that prickly feeling at the roots of my hair that I always get when I hear a wolf howl. Primitive fear, I suppose the books would call it. But all the same, I love it."

"Me, too. I guess it's because we've heard it ever since we can remember. There's three sounds that mean the North to me.

Guess what they are?" He stood before her smiling into the deep violet eyes that were raised to his.

"Why—three sounds? Let's see—the howl of a wolf, that's one. And the sound of the ice going out in the spring, that's two. And I suppose the other is the whine of mosquitoes on a still night. Or maybe it's the roar of the wind in winter."

Brent Cavalier laughed. "You got the wolf howl all right—but the others—they are either dangerous, or damn disagreeable. The three sounds that mean the North to me are the howl of a wolf, the bellow of a cow moose, and the honking of geese high in the air—before you can even see 'em against the blue. How've you been, Janet? You look prettier every time I see you.

How about it—you going to marry me this trip—or have I got to come clear down here again?"

"Sh-sh-sh. Daddy will hear you—and Father Cassat is here, too."

"Good! Fine! Nothing to prevent our getting hitched, right now."

The light faded from the girl's eyes. "You know what will prevent it," she replied in a low voice, and disappeared into the trading room.

The young man followed, but the girl was nowhere in sight and he noticed that the door to the living quarters stood open. He advanced toward the huge stone fireplace before which Colin Duncan and Father Cassat sat smoking. At sight of him the little priest smiled. Everyone smiled at Brent Cavalier, the happy-go-lucky, devil-may-care son of Tom Cavalier the old sourdough who had been drowned in a whitewater rapid several years before—everyone except Colin Duncan, who eyed the young man with dour disapproval.

**IGNORING THE** glance, Brent smiled at the surly Scot. "Hello, Colin! Looking gay and happy as ever, I see," and turned to the little priest who had removed the long stem of his porcelain bowled pipe from his lips. "How are you, Father? How are the Siwashes coming along?" Reaching into his pocket, he withdrew a small moosehide sack and tossed it into the lap of the long black robe. "Here's a little dust to help lick the devil. But mind you—don't spend it all on the Siwashes. I noticed that parka you were trailing around in last winter was getting worn damn thin in spots. And along last spring I heard Black John Smith giving you hell for traveling in leaky mukluks."

The priest smiled. "Ah—Black John—a merry rogue. But one, I have found, whose good deeds outshine his darker ones. He is always ready to contribute liberally for the relief of suffering, be the sufferer white man or red." He sat balancing the little sack of dust in his hand. "But you, my son—are you sure you can spare this?"

The younger man laughed, and slipping his hand into the pocket of his mackinaw flashed a thick roll of bills. "Sure I can spare it. See? I'll always have plenty as long as the boys keep on trying to make their little ones beat my big ones—and they always will. Beats the devil how men hate to lay down a hand."

Colin Duncan removed the short black pipe from his mouth and spat into the fire. "A fool and his money are soon parted," he growled.

"That's right, Colin," Brent grinned. "That's just what I keep telling the boys when they run a flush up against a full house. But you can't make 'em believe it. And I'll bet Father Cassat has the same trouble dinging religion into the Siwashes. But it's a good thing they do convert hard, or we'd both find ourselves out of a job—ain't that so, Father?"

The little priest smiled. "Our professions are in nowise akin," he said. "You are young. It is my belief that you will see the error of your ways. You are of good stock. Your mother and your father I knew well. They were people of sterling worth."

"Aye, they were that," seconded Colin. "Tom Cavalier was a God fearin' mon—an' a hard workin' one. 'Tis a shame his son shud turn out to be nowt but a wastrel an' a ne'er-do-weel."

The younger man nodded, his eyes on the face of the Scot. "My dad *was* a hard working man. All his life he worked hard—and what did it get him? He fought the North for twenty years—and what did it get him? We got along—always had enough to eat, and clothing to wear, and a roof over our heads—but that's all. He never made a strike. He never had any luck. I am lucky. I study the run of the cards, and I study the men I play against. I work with cards instead of a shovel and windlass. I'm only twenty-five, and I have more dust than my dad ever had—and I don't break my back getting it."

"Ye're a gambler an' a profligate. Ye toss gold aboot like it was dross."

"You mean that dust I just gave Father Cassat? That's just my ante in the game of living. He'll find good use for it. And at that, I'll bet it's a damn sight more than you ever gave him, with all your God-fearing talk! Listen, Colin—you don't like me, and I know it. And what's more, I don't give a damn whether you do or not. There is only one thing I want here—and that's Janet. I love her and I've got a reason to believe she don't think so badly of me. You say I'm a wastrel and a ne'er-do-well—and maybe I am, from your angle. But I'll tell you right now that if Janet marries me, she'll live better, and have a damn sight more money than she's ever had here. She'll enjoy life, too. She won't be cooped up all her life in a stinking trading post."

The Scot leaped to his feet, his face glowering. "Be gone! An' never show ye're face here again! I wad sooner see Janet dead an' laid oot in her coffin, than married to the likes of ye! Ye're a gambler! An' a gambler is naught but a thief!"

"You're a liar! And if you were a younger man I'd knock your teeth down your throat!"

Father Cassat rose and stepped between the two, his silvery locks cascading about the shoulders of his long black robe—a frail helpless body to interpose between the two angry men. He held up a thin white hand upon the back of which veins stood out like a pattern of thick blue yarn. "Peace," he said, in a voice that rang sharp with authority. "You are both at fault. You, Colin, because you have wrongly accused Brent of being a thief. Gambler he is; but no thief. I have traveled the length of the river, and into far camps beyond the rivers—and everywhere I go men speak of Brent Cavalier with respect. He is known as a square gambler—one who would scorn to turn a dishonest card. Time and again he has been known to give back the money he has fairly won from some man who could ill afford to lose it."

He turned to the younger man. "And you, Brent—you are wrong in coming here and baiting Colin under his own roof."

"I didn't come here to bait him. And I didn't come here to be called a thief, either. I came to ask Janet to marry me. She is of age. And if she'll have me, you can marry us right here and now, despite what Colin says." A slight sound caught his attention and he turned toward the rear of the room to see the girl standing framed in the doorway of the living quarters, her face dead white in the semi-darkness of the room. "How about it, Janet?" he asked. "Shall Father Cassat marry us—here—now?"

"No. I have told you many times that I would never marry you unless you gave up the cards. My father is right—you are a gambler. And a gambler is no better than a thief, in that he takes money from others that he did not earn."

For long moments silence reigned in the room—a heavy, tense silence, as the four stood without moving. Then Brent spoke. "All right, Janet. If that's the way you feel—if that's your final word—why—that's the way it is. Maybe sometime you'll change your mind. When you do, I'll be waiting for you."

A choking sound came from the doorway. "Oh—Brent—why—why won't you give up the cards? We—we could go off on some creek and I know we could make a strike! You're lucky—we could—"

"No, Janet. I've lived on cricks all my life. I know how hard my mother had to work—and I know how little she got out of life. I'd die rather than have you go through with that. My mother was a broken old woman when she died—at forty-five. Only a few men make strikes. The odds aren't right. They are much better with the cards."

"D'ye see, girl," Colin said. "He wad ruther tak' what does na belong to him, than engage in honest toil. Ye are decidin' wisely in follerin' ye're head ruther than ye're heart."

Brent turned on the speaker. "I never took a dollar that didn't belong to me," he said in a low hard voice. "And that's a damned sight more than you can say! Oh, I've watched you slip big ones in with the little ones when you were sorting the Siwashes' fur. And your scales are set right now at fourteen ounces to the pound. And the blankets you sell for wool are twenty-five percent cotton—I happen to know where you buy them. And you call me a thief! You—with your short weights, and your God-fearing patter!" Abruptly he turned on his heel, and the next moment he was gone.

When, a few minutes later, Janet Duncan reached the bank, Brent Cavalier's canoe was well out in the river. "Brent!" she called. And again, "Brent!" But the sound of her voice was lost in the vastness that is the North. And the canoe forged on upriver, propelled by the strong steady paddle-strokes of the man who didn't look back. For a long time the girl stood there, her skirts whipping about her knees, her eyes on the blurring canoe. When it was but a dancing speck in the distance she turned toward the trading post. A sound reached her ears—the honking of wild geese. She raised her eyes and searched the sky. Presently a long, V-shaped line traced itself against the blue—a line that wavered and shifted, but held steadily southward. She watched it until it disappeared, and the honking faded into silence. When her eyes again sought the river the canoe was no longer in sight, and with a dry inarticulate sob, she turned away from the river.

## II

CARMACK'S STRIKE ON Rabbit Creek, which men renamed Bonanza, had attracted men from the established camps of Forty Mile and Circle, and a new camp had sprung up in the shadow of Moosehide Mountain at the junction of the Klondike with the Yukon—Dawson, the sprawling city of tents and log cabins and whipsawed shacks that was soon to become the metropolis of the Canadian Yukon.

These were the tents and the shacks of sourdoughs—men from "downriver" located Bonanza from mouth to source, and claims were filed on Hunker, Sulfer, Ophir, Gold Hill, the Klondike—creeks that a few short months before had never even been heard of. For nearly a year was to elapse before the *Portland* was to dock at Seattle with the cargo of dust that sent the chechakos from the States surging into the country like a devastating swarm of locusts.

News of the strike had gone up and down the big river. Men spoke of two—ten—twenty dollars to the pan—then fifty—and a hundred dollars. Lies, mostly, when they were told—but so rich was the gravel of Bonanza that the truth overtook and passed the lies. When someone panned ten dollars, by the time the news reached Circle, and Eagle, and Rampart, rumor had swelled it to twenty dollars—and by the time the stampeders, attracted by the lie reached Dawson, men were actually panning ten dollars, and twenty, and thirty.

Tom Chisholm set out a bottle and glasses as the younger man stepped into the saloon. "Hello, Brent! Fill up. Where you be'n? Ain't seen you around for a week or so. Be'n off somewhere's tryin' to make a strike?"

"I've be'n downriver," Cavalier replied, filling his glass and shoving the bottle toward the other.

"Downriver! Hell, man, there ain't nothin' downriver fer you!"

Brent nodded slowly as he watched the little beads rise and

range themselves around the rim of his glass. "Guess you're right, Tom," he said somberly.

"Sure I'm right. A few old shellbacks has still got faith in the lower country, but I'm tellin' you that when Carmack shook that dust out of the grass roots on Bonanza it spelt the end fer Birch Crick, an' Coal Crick, an' Forty Mile. 'Course I know how you feel—born an' raised on Birch Crick, you hate to admit that the upper country's got it backed off the map. But you've got to admit it, Brent."

"Birch Crick don't mean anything to me, except a lot of hard work. It killed my dad and my mother. I don't care if I never see it again." The younger man's eyes were still on his glass and there was a note of sympathy in Chisholm's voice as he said:

"Still an' all it's home to you, Brent. It's where you was born an' raised, an' it's where yer dad and yer ma lays buried. You don't mean that—about never wantin' to see it agin. Looks like yer feelin' kinda down on yer luck. Did the boys down to Forty Mile give you a trimmin'? If that's all's ailin' you, you can forgit it. A bunch of the boys'll be in this evenin', an' there'll be a stiff game goin'. I'll stake you to a roll—all you want."

"Thanks, Tom," Brent said, and raising his glass, tossed off the liquor. "I took a trimming, all right—but it wasn't at Forty Mile. And I've still got a roll."

"Some proposition peter out on you?"

"Yeah. The best proposition in the North."

"Cripes sake, Brent—it's time you was gittin' wise to yerself! I'm tellin' you there ain't no proposition in the hull damn down-river country that kin hold a candle to what we've got up here. If you'd stop an' think a minute, you'd know damn well I'm right. Where's the sourdoughs at—men like Bettles, an' Swiftwater Bill, an' Burr MacShane, an' Camillo Bill, an' Moosehide Charlie, an' a dozen others I could name—men that knows gold? They ain't wastin' their time downriver, by a damn sight—they're right here. An' if Tom Cavalier was alive today, he'd be here, too, along with the other old-timers. An' believe me, he'd have his stakes in right now, on Bonanza, er Hunker, er one of the other cricks that's goin' to pay out in millions. Take a tip from me, Brent. You're goin' to make more money minin' than you ever could with the cards. 'Cause I'm tellin' you, when news of this strike hits the outside, an' the dust's shipped out to prove it, there's goin' to be the damndest stampede the world ever seen. The chechakos'll come pilin' in on us till there won't be claims enough to go 'round."

"What do you mean—I'll make money mining? I'm telling you, Tom, I wouldn't stake the best claim on Bonanza, or any other crick—even if I knew it was the best claim. I've shoveled gravel, and cranked a windlass, and chopped wood, and sloshed around sluices, and fought mosquitoes all the while when I was a kid, till I had calluses on my hands half an inch thick."

Chisholm grinned. "I don't see no calluses on 'em now, Brent."

Cavalier spread his hands out on the bar and regarded the soft palms and long supple fingers. "No, and by God you never will see any on 'em again! I'm through with mining for good and all. When I can't make a living at cards, I'll starve."

"You might think yer through with it, but you ain't—by a damn sight."

Brent glanced up quickly. "What do you mean?"

Chisholm's grin broadened. "Meanin' that Joe Husby located right in the middle of one of the sweetest propositions on Hunker."

"Joe Husby?"

"Yeah—you remember the old fella that use' to hang around Bergman's down to Forty Mile, doin' odd jobs, an' trappin' a little, now an' then."

"Oh—sure. Didn't even know his name. Never heard him called anything but Joe."

"Well, you mightn't of knowed his name, but he know'd yourn, all right. You kin go down to the recorder's an' see fer yerself."

"What do you mean?"

"Don't you rec'lect grubstakin' him 'long about six months back? Right here in this room, it was. Joe he drifted upriver along with the rest of us, an' I had him workin' here—cleanin' spittoons, an' sweepin' out, an' what-not. You'd be'n settin in a game that busted up, 'long about four o'clock in the mornin', an' you was standin' here at the bar takin' a night-cap, an' Joe he was beggin' Sam Booth to grubstake him, on account he done Booth a favor, one time—an' Sam turned him down cold. So when Sam went out you peeled a few bills off'n yer roll an' tossed 'em to Joe. 'Here's yer grubstake' you says to him. 'Hit out an' see what you kin do with it.' An', by God, what he done with it is plenty! Don't you rec'lect that time? I do. I was standin' right here behind the bar."

Cavalier shook his head. "Don't remember a damn thing about it. I've grubstaked a lot of the old-timers, here and there, but never gave it a second thought. The poor old devils were down on their luck—why shouldn't I? Hell—it's just my ante in the game of living."

Chisholm nodded slowly. "Uh-huh. Well, this time you shore as hell cashed in on yer ante. Joe recorded you on that claim—full pardners. That's what I meant when I said you ain't through with minin'."

"But I tell you I am through. I won't want that claim—or any part of it."

"You mean you ain't goin' out there an' help Joe work it?"

"That's just what I mean."

"Would you sell your half?"

"Sure I'll sell. That is, I'll sell to any square guy. This old Joe looks to me like a man that's had his share of tough breaks already. And he prob'ly isn't very long on brains. I won't sell to anyone that would take advantage of him—try to beat him out of his share. He's got a right to have an honest pardner."

"How would I do?"

"You? Why sure, Tom. You're square as hell. You'd see that poor old cuss got what's coming to him."

"Thanks," said Chisholm. "Yer a square shooter, yerself, Brent. Most fellas would sell where they could git the most money—an' to hell with what happened to Joe. What's yer figger?"

Brent grinned. "How the hell do I know? You know more about the property than I do. What's your offer?"

"First off, I'm tellin' you that not me, nor no man livin' knows what that claim's worth. I think yer a damn fool fer lettin' it go. But that's your business. It might pay a million. Then, agin', it might peter out. Any proposition's a gamble."

"Well—I'm a gambler. What's your offer?"

"God—it's pretty hard to say. I ain't got no hell of a lot of cash on hand. An' this saloon ain't good to back up no hell of an amount."

"To hell with the saloon. Your word's good."

"You mean you'll take my onsecured note?"

"Sure I'll take it."

"Okay. If the claim's anywheres near as good as what they say it is, you'll git every damn cent of yer money. But if she peters out you'll shore be left holdin' the bag—'cause the chances is, I'd never be able to make the note good."

"I'll take a chance. And if the claim peters out, I'll tear the note up. If I kept the claim and it petered out, what good would it be to me? Make out your note."

"But I ain't made you no offer."

"Hell—I can read. I'll see the figure on the note, won't I?"

Chisholm grinned. "Well, I'll be damned! My figger is a hundred thousan'—twenty thousan' in cash, an' my note fer the balance. An' I'm givin' you fair warnin', I might be practically stealin' the claim, at that price. How about it?"

"Okay. Fork over the cash, an' write out the note, and I'll be on my way."

"On yer way! On yer way where?"

"Outside. That twenty thousand, with what I've got on me ought to give me plenty of working capital. Guess I'll slip out and see how the game's played in Seattle and Frisco."

"Outside!" Chisholm exclaimed. "You mean yer goin' out of the North?" he asked.

"That's right. To hell with the North. I hate it."

WITHOUT A word Chisholm opened the iron safe and counted out the money. Then he drew his note and signed it. The younger man pocketed the bills and folding the note, placed it in his wallet. He held out his hand. "So long, Tom," he said.

The other took the hand. "Won't you be waitin' to say good-by to the boys? They'll be sorry to see you go."

The other shook his head. "No, Tom—you tell 'em good-by for me. I—I've known most of 'em all my life. I—I'd—rather not say good-by."

"Okay, lad. I'll tell 'em. But—you'll be comin' back. Yer the breed of the North, Brent. You'll be comin' back home—an' when you do come, if that claim's what I think it is, there'll be eighty thousan' waitin' fer you here in the safe."

### III

AFTER SUPPER THE sourdoughs drifted into Tom Chisholm's saloon and Bettles suggested a game of stud. "Kind of a shame not to be improvin' our time whilst Black John's amongst us. He'll be pullin' out fer Halfaday tomorrow, an' it would be a damn shame to let him get out of Dawson with any dust in his poke."

The big man grinned. "If I was frivolous minded I wouldn't want no better proposition than jest settin' in a game with you damn frost hounds. Couple more nights of stud with you boys an' I'd have to hire a Siwash to pack my dust over the portages."

"You done all right, last night," Moosehide Charlie admitted, "but luck like that's bound to turn. Come on, let's git goin'.

There's five of us here, an' someone else'll be showin' up. Where the hell's Brent Cavalier? I ain't saw him around fer a week."

"I'll buy a drink first," Burr MacShane said. "Brent's prob'ly up on Hunker. Didn't you hear about him grubstakin' old Joe Husby, an' Joe locatin' one of the best propositions up there?"

"Brent's grubstaked a hell of a lot of them old-timers," Camillo Bill said. "It's about time one of 'em come through."

"Accordin' to what they say about Husby's claim, Brent won't have to worry if none of the others come through."

"Hell, Brent didn't expect none of 'em to come through," Black John said. "He jest grubstakes them old down-an'-outers to make 'em happy. But I'm doubtin' that he'll work that location, no matter how good it is. Brent Cavalier's a gambler."

"Yeah," Swiftwater Bill agreed, "an' a damn good gambler, too. An' what's more he's square. He plays way ahead of the game because he uses his head. Most of them professionals use their fingers—but not Brent. An' it ain't because he couldn't if he wanted to. Hell, he knows all the tricks."

Black John laughed. "Brent would never turn a crooked card playin' with us fellas. But he shore as hell don't make no bones about it when he's playin' against a crook. I was lookin' on the time he busted Hank Cronk, down to Rampart. It was in Swede Sam's place. Doc Carter, an' Falkenberg, an' Old Man Minock, an' Cap Williams, an' Al Mayo was in the game, an' so was Cronk an' old Jim Bradley. Jim, he'd sold out a proposition he had on Coal Crick, an' he had a roll on him, an' he was pretty drunk, but his luck wasn't runnin' so bad, at that."

"Howcome you'd show up in Rampart?" Bettles grinned. "Had them Alasky marshals fergot about that Army payroll job—er was you goin' under some other name?"

"Yer question is irrelevant, immaterial, an' is beside the p'int. An' on top of that, the payroll prank to which you refer didn't take place till a month later," Black John replied. "As I was goin' on to say, old Jim's luck wasn't runnin' so bad, an' when the game broke up he still had his roll. Me an' Brent Cavalier was headin' fer Tanana, an' we'd stopped over at Rampart fer the night, an' was killin' time watchin' the game, which was full-up er we'd of set in."

"Hank Cronk seen how old Jim was pretty well oiled, so when the others quit, he begun makin' cracks about Jim's playin' till Jim got mad an' challenged him to a two-handed game—which was jest what Hank wanted. Swede Sam tried to talk Jim out of playin', but he had jest enough under his belt to be stubborn—so him an' Cronk started playin'. Brent an' I watched the game, goin' to the bar fer an occasional drink. An' pretty quick I noticed that Brent seemed to be feelin' his licker, which I thought was funny, because we hadn't had no more'n six er eight all evenin'.

"Well, to make a long story short, it took Cronk jest about an hour to clean old Jim out of every damn cent he had. Brent had be'n gettin' drunker an' drunker, an' every onct in a while he'd bust out with some advice, after lookin' in one hand er the other. Cronk, he'd told him to mind his own business a few times, but Brent, kep' a-hornin' in. So when Jim lost the last pot an' had to quit, Cronk looks over at Brent, which he wasn't hardly no more than a kid then, an' he says kind of sneerin'—'mebbe you'd like to get a piece of this change, if yer so damn smart.'

"Brent allowed he would, an' figgerin' he was drunk, I nudged him to keep out of it, knowin' that Hank was a damn crook, but I hadn't be'n able to get onto his trick. Ignorin' the nudge, Brent set down where Jim had got up, an' they started to play. Well—it took Brent jest an hour an' twenty minutes by the dock to clean Cronk out of every damn cent he had. Then he laughed at him, an' handed old Jim back his roll—an' stuck Cronk's roll in his pocket. An' on top of that, he up an' showed me an' Jim an' Swede Sam the hold-out trick Cronk had be'n usin'. An' between the two of 'em, they damn near killed Cronk before he could get out the door. An' they might as well have finished the job, because a soldier shot him deader'n hell a little while after that at Fort Egbert, fer runnin' a set of crooked dice into a crap game."

Tom Chisholm who had relieved his bartender during Black John's story, nodded. "Yeah, Brent's a swell guy anyways you look at him. Too bad he's gone."

"Gone!" Swiftwater Bill exclaimed. "What do you mean—gone?"

"Gone out of the country—gone outside."

"Yer crazy as hell!" Moosehide Charlie said. "Cripes. Brent was born an' raised on Birch Crick. What the hell would he go outside fer?"

"Claimed he was goin' to Seattle, an' Frisco, an' them places, to see how they played the game down there."

"But how about his half interest in Joe Husby's claim on Hunker?" MacShane asked.

"He ain't got no half interest on Hunker," Chisholm replied. "I bought him out this mornin', an' he hit on upriver. He'd be'n downriver fer a week, an' didn't know nothin' about Joe's strike till I told him. Then he said he wouldn't work no claim, an' didn't want no part of one, an' told me to make him an offer fer his half interest. I offered a hundred thousan', an' he took it without no dickerin'. Claimed he wouldn't of sold to anyone that might try to beat Joe out of his share. I warned him the claim was prob'ly worth a damn sight more'n I offered—but he took me up."

"But what the hell give him the notion of goin' outside—an' him born an' raised here?" Swiftwater Bill asked.

Chisholm shrugged. "Search me. All he told me was jest like I said—that he wanted to see how the game was played in them places. He seemed sort of low in his mind when he showed up here. Claimed he'd lost out on some proposition downriver. I offered to lend him all he wanted. But he wasn't broke, an' he claimed he didn't need no loan."

**BLACK JOHN** frowned. "He'll be comin' back," he opined. "Brent was a damn good gambler—fer these parts. But when he gets down there amongst them city crooks, they'll take him like Grant took Richmond."

"Who was Richmond? An' how much did this here Grant take him fer?" Moosehide asked.

"Nothin' but a course in hist'ry would cure your case," the big man grinned. "But, at that, it's too bad Brent took along that hundred thousan'. Them damn crooks might get every cent of it. Brent'll shore get his eye teeth cut—but he'll pay a hell of a price fer the cuttin'."

"I only paid Brent twenty thousan' in cash," Chisholm said. "When he gits back he'll have eighty thousan' waitin' fer him— if that claim's any good."

"I believe like John that them city gamblers will clean him," opined Camillo Bill. "But whether they do er not, Brent'll be comin' back. No one that was born an' raised here would stay back there in the States very long. Why the hell would they?"

Father Cassat stepped into the room and approached the group at the bar. "Is Brent Cavalier here?" he asked.

Black John smiled down at the little priest. "No, Father," he said. "Fact is, we was jest talkin' about Brent. He's gone outside."

"Outside? That is indeed a pity. I have a message for him."

"Guess it'll have to keep till he comes back," Swiftwater Bill said. "But hold on—who's the message from, Father? If we know'd that we might be able to figger out why he went outside."

"It is from Janet Duncan. I happened to be at the post when Brent came and asked Janet to marry him. But Colin accused him of being a wastrel, and no better than a thief, and ordered him off the place."

"Then that's what Brent meant when he said he'd lost out on the best proposition in the North," Chisholm said.

"He wasn't so far off, at that," Burr MacShane said. "She's a fine woman—Janet Duncan."

"A fine woman, indeed," the priest agreed. "She told Brent that if he would forsake the cards, she would marry him and they could go off on the creeks and seek their fortune. But Brent pointed out that he had seen the hard work of the creeks kill his own mother and he refused to subject her to a like fate."

"Colin Duncan's got a crust to be callin' Brent a thief, when everyone on the river knows he's be'n skinnin' the Siwashes out of their eye teeth fer years," Moosehide Charlie said.

"All of which raises a p'int of ethics," Black John grinned. "Which is better, Father—a square gambler er a crooked trader?"

The little priest returned the smile: "I cannot condone gambling as a profession," he replied, "neither can I countenance cheating in business."

"Which don't answer my question none whatever," the big man chuckled. "That's the trouble with you theologians, Father—you won't let no one pin you down. We all know what you think—why not come right out with it?"

"Well, then, I will say that upon the premises you have stated, the better man of the two is he who does the greater amount of good in the world."

BETTLES LAUGHED. "It shore takes an outlaw to figger out them fine p'ints of ethics, don't it, Father? But gettin' down to cases, Brent's courtin' has sort of wound up in a stalemate, eh?"

"As he left the trading post he told Janet that if she ever changed her mind he would be waiting for her. And when I departed, shortly thereafter she followed me to the river, and as I stepped into my canoe she told me that if I should run onto Brent upriver I might hint to him that possibly she had already changed her mind. I am sorry that I am not able to deliver her message. For while I do not uphold his profession, I cannot help but believe that Brent Cavalier does far more good than he does harm in the world."

"Yeah," Black John agreed, "an' a damn sight more good than old Colin Duncan would ever do—if he could live twice. But

I wouldn't worry if I was you, Father. Brent'll be back. An' I'll bet even money that you'll get the job of marryin' them two, yet."

## IV

BRENT CAVALIER CLOSED a heavy door behind him and stepped out onto the sidewalk. From midnight on into the gray of the morning he had dealt faro in the gambling house of Coffee John. The feel of spring was in the air that he drew deeply into his lungs—air sharp with the tang of frosty nights followed by days of bright sunshine that melted the snow and sent torrents of water rushing down hillsides to swell the swollen creeks and rivers. A milk wagon lumbered past, the iron-shod hoofs of the horse beating a measured clomp, clomp, clomp on the rough cobbles. Brent walked slowly in the direction of the street car line that would take him to his lodgings.

At the corner a policeman greeted him cheerily. "Hello, Brent! Swell mornin', ain't it? Guess spring's here to stay. Seen a robin yesterday in the park. Makes a man feel like gettin' out in the country."

"That's right," Brent agreed, "far, far into the country. Why do people stay in a city?"

"Why—hell—Brent—we've got to. Our job's here. It ain't like if we was farmers, er somethin'. I'm goin' to get me a farm, some time, an' then I won't give a damn if I never see a city agin. I was raised on a farm. Was you raised in the country, too?"

Brent nodded. "Yeah. Yeah, I was raised in the country."

The officer grinned as his glance took in the polished shoes, the tailored suit, and came to rest on the diamond that flashed in the stickpin. "Wouldn't no one know it unless you told 'em. Cripes, if I made the money you do, I'd buy me a farm tomorrow!"

Brent smiled and passed on. "Guess it gets into everyone's blood—the feel of spring," he muttered. Two blocks farther on he paused at the curb to wait for his street car. He glanced toward the east where, with startling suddenness, the pearl and salmon tinted sky burst into a riot of blazing color that was the false dawn.

The street car rounded the corner and ground to a stop. The gate swung open and the conductor smiled a greeting as he took Brent's nickel. "Mornin' Brent. Well, was they bettin' 'em high, last night? Gee, I wisht I made my money as easy as you do. Goin' to be a swell day, an' by gosh, if I fergit them garden seeds, the old woman'll skin me alive. Don't s'pose you ever messed around in a garden none?"

Brent shook his head. "No, I never had a garden."

"Lotta hard work. Kinda fun though, take it a day like this. Makes a fella feel like gettin' outdoors." There were no other passengers on the early outbound run, and the conductor dropped into the seat across the aisle. "See by the paper where they're shovellin' out a hell of a lot of gold up there in the Klondike. I know four, five fellas that's went from here. Bet they'll wisht to God they was back when winter hits 'em. That must be a hell of a country up there in Alasky. Accordin' to the papers it's about nine months winter an' three months late fall. They say folks is ganged up in Seattle till hell won't have 'em, waitin' to git on a boat. What I claim, this here country's got winter enough to suit me." He glanced out the window and reached for the signal button. "Hell fire, we run by yer stop! You'll have to walk back a couple of blocks."

Brent smiled. "Never mind stopping. I'll go on to the end of the line. Wouldn't mind taking a walk in the country on a morning like this. Give me an appetite for breakfast."

As he left the car the conductor grinned. "Don't git lost. Remember there ain't no street signs on them country roads."

The sun rose in a cloudless sky. The houses became farther and farther apart. The sidewalk ended and, almost before he realized it, Brent found himself on a country road. Clear liquid notes fell upon his ear. He glanced upward and there on the topmost branch of a leafless tree a robin caroled his greeting to the sun. The wailing note of a mourning dove sounded from a thicket. A prairie horned lark flitted ahead of him, and beside an ice-skimmed pool of surface water in an adjoining field a flock of killdees screamed angrily as they rose in erratic flight.

Brent stretched his arms above his head and breathed deeply of the clear crisp air. "Spring is here," he said aloud. "But—it's still winter on the Yukon." He walked on, past open fields, past neat farmsteads where cows were being turned onto pasture after their early milking. A wooden bridge spanned a burbling brook, and turning from the road he sat down on a grassy bank.

**FORTUNE HAD** smiled on Brent Cavalier during the year and a half that had elapsed since he stepped from the trading post of Colin Duncan, and with a heavy heart, hit for the outside. Vancouver knew him, and Frisco, and Seattle, and Butte. Wherever money could be bet on the turn of a card, there Brent Cavalier might be found, playing now with reckless abandon, and again with the cold calculating logic of an actuary. Men instinctively liked him, albeit many gamblers refused to face him across a table. He was known as a square gambler—as one who would scorn to turn a dishonest card—yet they feared his play. He would sit in a game for hours, calling occasional bets, tossing away hands. Then, suddenly he would launch an attack, tossing in yellow chips by the handful, laughing as he raked in the pots. Smiling, debonair, boyish, he won not only the regard, but the respect of the cold-eyed followers of the blind goddess. For these men knew that beneath his disarming boyishness this man was hard—hard and lightning fast. For it was told in the gambling houses how one night in Butte he raised a pot relentlessly until everyone dropped out save a single player—one known from Chicago to Frisco as a killer, having beat two raps of manslaughter, and one of murder. When the man shoved in his last chip and demanded a showdown, Brent smilingly tossed his hand face downward upon the table and reached for the pot. A gun appeared in the man's hand, but before he could pull the trigger a shot rang out and the gun thudded among the chips on the table, as the man slumped sidewise and thumped to the floor. As Brent dropped his pistol into the side pocket of his coat, the wide-eyed onlookers turned over the two hands— the gambler's cards showed four kings and an ace—Brent's, a pair of sevens. When they demanded to know why he had reached for the pot, Brent smilingly stooped, and stripping the coat from the dead man, exposed an expensive mechanical hold-out device concealed by the sleeve. He demanded that the law be called in, and when the facts were explained it was so clear a case of self-defense that he was not even arrested.

Stories of his prowess spread, some true, many false, until his fame spread far beyond the circle of his acquaintances and reached the ears of Coffee John in Minneapolis.

Justly, or unjustly, Coffee John's place had fallen into disrepute. There was talk of crooked wheels, and of faro being dealt from a double-slotted box, and of house men sitting in the poker games who were "handy with the cards." Business declined sharply, and in desperation Coffee John boarded a train for Seattle and sought out Brent Cavalier. What passed between the two neither ever revealed. What men did know was that word passed among the gambling fraternity that Brent Cavalier had taken over the management of Coffee John's place, that four of the establishment's eight roulette wheels had been re- placed by new ones, and that from midnight on Brent Cavalier himself dealt faro. Also it was said that not one of the half- dozen professionals who had played for the house at the poker tables were now allowed within its doors. Business immedi- ately picked up—and once again Coffee John prospered.

**BRENT CLASPED** his hands behind his head, stretched out on the grassy slope, and idly watched the effortless flight of a red-tailed hawk that swung in wide circles high in the air. "I wonder what Janet is doing right now," he mused. "Why couldn't she see that it was for her own good I would not go to the creeks? Gambling is a business, the same as any other business—honest, or dishonest, as a man conducts it. What has love to do with business? There are dishonest bankers, and even great rogues among the clergy. And her own father, old Colin, is crooked as they make 'em in his dealings with the Siwashes. Yet, because I am a gambler, she will not have me. And it is the same here. Known usurers, grafting politicians, market manipulators, and business sharpshooters of all kinds are accepted socially—but an honest gambler is ostracized. Why? If God knows the answer, He sure never shared the secret with me. I suppose it would be called the irony of fate. Why does she have to be like all the rest? If she would marry me, I'd say to hell with 'em all. She would live better than she's ever lived. She'd never have to turn over her hand if she didn't want to. And she would turn down a life like that to go to the creeks— live in a tent or a pole and mud shack—work her fingers to the bone—live like a damn squaw—and die of old age at forty-five, like my mother did. I could take it—but I'll be damned if I'll see her go that way. Happiness could never lie along that road— and why love at all, if not for happiness? Oh, well—Janet will marry some prospector, or trader—and learn her mistake the hard way. And I—I will never marry. Here in the city the kind of a woman who would marry a professional gambler, no honorable gambler would want. Damn the city—any city—they're all alike!"

Brent realized that he was hungry. He unclasped his hands and sat up. As he was about to get to his feet every muscle in his body suddenly tensed. Clear, melodious, from somewhere in the vaulted blue the sound came floating earthward from the illimitable heights—the honking of wild geese. Louder and louder the discordant notes welled on the still air, and straining his eyes to the southward Brent's keen eyes picked up a thin V-shaped line—and another and another—wild geese winging their way northward. The thin lines grew more distinct, wavered, merged, and with discordant clamor separated, reformed and winged noisily on into the North.

For long moments Brent Cavalier sat as one in a trance, his eyes glued to the V-shaped wavering lines that thinned to hair-like fineness and blended into the blue as the sound of the honking diminished, and finally ceased. The North—whitewater rapids—towering mountains—the smell of spruce fires—the whine of mosquitoes—the bite of the strong cold—Bettles, Camillo Bill, Tom Chisholm, Black John Smith—poker games by the light of huge swinging lamps—the bellow of the cow moose—the wolf's long howl—and the honking of wild geese high in the air. An intense nostalgia came over him. The words of the street car conductor came to his mind, "They're shovellin' out a hell of a lot of gold up there in the Klondike"—the creak of a windlass on frosty air—the thud of a dust sack tossed onto a bar—"here's how, boys, drink up an' have one on me."

Brent Cavalier got to his feet and walked back to the rutted road. White farm houses, red barns, pavements, street cars, tall buildings ceased to be. In their place were the wind-tossed waters of blue lakes, the spires of spruce trees on steep hillsides, bleak snow-covered barrens, and the grinding of ice in the rivers. Brent Cavalier was of the North. What was it the conductor had said? "They say folks is ganged up in Seattle till hell won't have 'em, waitin' to git on a boat."

**THREE DAYS** later, in the dining-room of a Seattle hotel Brent stepped to a table and laid his hand on the shoulder of a man dressed in the uniform of the Northwest Mounted Police. "Hello, Downey! What in the devil are you doing here?"

The young officer looked up with a puzzled frown. "I s'pose I ought to know you—but damned if I can place you," he said.

"So—if a man changes his shirt and grows an imperial and a mustache, the police no longer know him, eh? It was Black John, himself, I believe, who said whiskers cover a multitude of sins—and I guess he's right."

Downey grinned. "He ort to know," he said dryly. Then, his eyes still on the other's face, he suddenly exclaimed, "By God— Brent Cavalier! How are you, Brent? We heard how you've be'n takin' these city slickers like nobody's business. An' it must be true. You shore as hell look prosperous."

Brent grinned. "They use their fingers instead of their heads— tricks instead of logic. When occasion demands, I use both. They can't—they're heads aren't much good—and they have no logic."

"Sounds reasonable. Set down, if you haven't et. I jest put my order in."

Brent seated himself and when the waiter returned, gave his order. "How are all the boys?" he asked eagerly.

"Well, the old-timers are same as ever. But you wouldn't know Dawson now. Hell, we're a reg'lar city! Chechakos thicker'n fleas on a Siwash dog. You'd ort to come up an' look us over some time. The boys would be glad to see you. But I s'pose you'll stick to the cities."

"Yeah? You're a damn poor guesser, Downey. I'm on my way to Dawson right now—or I was till I hit this damn town and tried to get passage on a boat. A man can't get a ticket for love or money. I'm hitting for Vancouver to try my luck there."

"You always was lucky, Brent, an' it looks like yer luck's holdin'. You can have my ticket on the *Mexico*. She sails in the mornin'. I got a wire an hour ago. I've got to go to Ottawa. Can't keep out of God's country, eh? The boys figgered you'd be back."

"Yes—I'll be back."

"Kind of miss the high life, won't you?" the officer asked with a glance at the other's attire.

"High life—hell! Downey, I'd rather win ten dollars over one of Tom Chisholm's tables, than ten thousand at Dick Can-field's—and that's the God's truth."

"Yeah. I know. Kind of gets in a man's blood—the North."

"You bet. Hell, I was all right, Downey—had a good thing

in Minneapolis, till I took a walk out in the country the other morning."

Downey grinned. "Hear a wolf howl?"

"Wild geese—hundreds of 'em—high up, and headed North. Headed home. Honking. And me in a damned city! Those geese winter well down south! They could stay there and mate and raise their broods where there is plenty of food. But they don't do it. They fly thousands of miles—to get home. And I'm going home, too. I've done well here. And I've lived more comfortably than I ever lived in my life—and I could keep on doing well, and living comfortably. But—I'm going home."

"You won't do so bad back there, either. The games run into big money. An' Tom Chisholm's holdin' eighty thousan' in his safe fer you, an' ten percent interest on top of it. He's already taken out a couple hundred thousand out of that half interest you sold him on Hunker. An' Joe Husby's taken out the same. You wouldn't know Joe, now. You shore done him a good turn when you grubstaked him, that mornin'."

"I'm glad of it. The poor old cuss. I'll grubstake some more of 'em, too. Not that I give a damn for the claims. It gives 'em something to do. It's my ante in the game of living."

"You'll find the old-timers the same as ever," Downey cautioned. "But lay off the chechakos. They're another breed of cats. There ain't one in a hundred of 'em's worth the powder to blow 'em to hell. Tom Chisholm would have shipped you down that eighty thousan', but he didn't know where to send it."

"That's okay. I haven't needed it. I'll give the interest money to Father Cassat. He'll find some good use for it. Just another ante in the game of living. But I'll make him get himself a decent outfit before he gives it all away to the Siwashes. Boy, it will feel good to be on that boat, headed North! You say all the old sourdoughs are okay? It'll sure be good to see 'em again."

"Yeah, most of 'em's the same as ever. Jimmie the Rough got drunk one night last winter an' froze to death on Front Street. Old Colin Duncan died along in the spring. That girl of his—

Janet, she's runnin' the post. Goin' to marry young Sam Radway next month, accordin' to the talk. Good girl—Janet. Them downriver Siwashes has be'n gettin' a better break, since she took over."

"Yeah," Brent said. "Yeah—I expect they have. This young Radway—who is he?"

"He's a young fella that come in with the first run of chechakos. Seems to be all right. Damn sight better'n the heft of 'em—but that ain't sayin' much. Located a pretty fair proposition on Ophir. Hard worker. Goes on a drunk now an' then an' bets 'em high, wide an' han'some when he gets in a game. But in a day er so he's back on the job. The talk was when I come away that he's figgerin' on buyin' into old Matt Strang's layout on a feeder that runs into Bonanza. Ort to be a good thing, when they run a flume in there."

"So old Matt struck it lucky, eh? Hell, he's been drunk ever since I can remember."

"Well, Matt shore pours down a lot of licker. I never seen him real drunk, but I never seen him what you could call right down sober, neither."

The talk drifted to other things, and an hour later, with Downey's ticket in his pocket, Brent purchased an outfit, called a cab, and boarded the boat for Skagway.

## V

**THE LITTLE GROUP** of sourdoughs who stood before Tom Chisholm's bar eyed the well-dressed stranger who stepped into the room, crossed to the bar, and ordered a drink. Noting that the glasses on the bar were empty, the lips between the neat imperial and the well-trimmed blond mustache smiled. "Will you gentlemen join me?" he asked.

"We don't mind," Bettles said. "Boys, fill up, an' we'll have one on Buffalo Bill!" The allusion caught their fancy and all, including the stranger, laughed.

Moosehide Charlie concurred. "Shore we'll have one. Don't know we've ever be'n called gentlemen before," he added, as his glance swept the rough attire of the others and came to rest on the stranger's perfectly cut tweeds.

The stranger returned the smile. "It has been my experience that there are nearly as many gentlemen in overalls as there are rogues in tailored clothing."

Shrewd blue eyes twinkled above the heavy black beard as Black John Smith raised his glass. "To a true word well spoke," he said.

Glasses were emptied and refilled. "Jest get in?" Burr Mac-Shane asked, by way of conversation.

"Yes, an hour ago, on the *Hannah*."

"Lookin' around fer investments, I s'pose?" Camillo Bill asked. "Not that it's any of my business."

"Yes. I have a little money to invest, if I can find the right proposition."

"Know anything about minin'?" Moosehide asked.

"A little."

"You don't look like you ever done a hell of a lot of it. If I was you I'd go kind of easy on the investment business till yer shore you're gettin' a run fer yer money. The country's full of crooks an' tin horns sence the damn chechakos come pilin' in on us. They'll try to sell you anything, from the gold-paved streets of heaven, to a half interest in the moon."

The stranger laughed. "Thanks for the advice. I'll keep my eyes open."

"If yer as good sizin' up minin' property, as you be folks, you'll ondoubtless git along," Black John opined. "But seems like we're wastin' time. How about a little game?"

The sourdoughs agreed, and Swiftwater Bill turned to the stranger. "Yer welcome to set in, Buffalo," he invited, "an' it ain't no more'n fair to warn you that the stakes might run a mite high when the cards git het up. If a man's luck's runnin' porely, he might git nicked kinda deep. But whichever way she goes you kin be shore you've had an honest run fer yer money which, sence the damn chechakos stampeded in on us, is more'n you kin say fer most games in this camp."

The stranger sat in, and the game proceeded without incident, and with varying fortune for a couple of hours. Instinctively the sourdoughs liked this man, who played his cards conservatively and soundly, matched drink for drink with them, and held his liquor well.

Along toward midnight two men entered and stepped to the bar. The younger of the two, a bit the worse for liquor, thumped on the bar and loudly demanded a drink.

Swiftwater Bill glanced up. "There's Sam Radway an' he's lickered up," he said, in an undertone. "An' that damned Snake Rodgers has got him in tow."

Camillo Bill nodded. "Yeah, an' the next thing, he'll be wantin' to set in the game."

"We hadn't ort to let him in," Moosehide opined. "He bets 'em like a damn fool when he's soused."

"That's right," Bettles agreed. "An' him due to marry Janet Duncan, come Saturday, an' it's Tuesday night. Hell, he won't be in no shape to git married, if he's startin' a drunk. He can't hold no licker."

"He don't go on a bender only two, three times a year," Burr MacShane said. "In between he's a damn hard worker. Smart, too. Got a good thing there on Ophir."

"Yeah, he did have," Camillo said. "He sold out the other day to Charlie Blunden. He's buyin' a half interest in old Matt Strang's layout. Goin' to close the deal tomorrow, so Matt told me. He's payin' thirty thousan' fer it. They're puttin' the money in a flume."

"Ort to be a good buy at that price," Swiftwater opined. "Onct they git a flume in on that feeder old Matt's claim might pay out big. But—thirty thousan'—seems like Charlie Blunden paid about twict what I'd give fer Radway's location on Ophir."

"Yeah, an' it's twict what Charlie give fer it, too," Bettles said. "Janet Duncan's puttin' in the fifteen thousan' old Colin left— an' it's every damn cent she's got—except the post."

"Yeah, an' by God, if Radway sets in the game here, the way he's liable to bet 'em, he might lose the whole damn thirty thousan' that he's s'posed to turn over to old Matt tomorrow," Swiftwater said. "I claim we hadn't ort to let him set in. He shore as hell can't blow no thirty thousan' fer drinks between now an' mornin'."

**BLACK JOHN SMITH** eyed the speaker. "Yer reasonin' is faulty, Swiftwater," he said. "I claim we'd ort to let him in. At least, he'll get a square deal here. What will happen to him if we don't let him in, an' him hell-bent to play? Why, Snake Rodgers'll steer him down to the Klondike Palace, er off to some cabin somewheres an' trim him shore as hell. I'd hate like hell to see Snake Rodgers git Janet Duncan's money."

"John's right," Bettles agreed. "He hadn't ort to be let play when he's drinkin'. But cripes, he's of age. There can't no one stop him. If he's bound to play, he might better set in a square game than a crooked one."

"Okay," Swiftwater said. "Here he comes—but if that damn Snake Rodgers wants in, I'm cashin' out."

"He won't," Black John grinned. "He don't want none of our meat."

Young Radway barged toward the table, eyes bright, an' face flushed. "Hi, boys!" he shouted. "Got room fer another player? Move over, Moosehide, an' let a good man pull up a chair!"

Bettles, dean of the sourdoughs, eyed him soberly. "Yer welcome to set in, son," he said. "But I don't mind tellin' you we'd ruther you wouldn't."

"What the hell! Ain't my money as good as the next man's?"

"It ain't that. We happen to know that you're due to pay over every damn cent you could scrape together to old Matt Strang tomorrow. It looks like a good investment. Hadn't you better lay off an' make it?"

"I'll make it all right. Hell, my luck's runnin'! You bet! Goin' to marry the best damn girl in the Yukon, Saturday. Goin' to buy into the best damn proposition on Bonanza tomorrow. An' tonight, down to the Klondike Palace, I toss a poke of dust on the wheel an' win four to one! What I claim, a man's got to bet 'em high while his luck's runnin'."

Bettles shrugged. "Okay," he said bluntly. "You've had yer warnin'."

Radway started with a thousand dollar stack of chips. He played recklessly, won several big pots, but lost steadily. Three or four times he called for drinks, but the sourdoughs declined to drink, only the stranger joined him. And presently he, too, began to show his liquor. His voice thickened, he handled the cards clumsily, but his play remained conservative. At the end of an hour Radway had bought another stack, and another. As he called for a fourth stack, Black John glanced across at him.

"Yer luck's changed, son," he said. "It's the way luck goes— holds fer a spell, an' then it breaks. You was right in sayin' that a man ort to bet 'em high while his luck's runnin'. But when his luck changes, a wise man drops out."

"That's right," Bettles seconded. "An' on top of that, any man's a damn fool that let his licker bet his cards—instead of his jedgement."

Radway, whose repeated losses had ruffled his temper, burst into flaming rage. "To hell with you! All of you! Who the hell do you think you are—tellin' me how to bet my cards! An' what business is it of yours how I spend my money? To hell with your game! By God, I'll go find a game where they mind their own business!"

He got up abruptly and strode to the bar. "Give me a drink," he demanded. Snake Rodgers who had been an interested spectator, edged nearer to him. "That's right, Sam," he said. "What's it any of their damn business how you play yer cards, er how you spend yer money? Hell, you ain't no kid. You know what yer doin'. Come on down to the Palace an' set in a good game."

As the two filled their glasses the stranger cashed in and stepped to the bar. "Mind if I join you?" he asked, a slightly maudlin note in his voice. "Guess I'll go 'long and get in a good game, too."

"Sure thing," Rodgers said. "You'll get a run fer yer money down to the Palace."

AS THE three swallowed their liquor and headed for the door, the stranger said, "Show me where this Klondike Palace is, and I'll join you in a few minutes. Got to stop in the restaurant first and get a bite to eat."

As they left the room, Bettles glanced at the others. "Well, what do you know about that! Buffalo Bill seemed like a good guy, too."

"Y-e-a-h," Black John drawled. "That's right. He did." Play was resumed, but somehow interest flagged, and a half hour later the big man yawned. "I've had enough," he said. "I'm cashin' in. Guess I'll sort of stroll down to the Palace an' watch a good game."

Camillo Bill frowned. "It's a damn shame," he said, "onct they git Radway in the Palace they'll take him fer every damn cent he's got on him. An' that's prob'ly every damn cent him an' Janet Duncan has got in the world."

"Ain't there no way we kin stop it?" Moosehide Charlie asked. "How about the police? I don't give a damn about Radway, but like Camillo says, it's a damn shame fer him to lose all Janet's money. There ain't no jestice in that."

Black John grinned. "There ain't nothin' the law can do. If he's got Janet's money, she turned it over to him of her own free will. An' a man's got a right to drink—an' he's got a right to play cards, ain't he? If he didn't have, us boys would be in a hell of a fix fer amusement. The longer you live, Moosehide, the plainer you'll see that the law's a damn bunglesome method of workin' out jestice."

"Radway's a square shooter," Burr MacShane said. "I kinda hate to see him get trimmed. His word's as good as his bond. I sold him a location on Eldorado that petered out on him. An' after he made his strike on Ophir, he come an' paid every damn cent that was owin' on it. I told him to forget it—but he claimed a bargain was a bargain. He claimed it wasn't my fault it petered out, an' that if it had turned out the other way, he'd damn well of hung onto it. A man can't help but respect a guy like that."

"Yeah, he's likable, all right," Bettles agreed. "If it wasn't fer these damn drunks he gets on."

Black John chuckled. "We'll now listen to a temperance lecture by the Reverend Mr. Bettles, who has made a personal study of licker from every known angle."

"Is that so!" Bettles exclaimed. "Well, what I claim, it ain't the amount of licker a man drinks that cuts any figure—it's how he handles what he does drink. It's too damn bad Janet Duncan turned down Brent Cavalier. He was a square shooter—an' he could handle his licker, to boot."

"I figgered Brent would be showin' up before this," Moosehide said.

Camillo Bill shook his head. "Nope. I don't expect we'll be seein' Brent no more. I run onto his trail last winter when I went outside. He's got him quite a reputation amongst them west coast gamblers. I tried to look him up, but he'd gone east—to Chicago, or Minneapolis, er somewheres. They claim he knows all the tricks. An' it ain't that they're afraid he'll use 'em agin' 'em—but they're afraid to use theirs agin' him. Fella tried it in Butte, one night—an' they picked him up off the floor. Brent, he's makin' good back there in the States. Why the hell should he come back here, when he kin live a damn sight more comfortable where he's at?"

Bettles glanced about him. "Why do any of us stay here?" he asked. "There ain't a man here but what's got all he'll ever need in the way of dust. Hell, we could go outside an' live comfortable, too—but we don't go outside—er if we do we come back as quick as God'll let us. I'm tellin' you there's somethin' about this country that gets into a man's blood. An' Brent, he's more sourdough than any of us—he was born here. I figger Brent'll come back. Ain't that right, John?"

The big man nodded. "More'n likely," he agreed. "Guess I'll be driftin' down to the Palace. If them birds are goin' to take Radway fer his roll, I might as well see the show."

At the end of an hour Camillo Bill cashed in his chips. "Must be somethin' worth seem' goin' on down to the Palace, er John would of be'n back. He'd never hang around that dump jest fer fun. Guess I'll go down an' have a look."

"We'll all go," Bettles said. "It wouldn't hurt to have a bunch of sourdoughs in there in case Radway was gettin' a raw deal."

## VI

THE SOURDOUGHS STEPPED into the Klondike Palace to find Black John alone at the bar. Chechakos, hangers-on, dance-hall girls were crowded about a table toward the rear, at which, in an atmosphere of tense silence, two men were playing cards.

"What the hell?" Bettles asked, as they joined the big man. "Only a two-handed game? Where's Snake Rodgers? An' who's the gent playin' agin Radway?"

"There was five, six, in it," Black John explained. "But the rest dropped out. The stakes got a little too rich fer their blood. The play in here is mostly amongst chechakos an' tinhorns like Rodgers an' when the bets got to runnin' into the thousan's, they quit, Snake along with 'em. The bird that's playin' agin Radway claims to be a business man lookin' fer investments—like our friend over to Chisholm's place."

"You mean Buffalo Bill? What's become of him?" Camillo Bill asked. "Thought he claimed he'd be down here to set in the game."

"He's here all right, but he ain't settin' in the game," Black John said. "He's there on the sidelines lookin' on. You'll hear from him directly. He horns in, now an' then, with a little free advice."

"How's Radway doin'?" asked Moosehide.

"It won't be long, now," the big man replied. "The business man's luck seems to be runnin' good, an' Radway must be about to the bottom of his roll."

"Business man, hell!" Camillo Bill snorted. "He's a shore-thing artist if I ever seen one! Look at that big diamond flashin' in his necktie, an' them long slick fingers, an' them fishy blue eyes." A voice broke the silence, low pitched, but distinctly audible in the tense silence. "Make it a hundred."

Radway scanned his cards. "Raise it five hundred," he said, in a voice that sounded high-pitched and jerky.

*"And* a thousand."

Radway studied his cards. "Call," he said, hoarsely, and tossed some bills into the pot. "That's good," he croaked, as he scanned the hand the other spread face up on the table.

As he gathered the cards to deal, Buffalo Bill, who stood close beside him, chuckled. "You shouldn't have called. Raise, or throw 'em away. That's the way to play 'em," he advised in a slightly maudlin tone.

"Damn it—shut up!" Radway cried hysterically. "You've been butting in here long enough."

"If you know so much about the game maybe you'd like to take a hand," the cold-eyed gambler said.

"Nope. Spoil a good game. Six, seven handed's a good game. Not three-handed. Two handed's best game—just one man 'gainst 'nother. I 'pologize, my friends." Pausing he drew a silver flask from his pocket and tendered it to the players. "Have a li'l drink, jes' to show there's no hard feelin's."

Both drank and the man returned the flask to his pocket. As Radway dealt, he drew it out and took a drink himself and again returned the flask to his pocket.

**EACH WON** a couple of inconsequential pots. Then, on the gambler's deal, after several raises, he tossed in a roll of bills. "Raise it five thousand," he said tersely.

Radway scanned the pips of his cards. His eyes strayed to the pot, and to the pile of bills before the other. He moistened his lips with his tongue.

As he was about to toss the hand away, the flask-toter again offered advice. "Call him," he said. "He's bluffing, sure."

Radway looked up angrily as the voice of the gambler broke the silence. "Maybe you'd like to take his hand and call," he sneered, "since you're so damn sure I'm bluffing. I guess if Radway's through with 'em he'll let you play 'em. It'll only cost you five thousand."

A few of the onlookers chuckled, but elapsed quickly into silence as the stranger turned to Radway. "What do you say? I will show you how to play them. A hand like that should not be lightly tossed away."

"Call him, if you know so damn much. But quit butting in. If you want to sit in this game—pull up a chair."

"Oh, no. I need my money to buy options. But five thousand—what is that? Even if I lose, it is nothing."

Audible gasps, and low-voiced exclamations escaped the crowded onlookers as the man drew a huge roll from his pocket and stripped off five one thousand dollar bills which he tossed into the pot. "I call your bet," he said.

The other spread his hand. "Queens full of sixes," he announced. Buffalo Bill eyed the cards with a look of pained surprise. He scanned the hand that Radway had passed him. "You drew three cards," he said, "and I have here three aces." He tossed them onto the table as the other raked in the pot. "Oh well, it was worth the money to find out. But I thought I had you beaten. Three aces is a good hand."

Where this stranger had been regarded tolerantly as a drunken nuisance, he now commanded glances of respect because of his fat roll. The gambler renewed his invitation for him to sit in the game, but the man declined, repeating that a two handed game was best. Again he tendered his flask, and again the two players drank.

At the bar Black John grinned. "That ort to settle Radway's hash," he opined. "The hard-eyed gent will make quick work of him, now, to get at Buffalo's roll."

"Cripes, we'd ort to get Buffalo out of here," Camillo Bill said. "He ain't a bad guy, an' that damned crook will go through his roll in no time—drunk as he is."

The big man's grin widened. "Figure he's drunk, eh?"

"Why—hell's fire—look at him! He was startin' to feel his licker back there in Tom's place. An' he's shore got him a snootful now. An' if he keeps on nickin' away at that there flask he won't know a pair of deuces from a royal flush in a half-hour's time."

"Well—mebbe," Black John admitted. "But if yer right, it'll be the first time I ever saw a man get drunk on tea."

"Tea! What do you mean—tea!" Bettles demanded.

THE BIG man laughed. "You wouldn't be expected to know, Bettles, but tea is a drink that's favored by women an' children."

"It's held to be non-intoxicatin'. You rec'lect that when the stranger left Chisholm's place he said he was goin' to stop in fer a bite to eat before he come down here? Well, I happened to glance into the restaurant window as I come by, an' I seen him fillin' that flask with tea."

"But cripes, John," Camillo Bill exclaimed, "if it was tea in his flask them other two would of noticed it! You jest seen Radway an' the other guy take a drink out of it."

"It—or another jest like it," Black John observed dryly. "Didn't you notice that he never took a drink without puttin' the flask back in his pocket an' takin' it out agin?"

"You mean he switched flasks on 'em? What the hell's the idee?"

"That," replied Black John, "is what I'm stickin' around to see."

Burr MacShane jerked his head toward the table. "Looks like Radway's playin' his last hand, right now," he said.

The voice of the gambler who faced Radway across the table cut the tense silence. "And another two thousand on top of that."

The eyes of the sourdoughs were on the younger man's face, white and drawn in the glare of the lamplight. His glance shifted from the handful of bills the other had tossed into the pot, and his fingers trembled slightly as he scanned the pips of his cards. Nervously he counted the bills in front of him, and tossed them into the pot. "I've only got seventeen hundred left," he said, in a low tense voice. "If it was seventeen thousand I'd get my money back, right here. You drew three cards—you can't always catch 'em. I call for my pile. I've got tens full on jacks; can you beat 'em?"

WITH A smile the other tossed his cards face up onto the table and raked in the pot. "I was lucky," he said, "I caught two little deuces to the pair I held in my hand. Better luck, next time, my friend."

Radway's eyes had a set, glassy look as they stared at the four deuces. His chair rasped harshly on the floor boards as he shoved it back from the table. For a moment he stood there, his doubled fists resting heavily on the table. "There won't be any next time for me," he said, in a low, husky voice. "I'm done—cleaned out. And when I say done—I mean done—with the cards and the booze forever. I've learned my lesson—and it's been a damn dear one. But it's one I won't forget." Then abruptly he turned from the table, and the crowd parted to let him pass.

Beside the table Buffalo Bill stood, weaving slightly on his feet and pointing unsteadily at the four deuces. "You were a damn fool fer betting four li'l deuces so high," he said to the gambler. "He only drew one card. Any fours would beat you."

The other looked up with a smile. "You're right, brother. I did bet 'em a little high. But hell—he'd be'n having a tough run of luck, and I wanted to give him a run for his money. I ain't like some guys—never give a man a break."

"Tha's right. You're a good sport. Like to see good sport. Too bad he went broke. Luck's boun' to change. Good luck and bad luck. He might have got his money back."

"Sure he might," the other agreed. "The way the cards have be'n running seems like I couldn't lose. But, like you said, luck like that's bound to change. I'm willing to take a chance, though. How about giving that roll of yours a little play?"

"Two-handed game? Jus' you and me?"

"That's right. And to show you I'm a sport—that's a damn unlucky seat he just got out of. If you want me to, I'll take it, and let you have mine."

The other chuckled inanely. "Oh no you don't! You know luck's boun' to change. Can't fool me. When it changes, then this seat'll be the lucky one."

"Okay, brother—suit yourself," the gambler replied indifferently, as Buffalo Bill seated himself in the chair vacated by Radway, and drew the flask from his pocket. He tendered the flask to the other.

"Firs' we'll have li'l drink, eh?"

As the man tilted the flask Moosehide Charlie nudged Black John. "If that guy ain't drunk he's a damn good actor. He'd ort to be in some show."

"I've got a hunch that the show he's goin' to put on'll be worth the price of admission," the big man grinned. "I'm kinda glad I come down here."

The man returned the flask, and picking up the cards, riffled them, and tendered the deck.

"Cut for deal," he said.

The other cut and showed a five spot. "Beats your four," he said. "Looks like luck's turned. Any time a man wins deal on a li'l five spot, he's lucky."

"That's right. But you forgot to take your drink. What you trying to do—hold out on me?"

THE MAN chuckled and fumbled in his pocket for his flask. "Hell of a note—forgetting to take a drink," he said, as he unscrewed the cap. "Here's how. Unlucky in love, lucky at cards, as the saying goes. I'm sure unlucky in love—so I'm boun' to be lucky at cards." He returned the flask to his pocket, picked up the deck, placed his roll on the table before him and tossed a bill into the pot without looking at it.

"A hundred?" the other asked, "for the ante?"

"Oh sure—hundred or a thousand—what's the difference? Don't like a piker game. We're good sports—like to bet 'em high."

The other shrugged and tossed in a bill, scanned his cards, and dropped in another. "Make it another hundred to draw cards," he said.

Buffalo gathered the cards clumsily and examined the pips. "Five hundred more," he said, tossing the money into the pot.

The gambler saw the raise, and each drew three cards. "Here's five hundred that says I've got you beat," he said.

Buffalo stared at the three cards that he picked up from the table. "And here's five thousand says you haven't," he replied, peeling the money from his roll and tossing it in with a flourish.

The other stared at his cards, and tossed them away. "I made jacks up," he said. "But they ain't worth no five thousand."

Buffalo chuckled and raked in the pot. "Any pair was worth five thousand, my friend," he said, spreading his cards face up. "I drew to the ace and king of hearts, and caught three little spades. Any hand's good—if you bet 'em right." Audible gasps escaped the lips of the onlookers who crowded the table, as the man went on with his patter. "Guts and money—that's what it takes to play poker. Cards don't count—just guts and money.

Can't win if you throw away good hands."

The cold blue eyes of the other hardened as he gathered the cards for the deal, and men noted that his face had flushed under the other's taunting words.

For half an hour the game proceeded with varying luck, Buffalo playing recklessly, handling the cards clumsily, tossing away good hands, and winning pots on sheer bluff, always heckling the other with taunting patter, until finally, goaded to fury, the man tossed in a thousand dollar bill on his own deal.

"Cover that, damn you!" he cried. "And anyway, shut up! You drive a man nuts with your damn gabble. Play your cards and keep your damn mouth shut!"

Buffalo laughed. "Oh-ho, so now he gets angry! You should not lose your temper, my friend. I am a couple of thousand ahead, so he gets mad. I have seen men do that before—and always they lose. When a man loses his temper, he loses his judgment, too. Guts, and judgment, and cards, and luck—they all become mixed up in a grand mess, and he cannot tell one from the other. Here is your thousand, and I make it ten thousand to draw cards—and when you lose this pot, you will be so mad you will burst."

At the bar Black John winked at Swiftwater Bill. "This looks like the blow-off," he said, as the dealer, a murderous glitter in his eyes, picked up his roll, "let's step over an' get us an eye-full." Unnoticed by the fascinated onlookers, the sourdoughs took places at the edge of the crowd. "You're half in," the dealer said, tossing twenty thousand into the pot, "maybe that'll shut yer damn mouth for you!"

BUFFALO PICKED up his cards and examined them carefully. "I have a good hand here," he said. "I once won fifty thousand on this very hand—in Frisco it was, a year ago. In a two-handed game, too—just like this game. The man was a professional gambler, they said. But he lost his temper—and so he used poor judgment in betting his cards. Yes—it was this very same hand. I—"

"Shut up!" cried the other, his voice shaking with rage. "Are you going to call that bet?"

"Call it? Oh, no, my friend. Raise it, or throw 'em away. That's my motto. They're either good, or they're not good. If they're good, a man should get all he can out of them. If they're not good, he should throw them away. You follow the logic, I hope? Well, this hand seems good. I raise you another ten thousand, and then we will draw cards."

The other saw the raise, and picked up the deck. "How many?" he asked.

"Me? I have a hand here that could not be helped—so why should I draw cards? I think these will do. Help yourself—and I warn you that you better make a good draw."

The man discarded and drew one card. Glancing at the pip, he pushed some bills into the pot. "Ten thousand," he said.

The other smiled. "What—only ten thousand? Only the amount of my original raise? Then, my friend, it must be that you did not help your hand. So I will raise you fifty thousand." He picked up his roll and counted it. "But, I have not so much here. This is only thirty-one thousand. Wait till I see if I have some loose change in another pocket." He fumbled through one pocket after another, finally producing another huge roll from a side pocket of his trousers. "Ah, yes, I thought I must have more, if I could only find it. There, nineteen thousand—that makes the fifty thousand. Do you call, my friend—or do you care to raise? I have more here. If you raise, we will make it a good pot."

In a cold rage, the other counted his bills. "I've only got forty-one thousand," he said, tossing it into the pot. "I call for that."

"What—only forty-one thousand? You took twenty-six thousand from the young man who went broke. Can it be that you had only fifteen thousand of your own besides the thirty-one thousand that you already have in the pot? Had I known that I would not have bothered to sit down. I do not like a piker game."

"Show your cards!" the other cried furiously. "And by God, they better be good!"

"Oh, yes—my cards. Here they are—four kings," he announced, and reached to draw the huge pile of bills toward him.

The other spread his hand. "Not so fast! Why don't you stay out till you get something?" he sneered, his voice dripping venom. "How do you like the looks of these four snake-eyes?"

Buffalo's glance met the glare of the cold blue eyes. "I like them," he said, as he continued to draw the pot toward him.

Instantly the other's right hand flew to his hip pocket and came up with a revolver which thudded onto the table top as his eyes stared into the muzzle of the blue-black automatic in Buffalo's hand. "What the hell! What's the matter with them four aces?" he asked, in a voice that trembled with rage and sudden terror as his glance shifted to the closely packed faces. "How about it, men—four aces beats four kings, don't they?"

**BUFFALO SMILED.** The maudlin note that had accompanied his taunting chatter was gone from his voice as he said, "No man will dispute the fact that four aces dealt from a deck that has been set up, will not beat anything."

"What do you mean—set up?" the man's voice was shrill now—and his face had gone deathly white.

"I mean that the deck here on the table—the deck from which you dealt the last hand, is not the deck with which we have been playing."

"You lie!"

"No. I do not lie. Because from the other deck you could not possibly have dealt four aces—for the simple reason that there are only three aces in it. The other ace is on the floor under my right foot. I am rather clumsy in handling the cards, as you may have noticed, and on the deal before this one, I dropped an ace on the floor—but I did not bother to pick it up. I thought we could get along without it. It is the ace of clubs. I must keep you covered, or I would reach down and get it. Maybe one of these men will do it for me. Ah—yes—thanks," he said, as he shifted his foot to allow a man to recover the card. "So," he continued. "If you will now submit to a search of your pockets by any one of the sourdoughs I see standing at the edge of the crowd, you may yet win this pot—but not if they should find a deck of cards in it with the ace of clubs missing. Do you care to submit to the search?"

The cold eyes took on a glassy look as the man moistened his lips with his tongue. "Who—who are you?" he croaked, after long, tense moments of silence.

"Me? The sourdoughs christened me Buffalo Bill. But Brent Cavalier is the name. I—"

"Brent Cavalier! You—Brent Cavalier? The gambler? The guy that killed Stony Brooks that time, in Butte!"

"Yes. A regrettable incident. But a most necessary one."

"Brent Cavalier," cried Swiftwater Bill. "By God, I know'd he'd come back!"

At the edge of the crowd Bettles turned to Black John. "Damn you John—I'll bet you knew it was Brent!"

The big man nodded. "Yeah. In that game at Tom's place—I spotted him. You see, I rec'lected how Brent used to sort of squint one eye when he looked at his hole card. An' Buffalo, he done the same. So I mistrusted he was Brent—that's why I figured we'd see some fun. An' then when he begun buttin' in an' makin' the other guy mad—I knew he was Brent. You see, I remembered how be busted Hank Cronk that time down to Rampart."

## VII

**LATE THE FOLLOWING** morning, as Black John was about to step into Tom Chisholm's saloon, he turned at the sound of a voice.

"Hello, Father! Didn't expect to see you in Dawson. Last time I run acrost you, you was headin' up Sixtymile to christen some Siwash kid. I trust the venture was a success."

The little priest smiled. "Ah yes, a lamb here, and a lamb there—I gather them into the fold."

"Yeah, but lookin' the Siwashes over, it seems like quite a few of 'em jumps the fence an' turns ort to be black sheep."

The smile faded from the thin lips. "It is not only among the Indians that black sheep appear."

The big man grinned. "Meanin' me?"

"No, John. There is much in your nature that I cannot condone. But there is much of good in it, too. You are a great rogue—as you very well know. But also you are a power for the right, in a land where there is much of wrong. At least, you are honest with yourself."

The grin became a chuckle. "That's right, Father—I can't remember of ever beatin' myself out of a dime. But what's on your mind? You look like you'd lost yer last friend."

"Not my last friend, I hope. But one who, despite his calling, I have always regarded as a friend. I speak of Brent Cavalier."

"What's Brent be'n up to now?"

"It has reached my ears that he has returned to the North, and that last night he inveigled young Radway into a game of cards, and while Radway was drunk, he won all of his money. The sad part of it is that he won not only Radway's money, but also fifteen thousand dollars that belonged to Janet Duncan—the entire fortune, save the trading post, left her by her father. I was to have married those two on this coming Saturday. Janet had entrusted him with the money which, with a like amount of his own, he was this day to have paid over to Matthew Strang for a half interest in his location."

Black John nodded. "Yeah, Brent got the money, all right. In the Klondike Palace, it was. I was lookin' on when he done it."

"Could you not have prevented it, John?"

"Nope. An' I wouldn't, if I could. What I claim, if a man's damn fool enough to try to beat a professional gambler, he'd ort to lose."

"But young Radway was drunk."

"Yeah—but that didn't seem to help his case none."

Father Cassat sighed. "I am sore of heart. It is true that Brent Cavalier was in love with Janet. I, myself, heard her refuse to marry him unless he would forswear the cards. The girl loved him, too. For as I left the trading post after Brent had gone, she asked me to hint to Brent that she might change her mind. But when I reached Dawson, Brent had gone. She waited for a year, and believing that he would never return to the North, she promised herself to Radway."

"Yeah, I heard about it. What do you think, Father—does she love Radway—or is she jest marryin' him to spite Brent?"

"She loves Radway dearly. That I know, else I would not consent to marry them. I have made careful inquiry, and I find that Radway is a fine lad—honorable and industrious. His only fault seems to be that two or three times a year he goes on a spree. It was my hope that after his marriage he would settle down to a life of sobriety."

White teeth flashed behind the black beard. "Be a kinda dull way to live. But it might be all right after a man got used to it. So you think mebbe Brent put a crimp in this here weddin', eh?"

"I am afraid he has ruined two lives," the priest replied gravely. "I am sorely disappointed in Brent Cavalier. Upon his return he doubtless heard of the impending wedding, and took this method of wreaking vengeance upon the girl who had rejected him. But—such a vile and sordid revenge! A revenge unworthy of any but the lowest of scoundrels. I cannot see how such a one could hold up his head among men."

"He was holdin' it all right the last I seen him," Black John said.

"Then he has sunk lower even than I thought. It seems that the year and a half he has spent outside has hardened him."

"Yeah, he's hard, all right. I noticed that, last night."

"Have you seen young Radway this morning?"

"No. I jest got up. Was jest about to step in fer an eye-opener when you came along."

"I have been searching for him high and low. But no one has seen him. When he left the Klondike Palace last night, he seems to have disappeared from the face of the earth. Further search would seem a waste of time! I shall go downriver and break the news to Janet. It is better that she hear it from my lips than from those of another. Poor girl. My heart bleeds for her. It may be that I may soften the blow by some words of comfort. It is a duty for which I have no liking. It seems that during all my life I must needs see more of sorrow, and unhappiness, and pain than of joy and gladness."

Black John nodded. "Yeah, I s'pose that's right, Father. But anyhow you've got the satisfaction of knowin' that you've done more to ease this here sorrow, an' pain, an' onhappiness than any damn man in the Yukon. An' there ain't a sourdough in the country but that knows it."

"Thank you, John. From your lips, that is a compliment indeed. I only hope that I am worthy of it. I must go now and carry my pack to my canoe."

"Don't be in sech a hell of a hurry. You ain't the only one that likes to do a good turn, now an' then."

"What do you mean?"

"Meanin' that if you'll wait till I throw a couple of drinks into me, an' get outside of a good big breakfast, I'll go along. Fact is, I've know'd Janet Duncan ever sence they was pinnin' 'em on her three-cornered. 'Uncle John,' she used to call me, when I'd stop in now an' then to have a drink with that damn old penny-pinchin' dad of hers. I ain't much good at utterin' words of comfort—that'll be your job. But it jest so happens that, owin' to a little deal I put over on a fella not long ago, I've got a little loose change that ain't workin', an' if these young folks is willin' to accept a loan off'n me, I'll be glad to stake 'em to that there half interest in old Matt Strang's claim. Like I said, I watched that there game last night. An' when young Radway lost the last pot, I heard him say he was through—done with cards an' booze forever. I've heard that said before—plenty of times. But not jest like he said it—an' not only I heard the words, but I watched his face when he spoke 'em. It was sort of like he was makin' a promise to himself—an' damned if I don't believe he'll keep it."

The eyes of the little priest were shining, lighting up his whole face. "Oh, John," he exclaimed, "will you do that?"

"Why not? It's a good investment, ain't it?"

"If we could only find young Radway," the priest said, his brows knitting. "Deep in my heart lurks the fear that he may have left the country, or worse—drowned himself in the river."

"Not on yer tintype, Father. If you was a bettin' man, I'd lay you two to one I know where he is, right now."

"Where?"

"Down to Duncan's Post, tellin' Janet what a damn fool he was. You claim he's honorable. Well, ain't that what an honorable man would do? It's a tough job. It takes guts. But if I didn't think he's got guts, I wouldn't be offerin' to stake him to thirty thousan' dollars, would I?"

"Trust God you are right, John! And in going down there you are accomplishing far more than I could accomplish. All I have to offer is words of comfort—while you may be the means of saving those two from despair."

"Ferget it."

"I cannot forget that which I have known for a long time— that in your nature there is far more of good than of evil."

The big man laughed. "Hell's bells—an' me an outlaw! Trot along, Father. I'll meet you down to the river."

# VIII

**THE SUN HUNG** low in the west as Black John and the little priest drew the canoe clear of the water and ascended the steep bank to the trading post. Two figures rose from their seats on the low log stoop. The girl hurried across the little flat to meet them. "Ah, Father Cassat," she cried, her eyes shining. "And—if it isn't Uncle John! It's a long time since I've seen you!"

"Hi, Janet!" boomed the big man. "Yeah, it's quite a while. I sort of steer clear of the lower river. 'Fraid I might bust a paddle an' get carried down acrost the line an' run into one of them U.S. Marshals. A man's got to be kinda careful of the company he keeps."

The girl laughed. "From what I hear, the company you keep up there on Halfaday ought to be kept in some jail!"

"Well, most of 'em has be'n, take it one time er another," Black John grinned, as young Radway joined the three.

Father Cassat offered his hand. "How are you, my son? I—I heard of your—er—misfortune, and searched in vain for you in Dawson. So I came to speak a word of comfort to Janet."

The younger man's face was grave. "I hit out that night and came down here to tell her about it—about what a fool I'd been."

Black John noted the look in the violet eyes as they rested for a moment on the young man's face—the look with which a mother regards a wayward son. Then the eyes returned to the face of the priest.

"He told me all about it, Father. And he has given me his promise that he is through with cards and liquor forever. And I believe him. He offered to release me from my promise to marry him. Told me he was not fit for any woman to love. He said he would repay every cent, if it took him a lifetime to do it. But—I would not let him release me. I believe the lesson he learned was cheap at the price. Because it's a lesson he will never forget. I love him.

"It took a man—a real man—to come straight to me and tell me what he had done. So we will be married and stay here and run the post."

The priest nodded and glanced at the big man at his side. "John told me we would find him here," he said.

The girl's eyes lighted. "Then you, too, believe that he is a man!"

"A man—an' a damn good one. He's got guts," Black John replied.

The girl turned to the priest. "There is no use in waiting till Saturday. Will you marry us, Father—now? And then we will all come out and sit on the porch and watch the sunset."

IT WAS a simple ceremony there in the dim-lit trading room, and when it was over, the four seated themselves on the porch and watched the sun sink in a blaze of glory behind the distant peaks.

Father Cassat lighted the tobacco in his long-stemmed porcelain pipe and drew the smoke deep into his lungs. "I believe that you have chosen wisely, my daughter," he said, his eyes on the face of the girl. "I am very glad that I did not overtake Brent Cavalier and give him your message, that day, a year and a half ago." He paused abruptly, and glanced toward the groom. "There! I am afraid I have shown little tact!"

The girl laughed. "That's all right, Father. I told Sam all about my passing fancy for Brent Cavalier. I, too, think I have chosen wisely."

"Yes, I am sorely disappointed in Brent. Gambler though he was, there was something likable about him. He was a happy-go-lucky lad, generous with his money and, while he remained in the North, honorable in his profession. It seems that the life of the cities has changed him for the worse."

"What do you mean, Father? Have you had news of him?"

"News of him!" The priest exclaimed, with a glance toward Radway. "Did you not tell her that it was Brent Cavalier who enticed you to play when he knew that you were drunk, and who, doubtless by some dark trick of the gambler's art, robbed you of your money?"

The younger man flushed. "So that was Brent Cavalier! I did not hear his name. I went to the Palace with Snake Rodgers, and that man sat in the game, which was six-handed until he and I got to betting them high. Then the others dropped out."

"Brent back in the North! And—and he—did that!" the girl cried. "I see it all, now! He learned of our approaching marriage, and he did that to hurt me. Or maybe he thought that by winning all of Sam's money, he would make our marriage impossible—and that I would then marry him!"

"How could he possibly think that I would ever marry a man who would stoop to a trick of that kind?"

"There's a canoe comin' down the river," Black John observed. "Looks like it's swingin' in to the landin'."

THE FOUR waited expectantly as a figure appeared above the rim of the bank and approached across the flat. In the fast gathering twilight the man's features were indistinguishable until he had advanced to within a few feet of the porch. Then, suddenly the girl leaped to her feet, her face flaming. "Brent Cavalier! How dare you come here?"

Black John noted with a smile that mustache and imperial were gone from the man's face, as Sam Radway rose and stood beside Janet.

"Brent Cavalier!" he cried, a puzzled look in his eyes. "Why— this is not the man who got our money."

Father Cassat glanced up into the speaker's face. "What!" he exclaimed.

"No! This is not the man who played. If he wasn't smooth shaved, I'd say he looks like the fellow they called Buffalo Bill, who hung around the table and kept butting in all the time. But he didn't play—except one hand that I tossed away, and he lost on that."

The little priest turned to Black John. "But you yourself told me that Brent got the money—that you witnessed the game!"

"Yeah," the big man grinned, "Brent got the money, all right. But he didn't get it off'n Radway. I seen the games—both of 'em."

"Both of them?" asked the girl. "What do you mean?"

"Why, the game where the tinhorn took Radway—an' the next game where Brent took the tinhorn. They was two separate transactions. An' believe me, they was worth watchin'—'specially the last one."

CAVALIER LAUGHED. "The damn dirty crook," he said. "I stuck around till I got onto his tricks—second dealing, mostly. When I offered him my flask I managed to stumble against him as his head was tilted back, and I located an extra deck of cards in his pocket. When I flashed my roll I knew he'd make a play for it, and I figured he'd clean up on Radway with his second dealing, and save the cold deck to run in on me. I kept nicking at him till he got mad, and watched him till I knew just what hand the blow-off would come. Then I tapped him for his pile." He turned to the girl. "I understand that you and Radway are going to be married Saturday, Janet. So I thought I'd drop down for the wedding."

"Yer too late, Brent," Black John said. "The Padre tied the knot about fifteen minutes ago."

"Then—may I offer my congratulations?" Brent asked, a smile on his lips. "I thought, a year and a half ago, that you were making a mistake in turning me down, Janet. But now—I'm not so sure. You've married a good man, girl—and I wish you all the luck in the world."

"Why—why—thanks, Brent. I—I—know I have."

"I wouldn't give up the cards, Janet. But he will—and the booze along with 'em. I heard him say so, that night. A man in my business learns to size men up. We can't afford to make mistakes. I know he meant what he said." Pausing, he drew a long envelope from his pocket and handed it to the girl. "A little wedding present," he said. "For old times' sake."

The girl tore open the flap and glanced at the document, holding it to catch the fleeting light. "Why—why—it's a deed to Matt Strang's location!"

Cavalier nodded. "That's right. I heard that you two had expected to buy in there."

"But, Brent, we were only buying a half interest. And this is a deed to the entire location!"

"Yes. Thirty thousand of it was your own money—that I took off that crook. I took the rest of it off him, too—and that part is my wedding present."

Tears welled into the violet eyes and overflowed onto the girl's cheeks. "But—Brent—how can we ever thank you?"

"Forget it. It's just a little ante in the game of living. I looked into the proposition before I bought it. You've got a good thing there—good enough so you'll never have to kill yourself on the cricks—like my mother did."

"But—we never could have afforded the whole location."

"It's better this way. It'll be easier for Radway, especially at first, if he don't have to be associated with a man who's half soused all the time." He paused, and smiled. "Well, as Father Cassat would say—God bless you, my children. I must be on my way." He turned to the little priest. "Oh, yes, Father—I nearly forgot!" Drawing a roll of bills from his pocket, he tossed them into the lap of the long black robe. "Here's another little ante in the game of living. A man can't afford not to ante, you know. It's the interest money Tom Chisholm paid me. Use it for the Siwashes, if you want to. But first see that you get yourself a good warm outfit for winter. Remember—I'll be in the country from now on. I'll keep an eye on you."

"God bless you, my son," the priest said. "You have made me happier than you know. Not because of this money—but because I have learned that you are as I remembered you."

"But, Brent," cried the girl, "surely you are not going away, now—tonight! We have plenty of room here. Surely you will stay with us at least until morning!"

The man shook his head as his lips smiled. "Can't do it, Janet. Some other time maybe. But the fact is I've got an important engagement downriver. It was exactly two years ago tomorrow night that Jack Wentworth and the doctor took me for nineteen dollars in a ten-cent limit game in Eagle. A gambler never forgets. And first and last, Janet, you know I'm a gambler. I'm going down and try to get that nineteen dollars back. I want to make an anniversary of it—and I'll just about make it, if I hurry."

The four accompanied him to the riverbank, and just as he stepped into his canoe, a sound floated down out of the dark— the sound of wild geese honking. Brent Cavalier turned, and his eyes met the eyes of the girl. "Good-by, Janet," he said, after a long moment of silence, "Maybe before morning I'll hear a wolf howl."

He shoved off, and the four stood there looking out over the mighty Yukon until the canoe disappeared in the gloaming.

# HALFADAY EVIDENCE,
# PACKAGE STYLE

**ONE DAY EARLY** in June, Old Cush, proprietor of Cushing's Fort, the combined trading post and saloon that served the little community of outlawed men that had sprung up on Halfaday Creek, hard against the Yukon-Alaska border, scowled at the four sixes that Black John Smith had rolled onto the bar, gathered the dice, and returned them to the leather box. "The drinks is on me," he announced, as he set out bottles and glasses. "I see by that paper Red John fetched up from Dawson, where Admiral Dewey claims he's goin' to run fer president. What I claim, John—if a man licks some Spanish over there in Manila somewheres, why would he make a good president?"

"W-e-e-l-l, you've got to remember, Cush, he married a rich widow since he came back, and a grateful nation donated him a house and lot, there in Washington—he prob'ly figures he can afford to."

"Why would a nation be grateful if someone married a rich widder?"

The big man grinned. "The gratitude was for lickin' the Spaniards—not for marryin' the widow."

"Huh! If a man's got a rich widder, an' a house an' lot in Worshin'ton, it ain't no sign he'd make a good president—even if he did lick some Spanish."

"I guess the country's safe enough. Dewey ain't kiddin' no one but himself. Look—here comes someone."

A man crossed the clearing, a limp packsack dangling from

one shoulder and paused in the doorway, his mild brown eyes surveying the room. He was a small man, with a sprinkling of gray showing in his brown beard. The eyes focused on Black John. "I guess mebbe I got to the wrong place," he said. "I seen an Injun yesterday an' he told me this here is Halfaday Crick an' there was a tradin' post here so I come on up, figgerin' on buyin' me some grub. I run out a few days ago, an' I've be'n livin' on fish an' some birds I killed with rocks. But this here looks more like a saloon."

The big man smiled. "Come on in. You can get all the grub you want. That door yonder leads to the tradin' room. Cush rigged the bar in front because most of his customers like to wet their whistle before an' after they do their tradin'."

As the man crossed the floor Cush slid a glass across the bar and shoved the bottle toward him. "Fill up," he said. "The house is buyin' one."

"I ain't much of a hand to drink," the man said, as he poured the liquor. "But like if a man's tired, a little whiskey does him good."

Black John nodded. "Yeah, it's always be'n my thesis that a modicum of liquor, judicially applied, has beneficial results."

"Be you a preacher?" the man asked.

"No. My pa was, an' I've always held to the theory that one preacher to a family is enough. Smith is the name—Black John, in the vernacular, owin' to my whiskers bein' that color. An' the man behind the bar is Lyme Cushing, popularly known as Cush."

"Oh, then you're the man Mister Downey told me about! An' the Injun was right!"

"This is Halfaday Crick, all right. But why should Downey send you up here?"

"Well I went to the police station to ask 'em where I could

dig me some gold. Mister Downey was right nice an' he talked to me, an' when he found out I was alone he says how the best thing I could do was hit fer here an' you'd see that I got a location somewheres."

The big man grinned. "A touchin' tribute to my innate integrity."

"You know a lot of big words, all right—"

"Huh," Cush grunted. "It would be a damn sight better if he know'd a few little ones to mix in with 'em. Then someone might know what he was talkin' about."

"My name's Barlow—Nate Barlow. I come clean up here from Goshen, Indiany, to try an' dig me some gold. It's on account of my wife bein' sickly an' not able to help with the work no more, an' doctors an' medicine costin' so much I mortgaged the farm an' hit out fer this here Klondike I be'n readin' about in the papers. I figgered if I could dig me a lot of gold I kin go back an' pay off the mortgage, an' mebbe git my wife cured up. I met a couple of fellas on the boat, which they was farmers, too, an' we throw'd in together an' come in over the pass an' built us a boat on Lake Bennett an' come on down to Dawson. When we got there I run onto Bill Sykes which he usta live in Goshen. He run a feed store there but he skipped out about six er seven year ago, on account they claimed he robbed some fella. But Bill claims he never done it. He says how he couldn't prove no alibi on account of he might got in worser trouble, yet. So he hit out fer the coast an' come on up here. He claims he put in six year down the Yukon in Alasky, an' his pardner robbed him, so he come to Dawson. He claimed he know'd all about diggin' gold, so I told them other two I was goin' to throw in with Bill.

"I wanted to start right in diggin' gold but Bill says they worn't no hurry. So we went in a place they call the Klondike Palace. It's a saloon, but besides that they was a lot of men gamblin' in there. Some was playin' cards, an' other ones was crowdin' around a kind of table with numbers on it, an' a kind of a wheel with a little ball that a man would spin around an' it would stop on some number, an' the one that bet on that number would win an' the rest would lose.

"An' not only that, but off to one side in another big room a feller was playin' a pyanner, an' some men an' wimmin was dancin'—an' the way them wimmin was dressed was somethin' scand'las! Cripes, their dresses was short to start out with, an' when their pardner would whirl 'em around a man could see they didn't have nothin' on but a little short pair of pants that didn't come nowheres near down their leg—an' most of 'em was good lookin' to boot.

"'This ain't no place fer us,' I says, 'let's git outa here.' But Bill still says they worn't no hurry. 'You buy a drink,' he says. 'I would if I wasn't broke.' So we went to the bar, an' danged if they wasn't some of them dance wimmin, standin' there drinkin' with their pardners, same as if they was men! I know'd my wife wouldn't like it if I was in sech a place—an' I didn't neither. But I pulls out a roll of bills an' peels off a twenty an' slaps it on the bar an calls fer two drinks.

"They was two, three bartenders dressed up in white coats, an' one big man which stood near the end of the bar in front of the safe. He didn't have on no white coat, an' he had a big diamon' in his necktie, an' he stepped over in front of us an' says how the bartenders was busy he'd serve us hisself. He set out a bottle an a couple of glasses, an' was right friendly.

"**HE SAYS** he's the owner of the place, an' his name is Malone, an' he tells us to make ourself to home there whilst we was in town. He give me my change, an' then he says to have one on the house. I don't never take only the one drink the same day, but Bill, he tuk another one, an' I waited.

"Spite of Malone bein' friendly I didn't like him, on account of him claimin' the bartenders was busy, when one of 'em had headed our way already, an' I seen Malone wink at him, an' he turned back. I figger when Malone seen that roll of bills, he figgered I would spend a lot of money there. When Bill drunk his drink Malone bought another one, an' when Bill drunk that one Malone says, 'Well boys, stick around an' have a good time. You can git anythin' you want around here—licker, girls, a run fer yer money—it's plenty lonesome out on the cricks—have a good time whilst you kin.'

"Well, I gits Bill off to one side an' tells him we better be hittin' out an' dig us some gold. But he claimed that, what with so many folks around it don't stand to reason we could find no gold jest hittin' out by ourself. He says how he don't know nothin' about the country on the Canady side. We'll stick around a few days an' sort of git the lay of the land. Malone, he's a good fella, an' he'll put us wise to where to go.

"I told him about Malone winkin' at the bartender when he seen that roll of bills, an' we better go to the police an' ask 'em where to go. But them three drinks Bill had drunk was takin' holt, an' he claimed I jest suspicioned Malone winkin'. He claimed that a saloon is a good place to find out where the gold's at, 'cause that's where the boys comes in an' shoots off their mouth.

"Well, you see I know'd Bill was quite a hand to drink, back there in Goshen, an' on top of that, I seen how he was eyein' them dance wimmin, an' I rec'lected how Bill's wife told my wife one time she didn't dast to keep no hired girl on account of Bill foolin' around with 'em. 'Course, Bill's wife ain't so good lookin'—an' she's got a hell of a tongue on her, to boot—but at that, he married her, an' he hadn't ort to go foolin' around other wimmin.

"I told Bill I come up here to dig gold an' not to hang around no saloon, an' if he wouldn't go 'long with me, he could stay there. But, like I says, them drinks had took holt, an' he wouldn't go. So I loant him fifty dollars, an' went over to the police station an' Mister Downey told me about gittin' a free miner's certificate, an' how to stake out a claim when I find some gold, an' he says to hit up the White River where this here Halfaday Crick runs into, an' tell you he sent me, the chances is you'd tell me where I could dig me some gold.

"So I bought me some grub an' a pick an' a gold pan, an' a shovel, an' a canoe, an' Mister Downey showed me how to work the pan an' find the gold in the bottom. An' he went down to the steamboat with me an' told the captain to put me off at the mouth of the White River—an' here I be. But it took me longer'n what I figgered an' I run outa grub."

THE BIG man nodded, gravely. "There's plenty of rapids on the White, an' a lot of portages. Not knowin' any more about the country than you do, you done all right, for a chechako."

"Fer a which?" the man asked, a puzzled frown on his face.

"A chechako—that's what we call newcomers hereabouts. The old timers are called sourdoughs. I can see why Downey sent you up here—knowin' we always work hand an' glove with the police. But about puttin' you on a good location is somethin' else again. This placer minin' is about ten percent savvy an' ninety percent luck. You hit up a crick, pan the gravel, here an' there, dig down into the ground here an' there, an' look for colors—gold, of course bein' yellow, an' heavy.

"You ain't got the savvy. That'll come with experience. But you might have the luck. There's plenty of feeders—little cricks—runnin' into Halfaday. Some have been prospected, an' some haven't. Good locations have been found, both on the feeders, an' on the crick itself. My advice is to hit out an' prospect the feeders—the main crick has been pretty well prospected. You can get your supplies here. If you make a strike, stake out your claim, an' hit down to Dawson an' record it. Then come back an' put in the rest of the summer puttin' up a shack an' choppin' wood."

Barlow smiled. "Oh, I don't need no shack. I've got my tent. And I kin chop enough wood in jest a few minutes to last me all day."

Black John returned the smile. "You've got quite a bit to learn,

Nate. Summer's the time to prospect, but the real minin' is done in the winter. The gold lies deep in the gravel. You've got to sink a shaft to get it, an' in the summer your shaft would fill up with seepage. You'll need a shack, all right, an' you'll need plenty of wood. You've got to burn in. The gravel's froze hard, an' you've got to build your fire, thaw out a few inches, shovel the thawed gravel onto your dump, an' keep on clean down to bedrock. Then in the spring you sluice out your dump."

The man's eyes widened. "Gosh sakes! You mean I've got to stay up here all winter? Cripes, I better hurry up an' find me a claim, an' then write a letter to my wife an' tell her. We didn't figger I'd be gone that long, an' if I don't git back, come fall, she might worry. I'm sure much obliged to you fer tellin' me about that, Mister Smith," the man said, and turned to Cush. "I'll need some grub, Mr. Cushing. I haven't got much money left," he added, drawing a leather wallet from his pocket and counting some bills onto the bar. "Only forty dollars, so I'll have to go kinda light on the grub. But if I find some gold, I can buy more."

**A GLANCE** passed between Cush and Black John. "Better stick them bills back in yer pocket," Cush said. "Yer credick's good here fer whatever you need. You kin pay me when you make a strike."

"I'd rather you'd take the money, an' if it ain't enough you can charge me with the rest, if you will. I like to pay as I go."

"Okay," Cush said, and gathering the bills tossed them onto the back bar. "Come on in the storeroom an' we'll fix you up."

Shouldering his pack a short time later, the man turned toward the door. "I'm sure glad I took Mister Downey's advice," he said. "You're all good men, up here, on Halfaday Crick."

Black John grinned. "W-e-e-l-l, the observation should be taken with a dose of salts, as the sayin' is."

"An' jest think—when I told a man on the steamboat where I was headin', he looked at me kinda funny an' he ask me if I'm a outlaw. An' when I says 'hell, no—I'm a farmer,' he told me I better stay off'n Halfaday Crick 'cause you was all outlaws up here. I guess he was kiddin' me, 'cause I know'd the police wouldn't send no one where they was outlaws."

"As a matter of fact, an outlaw of one kind an' another has sojourned amongst us, but in most cases sech sojourns has be'n temporary in the extreme. They've passed on—some to infest other communities, an' others to their final reward, as the grave-yard out back can testify. Halfaday is the moralest crick in the Yukon. But to change the subject, it's drawin' on towards evenin', an' seein' that I've got a spare bunk in my cabin, you better stay over an' hit out in the mornin'."

The man shook his head. "Thanks jest the same, but I'll be shovin' on. There's quite a few hours of daylight left an' the quicker I git to work diggin' me some gold, the quicker I kin git back home an' pay off the mortgage an' git my wife cured. I'll do like you say an' hit up one of them little cricks. I passed a lot of 'em comin' up here."

When the man had gone Cush shook his head. "That pore devil ain't got one chanct in a thousan' of makin' a strike. Trouble with them chechakos they read in the papers about the Klon-dike, an' the amount of gold the ships is fetchin' back, an' they think all they've got to do is hit up here an' begin shovelin' gold into a sack!"

"That's right," Black John agreed. "His chances ain't good—but you never can tell. He's a right thinkin' hombre, an' he's got guts, or he never would have shoved on up here alone. I'd like to see him make good."

## II

"Y'KNOW, JOHN," CUSH said, one morning as he gathered the dice from the bar and set out bottle and glasses, "I be'n thinkin' about that there Nate Barlow—you remember that smallish lookin' feller that stopped here along in June claimin'

Downey sent him up to Halfaday, an' you told him he better hit out an' prospect the feeders. Well, here it is damn near August, an' he ain't never showed up no more. I don't figger he had grub enough to last him this long. I kinda liked the little cuss. It would be too bad if somethin' has happened to him—like gittin' lost, er somethin'."

Black John filled his glass and nodded. "Yeah, I got to wonderin' about Nate a couple of weeks ago, him bein' a sort of protégé of mine."

"He ain't no Portugee. Portugees is some kind of Spanish, er Greasers, or somethin'. Barlow come from Indiany."

The big man grinned. "Okay, we'll call him a Hoosier, then. Like I said, I got to wonderin' about him, so a couple of weeks ago I hit out down the crick, rememberin' that he said he'd prospect some of them feeders he passed comin' up. I found where a canoe had been cached in the brush a hundred yards up a rocky gulch a couple of miles below here. So I followed up the gulch, an' after about a mile of slippery rock rapids she flattens out. I found campfire ashes here an' there, an' places where someone had be'n gougin' into the gravel, an' then, about three miles back from the head of the rapids I found Nate's stakes. He'd listened to what Downey told him, all right. His stakes were accordin' to regulations, an' the proper distance apart for a Discovery claim."

"You say you found his stakes. Didn't you find him along with 'em?"

"No. But I found a note fastened to his Number One stake with a sliver of wood, sayin' he'd hit out for Dawson to record his claim."

"You say this here gulch he went up flatted out a ways back. The damn fool didn't sock in his stakes in no moose pasture, did he?"

Black John nodded. "He did. When he hit for Dawson he was travellin' light. I found his pick, an' pan, an' shovel cached in a bunch of willows, an' I done a little snoopin' around here an' there on his location. I figure Nate's the same kind of a damn fool Carmack was when he staked that moose pasture on Bonanza."

CUSH'S EYE suddenly widened. "Good God, John—you don't mean he made a strike like Carmack! If he did, why the hell ain't we up there gittin' in on it?"

"I don't believe Nate's struck another Bonanza. But I do know he's got a damn good proposition there. I've slipped over there several times since an' prospected the whole crick. There's room for maybe fifteen or twenty locations between the head of the rapids and the point where the flat butts up against a mountain. Far as I can see, Nate's staked the best location on the crick. Some of the others will pay out fairly well, but they're nothin' to get excited about."

Cush refilled his glass and shoved the bottle. "Luck's a funny thing," he philosophized. "Seems like the damner fool a man is, the luckier he might be. Take this here Nate, now— He didn't know nothin' about the country, an' nothin' about prospectin', an' he hits out an' makes him a strike on the first crick he comes to. What I can't figger—with that there feeder layin' there all this time, why ain't none of the boys here on Halfaday located it?"

Black John grinned. "You just p'inted out the reason. They know the country, an' they know somethin' about prospectin'. Knowin' the country, they all passed up a gulch that's so damn rocky they couldn't get a pick into it—an' even if they'd shoved on up, like Nate did, they know better than to prospect a moose pasture—just like plenty of sourdoughs had passed up that moose pasture on Bonanza till Carmack got to foolin' around with a shovel under that birch tree."

"Guess that's right," Cush admitted. "Looks like the more a man don't know about nothin' the better liable he is to git along."

"It'll take time to figure that one out," Black John chuckled, "but you're ondoubtless right."

"Huh," Cush scowled. "If all a man knows is big words it ain't no wonder he can't onderstand no little ones. Anyways, I'm glad Nate struck it lucky, so he kin pay off his mortgage an' git his wife cured. It's nice to have someone on the crick which ain't some damn crook claimin' his name is John Smith."

He paused abruptly and pointed toward the open doorway. "Look, here comes One Armed John hell-bent across the clearin'. I'll bet he's found another corpse—an' hot as it is, it'll prob'ly stink! By God, next time I git to Dawson, I'm gain' to tell 'em to git someone elst fer coroner!"

**AS CUSH** slid out another glass, One Armed John burst into the room and crossed to the bar. "Hey," he cried, "they's a gang come up the crick! They's seventeen of 'em in canoes! I counted 'em. An' what do you think they done?"

Black John refilled his glass and shoved the bottle along. "In the leadin' canoe there was a smallish man with a littly gray showin' in his beard?"

"That's right—him an' another one! But how did you…?"

"An' what they done was to head up that rocky gulch about a mile or so above Pot Gutted John's cabin?"

"Why shore! But how the hell did you know? I be'n sneakin' along through the bresh watchin' 'em an' when they started up that there gulch I run fer here to beat hell. How could you know what they done—an' you standin' here?"

"The feat was accomplished by deductive reasonin'."

One Armed stared blankly into the big man's face for a moment, then filled his glass. "Oh—like that—huh?" he mumbled. "By God, John—no wonder you kin outguess all these damn crooks! You allus know what they do, even before they done it."

The big man turned to Cush. "Looks like our friend Nate sort of shot off his mouth down there in Dawson," he said. "Well, this new addition to our little community will mean more business for you."

"Huh," growled Cush. "Prob'ly a bunch of damn chechakos. Why the hell couldn't they stayed where they was? I got all the trade I want, now, without a lot of chechakos pilin' in on me. First thing you know the country'll git all settled up an' go to hell jest like back there in the States. You say they ain't only a few claims on that flat that'll pay out. Then the rest of them damn cusses'll go broke an' want credick, an' I'll git stuck."

"Oh, I don't know, Cush," the big man grinned. "Some of 'em might be well heeled."

"Why would someone which he was well heeled be hittin' out to hell an' gone on the say-so of some damn chechako like Nate? Nussir—they're a bunch of bums, an' they'll be damn lucky if we don't have to hang a few of 'em before they git outa here. By God, the first one of 'em outside of Nate, that asks fer credick's goin' to git a bung-starter right between the eyes!"

## III

"FIFTEEN-TWO, FIFTEEN-FOUR, AN' three is seven—an' that's all I need. The game's on you, an'...."

"Hold on, there!" Black John interrupted. "You needed ten p'ints, an'...."

"Yeah," Cush retorted, "an' I got ten p'ints! I paired yer four, an' when you couldn't git in with them two queens, I got a go, an' them seven I counted makes ten. The game's on you, an' yer lackin' of seventeen holes, an' that's seventeen dollars, besides the drinks bein' on you fer losin' the game—an' they ain't no way you kin squinch out of it!"

"You're a hard man, Cush," Black John grinned, and glanced toward the doorway. "Look—here comes someone. It's Nate Barlow, an' he's got someone with him. An' by the way, that obviates my obligation to buy a drink, it bein' the immemorial an' well established custom that upon the advent of a stranger, the house sets 'em up."

Picking up the cribbage board and cards from the table, Cush stepped behind the bar and made an entry in his day book. "You squinch outa buyin' the drinks, all right—but them seventeen dollars is down in the book, an' all the big words you kin think up ain't goin' to rub 'em out."

The two men stepped into the room and ranged themselves beside Black John at the bar as Cush set out the bottle and glasses. "Hello, Mr. Smith," Nate said. "I want you an' Mr. Cushing should meet Bill Sykes. He's the one I was tellin' you used to live there in Goshen. Bill an' I's old friends, comin' from the same town—I don't come from the town, you might say, but my farm ain't only a couple mile out. It ain't so much of a farm—only a forty, but me an' the wife made a livin' off'n it, till she got to ailin'."

"Fill up," Cush invited. "This un's on the house."

"Glad to meet you boys," Sykes said. "Nate's be'n tellin' me how yer all good fellas, up here."

As the glasses were filled, Black John eyed Barlow. "One Armed John told us two, three days ago about a bunch of chechakos stampedin' up that rocky gulch, couple of miles below here. If you made a strike up there you hadn't ort to shot off yer mouth down in Dawson."

"I never told nothin' to no one except Bill, here. When you told me about prospectin' them little cricks—feeders, you called 'em—I paddled back down the crick an' hit up the first one I come to. They was only a little water runnin' down over the rocks, so I hid my canoe in the bresh an' went on up a-foot. After a while the rocks quit, an' I come out on a flat, so I begun to dig around here an' there. I panned out a little gold, like Mister Downey showed me how, an' then five er six days later I come to a place where all to onct I begun to git a lot of gold in most every panful of gravel. So I placed off the distance fer a Discovery claim an' put in my stakes, jest like Mister Downey told me, an' hit down to Dawson an' recorded my claim.

"I had my gold tied up in my other shirt, an' I tuk it in a store an' the man let me weigh it up on his scales, an' it come to right around six pound, shirt an' all. So I tuk it over to the bank, an' the man there weighed up the gold an' give me back the shirt. He claimed they was fifty-six ounces, an' it come to eight hundred an' ninety-six dollars. So I boughten a draft fer ninety dollars an' sent it to the Goshen bank fer to pay the first year's interest on my mortgage, an' I sent my wife a draft fer five hundred dollars an' kep' the three hundred an' six dollars that was left."

THE MAN paused and reaching into his pocket, counted some bills onto the bar and shoved them across to Cush. "An' here's the eighty-seven dollars balance I owe you, fer that stuff I got. Then I hunted up Bill, here, knowin' he was broke. He was in the Klondike Palace, an' I told him about findin' gold an' stakin' my claim, an' how he better come on back here with me an' stake him one, too. He claimed he needed a couple of drinks, an' borrowed twenty dollars off'n me, an' I went to the store an' boughten enough grub fer us to come up here on. When I got back to the saloon Bill was buyin' drinks for some guys, an' braggin' about the strike I made an' how I was takin' him up there with me, so he could stake him a claim, too.

"I wanted to start right out, but Bill he wouldn't come ontil he'd blow'd in the rest of that twenty, so I waited around, an' when it was gone he wanted to borry some more, but I wouldn't loan him none, on account I had to save them eighty-seven dollars I jest paid Mr. Cushing. We had to wait four er five hours fer the boat to start, an' when she did a lot of them guys that was in the saloon was on her, an' when she let us off at the mouth of the White River, they got off, too, an' follered us up."

Sykes downed his drink, and grinned rather sheepishly. "You know how it goes when a man gits a few in under his belt, he's apt to run off at the head. I'd ort to kep' my mouth shet—but I didn't. Anyways I guess they ain't no harm done. I got my stakes in on the next claim above Nate's. An' the rest of 'em's got the hull flat staked clean from them rock rapids to where the flat runs up agin a mountain. They ain't a bad bunch, barrin' one guy name of Frenchy Lalonde. He's got the next claim below Nate's. Another guy got there first, an' was cuttin' his stakes when Frenchy run him off. The guy wasn't goin' to go, but Frenchy pulls a gun on him, an' not only he run him off the claim, but he tuk the stakes the guy had cut, to boot. This here Frenchy, he's a bad actor. Claims he usta be a cowboy back in Montana. Carries a .44 Colt in under his shirt, an' every onct in a while he pulls it out an' takes a shot at somethin' jest to show folks how he kin shoot."

"Long as he confines his shootin' to showin' off I guess no one's got any kick comin'," Black John replied.

"Yeah, but with the law no closter'n Dawson, he could shoot one of us guys an' be to hell an' gone before the police got here."

"To hell an' gone is right," the big man replied, with a grin. "There's quite a few of these bad actors lyin' out back in the graveyard that kicked out on the end of a rope. They're the ones with an H on their slab. The Ms are the ones that got murdered."

"You mean you hung 'em without no police, er judge, er jury?"

"Oh, shore. Miners' meetin' tended to that."

"Miners' meetin'?"

"Yeah. It's an institution we've got that combines the functions of the police, an' judge, an' jury. It's a damn sight quicker, an' in most cases, a damn sight more efficient."

"I guess Frenchy wouldn't shoot no one," Barlow said. "He jest likes to show off." He turned to Cush. "Me an' Bill, here, we need some grub. Bill, he's broke. So if my credick's good you kin charge what he gits agin me, an' he kin pay me later. Me an' Bill, we're goin' to work together, puttin' up our shacks an' cuttin' wood. Then when we come to minin', this winter, we'll work one day on my claim an' one day on his'n. We figger it's better that way than each one workin' alone."

Black John agreed, and a short time later the two took their departure.

## IV

**OF THE SEVENTEEN** locations staked on Stony Creek, six failed to pay wages, and their owners quit and drifted back to Dawson before winter had fairly set in. Four others pulled out later. Frequent test pannings had showed Nate Barlow's Discovery claim to be far and away the best location on the creek. Frenchy Lalonde and Bill Sykes, on the claims adjoining Discovery, were doing well, with the remaining four taking out better than wages.

The Christmas jamboree was in full swing at Cushing's Fort when the seven men remaining on Stony Creek joined in the festivities. After a few drinks at the crowded bar where One Armed John was acting as assistant bartender, Bill Sykes slipped into a chair vacated by a man at one of the stud tables, to find himself seated next to Black John.

At the end of the bar Nate Barlow nursed his drink as he eyed the scene with evident amusement. Waxing more blatant with each drink, the swashbuckling Frenchy Lalonde, twirling his .44 six-gun, on his finger, offered to out-ride, out-shoot, or out-rope anyone present for the drinks on the house.

"Guess you won't git no takers, Frenchy," Red John opined. "There ain't nothin' big enough to ride in this country but a moose, an' we ain't got none handy. Our shootin' is mostly done with rifles, not with revolvers, or our mouth. An' about the only rope we use has got a hangman's knot on one end, with the other end throw'd over a rafter."

"Hard guys, eh?" Frenchy sneered, as he slipped the gun beneath his shirt. "Well, tellin' you about me, I'm hard, too. The outfit I rode with in Montana was hard. Hell, I was about the only man on the round-up that wasn't wanted fer somethin'."

"I kin believe that, all right," Short John grinned. "Who the hell would want you?"

Frenchy whirled and swung with his right—a blow that

landed harmlessly against the other's shoulder. The next instant he measured his length on the floor, as Short John stood looking down at him, he rubbed the knuckles of his left hand. "Yer hard, all right, Frenchy," he said. "I damn near broke my knuckles on yer jaw."

Frenchy rose slowly to his feet and tossed a limp poke onto the bar. "Fill 'em up," he said. "I know when I'm licked. The drinks is on me."

Cush weighed out the dust and returned the poke to the bar. Pocketing the empty poke, Frenchy poured his drink. The stud game broke up, and the players joined the others at the bar, Bill Sykes lining up beside Black John. A few minutes later Pot Gutted John tossed his poke onto the bar and ordered a round of drinks.

When the glasses were filled, Sykes smiled into the big man's face. "Seems like old times," he said. "We used to have a hell of a time around Chris'mas, down around Circle City an' Fort Yukon, an' them places."

Black John nodded. "Yeah, I guess the boys whoop her up most anywheres Chris'mas time. Gives 'em a chanct to kinda blow off steam. Was you down there long—in the lower country?"

"I put in six year one place an' another, on the American side. Done all right, too, ontil my pardner pulled out on me. Yup— the skunk tuk all the dust in our cache an' beat it whilst I was off huntin' moose. An' I never seen er heard tell of him agin. After that I fooled around along the river fer a couple of years, prospectin' an' workin' fer wages. Then I come on upriver an' run onto Nate Barlow. I know'd Nate around Goshen, Indiany.

"I come away from Goshen on account some guy got robbed an' claimed it was me done it. He lied like hell—but I know'd I couldn't prove no alibi, that night, on account I was out with another guy's wife, which this other guy would of shot me sure as hell if he know'd it—so I got to hell outa there an' hit fer Alasky.

"I rec'lect a couple year ago, down to Circle City, when the boys was in fer Chris'mas, they pulled off dog-sled races, an' snowshoes races, an' they was some Swedes there that raced on skis. But the damndest race I ever seen was in Chicago, one time. They was six of them there horseless buggies in it. They was goin' to be seven, but one run agin a street car an' knocked off a wheel. Thanksgivin' Day, it was, an' the road was covered with snow. Two of'em run with 'lectric batteries in 'em, but they didn't last long. The other four had gasoline engynes, an' two of them dropped out. Fella name of Frank Duryea win the race— fifty mile, it was, an' he made it in right around ten hours. Hell—any common horse could beat that! Them damn rigs won't never 'mount to nothin', they're only fer some rich guy to fool around with."

Black John nodded. "Yeah, I read about that race a while back in the paper. So you was right there an' saw it, eh?"

"Yer damn right I was! Fact is, it was me an' couple other fellas helped this here Haynes guy pull his buggy off'n the track where the street car hit it."

"Where the hell's my poke?" The voice of Pot Gutted John rose above the babble of conversation.

Cush eyed him across the bar. "I tossed it right there in front of you after I weighed out the dust fer the drinks."

"Well, by God, it ain't there now!" the other exclaimed, as all eyes swept the bar littered with empty glasses.

"Prob'ly shoved in yer pocket without noticin' it," One Armed John suggested.

"Like hell I did!" Pot Gut searched his pockets to no avail.

The voice of Nate Barlow broke the momentary silence. "I seen Frenchy pick up a poke off'n the bar."

Frenchy scowled. "Shore I did! It was my poke. Hell, I bought a round after Shorty, there knocked me down, didn't I?"

"Yeah, but this was only a couple of minutes ago. Mebbe you picked up his'n by mistake," Nate replied mildly. "Anyone might make a mistake."

Black John smiled at the belligerent Lalonde. "Better frisk yourself, Frenchy. Like Nate says, anyone could make a mistake. If someone else has to frisk you, the boys might not think it was a mistake."

With all eyes on him Frenchy explored his pockets and brought forth two pokes, his own, and Pot Gutted John's. "Well, I'll be damned!" he exclaimed. "I shore don't remember pickin' up that poke. Guess my head's kinda woozy yet, where Shorty whammed me on the jaw." He tossed the poke onto the bar and turned to Pot Gutted John. "It's my mistake, all right," he said. "I'm sorry it happened. Hell, if I aimed to rob a man I wouldn't go fer no half-empty poke, would I—an' right in front of a hull roomful of folks?"

"Not an' git away with it, you wouldn't," Pot Gut replied, pocketing the poke. "Better watch yer step, Frenchy. A few more mistakes like that might git a man a hangin'."

Black John ordered a round of drinks, and the incident passed off. When the glasses were filled, Sykes turned to Black John. "I hope Frenchy don't hold it agin Nate fer squealin' on him," he said in an undertone. "I wouldn't trust Frenchy no further'n what I could see him—after what he done to that there guy that was tryin' to stake the claim below Discovery, there on Stony Crick. Nate, he figgers he'll have all the gold he'll need after the clean-up, an' he's goin' to sell me his claim, an' go on back to Goshen. I shore wouldn't want nothin' to happen to him."

"Neither would I," the big man agreed. "But if somethin' does, we'll shore as hell hang the one that done it."

"Yer damn right—an' believe me—I want to git in on the hangin'!"

**SYKES TOOK** a seat at a stud table, and Nate Barlow stepped into the place he had occupied at the bar. "How they comin', Nate?" the big man asked. "Better get in on this drink—I'm buyin' one."

The other shook his head. "No thanks, Mr. Smith. I don't never take but the one drink the same day. I'm doin' all right there on Stony Crick. I take test pannin's every day er two, like you an' Mr. Downey told me to, an' seems like I'm gittin' more gold the further I go down. I figger I'll have all the gold I'll ever need, when I clean up my dump in the spring. I'll get my wife cured, an' pay off my mortgage, an' mebbe I wouldn't have to farm if I don't want to—jest set around an' take it easy."

"I'd sort of keep an eye on Frenchy, if I was you. He's prob'ly sore as hell 'cause you squealed on him fer pinchin' Pot Gutted John's poke."

"Oh, Frenchy's all right. He didn't go to steal the poke. He thought it was his'n—he said so hisself. He couldn't remember pickin' up his own poke on account of that man knockin' him down."

"Sykes was tellin' me you figure to sell out to him after the clean-up."

"Yes, like I was sayin', I'll have gold enough by spring an' on top of that, I'll have what Bill's goin' to pay me fer the claim."

"How much is he payin' you?"

"We don't know, yet. You see, his claim ain't nowheres near as good as mine, so he figgers, long as I'm pullin' out anyhow, he'll pay me whatever he's took out of his'n, an' I'll deed him mine."

"You might be able to get a damn sight more'n that fer it. If I was you I'd sort of look around before I sold out."

"Yeah, I might," Nate admitted. "But what's the use? There's only me an' my wife. We ain't got no kids. We'll have all we kin ever spend. An' when we die we can't take it with us, an' there ain't no one to leave it to. Besides, Bill, he's had kinda hard luck. His wife was allus raisin' hell with him, back there in Goshen. An' then he got blamed fer that robbery he claims he never done. An' on top of that his pardner, somewheres over in Alasky skipped out with all their gold. I kinda feel sorry fer him—comin' from the same town, an' all.

"I'm shore glad I come up here an' run onto sech good men—like Mr. Downey tellin' me to come up here an' see you—an' you tellin' me about prospectin' them little cricks—an' Mr. Cushing trustin' me fer my supplies. I'll be hittin' back, now. I had my drink an' I don't play no cards, so I'll git my pack of grub an' hit fer Stony Crick. I mebbe won't be seein' you till spring. But I'll stop an' say good-by 'fore I go back home."

## V

**THE SPRING CLEAN-UP** on Halfaday was well along when Bill Sykes and two men from Stony Creek burst into Cushing's saloon late one morning as Cush and Black John were shaking dice for the drinks. "By God, I know'd it would happen, sooner er later," Sykes cried. "Nate Barlow's murdered right there in his cabin, an Frenchy Lalonde's skipped out!"

Black John glanced at the three sixes Cush cast from the box, nodded, and reached for the bottle. "The drinks are on me," he said. "An' shove out three more glasses. These boys look like they need one." Glass in hand, he eyed Sykes. "How do you know Nate was murdered? An' how do you know that Frenchy skipped out?"

"How do I know! 'Cause I seen Nate layin' there on his floor, an' a puddle of blood kinda dry an' sticky like, an' a hole in the back of his head where it had run out of! I give one look an' run down the crick acrost Frenchy's claim hollerin' like hell, an' got these boys, an' a couple of more, an' we went back. We hollered fer Frenchy, an' when he didn't come out, we shoved his door open an' he was gone, an' his packsack was gone, an' we went on up to Nate's an' looked in the door, but we never went in nor touched nothin', 'cause we figgered you'd want to see things jest as they was. So two of the boys agreed to stay there an' see that no one went in er bothered nothin', an' us three come up here, hell-bent, to tell you."

Black John nodded. "You done right, Bill. Yer thoughtfulness is commendable. How's the clean-up comin' along, over on Stony Crick?"

"Frenchy, he finished his clean-up day before yesterday. He told me he tuk out seven hundred an' twenty ounces. I an' Nate, we worked together on our clean-ups, an' I only got three hundred an' forty ounces—but Nate, he tuk out twelve hundred an' sixty ounces. His Discovery claim is the best one on the creek by all odds."

"Do you know where Nate cached his dust?"

"Hell, no! That is, I didn't know till us boys went up there this mornin'. After we seen how Frenchy was gone, an' Nate layin' there dead on his floor, we kinda looked around them two claims, an' pretty quick we found a kind of a hole-like in the rim wall where a kinda flattish rock had be'n shoved away, an' they wasn't no gold in there—only one empty poke. It was Nate's poke, all right. I seen him makin' 'em. He sewed 'em with stout black thread. It shore looks like that was Nate's cache, all right. An' when we looked in Frenchy's cabin to see if he was there, I seen where one of the puncheons in his floor was shoved to one side, so when we started fer here, us three looked in there agin an' we seen a holler place in under that puncheon which was prob'ly his cache. By God, he murdered Nate, an' robbed his cache! Then he come back to his cabin an' got his dust an' his pack, an' hit out. He musta did it last night, 'cause he was there on the crick yesterday, wasn't he?"

The others agreed, and again Black John nodded. "Yer deductions sound reasonable, under the circumstances, to the casual observer."

Sykes frowned, slightly. "How's that agin?"

"Meanin' that it looks like Frenchy is the guilty party."

"Yer damn right he is! I mistrusted somethin' might happen ever sence Chris'mas time when Nate says he seen Frenchy pick up Pot Gutted John's poke off'n the bar. Frenchy claimed he done it by mistake, but they was a lot of us know'd different.

He's nothin' but a damn thief, an' he told me a while back that he'd git even with Nate fer shootin' off his mouth. An' it shore as hell looks like he done it."

"Confronted, as we are, by the motive, the opportunity, an' the overt act," Black John said, "it is reasonable to assume that the malefactor has accomplished his purpose."

"Cripes sakes," Sykes exclaimed, "you talk like some damn preacher, er lawyer, er somethin'! What does all them big words mean?"

"They mean 'yeah'," Cush explained, as he mopped at the bar. "John, he never misses the chanct to make twenty big words do the work of one little one."

The big man grinned. "Fill 'em up again, Cush. We'll throw this one into us, an' be on our way. I'm goin' back with these boys an' sort of look things over."

"Mebbe," Cush said, "I'd ort to go along an' fetch a coroner's jury to set on Nate. It's goin' to be rough goin', what with the rheumatiz givin' me hell in the left leg."

"It won't be necessary for you to go over to Stony Crick. I'll go back with these boys an' we'll look things over, an' fetch Nate back with us. You notify a half a dozen of the boys to show up tomorrow for a jury an' we'll hold the inquest here in the saloon." He turned to the others. "You men from Stony Crick will have to be here to testify as to what we find out."

"Yer damn right we'll be here!" Sykes replied. "Us, an' all the rest of the boys from Stony. Nate Barlow was my friend. He was friends with all the boys on the crick except that damn Frenchy. I'd shore enjoy seein' the son of a bitch hung that killed him."

"I've got a hunch that you'll be there at the hangin'," Black John replied.

"You mean you figger the police will ketch up with Frenchy?" Sykes asked eagerly.

"Well, the boys in the Mounted are pretty good, especially

if Corporal Downey gets on the job. Drink up, an' we'll get goin'."

## VI

**THE FOUR ARRIVED** at Nate Barlow's claim to find all of the remaining Stony Creek men seated on the ground in front of the cabin.

"We ain't went inside," one of the men explained. "Everythin's jest like it was."

Black John opened the door and stepped into the room, followed by Sykes. The others grouped about the doorway muttering angrily as they eyed the body sprawled on the floor.

Black John stooped and examined the wound. "Shot in the back of the head with a heavy calibre gun—a revolver, most likely—the bullet didn't go on through."

Sykes nodded. "That's right. Frenchy had the only revolver on the crick. He was allus shootin' around with it. A .44 Colt, it was. Ain't that so, boys?" he asked, turning to the group at the doorway. All agreed, and Sykes stooped and picked up a small object from the floor near a leg of the stove. He handed it to Black John. "An' that proves it!" he exclaimed triumphantly. "A .44 ca'tridge—right where Frenchy throw'd it after he shot Nate!"

Black John sniffed at the brass cartridge and with the point of his knife he scratched an X on the shell, and held it up. "You men could identify this shell if necessary." They nodded and Black John thrust it into his pocket. "It's be'n fired recently—not later than last night, I'd say." He turned to the group at the doorway. "Any of you boys hear any shootin'?"

"I did," one replied. "'Long jest afore dark, it was. It come from up this-a-way. Five, six shots, it was."

Two or three others nodded, and one added, "Yeah, I heard 'em. But I didn't pay no heed. Frenchy, he was allus shootin' around with that big revolver—allus wantin' to bet someone he could out-shoot 'em, er that he could hit a tin can, er somethin'. Then, quite a while later—after dark, it was—I heered one more shot an' I figgered mebbe Frenchy had took a crack at a owl, er mebbe a wolf snootin' around his meat cache."

"That's right," Sykes agreed. "I heered them shots, too. But like Clem there says, Frenchy was allus shootin' at somethin' er other. Way it looks now, he went out an' practiced up, an' then after dark he snuck up to Nate's cabin an' let him have it."

"Pretty good shot was he?" Black John asked.

"Yer damn right he was," Sykes replied. "I've saw him set up a tin can fifteen, twenty steps off an' hit it the first shot, an' then keep it rollin', shootin' one shot after another till his gun was empty an' never miss onct."

"You said somethin' about findin' Nate's cache. I'd like to have a look at that."

"We don't know if it was his cache, fer shore," Sykes said. "I jest says we figgered it was."

The two stepped from the room and Sykes led the way, others following. At the foot of the rim wall a short distance back from the cabin he paused and pointed to an aperture at the base of the wall. "Everythin's jest like we found it, ain't it, boys?" The others nodded agreement, and he continued. "You kin see fer yerself there's one empty poke layin' there, an' like I says, I know it's Nate's poke 'cause I seen him makin' 'em. The way I figger— Frenchy he snuck around till he found out where Nate cached his dust, then he slips over after dark las' night an' shoots Nate, an' come over here an' robbed the cache an' throw'd his dust an' some stuff in his packsack an' skipped out. That there flat rock layin' there—looks like that was the cover to the cache."

"Kinda looks that way, don't it?" the big man replied. "Let's go take a look at Frenchy's place. It don't pay to overlook nothin' in a case of this kind."

Stepping into Frenchy's cabin, Black John glanced around, as Sykes pointed to an empty hollow beneath a floor puncheon that had been thrust aside. "Like I says—that's prob'ly wher' Frenchy cached his dust."

"Yer ondoubtless right," Black John agreed, and turned to the others. "Accordin' to what Nate told me, you boys hit out from Dawson on this stampede on pretty short notice. Didn't have much time to throw an outfit together. You must of travelled light."

"You bet yer life!"

"I'll say we did!"

"Cripes, when Sykes, here, got to shootin' off there in the Klondike Palace about this here strike Nate made, we had to ketch that boat they was pullin' out on! Yer damn right we was travellin' light!"

"Well, I guess that's about all we can find out here," the big man said. "We'll hold the inquest up to Cush's in the mornin', Cush, he's the coroner, an' he'll app'int a jury an' set on the case. You boys'll all have to be there, an' tell what you know—like seein' Nate layin' dead on his floor with a bullet in his head, an' about findin' his cache, an' how things look here at Frenchy's. We'll make a litter out of a couple of poles an' a blanket, an' two of you can pack Nate up there. Better start now. Four of you better go so you can spell one another off. The goin's kinda rough in places. Nate can lay in the storeroom over night."

**FOUR OF** the men volunteered, and when they pulled out, Sykes stepped close to Black John. "How about a little drink? I got part of a bottle left there in my cabin. Couldn't ask all the boys. Ain't got enough left fer only a couple good slugs fer the two of us."

Black John followed the man to his cabin, and seated himself as Sykes set a bottle and a tin cup on the table. "I hain't only got the one cup," he said. "Like the boys was sayin', we come up here travelin' light. Help yerself."

"After you," the big man said.

The other grinned. "What the hell—you don't think that

licker's p'izen, do you?"

"I don't know. I can tell better after seein' you down a good stiff drink of it."

Sykes poured out half a tin cup of liquor, swallowed it, and shoved the cup across the board. "Guess you know it's all right, now. I s'pose though, a man's got to kinda keep his eyes open, at that."

Black John nodded. "That's right. His eyes an' his ears, too." He poured and downed a liberal drink, and returned the cup to the table. "So you put in six years down around Circle, eh? I s'pose you know Bob Steele, that runs the big store out there?"

"Hell, yes! I know Bob well. I've bought a lot of stuff off'n Bob."

"An' Bergman, that runs the saloon there?"

"Oh, shore. Many's the drink I've had in Bergman's place."

"You must have prospected on the Charley River, then. You know—it runs into the Yukon right acrost from Circle."

"That's right. I prospected the Charley from one end damn near to the other. It was on the Charley that my pardner robbed me."

"I put in a couple years on the Charley," Black John said. "Eight, ten years back. Had a location right below the water-fall—you know that big fall jest above where the river widens out into a kind of a lake."

"Oh, shore I know. Yeah, I've paddled acrost that lake an' portaged around that falls many a time. Our claim was way above there. Sometime me an' you'll have to git together fer a good talk."

"Yeah, that's right. Well, I'll be shovin' along. Don't fail to show up at Cush's in the mornin'. We'll need your testimony at the inquest bein' as you're the one that found Nate. When we get the official coroner's verdick that it was Frenchy killed Nate, the police will take right out after him instead of runnin' around in circles huntin' for someone else."

"Oh, I'll be there, all right. Have another drink before you go."

The big man grinned, as he poured some liquor into the cup. "A man can't walk on one leg, as the sayin' goes—an' I've got some walkin' to do. Here's how!" He downed the drink, stepped from the cabin, and headed down the creek. He crossed Nate Barlow's Discovery claim, and at the lower boundary of Frenchy's No. 1 Below, he turned abruptly into the bush, and seated himself on a stone that gave him a view of the creek. "The shots the boys heard just before dark they said sounded like they came from up here. So they couldn't have be'n fired very far one side or the other of the crick. It shouldn't take me very long to catch up with Frenchy," he muttered, and a few minutes later, satisfied that Sykes had not followed, he began a careful search of the bush, covering every inch of the ground for some two hundred yards back from the creek. Finding nothing, he crossed the creek, and some ten minutes later, he stood beside a rock crack, some two feet wide and ten feet deep that slanted sharply into a ravine. Near the edge of the crack he found an empty tin can pierced by several bullet holes. Some fifteen yards along the rock, he stooped and picked up half a dozen empty .44 calibre shells. Then dropped to his knees and examined closely a dark red stain on the rock, and on a small patch of caribou moss. It was but the work of a moment to follow the trail where a heavy object had been dragged to the edge of the crack. Lowering himself into the crack, he threw aside some loose stones that covered Frenchy's body. Grasping it by the feet, he easily dragged it down the slope into the ravine, where he shouldered it and struck out for Halfaday. Leaving the body in his cabin he stepped over to Cushing's to find the four who had carried Nate Barlow's body, together with half a dozen of the residents of Halfaday lined up at the bar discussing the murder.

"Ain't it hell," Cush said, as he set a bottle and glass before Black John, "a damn coot like that there Frenchy, murderin' a good guy like Nate Barlow? But where you be'n all this time? These boys fetched Nate in couple hours ago—an' you was travelin' light."

"Oh, I stuck around a while over there on Stony Crick, just in case I might pick up some loose ends."

"Loose ends! Hell fire, it don't look like we need no more loose ends than what we've got! Nate, layin' there on his floor with a .44 hole in the back of his head, an' Frenchy ownin' the only .44 on the crick, an' him gone with Nate's dust an' his own to boot!"

The big man grinned. "Looks like there's a loose end or two to pick up right here. You say Nate's got a .44 hole in his head—how do you know it's a .44 hole? Did you get the bullet?"

"Cripes, no! It's in his head. It never come out in front."

"Then you're just guessin' it's a .44."

"'Course it's a .44! Everyone on Stony Crick an' most of us here on Halfaday know'd Frenchy had a .44. He was allus pullin' it, an' wantin' to bet on his shootin'.'"

"Nevertheless, we've got to make shore. A .45, or a .38 would make a hole in a man's head, too. A coroner should never jump to a conclusion. Where have you got Nate?"

"He's in the storeroom. An' if you think I'm a-goin' to mess around in his head huntin' that bullet, you kin go jump in the crick."

"The bullet won't be hard to find. Where's your meat saw?"

"Git it from the klooch," Cush growled, "an' tell her to be damn shore she worshes it when you git through."

Nearly an hour later Black John reentered the saloon and laid a slightly mushroomed bullet and an empty brass shell on the bar. "It's a .44, all right," he said, as the men crowded around. "You can see it fits this shell Bill Sykes picked up off Nate's floor. There's no question about it's bein' Frenchy's gun that killed him."

# VII

NEWS OF THE murder had spread and some twenty men from Halfaday joined those from Stony Creek in Cushing's saloon the following morning. Promptly at ten o'clock, Black John thumped the bar with his fist. "Drink up, men. Cush'll clear the bar an' won't serve no more drinks till after the inquest. Bein' coroner, he app'ints you four men that fetched Nate Barlow's corpse over from Stony Crick, an' Red John, an' Pot Gutted John fer a jury to determine, to the best of your ability the cause of Barlow's death." He turned to Cush. "Just to keep the record straight, how do you pronounce him?"

"Huh—I pronounce him Barlow—same as anyone else would."

"I mean, is he alive, or dead?"

"If he ain't dead by this time he shore as hell ort to be—with the back of his head shot, an' the front of it sawed."

"Nate, havin' be'n duly pronounced dead, will henceforth be known as Exhibit A." He laid an object on the bar. "This is the bullet I removed from Nate's head. It is Exhibit B. An' this empty shell that Bill Sykes picked up off Nate's floor in the presence of me an' four of the jury, is Exhibit C. For the first witness Cush calls Bill Sykes. Stand out here, Bill, where the jury can hear you. Hold up yer right or left hand. Do you swear to tell the truth, the whole truth, or any part of it, s'elp'e God?"

"That's right."

"Did you, or did you not, go to Nate Barlow's cabin yesterday mornin'?"

"I did."

"Was Nate there?"

"Shore he was."

"What was his status at the time?"

"What was his which?"

"Was he alive or dead?"

"He was deader'n hell. They was a bullet hole in the back of his head, an' a puddle of blood on the floor. So I run down the crick hollerin' an' these four here on the jury went back there with me, an' they seen jest what I seen. So two of 'em stayed there to keep anyone from messin' things up, an' the other two come over here with me an' told you about it."

THE FOUR nodded solemn agreement, and Black John picked up the empty shell from the bar. "An' when I went back with you an' we stepped into Nate's cabin, did you, or did you not, find this shell on the floor?"

"I did."

He handed the shell to one of the jurors. "Pass this around amongst you an' examine it closely." When it was handed back he asked, "Did you men notice what calibre it is?"

"It's a .44," they answered in chorus.

The big man nodded, picked the bullet from the bar and held it for all to see. "This is the bullet I removed from Nate Barlow's head. It had passed through his head an' laid against the bone of his forehead." He paused and fitted the base of the bullet into the shell. "You can all see that it is a .44 bullet. Now does anyone here rec'lect seein' a .44 gun in anyone's possession?"

The name of Frenchy Lalonde roared from every throat, and Black John pounded for order. When some semblance of quiet was restored the big man turned to Sykes. "Did you visit Lalonde's cabin after findin' Nate's body?"

"Shore I did, an' these guys went along. Frenchy was gone, an' so was his pack, an his cache was empty, an' so was Nate's— that is," he added, "we found what looked like Nate's cache. You seen it there at the bottom of the rim wall."

Black John nodded. "That will do. Witness excused." He turned to the jurors. "Cush app'ints Pot Gutted John as foreman of the jury, an' he will announce the verdick which you will have five minutes to reach." The men whispered among themselves and a moment later Pot Gutted John stepped forward. "We don't need no five minutes. Hell, anyone kin see what come off. Our verdick is that Nate Barlow was murdered an' robbed by Frenchy Lalonde."

"Okay," Black John replied. "Inquest adjourned. I just counted noses, an' find there's exactly fifty-two men here." Stepping to a table, he picked up a deck of cards, shuffled it and laid it on the bar. "Every man draws a card. The four drawin' the deuces are ordered to dig Nate's grave, an' the two drawin' the black treys will prepare the slab. Red John bein' handy at it, will burn Nate's name on it, along with the check latter M, for murdered. Step up, boys, an' draw your cards."

**LATE IN** the afternoon, with Nate Barlow laid away beneath the new slab in the little cemetery, Bill Sykes, a bit the worse for numerous drinks, edged in beside Black John at the bar. "I be'n out pickin' a big mess of posies an' laid 'em on pore Nate's grave," he said. "I shore hate to think about Nate bein' dead, comin' from the same town, an' all. We be'n friends ever sence we was kids, you might say. When I go back I kin tell Nate's woman about him gittin' a good funeral."

"Figurin' on pullin' out?" Black John asked. "Thought you were goin' to buy Nate's location."

"Yeah, I figger on goin' back to Goshen an' buyin' it off'n his widder. I'll give her a good price fer it, all right. Then I'll come back. I'd shore like to stick around an' see the fellow that murdered Nate hung."

The big man nodded. "Yeah—it's a sight I'm goin' to enjoy, myself."

"But I don't darc to wait er someone elst might buy Nate's claim. It'll take damn near two weeks to git word to the police an' then it'll take 'em another two weeks to git up here, an' it might be another month er so before they ketched Frenchy, an' what with the trial, an' all, cripes it might be late in the fall before they hang him."

The big man grinned. "I look for Corporal Downey to show up about day after tomorrow."

"What!" The word exploded from Sykes' lips, and his body stiffened as he glanced, wide-eyed into the other's face.

"Yeah, you see, I know that Downey is over at Sebastian's village on Ladue Crick, so I sent a man over to notify him of the murder before I went back to Stony Crick with you. He's over there on a hooch case, but he'll drop that damn quick when he hears about this murder. Like I said, he'll probably get here day after tomorrow, an' when he gets on the job he won't quit till he cleans up this murder—you can bet your life on that."

"But, hell, John—it's already cleared up! Cripes, didn't the coroner's jury jest claim it was Frenchy done it?"

"Yeah, but Downey ain't a coroner's jury. He's a policeman. Hell, he's liable to hang around over there on Stony Crick for a week lookin' things over, an' when he's through he'll know what happened over there—an' don't you forget it."

The crowd in the saloon thinned as the men went back to their claims, and as the sun sank behind the mountains, the men from Stony Creek headed for the door. "Hey, Sykes, you comin' along? We're headin back 'fore it gits dark."

The man downed his drink at a gulp. "Yeah, I'm comin'," he replied, and turned to Black John. "Well, so long. I'll be hittin' back with the boys. If this here Downey's goin' to git here that quick, I'll probably stick around an' see if I kin mebbe help him out."

WHEN THE men had gone Cush eyed Black John across the bar. "What's this here line of guff you was handin' Sykes about Downey bein' over on Ladue Crick, an' you sendin' a man after him? I ain't heard about no hooch case over there, er Downey bein' there neither."

The big man grinned. "The proposition was merely a hypothetical premise—"

"I don't give a damn about no hypocritical promise!" Cush

interrupted. "An' likewise I ain't goin' to stand here an' listen to no sermon! All I says—what the hell did you lie to Sykes fer? Fact is, Downey'd jest be wastin' time if he come up here. What he better be doin' is spreadin' his men up an' down the river on the lookout fer Frenchy. Yer gen'ly smart as hell figgerin' out these cases, John—but yer slippin'. When Sykes an' them other two come bustin' in here an' told about Nate bein' murdered, an' Frenchy pulled out, what you'd ort to done was to took out hell-bent after Frenchy, instead of putterin' around over on Stony Crick. I done some figgerin' after you'd went an' I seen where Frenchy would be packin' right around a hundred an' twenty-five pound of dust, what with Nate's twelve hundred an' sixty ounces an' his own seven hundred an' twenty—an' his grub an' trail outfit on top of that. You could of hit out light an' overtook him at the Fish Rapids easy—instead of which you went over there on Stony Crick an' found out what everyone know'd a'ready."

"Well, lookin' at it from your angle, maybe yer right."

"Yer damn right I'm right! An' quick as you'd hit out fer Stony Crick I sent Short John down to notify the police so's they could pick Frenchy up on the big river 'fore he kin git outside with Nate's dust."

Black John shook his head slowly. "The police'll never pick him up, Cush. You've just went ahead an' put 'em to a lot of bother for nothin'."

"Why won't they pick him up? Cripes, Short John'll hit the river damn near as quick as Frenchy will—an' even if Frenchy ketched a steamboat, the police kin notify Whitehorse to be on the lookout fer him."

"They won't pick him up because, onfortunately for him, Frenchy has already arrived at his ultimate destination—an' not by way of the river."

"You mean he hit out over the Dalton Trail?"

"No. Meanin' that he didn't hit out."

"Wher' the hell's he at, then?"

"At the present moment he's over in my shack."

Cush's eyes widened as he poured and gulped down a drink. "In yer shack! An' you stud there an' went on with the inquish when you could of turned it into a miners' meetin' an' hung Frenchy higher'n hell!"

"Oh shore. We can hang him yet, if you want to. But I wouldn't see much object in it."

"Why, 'course not," Cush replied, with elaborate sarcasm. "A man murders someone in his own shack an' hits out with his dust—an' there ain't no object in hangin' him fer it. Mebbe we'd better git him over here an' buy him a drink, er give him a medal, er somethin'."

"The fact is, Cush," the big man grinned, "Frenchy's dead. He weighs right around a hundred an' fifty pounds. I packed him over here from Stony Crick on my back."

"Dead! You mean you run him down an' shot him?"

"He's shot, all right—but I didn't shoot him. He was shot in the back of the head with his own gun."

"You mean, after he shot Nate, he turned his gun on hisself? But—hold on—how the hell kin a man shoot hisself in the back of the head?"

"He didn't shoot himself. The same man shot him that shot Nate Barlow. The fact is, Cush, Bill Sykes shot 'em both."

"Bill Sykes!" Cush gasped. "Bill Sykes shot 'em—an' you know'd it all the time—an' you stud right there an' let him hit out fer Stony Crick with all them others instid of callin' a miners' meetin' an hangin' him!"

"That's so—we could have done that, couldn't we? Looks like we overlooked a bet, don't it? Must be, like you said, I'm slippin'. Oh well—what's the difference. We can call a miners' meetin' an' hang him some other day."

Cush's eyes narrowed as he stared intently across the bar. "Some other day! You drunk—er gone crazy—er what?"

"I ain't drunk. An' not bein' a psychiatrist, I'm prob'ly incompetent to pass on my own sanity."

"Accordin' to the way you talk you ain't got no sanity fer anyone to pass on. By God, if Bill Sykes murdered them two we'd ort to call a miners' meetin' an' hang him tomorrow!"

"Oh, well—just as you say, Cush. We might as well get it over with. I guess tomorrow would be as good as any day. You pass the word along an' we'll hold the meetin' tomorrow afternoon."

"But, how about Sykes? He's liable to be to hell an' gone by then."

"Oh, Bill will be here, all right. Cripes, he's told me two, three times he'd like to see the son hung that murdered Nate Barlow. If we use this rafter here, an' don't blindfold him, he can get a good view of the proceedin' in the back bar mirror. Well, I'll be goin', now. Don't forget to get word to the Stony Crick boys. They'd like to get in on it, seein' the murders were pulled off over there. I'm slippin' down the crick a ways. There's a moose crossin' down there, an' along about daylight I might pick up somethin'."

Cush eyed the big man with a puzzled frown. "I don't know what's got into you, John. Here's two murders on the crick—an' you claim to know who done 'em—an' you let the damn cuss walk outs here right under yer nose—an' then go moose huntin'! An' allus before this, you was hell-bent to hang someone fer committin' only one murder!"

Black John shrugged. "Well, you said I was slippin', Cush—an' maybe yer right. I'll be here for the meetin', though. An' if I get a moose, I'll fetch you over a hind quarter."

# VIII

**SHORTLY AFTER DAYLIGHT** the following morning Black John stepped from the bush and greeted the man who had swung a pack from his shoulders and stooped to drag a canoe into the water at the mouth of Stony Creek. "Hello, Bill! Where you headin'?"

The man straightened suddenly, and Black John noted the bulge in the front of his checked shirt—noted also that the tight-pressed lips forced a smile. "Why—hello, John! Me, I'm pullin' out. I can't stick around till the police picks up Frenchy, much as I'd like to. I'm hittin' back to Goshen to buy Nate's claim, off'n his widder. But—what the hell you doin' down here this time a day?"

"Oh, my meat was runnin' kinda low, an' I figured I might get a shot at somethin'."

"It's lucky you seen me, then," the man said. "'Cause I seen a big bull moose about a mile back along the trail. He never seen me, an' I stud still, an' he walked acrost the trail an' bedded down right there in the bresh. You could sneak up on him from here. Like I says, it's about a mile, er mebbe a mile an' a half back, right where a big tree is broke off an' the trail goes around it. You can't miss it."

The big man smiled. "How do you know it was a bull?"

"Cripes I got a good look at him! He had horns on him this wide," Sykes replied, stretching his arms to capacity.

Black John carelessly thumbed the hammer of the rifle cradled in his left arm. "Kinda heavy pack you've got there, Bill," he remarked, casually.

"Yeah, I'm takin' my dust an' all my stuff along—all of it I could git in the pack."

"It couldn't be that you're packin' some other dust along with your own—say about twelve hundred an' sixty ounces of Nate's, an' seven hundred an' twenty of Frenchy's?"

"What the hell do you mean?" the man cried, his eyes suddenly widening.

"Meanin' just what I said."

"You know damn well that Frenchy bumped Nate off an' skipped out with his dust! An' so does everyone elst. By God, we proved that at the inquest, yesterday!"

Black John nodded. "Everyone else thinks so—everyone, that is, except you an' me. You see, Bill, Frenchy didn't skip out. He's up in my cabin, right now—waitin' to testify at the miners' meetin' this afternoon."

All the color drained from the man's face. "Up in yer cabin— waitin' to testify—it's a damn lie! He...." The words ceased abruptly, and the man wet his lips with his tongue, and suddenly his hand flew to the front of his shirt, then dropped to his side as his horror-stricken eyes fixed on the muzzle of the rifle scarcely two feet from his chest.

Reaching out, Black John jerked a six-gun from the front of the other's shirt, and stood there looking down at it. "A .44— Frenchy's .44. Come on, Bill—pick up yer pack. We don't want to be late for the meetin'."

The man suddenly found his voice. "By God, you can't ever prove nothin' on me! Frenchy's dead, an' if he's up in your cabin you packed him there. He shot Nate an' robbed him, an' I heer'd the shot an' run to Nate's cabin, an' ketched Frenchy robbin' his cache, an' when he seen me comin' he turned an' run, an' I shot him in the back of the head, an' drug him over an' dropped him down a rock crack an' piled stones on him. Then I tuk Nate's dust, an' Frenchy's along with it, an' I was hittin' out right now fer Dawson to turn the dust over to the police!"

"Why didn't you tell me that before? An' why didn't you tell it to the coroner's jury?"

"I'll tell you why—an' I'm givin' it to you straight. When Nate come back to Dawson an' filed his claim, an' Cuter Malone found out we was headin' fer the Halfaday Crick country, he told us that you was all outlaws, up here, an' you was the king of the bunch. So I figgered if you boys know'd I had all that dust, you might knock me off an' grab it, 'fore I could git to the police with it—that's why."

Black John nodded. "Sounds reasonable—about Cuter tellin' you we're all outlaws, up here. Somehow, seems like the crick has got a bad name—in some quarters. So if you can put that acrost to the boys, this afternoon, they'll ondoubtless turn you loose to take the dust to the police."

**AT PRECISELY** two o'clock that afternoon, Black John thumped the bar with his fist. "Miners' meetin' called to try one, to wit, Bill Sykes for the murder of Nate Barlow, an' the theft of twelve hundred an' sixty ounces of dust from his cache, an' also for the murder of Frenchy Lalonde, an' the theft of his seven hundred an' twenty ounces. Normally these two crimes would be handled separately, but bein' as they run so closely parallel, I deem it proper to bunch 'em.

"Nate Barlow is dead. Most of you were here an' helped bury him yesterday. The bullet that killed him is here on the bar, along with the empty shell Sykes picked up off Nate's floor in the presence of me an' four Stony Crick boys. They are Exhibits A an' B, respectively. Frenchy's body is over in my cabin, an' I hereby delegate Pot Gutted John an' Red John to fetch it here. It is Exhibit C. This packsack here belongs to Bill Sykes. He was hittin' out for the big river with it, when I happened to run acrost him this mornin' at the mouth of Stony Crick. In it are twenty-three hundred an' twenty ounces of dust, an' accordin' to Sykes, twelve hundred an' sixty of 'em come from Nate Barlow's cache, seven hundred an' twenty from Frenchy's, an' the remainin' three hundred an' forty belong to him. This pack-sack an' its contents is Exhibit D. An' this .44 Colt I'm layin' down on the bar is the one I took out from in under Bill's shirt this mornin' down by the crick. It is Exhibit E.

"Most of you boys was here yesterday at the coroner's inquest, so we can skip all the details that were brought out at that time. I will state that before I returned from Stony Crick I nosed around a bit and found Frenchy's body covered with stones in a rock crack. He had be'n shot in the back of the head. I packed it over here an'—" He paused and glanced toward the door where Pot Gutted John and Red John were carrying in the body. "Lay it here on the bar, boys an'—"

"Not by a damn sight!" Cush cried. "Not no corpse on the bar—an' it dead three, four days! Lay it on the floor—an' leave that door open, too!"

"Okay," the big man continued. "I will now state that, with the findin' of Frenchy's body I became convinced that Bill Sykes was the murderer of both Frenchy and Nate, so this mornin' I slipped down an' intercepted him as he was hittin' out with this pack of dust, an' I hereby charge him with the two murders. He will now be given the chance to try an' lie out of it. An' I'm warnin' you beforehand that as a liar Bill has got both Ananias an' Baron Munchausen backed off the map." He paused and turned to Sykes. "Stand out here, Bill, an' tell the boys what you can think up in the way of defense. No use swearin' you in. You couldn't tell the truth if you tried."

**SYKES STEPPED** forward and faced the assembly with his back to the bar. "I never told a lie in my life," he began. "At least not many. I did lie to Black John an' the coroner's jury about Frenchy skippin' out. I shot him, an' I'll tell you why. I an' some of the other boys on Stony Crick heer'd some shots the other evenin', an' after dark I heer'd one more shot that sounded like it come from Nate's cabin, so I run up there an' seen Nate layin' dead on his floor, an' when I come out I seen someone over by the rimwall, so I run over there, an' damn if it wasn't Frenchy robbin' Nate's cache. He tuk one shot at me an' then started to run so I cracked down on him with my rifle an' ketched him in the back of the head. Then I drug him over an' dropped him in a rock crack an' covered him with stones. I tuk Nate's dust, an' Frenchy's along with it—which I found his cache in under his floor—down to my place to keep it till I could take it down to Dawson an' turn it over to the police. The reason I lied to Black John, about Frenchy skippin' out with the dust was 'cause when we was down to Dawson, Cuter Malone told us that you boys up here was all outlaws, an' I figgered that if you know'd I had all that dust, you'd prob'ly knock me off an' grab it. It was Frenchy murdered Nate—an' me shootin' him ain't no murder, no ways you could look at it, after him crackin' down on me."

The man ceased speaking and Black John eyed him. "Is that all you've got to say?"

"Yeah, that's all. An' by God, it's enough to prove I never murdered no one, an' stole their dust! I was packin' that there dust down to the police so's they could git it to the rightful owners."

"Your zeal for righteousness is commendable, Bill. You say you shot Frenchy with your rifle? Would it be this rifle that's strapped to your pack, here?"

"Shore. That's the onliest rifle I've got."

"What calibre is it?"

"It's a .30-40. You kin see fer yerself."

"Oh, by the way, Bill—that bull moose you told me you saw this mornin'—how big did you say his horns was?"

"Biggest ones I ever seen. An' you could of got him, too, if you'd went up there. They was this wide," he spread out his arms at full length, and was greeted by a roar of laughter from the crowd. The man scowled. "What's so damn funny about that?"

"The funny part is that no bull moose has got a spread of horns this time of year," Black John explained. "They're jest beginnin' to show up in the velvet."

"Musta be'n some tree branches I seen, then, showin' up over his head. But they shore looked like horns to me."

"Your lie didn't work, Bill. You could not send me off on no wild goose chase—or moose chase, rather—I was after more important game than moose this mornin'. You see, Nate, I've known you were a damn liar ever since the first time you showed up here. You told Nate you'd spent six years along the Yukon, an' yet, when I mentioned a miners' meetin', you didn't know what it meant. Then, again at Chris'mas, when you told me about takin' in that horseless buggy race back there in Chicago...."

"By God, I did take it in! It was on Thanksgivin' day, an'...."

"Oh, shore. I know damn well you took it in. You knew how many was in the race, an' how many finished, an' who won it. You knew the distance they ran, an' the time they made it in. You even knew that one of the damn things run into a streetcar an' knocked a wheel off. You see, Bill, I read about that race in a Sunday paper that someone fetched up to Forty Mile. An' you're right about it bein' run Thanksgivin' Day—it was Thanksgivin' day, 1905. You see, you'd already told me about puttin' in six years down around Circle City. Your eyesight would have to be damn good to have watched that race from Circle. You saw that race, Bill—but you never saw Circle. When I saw that you were a liar, I gave you a chance to waller in a little deeper. I asked you if you knew Bob Steele, the storekeeper there, an' you said you'd bought a lot of stuff from Bob. As a matter of fact, Bob never run a store at Circle. Then I mentioned the Charley River runnin' into the Yukon right acrost from Circle, an' told about workin' a location just below the big waterfall just above where the Charley runs through that lake. An' you said shore you knew where that fall is, an' the lake. You claimed you'd prospected the Charley from one end to the other.

"As a matter of fact, Bill, the Charley don't run into the Yukon acrost from Circle. It runs in a good sixty miles above there— an' from the same side that Circle's on. Besides that, there's no big falls on the river, an' it don't widen out into any lake. When I mentioned Bergman's saloon bein' in Circle, you said you'd had many a drink in there. The fact is, Bergman's saloon is in Forty Mile—not Circle.

"But you ain't bein' tried for lyin', Bill—the offence not bein' hangable on Halfaday. Bein' as you've just given us your version of what come off over there on Stony Crick, I figure it's no more'n right to give the boys your status regardin' truth an' veracity." The big man picked up the brass shell from the bar and held it up for inspection. "Have you ever seen this shell before, Bill?"

The man examined it. "Shore I have. It's the one I picked up off'n Nate's floor—right where Frenchy throw'd it after shootin' Nate. You was right there an' seen me do it—an' so did Jones, an' Roberts, an' Shafer, here. I know it's the same one, 'cause there's the marks on it you made with yer own knife.

"Ain't that so, boys?" he appealed to the four, who replied in the affirmative.

"Now, Bill, you claimed it was after dark when you heard that shot an' run up to Nate's cabin, an' found him dead on the floor. Is that right?"

"Shore it's right. Other ones on Stony Crick heer'd it, too."

"But it wasn't too dark for you to see the sights on your rifle when you shot at Frenchy there at Nate's cache?"

"I don't know if I seen my sights, er not. Like I says, he tuk a shot at me, an' I shot back an' was lucky enough to hit him."

BLACK JOHN picked up the revolver from the bar. "This gun, now—it's a .44 Colt, the same kind of a gun Frenchy was known to own. Yet, when I took it out from under your shirt, this mornin', you claimed it was yours."

"That is my gun!" Sykes cried. "I bought it in Chicago."

The big man's eyes swept the crowd. "Any one here ever seen Sykes with a six-gun? Anyone know he had one? If so, let him speak up." Negative muttering and shaking of heads greeted the words. "I had that gun all the time," Sykes interrupted. "Jest 'cause I never flashed it around like Frenchy done, ain't no sign I didn't have it."

"Okay," Black John said. "Then it's your gun." Pausing, he picked up the bullet from the bar. "Here's the bullet I dug out of Nate Barlow's head." Pausing, he drew another bullet from his pocket and held the two out for inspection. "An' this other one, I dug out of Frenchy Lalonde's head. The two are identical. Frenchy was killed with a .44 revolver—not with a .30-40 rifle. He was shot in the back of the head at close range—just as Nate Barlow was shot—by the same gun in the hand of the same man." Lifting the revolver from the bar, he cocked it and fired a shot into the floor. Removing the empty shell, he pointed to the dent left in the percussion cap by the firing pin. It was a dent flattened slightly on one side, due to an imperfection of the pin. "Step up, men, an' compare these bullets, an' the dents in the caps of these empty shells. Both Barlow an' Lalonde were killed with this gun, which Sykes has just sworn was his." He paused and fixed his eyes on Sykes, whose face had gone dead white. "As a matter of fact, I suspected you from the first. Your eyes had a kind of a glint in 'em when Nate spoke of quittin' an' headin' for home with his dust. You went out of your way to plant the fact that Frenchy had it in for Nate—told me he had threatened to get even with him for callin' attention to the incident of Pot Gut's poke. Then, there in Nate's shack when you picked up that empty shell from the floor—right where you'd planted it—I knew it was you who had killed him. No one who didn't want to deliberately plant evidence, would stop to reload his gun after committin' a murder. Then, when you wanted it to appear that Frenchy had skipped out, you stuck his blankets an' his extra clothes in his packsack, an' left his fryin' pan, tea pail, an' his cup, an' plate an' eatin' tools. You men all hit out from Dawson travelin' light. You can bet Frenchy never packed two outfits of cookin' tools. You knew damn well that Frenchy was a good shot, yet you told me you figured that shootin' you heard before dark was him out practicin' up, before headin' up to Nate's to kill him. A good shot don't need much practice, Bill, to hit a man in the back of the head at a range of six inches. What really happened was, you took Frenchy up on a shootin' match—an' when your turn came to handle the gun, you waited till his back was turned an' let him have it—then went up an' killed Nate." He paused and let his glance travel over the crowd. "That's the evidence, men. What's your verdick—guilty, or not guilty?"

A loud roar of guilty filled the room. There was no dissenting vote, and Black John eyed the cringing man.

"Fact is you're a liar, Sykes—not a good liar—just a damn liar. You're such a dumb liar, that every time you opened your mouth you widened the trail that led right straight to your door. An' on top of that you're prob'ly the lowest-lived, orneriest cuss it's ever be'n our privilege to hang. You've come to the end of your rope, Sykes—there it is—Pot Gut has jest finished the noose. I remember you told me that you'd like to see the man hung that shot your friend, Nate Barlow. We won't blindfold you, Sykes—jest look in the mirror while you're swingin' high from that rafter, an' you'll get your wish."

Late that evening when the two were alone in the saloon, Cush eyed Black John across the bar. "Well, we got that damn Sykes hung, all right—but if you know'd it was him that shot them two, why the hell did you let him go back to Stony Crick with them others last evenin'? We could of stuck him in the hole till today an' be'n shore of havin' him."

The big man grinned. "I knew he had all of Nate's dust an' Frenchy's, too. But I didn't know where he'd cached it. By tellin' him I expected Downey to show up in a couple of days I knew he'd hit out at daylight with the dust an' most likely with Frenchy's gun. I figured it would be a damn sight easier to get Sykes an' all the evidence in one package, than to have to hunt all over hell for the dust an' the gun—an' maybe never find either one. An' by the way, Cush, we'll jest lump Frenchy's dust in with Nate's an' have Downey forward it to his widow. Sykes' three hundred an' forty ounces we'll split between us to cover expenses."

# TARGET PRACTICE
# ON HALFADAY

**OLD CUSH, PROPRIETOR** of Cushing's Fort, the combined trading post and saloon that served the little community of outlawed men that had grown up on Halfaday Creek, close against the Yukon-Alaska border, carefully folded a well thumbed copy of the *Police Gazette,* and placed it on the back bar from which he removed a bottle, two glasses and the inevitable leather dice box, as Black John Smith crossed the floor and faced him across the bar.

Picking up the box Black John cast the dice. "I'm leavin' the three fives in one," he said.

Cush failed to beat the fives, and when his next three shakes netted only a pair of sixes, he shoved the bottle across the bar with a scowl. "Anyone could beat a pair of sixes in three," he said. "The drinks is on me." When the glasses were filled, he eyed Black John through his steel rimmed spectacles. "Y'know wimmin is the durndest folks they is," he observed.

The big man grinned. "Well, barrin' men—maybe you're right. I see you've be'n perusin' the *Gazette.* I was lookin' it over the other evenin', an' believe me, the chorus in that burlesque show, the way they're dressed, shore don't leave much to the imagination. Fact is, I couldn't see much wrong with 'em."

"That's the heck of it," Cush growled. "The more clothes they ain't got on the worster a man is off if he has nothin' to do with 'em."

Black John's grin broadened. "Syntax is a wonderful thing," he observed.

"Yeah, an' believe me, if they was a sin tax the jails would be full of wimmin that couldn't pay their taxes. Look at them first three wives of mine—one of 'em soakin' flypaper in under the bed to git the p'izen out to slip in my coffee, an' the next one skippin' out on me with that B. & O. conductor down there in Cincinnati, an' the other one wearin' that there Spanish stiletto in her stockin'! If that ain't sinnin' I don't know what the hell you call it! I'm lucky to be alive!"

"An' all this time, I suppose, you played the part of the model husband."

"I was model enough not to git p'izened, er to git run out on, nor yet to git my goozle slit some might with no Spanish stiletto! An' right there in the *Gazette* I was jest readin' a piece where it tells about some woman in Chicago which she hired some guy which he was paroled fresh outa prison, to knock off her husban', promisin' to pay him outa the insurance money, an' when he done it, she payed him off by turnin' him in to the police. An' she'd of got away with it hadn't be'n fer some smart detective the insurance company put on her tail. This guy plays up to her an' one night in a booth in a tavern she spills her guts to him over drinks, not knowin' the dick had planted a couple of witnesses in the next booth with only a curtain between. So both her an' the guy that done the killin' got life—an' what I claim—they'd ort to get the rope! An' that's what I mean about wimmin—men's damn fools to marry 'em in the first place."

## II

**A SHADOW DARKENED** the door and both eyed the man who crossed the floor, a limp packsack dangling from his shoulders, and came to a halt beside Black John at the bar. "This here's Cushing's Fort on Halfaday Creek, ain't it?" he asked.

The big man nodded. "Yeah, this is the place. The character behind the bar there is Lyme Cushing, in person. My name's Smith—Black John by identification."

"My name's John Smith, too."

"Not on Halfaday it ain't. Just reach in the name can there on the end of the bar an' draw out a name."

"Name can! What's a name can?"

"It's a device Cush an' I worked out when the crick got so cluttered up with John Smiths that we ran out of distinguishin' characteristics—like Long John, Short John, One Eyed John, Pot Gutted John, Red John, One Armed John, et cetra. We garbled the names out of a history book an' tossed 'em into that molasses can yonder. Now when a man comes along claimin' his name is John Smith, we call his attention to the error, an' advise him to draw a name out of the can, which name becomes his property until such time as he departs from our midst."

"You talk like some lawyer er somethin', which I know you ain't none, on account Cuter Malone, down to the Klondike Palace in Dawson, tellin' me who you was."

"Who I am, he ondoubtless meant. But we'll pass over the inaccuracy."

"This here name can," the man grinned. "It ain't sech a bad idee, at that." Reaching into the can he withdrew a slip of paper, and holding it to the light, read: "Alexander Burr. I guess that's as good a name as any."

Behind the bar Cush nodded as he slid a glass toward the man. "Okay, Alex, fill up. The house is buyin' one."

"Friend of Cuter's, are you?" Black John asked, when the glasses were filled.

"Well, I don't know's you could call me a friend of his'n. I run acrost him there in the Palace. Hung around there a few days, sort of gittin' my bearin's like. You see, I'm new in this here country. Don't know my way around yet. So I hung out around the Palace—playin' a little stud an' givin' the girls a fling. It was in one of them stud games I tumbled onto somethin'. This here guy, he's a young punk that clerks in the office of the Consolidated Dredge Company, an' he got in kinda deep. When the game busted up, I bought him a drink, an' sort of told him I was sorry—him losin' like he done. An' he tells me that I didn't know the half of it. Said the cards had be'n runnin' agin him fer quite a spell, an' it was company gold he was losin', him havin' dug into it, to try to win back what he'd lost. I kinda hints that mebbe we could rig some way to git it back without the company ketchin' on—like if he knows where they keep their gold, we might be able to glom into it some night.

"He didn't figger we could git away with a play like that, but he told me there was another way we might work it. He claims that the company aims to ship out fifty thousan' in gold on the tenth of next month. He says they ain't goin' to ship it on the steamboat from Dawson on the fifteenth, like they generally do, on account of some smart crook might spot the shipment an' make a play fer it. So they're goin' to send it up to Ogilvie by canoe on the tenth, an' load it on the boat there, figgerin' that no one would look fer a gold shipment from Ogilvie. He said that him an' a guard would hit out with it on the night of the tenth.

"I tells him it would be a cinch fer me to knock off this guard an' we could split the fifty thousan' fifty-fifty. He fell fer it, all right. An' the next day I got to thinkin'. It would be a cinch fer me to knock off that guard, all right, but what the hell would I do then? You see, I don't know the country, an' they tell me that this here Corporal Downey is a smart cop. I'd want to git that dust away from Dawson. But where? So I kinda feels Malone out, sizin' him up fer a guy that knows a thing er two. I don't tell him nothin' about this here job—only sort of asks him where I could hook up with some guy that knows his way around in case I run up onto somethin'.

"**YOU SEE,** I heard about you bein' the biggest outlaw in the country, an' how the police don't dast to show up here on Half-aday Crick. So I asks him about you, an' he says sure you be—but if I've got any sense I'll cut a wide circle around you. Then he names off two, three guys that hangs around the Palace, claimin' they'd be good ones to hook up with if I pulled off somethin'.

"I could see by the way his eyes flickered when I mentioned yer name that he hated yer guts—so right then I decided that you was the man I wanted. I'm a high-class worker, myself—an' I don't aim to throw in with no damn punk. So I come on up here after findin' out where this Halfaday Crick is—an' believe me, it's a trip. So, now I got here, how about me an' you hookin' up on this here fifty thousan' job? It's a cinch, an' we could fetch the stuff on up here where the police don't dast to show up, an' split her fifty-fifty."

Black John shook his head slowly. "N-o-o-o, Alex, I guess I'll pass it up. The amount's too piddlin' to contemplate."

"Too piddlin'! Man—there's twenty-five thousan' apiece in it! How you goin' to make twenty-five thousan' any easier?"

"The amount, as I see it, would be twelve thousan', five hundred apiece—not twenty-five thousan'. You forget that you promised the clerk a split on the fifty thousan'."

The man grinned and winked. "I ain't fergot nothin'. But you kin fergit the clerk. We'll knock him off when we knock off the guard! How about it?"

"We-e-e-l-l, such proceedure seems a bit onethical at first glance. However...."

"I don't know what yer talkin' about," the man interrupted. "Does that mean yer throwin' in with me?"

"Not necessarily. You see, Alex, there seems to be a slight misconception in your estimate of Halfaday. You said that you heard that the police don't dare to show up here. The fact is that very few rookie policemen do visit us. But Corporal Downey drops in on us whenever the spirit moves him. You see, here on Halfaday, we neither help nor hinder the police."

The man frowned, downed his drink, and tossing a bill onto the bar, glanced across at Cush. "Fill 'em up agin'," he ordered, and when the glasses were filled, the frown melted into a grin as he eyed the big man. "Pretty smart, at that—lettin' Downey drop in now an' then, when there ain't nothing fer him to see. I kin go along with that, all right. It jest goes to show you ain't no green punk. I kin see where me an' you's goin' to hit it off."

"Yeah? Well, tellin' you about me, Alex—my eyesight ain't quite so good."

"How do you mean like that?"

"Meanin' that I'm a bit particular, myself, about who I hook up with. You seem to know a sight more about me that I know about you."

"You don't need to worry none about me, brother. I'm the guy that knows his way around—an' don't you fergit it. Me an' a pal takes a Great Northern express car fer sixty thousan' near Chinook, Montana. An' we take a bank at Park Rapids, Minnesoty fer better'n forty thousan'. We split up, then, an' I hooks up with another guy down in Kansas City, an' we takes the Tulsa bank fer ninety thousan', an' then hops up into Michigan, an' takes a bank in Grand Rapids fer fifty thousan' more. How's that fer a recommend?"

"Accordin' to your figures, your share of the profit in the four jobs you mentioned would be a hundred an' twenty thousan'. The amount is worth contemplatin'. An' talk bein' as cheap as it is, it didn't cost you a cent to get it off your chest."

"You mean you don't believe me—you figger I'm lyin' about them jobs?"

"Well, I have be'n lied to by bigger men than you—littler ones, too, as far as that goes."

"All right then, I'll prove it," the man replied, and reaching into his pocket, withdrew a wallet from which he extracted several newspaper clippings which he laid on the bar in front of the big man. "Read them an' you'll know whether I'm lyin' er not. I cut them pieces outa different newspapers."

Black John read the clippings and returned them to the bar.

"I see that the express messenger an' the bank teller in Tulsa were shot during the holdups—both square between the eyes. Pretty good shootin', I'd say. An' also I see that the police are up in the air on all four of the jobs."

"Yer right they're up in the air. When I pull off a job I don't never leave nothin' fer the police to git holt of. An' as fer the shootin'—I cooled both them guys myself. I don't shoot less'n I've got to. But when I do shoot I don't never miss. You satisfied now that I'm okay?"

"I've got no doubt but what these jobs were pulled. But I didn't see anything that ties you in with 'em. Any one could have pulled 'em, as far as I can see."

"Well, why would I cut them pieces outa the papers if I didn't pull them jobs? Why would I care about 'em, if I didn't pull 'em?"

"**LOTS OF** people clip excerp's from newspapers that have no reference to themselves. For all I know you may be just a casual collector of odd bits of Americana."

The man's brow furrowed. "What you talkin' about, anyhow?"

Cush mopped at some spilled liquor. "When John onreels them big words they wouldn't no one but God know what they was about."

"So you don't figger I was in on them jobs, eh?" the man asked.

"Well, up to the present I have no concrete evidence of the fact. Carryin' around newspaper clippin's about the jobs don't prove that you were in on 'em, by a damn sight."

"Okay—then I'll show you some evidence." Slipping the packsack from his shoulder, the man reached into it, and produced three rolls of bills. And for the next ten minutes Black John and Cush watched in silence as he counted the money onto the bar. "There you be—one hundred six outa the one hundred twenty thousan' I got off'n them jobs. The rest I spent since we pulled off the last one. Now do you believe me?" he asked, as he returned the money to the packsack.

Black John nodded. "Yes, I'm inclined to believe that you told the truth about those jobs, Alex. There is just one other item that remains to be verified—your ability to shoot. You claimed, I believe, that you never miss."

Pot Gutted John, Red John, and One Armed John stepped into the room and ranged themselves along the bar. Black John nodded toward the newcomer. "Boys meet Alex Burr, an' Cush shove out the bottle. I'm buyin' a drink." When the drinks were downed, the big man continued. "Alex an' I were talkin' here, an' he claims to be a pretty good shot with a six-gun...."

"Not no six-gun," the man interrupted. "An automatic—a Luger. Tell you what I'll do—we'll rig up a target, an' I'll shoot any man in the house fer the drinks—er fer any amount he wants to put up."

Pot Gutted John eyed the others. "Black John's the best shot amongst us," he said. "Tell you what I'll do—I'll take you on fer an ounce a shot for six shots—John shootin' his six-gun, an' you yer Luger."

"I'll go you a ounce a shot fer them six holes," Red John added.

"Okay, boys, you're on," Burr replied.

A bull's eye and several surrounding circles were inked on a blank sheet of paper, and proceeding to the creek, the target was pinned against a clay wall with slivers of wood. With the target in place, Burr glanced at Black John. "What range?" he asked.

The big man shrugged. "You name it."

"How's fifteen steps?"

"Okay. You take the first shot. I'd like to know what I've got to beat."

Pacing off the distance, the man whipped out the Luger from its holster and fired the instant it reached the level of his eye. Red John who had been standing to one side, peered at the target. "He jest clipped the edge of the bull's eye!" he exclaimed. "John'll have to go some to beat that!"

Black John fired, and missed the bull's eye by an inch. Again the man fired, and again he hit the bull's eye. Black John was a good two inches off. It was the same with the four remaining shots—the newcomer made a clean sweep of the match, missing the bull's eye with only one shot—and that by a scant quarter of an inch.

Back at the bar, Burr collected his six ounces of dust from Pot Gutted John and Red John, and numerous drinks were had all around. When the three had departed, Burr eyed Black John. "How about it—am I good—er ain't I?"

The big man nodded. "You're a better man than I am, Gunga Din."

The other frowned slightly. "The name I draw'd outa the can was Alexander Burr," he corrected.

"That's right. I forgot," Black John smiled.

"You goin' to throw in with me on that there Consolidated job, or ain't you?" the man asked.

"W-e-e-l-l, I'll think it over. We've got a month yet. There's plenty of time to decide."

Burr glanced at Cush. "How about a place to stay? You keep boarders?"

"No, I don't keep no boarders."

"You can throw your stuff in One Eyed John's cabin," Black John said.

"Who is One Eyed John?"

"He ain't no one, now," Cush explained. "That's who he was before we hung him."

"Hung him! What did you hang him fer?"

"Durned if I recollect," Black John answered. "Prob'ly for somethin' he done. I forgot to mention it, Alex—but we don't allow any crime on Halfaday. It might fetch in the police an' make it bad for everybody. So, if anyone commits a crime here on the crick, we call a miners' meetin' an' hang him."

The man nodded approval. "Good idee, at that. We shore don't want no police snoopin' around. Where's this here cabin at?"

"Down the crick a piece—jest a little ways below the clearin'. Come on along an' I'll show you. Funny thing about One Eyed John. After we'd hung him Cush and I hunted all over for his cache. We knew he had quite a heft of dust—used to play stud quite a lot—pretty lucky, too. We hunted all over the cabin, an' hunted around in the brush, but couldn't find any evidence of where he buried it. No one's be'n in the cabin since we hung him—so if you should happen to run onto the dust, we'll split it with you, fifty-fifty. It would most likely be in the moosehide pokes."

The two left the saloon, and a few minutes later when Black John returned to the saloon Cush eyed him across the bar. "Ain't it awful what keeps driftin' in on us, John? But, that there Alex kin shoot! I never seen no better shootin' than what he done."

"He's a crack shot, all right," the big man agreed. "In fact accordin' to those newspaper clippin's, an' the concrete evidence he produced to back 'em up, I'm inclined to the opinion that Alex is a mighty competent workman in his line."

"WORKMAN! I'LL bet the cuss never done an honest day's work in his life! Him shootin' that poor express man, an' that bank clerk right between the eyes when they pulled them jobs! An' on top of that when you claimed the cut on that Consolidated job wouldn't be only twelve thousan' five hundred on account of havin' to split with that there clerk, he claims he'll knock off the clerk along with the guard.

"What I claim, the quicker we git shet of that double-crossin' cuss the better!"

"O, I don't know, Cush."

"You don't know! You shore ain't figgerin' on throwin' in with him, be you?"

"Well, I'm sort of debatin' the proposition."

"That's one debate you better lose, then," Cush growled. "An' what's more—when you git holt of that there hundred an' six thousan' he had in his pack, jest remember, I seen it as quick as you did—an' I git my half!"

One morning a few days later Burr stepped into the saloon where Cush and Black John were shaking dice for the drinks. "Well," he said, eyeing the big man, "about three weeks from now we'll be pullin' out an' git set fer that Consolidated job, eh?"

Black John nodded. "That would be about the right time— providin' I decide to get in on it."

The man scowled. "You still think mebbe I ain't so good as I claimed, eh?"

"Downey's a damn smart policeman. A man's got to be mighty careful who he throws in with on a job of that kind."

"All right. We've got time, yet. There's one more way I kin prove it. You fellas know I ain't got no gold—only them bills, an' I've got them hid. I'll hit out fer Dawson an' pull off a job alone—some prospector er someone—an' hit back here with my take. Not knowin' no more'n what I do about the country, if I kin git away with a job like that, you'll know I'm good! Ain't that so?"

Black John nodded. "W-e-e-l-l, I'm inclined to believe that such procedure would indicate a certain measure of competence on your part."

The man frowned and glanced across at Cush. "What's he talkin' about?"

"He said 'yeah'."

"Okay—then I'll hit out."

"Shove out the bottle, Cush. I'll buy a drink," the big man said. As the glasses were filled he glanced at the butt of the Luger that protruded from Burr's holster, and grinned. "Kind of odd, ain't it, that a man claimin' his name's Smith would be packin' a gun with an F cut in on the butt-plate?"

Burr returned the grin. "I got the gun off'n a guy named Fink down in Chicago. He's a punk strong arm worker with a record as long as yer arm—jewelry stores, pawn shops, loan offices. One time when he was down on his luck I loaned him twenty bucks on the gun—an' I ain't saw him since. Knowin' his record, I figgered that sometime I might pull some job, an' leave the gun where the cops could find it—an' right away they'd connect Fink with the job—what with his record agin him, an' plenty of stoolies knowin' it was Fink's gun. Like I told you, I'm a guy that knows his way around. I don't overlook no bets."

**BLACK JOHN** nodded approval. "Guess you've got what it takes," he admitted. "An if you show up here after a trip to Dawson with some dust in your poke, it would clear up any lingerin' doubt I might have about your ability. But make it snappy, or we might lose out on that Consolidated job. An' here's another thing—if you should slip up, an' Downey follows you up here, I don't know a thing about it. I shore won't front for any punk that would botch a job. O, by the way, you didn't happen to run onto One Eyed John's cache, did you? Like I said, he must have left quite a heft of dust around there somewheres."

The man shook his head. "Nope. I hunted all over fer it, after you tellin' me he musta had it hid somewhares. But I couldn't find it. Prob'ly buried it somewheres out in the bresh."

A half hour later after watching the man's canoe disappear down the creek Black John went to his own cabin, picked up a carefully wrapped package and proceeded to the cabin of One Eyed John where he pulled on the bit of string that was scarcely visible where it protruded from the wall at the base of one of the coat-hanging pegs, and removed a section of log, thrust his arm into the enclosure and withdrew the three rolls of bills the man had counted out on Cush's bar. He also produced a moosehide sack. He grinned as he returned the sack to the aperture. "They're nothin' but gilded iron filin's, but they shore look like dust to a chechako. So he couldn't find One Eye's cache, eh? Didn't figure on splittin' that dust fifty-fifty with Cush an' me. Figured we'd overlooked that bit of string when we hunted for the cache—so it would be a good place to cache his own roll along with the dust. The devious an' onderhanded ways of these crooks are sad to contemplate," he muttered, as he removed the paper wrapping from the parcel he had brought from his cabin and proceeded to count out one hundred six thousand from a huge roll of bills. Making the money into three rolls, he placed them in the cache, and returned the section of log to its original position. "I figured that bunch of counterfeit money I got off those two con men a year or so back would come in handy, sometime or other," he said, as he pocketed Burr's money and left the cabin. "Because if Burr ever tries to spend any of that money he's goin' to find out real quick that crime don't pay."

On the fifteenth day after his departure Burr returned to Halfaday, staggering under the weight of a pack which thudded to the floor as he ranged himself beside Black John at the bar. "That there gold is heavy—what I mean," he panted. "Shove out the bottle, Cush. I'm buyin' a drink."

**WHEN THE** glasses were filled Black John eyed the pack. "Looks like you did all right for the time you were gone," he observed.

"I'll say I done all right!" the man agreed after downing his drink. Reaching for the bottle, he poured another. "It's that there Consolidated gold I was tellin' you about—an' what I mean, it weighs close to two hundred pounds if it weighs an ounce. I hits Dawson an' runs onto that there Consolitated clerk, an' he slips me the word that they changed their shippin' date on that gold, an' how him an' that guard is hittin' out that night with it, 'stead of waitin' till the tenth of next month. So I hits up the river an' lays fer 'em. It's moonlight an' I knocks 'em off where they pulled in clost to shore roundin' a p'int, an' hauls their canoe ashore an' puts the gold in my canoe, an' shoves theirn out in the river—an' them in it. Then I hits out up the river with the gold."

"Shot 'em with a rifle?"

"Shoot 'em with my Luger. I don't own no rifle."

"Kind of careless, wasn't it—shovin' the canoe out into the river where it's bound to be picked up with their bodies in it?"

The man grinned. "I know what you're thinkin'—that the police'll dig them bullets out of 'em, if they didn't go on through, an' save 'em, an' if they'd ever pick me up with the Luger, they'd have me dead to rights, 'cause I happen to know they've got a way of tellin' what gun they was fired from. Ain't that right?"

The big man nodded. "That was what I had in mind."

"Okay. Now I'll show you how smart I was by doin' like I done. I know'd I had quite a ways to go yet, so I hung onto the Luger, case I'd need it—like if the police er someone would run onto me. If I didn't run onto no one I aimed to throw the gun in the crick when I got back here. I shoved on upriver an' when daylight come I pulled the canoe out an' drug it back in the bresh an' slep' till evenin'. Then I shoved on upriver. I done the same the next night, an' on the third evenin' I come to another p'int where there was a little fire goin' where someone was campin'. I run in clost an' seen how it was a young punk an' he was alone, an' was cookin' his supper. I was kinda hungry, too, not darin' to build no fire. I hadn't had only some bologny to eat, so I landed, an' the kid invites me to have somethin' to eat. Whilst we was eatin' he tells me his name's Farley, an' he's hittin' fer Dawson to git in on the big gold strike. Well sir, soon as he told me his name, I remember that there F that's cut in my gun-butt, so when the kid goes fer some more firewood, I slips the Luger into the bottom of his pack, an' then I thanks him fer the meal, an' wishes him good luck an' shoves on. An', what I mean—if the police picks him up with that gun in his pos- session he won't have a chanct in the world of beatin' the rope fer them two murders. How's that fer smart?"

"You've shore proved your worth, Alex. I don't know's I ever run across a more thoroughly depraved an' iniquitous personality."

"I wished I know'd as many big words as you do—but anyhow I know'd if I got the chanct I could prove I'm okay. I got to thinkin', comin' up the crick, how with that there Consolidated job outa the way, we'd ort to kinda look around fer some other one to pull. 'Course, me pullin' this here alone, you couldn't expect me to split with you on it. Ain't that right?"

"Oh, shore. A split on that dust don't interest me in the least."

"I figger like this—what with you knowin' the country, an' all, mebbe it would be a good thing if you was to make a trip down to Dawson an' kinda look around. Mebbe you could tumble onto somethin' we could pull off later."

BLACK JOHN nodded. "I think you've got somethin' there, Alex. You lay low, here, an' I'll pull out in the mornin'."

When the man shouldered his heavy pack and left the saloon, Black John followed, and it was well after dark before he returned to the saloon.

### III

IN DAWSON Black John stepped into the office of the police detachment to be greeted by Corporal Downey. "Draw up a chair John. How's things on Halfaday?"

The big man drew up a chair, filled his pipe, and elevated his heels to the flat top desk. "Oh, about so-so. Nothin' ever happens, up there. What's the news along the river? Anyone broke any laws, lately?"

"Oh, we're busy as usual. Along with a lot of other stuff we had a robbery—fifty thousan' in dust that the Consolidated was shippin' out. They figured that it would be safer to run the stuff up to Oglivie an' ship it from there, so they loaded it in a canoe, one night, an' started it upriver in charge of a guard an' a clerk. The next day the *Sarah* picked up the canoe floatin' downriver a few miles below with the bodies of the guard an' the clerk in it. But the dust was gone. I started men up an' down the river, an' before night Constable Breen came in with the murderer—practically caught him red-handed, as the sayin' is."

"Got the dust, too, eh?"

"No. But we'll get it. The bird that pulled the robbery is a young punk. Breen picked him up a few miles upriver. He claims he don't know anything about it. But he's just a kid. Time he's be'n in solitary for a while he'll crack. He's bound to. We've got an open an' shut case against him!"

"Got witnesses, eh?"

"No. No witnesses. But we've got the gun that killed the guard an' the clerk. He had it in his pack."

"H-u-u-m, you know Downey, some of these open an' shut cases could be a sight more open than shut."

"This one's shut tighter than a drum. We got the killer, all right. An', like I said, time he's be'n locked up alone for a month or so, he'll crack. If not, then maybe the judge or the crown prosecutor might be able to show him the difference between the rope, an' a life sentence."

"You say this character's nothin' but a kid, eh?"

"That's right—eighteen, nineteen. Nice lookin' kid, too. Don't look like a tough guy. Don't talk like one either. But he's hard, all right. Claims he never saw the Luger Breen found in his pack. Claims he never owned a gun of any kind. We checked with his home town police—Sauk Centre, Minnesota, an' they say the kid's never be'n in trouble of any kind. Names Farley. His dad's on the way up here. Maybe he can get the kid to talk."

"You know, Downey, I like kids. Maybe if you'd let me try, I could get somethin' out of him."

"Well—you might at that. Go ahead—he's there in the guardroom."

**TEN MINUTES** later Black John returned to the office. "Find out where he's cached the dust?" Downey asked.

"Nope. Claims he don't know anything about the job. Says he never saw the Luger till Breen pulled it out of his pack."

Downey shrugged. "Yeah—that's the same line he gave us. But, Doc Sutherland dug out the bullets that killed those two fellows, an' it didn't take long to find out they were fired from that Luger. When I told him that, he dreamed up a cock an' bull story about some fellow headin' upriver in a canoe stoppin' off for supper with him when he was headin' down. I don't know how he thinks he can get away with anything when the Luger's got his initial F cut in the butt plate."

Black John nodded. "Looks kind of bad for him, at that. But do you know, Downey, I believe the kid."

"Believe him!"

"Yup. I shore do. He looks honest, an' he talks honest, too. Tell you what I'll do—I'll lay you a wager that the kid's clean."

"A wager. What kind of a wager? An' how could you prove it?"

Black John grinned. "I ain't in the police. It's up to you to prove it—you or Breen. An' as for the wager—how about a round of drinks over Cush's bar the next time you show up there?"

Downey returned the grin. "Okay. Make it two rounds. I'll never get two drinks any cheaper."

"Two rounds it is. An' don't wait too long about showin' up at Cush's. I'm shore amin' to enjoy those two drinks."

"It might be quite a while before I get up to Halfaday—busy as we are down here."

"Busy doin' what?"

"Why, everything that's listed in the manual."

"Nothin' that couldn't be put off if you were on the trail of a murderer, is there?"

"What do you mean—on the trail of a murderer?"

"O, just an expression you run across readin' these police stories in magazines."

Downey eyed the big man shrewdly. "Do you mean that there's a murderer on Halfaday?"

"How would I know? On Halfaday we don't neither help nor hinder the police."

For several moments Downey sat silent, drumming on the desk top with his finger tips.

"I know you wouldn't want me to make a trip up to Halfaday for nothin'—nor for those two drinks—especially when you've got to buy 'em."

"No. I wouldn't suggest that you make the trip for nothin'. Fact is, I'd like to show you a target."

"A target?"

"Yup. Just a square of pasteboard with a bulls-eye an' some rings marked on it. It's pinned up against a clay bank—if the wind hasn't blown it down. An' it's got some bullet holes in it where a fella beat me in a shootin' match. An', by the way—you might bring those bullets along with you, the ones that Doc dug out of that clerk an' the guard. I've got a hunch that you'll be interested in that target, Downey—especially in the clay bank behind. An' I might add that you're in error about who'll be payin' for the drinks. Fact is, I'll bet you another round that you'll pay for 'em."

**DOWNEY SHRUGGED.** "All right. I'll show up on Halfaday. I don't know what it's all about—this target shootin', an' all—an' you bein' so sure I'll be buyin' the drinks. I know you've got somethin' up your sleeve."

"Yeah," Black John grinned. "It's my arm. But just remember—

'There are more things in heaven an' earth, Horatio,

Than are dreamt of in your philosophy.'"

"Get out of here! When am I supposed to show up on

Halfaday?"

"I'm hittin' back in the mornin'. Better wait a week or so. I wouldn't like the boys to think you were campin' on my trail. They might figure I'd committed some crime—like spittin' on the sidewalk, or leavin' my hat on in church."

As Black John stepped into Cush's saloon on the evening of his return to Halfaday, Burr called him to one side. "Did they pinch that kid?" he asked. "The one which I slipped my Luger in his pack?"

"O shore. Constable Breen picked him up before he hit Dawson."

The man grinned and winked. "Pretty slick work, eh? If them bullets didn't go on through them two guys they'll hang him, all right—'cause, like I told you, they kin tell they was fired from that gun."

The big man nodded. "Downey told me himself that they had an open an' shut case."

"They've got the kid dead to rights—but they'll never git the dust."

"I'm inclined to agree with you, Alex."

"Yer right they won't! An' now—how about another job? Did you run onto anythin', down to Dawson?"

"Yeah. I got somethin' lined up. You'll know when the time comes."

A week later Black John turned as a shadow darkened the doorway of Cush's saloon where half a dozen men were ranged before the bar. "Well, if it ain't Corporal Downey! Step up an' wet your whistle. The house is buyin' one. Are you on the trail of some law breaker? Or is this a social call."

"Just stopped in on a routine patrol. How are things on Halfaday?"

"O, about as usual. We're a quiet little community. Nothin' much ever happens along the crick. Guess you know all these boys except Alex Burr, here. Alex, he's a newcomer amongst us.

He's livin' in One Eyed John's cabin. He's the best pistol shot I ever saw. An' that reminds me—you remember that time down to Dawson when some of us got to shootin' at a mark for the drinks, and you come along an' beat us all? Come on, boys, we'll throw this one into us, an' then I'm bettin' Downey the drinks for the house that he can't beat me again. We've got a target down there by the landin'."

The drinks were downed and all proceeded across the clearing to the landing where Black John pointed to the target pinned against the clay bank. "If you don't think Alex here, is good with a pistol, take a look at those bullet holes. I shot him for the drinks, one day, an' he beat me. You can tell which is which—his Luger makes smaller bullet holes than my Colt."

**DOWNEY GLANCED** at the target. "A Luger, did you say?"

"Yeah, Alex favors a Luger. Me, I like a six-gun best."

Stepping to the target, Downey examined the bullet holes. "That's mighty close shootin'," he said. "How far back did you stand?"

"Fifteen steps," Burr replied. "John, there—he paced it off."

"Can you do it again—make as good a pattern as that?" Downey asked.

The man frowned. "I could, but I lost my gun."

"Lost it?"

"Yeah. Couple days ago when I was paddlin' down the crick, I dropped my paddle, an' when I lent over to pick it up the gun dropped outa my holster an' sunk in one of them deep bends."

"Why didn't you dive down an' get it?" Downey asked.

"I couldn't. I can't swim a lick."

"If I know'd where you lost it, I'd dive down an' git it," Pot Gutted John said. "That there was the best shootin' gun I ever seen!" He turned to the others. "Ain't that so, boys?"

All agreed, and Red John said, "Yer right, it was! I'd shore like to git holt of that gun myself. I'd know it if I seen it—it had a F cut in the butt."

"An F?" Downey asked. "Did you say an F?"

"That's right," Burr replied. "I loant a guy name of Fink twenty dollars on it back in Chicago one time when he was broke, an' he never showed up with the twenty dollars, so I kep' the gun."

Black John laughed. "You wouldn't need any mark on the butt to identify it, would you Downey? All a man would have to do is dig the bullets out of the bank, there. It's clay, an' they wouldn't be scratched up, as if it was sand or gravel. Then if you matched 'em up with a bullet fired from that gun you'd know if they were the same."

Moving swiftly Downey snapped the handcuffs on Burr's wrists. "Hey!" the man cried, his eyes suddenly widening. "What goes on here?"

"I can tell you better after I dig out a couple of the bullets fired from your Luger." It was but the work of a few minutes to retrieve the bullets, and drawing a magnifying glass from his pocket, Downey compared them with a pair of bullets he took from an envelope. Then he turned to Burr. "You're under arrest for robbery and murder. Even with this pocket glass I can see that these bullets I dug from the bank were fired from the same gun that killed a clerk and a Consolidated guard down on the river. The microscope will prove it conclusively. Instead of losing your Luger in the creek, Burr, you planted it in the pack of that kid, Farley, when you stopped to eat supper with him that evening on the Yukon." He turned to the big man. "Come along, John. We'll slip over to One Eyed John's cabin, an' hunt for his cache."

As the others returned to the saloon, Black John accompanied the officer and his prisoner to the cabin, where Downey stepped directly to the wall and pulled on the bit of cord. "I remember this cache," he said. "I located it once before." Reaching in, he withdrew three rolls of bills, and a mooschide poke. Carrying the bills to the light he examined them carefully, then turned to Burr with a grin. "You've got a swell collection of counterfeit bills here," he said. "What did you do—fetch a printing press along?"

"Counterfeit!" Burr exclaimed. "Them's good bills! I ain't no fool. I know you got the goods on me fer the Consolidated job. I know you kin tell that the bullets the doc dug outa them guy's heads was fired from my gun. But yer crazy if you think them bills is counterfeit. They're my cut on an express job an' three bank jobs me an' a pal pulls back in the States!"

Downey's grin broadened. "Your pal shore doublecrossed you on the split, then. Like I said, these bills are all counterfeit."

"I'm tellin' you my pal was a good square guy. He wouldn't doublecross no one!" the man cried.

"Okay," Downey said. "But where's the dust you got when you pulled the Consolidated job down on the river?"

The man met the officer's glance with a sneer. "It's hid where neither you nor anyone else'll ever find it without I tell 'em where it's at. I know my way around. I wasn't made in a minute. I know what with them two killin's agin me I'll git the rope— that is," he added, "onlest when the time comes I kin dicker with the jedge an' the D.A. That there fifty thousan' in gold I've got hid, might buy me the difference between the rope an' a life stretch."

Downey shook his head. "Not in this country, it won't."

"Okay—then that there gold'll lay right where it's at till it rots," the man replied.

Downey shot a sidewise glance at Black John. "I wonder?" he said, dryly. "An' if Burr's pal back there in the States was so good and square, what were that express company an' those banks doin' with all this queer money?"

"It's kind of funny, at that," Black John agreed, with a grin. "But when you come to think about it, Downey, it's a good thing that it was an express company, an' some banks, an' a dredge company that lost all that money an' dust—instead of some poor man. Come on over to Cush's. You remember we were goin' to shoot for the drinks—an' that reminds me—you still owe me three drinks on that bet we made down in Dawson—recollect?"

"Yeah," Downey replied. "I recollect. Come on—I'll buy the drinks. Then I'll hit out to Dawson with my prisoner an' turn that kid loose."

# TRIAL AND ERROR

**BILL HARTLEY FIRST** noticed the two men at Dyea where hundreds of excited chechakos milled about amid the countless tons of supplies dumped helter skelter onto the beach by the lightering crew of the *Portland,* now but a smudge of black smoke in the distance.

He noticed them particularly because they alone seemed unhurried and unworried amid the bustle and confusion of the beach, and because their clothing differed essentially from the clothing of those who had come in on the steamer. Young Hartley made mental note of their garb from parka to mukluks. It looked fit—designed to withstand cold and hard usage. At the first store or trading post he came to, he would buy an outfit like that.

Old timers, these—sourdoughs. Not old in years, but evidently wise in the ways of the North. But what were they doing here on the beach? They hadn't come in on the *Portland.* And manifestly they were not packers. Packing was a Siwash job.

Bill found himself watching with curious interest as the two moved aimlessly about, pausing to speak now with this one, now with that, of the new arrivals. A team of gamblers, he decided—looking for easy pickings among the horde of chechakos. Well, the pickings were here. No gambler, he himself had won upwards of five hundred dollars in a game on the boat. The two were approaching him. He didn't like their looks—the tall one with the cold sinister eye, and the short one whose eyes darted furtive glances to the right and to the left.

**BILL WATCHED** his Indian packer fix his straps to the last piece of his outfit and join the others on the trail to the Chilkoot. As he started to follow, the two men paused beside him. The taller was about to speak when Bill forestalled him.

"I couldn't tell which shell the little pea was under, if I saw you put it there. I couldn't pick out the jack of hearts no matter how closely I watched you throw 'em. And I don't play poker, or stud, or even seven-up with professionals. Besides that, I've got a string of packers on the trail, and I'm in a hurry to catch up with 'em."

The short man scowled, and the tall one smiled thinly. "Yer Johnny Wisenheimer, hisself, ain't you? But you got us wrong, brother. You didn't happen to meet up with a party name of Hartley on the boat, did you—William G. Hartley?"

Instantly Bill's mind leaped to the letter in his pocket—the two letters, in fact; missives that had caused him to throw aside his books, and hurry north before his last year in medical college was completed. He shook his head slowly, as though trying to place the name. "No," he said, "I don't remember of meeting anyone of that name. Hartley, you say? Where did he come from?"

"Yeah, Hartley. He come from Montana, but he's be'n to Minneapolis for the last three, four year learnin' to be a doctor."

"Friend of yours?"

"Yeah, we use' to be pals, but I ain't seen him in a long while. Want to let him in on a good thing."

"You sure he was on the *Portland?*"

"Yeah, we be'n watchin' the last four, five boats. Be'n expec-tin' him. He was on the *Portland,* all right—his name was on the list. He's prob'ly around here somewheres—but there's so damn many an' they mill around so damn much, it's hard to find any one."

"Yeah, an' he might of pulled out fer Sheep Camp, a'ready—

a lot of 'em has," grumbled the short man. "Why in hell can't Creech do his own dirty work!"

"Who's Creech?" asked Bill, grinning at the other's discomfiture.

With a scowl, the tall man hastened to answer. "Oh, he's another pal of Hartley's. He was comin' along with me to meet him, but he got laid up with a bad cold, an' hired Shorty, here, in his place. We got to be movin' along before all these damn chechakos gits to Sheep Camp. Onct he gits there it'll be a hell of a job to find him."

"So long," said Bill. "Oh, by the way, if I should run across him, who should I tell him is looking for him?"

"Why—er—tell him—jest tell him his old pal John is tryin' to locate him—he'll know."

Bill Hartley turned and hurried after his packers who had merged with the long line of other packers that stretched out as far as the eye could reach on the trail to the Chilkoot. "My old pal, John," he grinned to himself. "Not a bad one, at that— most anyone can think back to some pal named John. And so

Creech's work is dirty work, eh? I suspected as much—but it sure peeved my old pal John, when his partner spoke out of turn."

## II

**AT SHEEP CAMP** Bill's packers quit and he pitched his tent in the snow at the edge of the big camp preparatory to relaying his outfit up the steep pitch to the Summit, where the Canadian Northwest Mounted police had established a customs office in a tent.

Sheep Camp, on the American side was hell on wheels. Some two or three thousand chechakos crazed by the lure of gold were engaged in transporting their outfits and supplies up the steep slope to the Summit. Packers were not to be had. The order had gone out that no one would be admitted into the Yukon without a year's supply of provisions, and men who had never in their lives carried anything heavier than a suitcase toiled up the trail that was little better than a cat climb with hundred-pound packs on their aching shoulders.

Hundreds, inadequately supplied, were turned back upon Sheep Camp to obtain the required supplies as best they might.

Canvas trading posts charged exorbitant prices for commodities. Gamblers, whiskey sellers, and prostitutes plied their respective trades in tents. There was no law on the American side. Back in Skagway an innocuous and incompetent United States Marshal represented law and order; but at Sheep Camp even this feeble gesture was lacking, and robbery and murder were of nightly occurrence. Fights were so numerous that no one except the combatants paid them any heed.

**RETURNING DOWN** the slope toward evening, Bill's ears were greeted by a fusillade of shots. Hastening toward a crowd that seemed to be milling around a common center, he accosted a man who, from the vantage point of a loaded sled, was peering over the heads of the throng.

"What's the battle about?"

"Cache robber," replied the man tersely. "They was goin' to hang him—but they couldn't wait an' shot him instead. Served the skunk right. It'll learn 'em to leave caches alone."

**PROCEEDING TO** his tent, Bill built a small cooking fire on the packed snow before its open flap. It was May and the weather was fairly warm. Smoke ascended lazily from the stovepipes that protruded through the roofs of hundreds of tents. And before the doorway of hundreds of others, fires flickered. The pleasant odor of spruce smoke permeated the air.

Nesting his coffee pot beside the blaze, Bill sliced some salt pork into his frying pan. Somewhere, someone was playing an accordion, and the music seemed somehow to fit. He dumped a can of beans into the pan with the pork, and with his back to the tent pole sat listening to the weird strains that floated through the fire-studded dark.

Supper over, he lighted his pipe and drew two letters from his pocket. One, written in a firm but rather scrawling hand, he drew from its envelope and reread for the dozenth time since its receipt in Minneapolis just fifteen days before.

Cushing's Fort, Halfaday Crick, Y.T.
Dec. 14th

Dear Billy:
Can you shoot as good as ever? Things look damn queer. That last
year of schooling can wait.
Sam Hartley.

That was all—just three terse sentences. Yet to young Bill
Hartley they spoke volumes. It was a call for help—and a
warning to come heeled. Bill remembered his Uncle Sam
vividly—remembered him in high-heeled boots and spurs with
the wide brim of his Stetson laid back to the wind as he thun-
dered along the trail on his big black stallion, Pedro. Remembered him as a hard riding, hard drinking, hard cussing buckeroo
of the vanished West. The picturesque one of the two Hartley
brothers, owners of the old Heart Bar ranch. Bill's father, John
Hartley, had been of quieter mien, albeit he remembered whispered mutterings among the older hands in the bunkhouse,
that once Old John got his back up, he was the harder one of
the two—reminiscent mutterings that went back to a certain
raid on Heart Bar stock in the days when rustlers were loose
in the land. Bill never did get the straight of it. When he asked
for particulars the cow hands told him to run along. He had
expected to get the story some time from Uncle Sam, but before
that day arrived Sam Hartley had sold out his interest in the
Heart Bar to John, and had hit north, because, as he put it: "The
damn nesters is crowdin' in till yuh can comb 'em out of yer
hair!"

BILL HAD been fourteen, when Sam Hartley had left for the
gold country. But long before that Uncle Sam had taught him
to ride, and to rope, and to shoot. And he had been a hard task
master—but thorough. Bill grinned into the little fire, as he
recalled incidents and snatches of those early lessons: "Damn
yore little hide—you shut one eye that time! If that was a man
instead of a tin can he'd have yore guts blow'd out through yore

back bone while you was linin' up them sights! Keep that can rollin'! What the hell you tryin' to do—make them shells last till Christmas?" And in the corral: "Climb back up into the middle of that buzzard-head agin an' sink yore rowels in! He wasn't doin' nothin' but crow-hoppin'. Make him buck! An' leave off grabbin' that horn. What the hell you tryin' to do—take the saddle with you?" And on the range: "Build yore loop small an' throw her straight! What the hell you tryin' to do—ketch all the horses in Choteau County in one throw?"

It was with a thrill of pride that Bill realized that when his Uncle Sam was in trouble he had appealed to him—had sent halfway across a continent for a man he had not seen since he was a fourteen year-old boy. But a man, nevertheless, he knew would not fail him! Bill's lips tightened grimly as he drew the other letter from its envelope—a typewritten letter that he held close to the flame of the fire:

*Dawson, Y.T.*
*March 15th*

*Mr. William G. Hartley,*
*Minneapolis, Minn.*
*Dear Sir:*
*Your uncle, Sam Hartley, is dead. He left a will naming you as his sole heir to considerable property which includes gold claims and a large sum in dust. Come at once. As Sam Hartley's attorney I am advising you that your presence is necessary to clean this matter up before the appointment of a public administrator for the territory, which will be done sometime this spring. If you wait till the administrator is appointed it may be a year, or longer, before this property will be turned over to you, besides incurring a great deal of expense.*

*Respectfully yours,*
*Josephus B. Creech,*
*Attorney at Law*

Both letters had been delivered in the same mail, a fact that had caused Bill much speculation until he learned that there had only been one mail out from the Yukon that spring. He returned the letters to his pocket, and nodded slowly as a shot rang out from somewhere on the other side of camp. "Things could look damned queer in a country like this," he muttered. "I don't know what happened—but by God I will! And as for this Creech who, according to my 'old pal, John,' is another old pal of mine—I wouldn't trust him as far as I could throw a bull by the tail."

**REFILLING HIS** pipe, Bill gazed moodily into his fire. If Uncle Sam's dead, he reasoned, there's nothing to be gained by going to this Cushing's Fort, wherever Halfaday Creek is. I'll go to Dawson first and get a line on Creech, before he knows I'm in the country. That is, if his reception committee don't spot me first. I don't like the look in old pal John's eye—he's a killer if ever I saw one. The other's just a rat. And that reminds me— He rose, fumbled in a duffel bag and returning to the fire, drew a blue-black six-gun from its leather holster, balanced it in his hand, threw it open and spun the cylinder. He remembered the day Uncle Sam gave it to him—the day he left for the North. "Take it, Billy," he had said. "Some day it might come in handy. She's a sweet old hog-leg; but jest you remember this—there ain't no gun any better than the man behind it."

Opening a box of cartridges, he slipped a handful into his pocket, and five of them into the cylinder. Seating the hammer on the empty chamber, he slipped the gun into the front of his shirt and returned the cartridge box and the holster to his duffel bag.

After I pass customs tomorrow, he planned, Bill Hartley had better disappear. I'll use some other name until I get a line on things—and I guess it'll be just as well if I kind of drop back into the vernacular, too. Creech evidently knows I've been to college and good English might tip off my hand.

**HE LAID** a few sticks of wood on the fire, and as the flames flared from the dry spruce, the empty bean can caught his eye, lying there on the snow where he had tossed it. He picked it up, his lips twisting into a grin. "Here's where Bill Hartley disappears," he said aloud, and threw the can a dozen paces out onto the snow. At the same instant he drew the six-gun from his shirt, and three shots rang out. The third missed, and the can stopped, but a fourth shot sent it spinning into the dark beyond the firelight.

A tent flap a few yards distant flew open, and a head and shoulders appeared. "What the hell—?"

"Keep yer shirt on, pardner," said a voice much nearer Bill. "We was jest shootin' at a tin can." Bill whirled at the words to find himself looking squarely up into the muzzle of a forty-five, held carelessly in the hand of the tall man with the cold, hard eyes that he had seen on Dyea beach. The man stood within six feet of him, just at the corner of his tent.

"Gawd, I thought it was another lynchin'!" exclaimed the voice from the other tent nervously. Beyond, Bill saw other heads disappear as other tent flaps dropped into place.

The man at the corner of the tent grinned. "Just set where you be," he ordered. "So you are Bill Hartley, eh? I had a hunch you was. Shorty didn't. He's still huntin' you at Dyea."

"Sure," answered Bill, returning the grin. "I was kind of hurt that an old pal like you didn't recognize me back there on the beach. So Creech sent you two out to knock me off on the trail, eh?"

"Someone's be'n tellin' secrets," sneered the man. "Er else yer one of these here natural guessers. You might be, at that—you sure doped it out right about Bill Hartley disappearin'. It looks like a bad year on the Hartleys."

"You don't think you can get away with murdering me right here in camp, do you?" asked Bill, weighing the chance of a lightning fast shot in the face of the man's gun. The shot, he realized would have to be not only fast but sure. There was only one bullet left in his gun.

"They'll think we're still shootin' at tin cans," grinned the man. "Even if they don't, I'll tell 'em you robbed a cache. These damn chechakos'll believe anything you tell 'em. Jest drop that gun on the snow an' edge away from it. I might not git you the first shot, an' I ain't takin' no chances." As he spoke he took a step forward. His shin came into contact with one corner guy rope of the tent, and in a split second, Bill saw that his gun muzzle had deflected a trifle to the right. Like a flash he whirled and fired, and the man pitched heavily forward, his pistol thudding against Bill's knee. Instantly Bill was on his feet, the man's gun in his hand.

Once again the neighboring tent flap was thrown back and the head appeared. Deliberately Bill raised the pistol and pointed it at the tin can that lay on the snow at the edge of the firelight.

"Fer cripes' sake, cut out that racket! You kin do yer shootin' in the daytime!"

"All right, pardner," replied Bill. "We'll be rollin' in, now. Jest took a couple of more shots fer good luck."

**THE TENT** flap fell into place, and Bill Hartley stood looking down at the man on the snow. He lay very still. Reaching down, Bill grasped him by the collar, drew him into the tent, and deposited him on the trampled snow beside his bed roll. A glance had shown him that the man was dead—drilled through the heart.

Stepping outside, he picked up the coffee pot and carefully poured the remaining liquid and the grounds upon the red blotch that showed in the snow. The hot coffee melted its way into the deep snow, carrying the blood stain with it. Bill kicked fresh snow over the spot, and tramped it down. He doused his fire with snow, and stepping into the tent, set to work scooping away the snow in a long trench. Two and a half feet down he struck frozen ground. Rolling the body into the trench, he packed snow over it, carried what was left outside, and added it to the banking of the tent. The man's pistol he buried with him.

Unrolling his bed he seated himself on the tarp, and drawing his own gun from his shirt front, he threw out the empty shells and reloaded it.

"One for Uncle Sam," he muttered grimly. And pulling off his pacs and mackinaw, he slipped between his blankets.

## III

**TWO DAYS LATER** Bill Hartley passed customs, and on the Canadian side was lucky enough to hire packers as far as Lake Lindeman where he found several thousand men feverishly engaged in felling trees, whip-sawing lumber, and building boats. Hundreds there were who, with boats completed and outfits cached on the shore, impatiently awaited the breaking up of the ice to launch forth on the long trip to Dawson.

Unlike conditions at Sheep Camp, some semblance of law and order prevailed at Lake Lindeman. A little liquor found its way in despite the vigilance of the police, and gambling was rife, particularly among the idle hundreds who had nothing to do but wait for the break-up. The con men, the robbers, and the murderers of Sheep Camp were filtering through, and Bill kept his six-gun ready to hand in the front of his shirt. Men do not change their natures by crossing a boundary line and, police notwithstanding, it was on the Canadian side that things had looked queer to Uncle Sam—and it was on the Canadian side that he had died.

Again luck favored Bill. For two hundred and fifty dollars he bought a half-interest in a seaworthy boat from a man whose partner had died of pneumonia in a tent beside the lake. Upon Bill's suggestion, they moved into one tent, stepped a mast in the boat, and by ripping only two seams of the other tent, rigged a serviceable sail.

With the lake ice black and rotten, and warm winds melting the snow, the break-up was near at hand. Boats and whip-sawed lumber were worth what a man would pay for them, and men whose boats were ready to start stayed close by their outfits, prepared at a moment's notice to knock out the chocks and begin the mad water race for gold.

It was while thus waiting one day that Bill looked up to encounter the shifty eyes of the shorter of the two men who had accosted him on the beach at Dyea. "Hello," he greeted. "Did you find your man?"

The shifty eyes narrowed. "No, an' I can't find Slim, neither."

"Who's Slim?"

"My pardner, the one that was askin' you about Hartley. He got a hunch that you was him—an' he went up to Sheep Camp to find you."

"He's prob'ly there yet, then. I came on through. Maybe he found Hartley."

THE OTHER scowled. "He was in Sheep Camp all right. But he ain't there now. An' Hartley come on through. A week ago it was—the police looked up the records."

Bill grinned. "Then he's here somewhere along the lake shore. It's a cinch he couldn't have gone on. Did the police describe him to you?"

"How the hell could they remember what one feller looked like—with the damn chechakos crowdin' in on 'em like they be? They don't even know if Slim come back through. He ain't in the record—not havin' to pass customs." He paused and with a sweep of the arm included the lake shore where for miles in either direction the tents of the chechakos dotted the landscape. "An' how in hell am I goin' to find 'em in all this mess—an' the break-up due any day? When it comes they'll all shove off fer Dawson—an' I ain't even got no boat. Me an' Slim come up on the ice."

As the man talked Bill sized him up as one of small calibre. Creech had evidently relied on Slim for the brains of the expedition. Here might be a chance to drive an entering wedge into the mystery of Uncle Sam. He'd take a chance. "Tough luck," he agreed. "An' Creech expectin' you back in Dawson."

"What do you know about Creech?" asked the man quickly, slanting Bill a sharp glance.

"Why—nothin'—except what you said down there on the beach—that you wished Creech would do his own dirty work. I kind of wondered about that. Why would huntin' an old pal be dirty work? I supposed that Creech was someone who had sent you up from Dawson."

"Yeah—that's right. He's another old pal of this here Hartley—like Slim. They hired me to come along. An' about the dirty work—you don't need to go wonderin' about that. If you don't think that mushin' a thousan' miles up through the snow to hunt out one damn chechako out of a million is dirty work—jest you try it, yerself. I got to be goin'. I'll be lucky to find him er Slim either before the break-up, in a mob like this."

"I'll say you will," answered Bill dryly. "Damn lucky."

**THAT NIGHT** the break-up came with an offshore wind. Open water leads showed in the black ice—leads that widened as the wind-tossed water lapped and pounded at the honeycombed ice, breaking it into tiny tinkling pencils. Daylight broke upon blue water studded by white-capped waves as far as the eye could reach—broke, too, upon a scene of indescribable bustle and confusion on the beach where hundreds of men toiled frantically in the loading of hastily launched boats. Leaky and overloaded boats sank. Ill-constructed boats tipped over, precipitating crews and supplies into the icy waters. Badly maneuvered boats collided and drifted apart as their cursing crews belabored each other with clumsy oars. Boats propelled by oars, by paddles, and by sails of every rig, cut and material dotted the wind-tossed waters. The last leg of the big stampede was on!

Thanks to proper construction, careful loading, and competent handling, the boat carrying Bill and his partner got away well in the forefront of the unending flotilla. Day after day, down through the lakes, and the connecting fast water, down through the Box Canyon, and the White Horse, on through Lake Laberge, and down the mighty Yukon she forged into the North, passing many, being passed by few—until, upon a June day, she tied up to the bank along with hundreds of other boats. Here, on the swampy flat in the shadow of Moosehide Mountain, the big gold camp of Dawson sprawled like a newborn thing awed by its own existence.

Here Bill bade good-by and good luck to his partner, and pitched his tent on the outskirts of the camp. He decided, for the present, at least, to play a waiting game—to find out by observation and by guarded inquiry what manner of man he had to deal with in the lawyer, Creech. And to learn, if possible, the particulars of his uncle's death.

**SAUNTERING ALONG** Front Street, after putting his camp in order, he was confronted by a crudely painted sign nailed above the door of a frame shack sandwiched in between a restaurant and a saloon.

JOSEPHUS B. CREECH
ATTORNEY AT LAW.

The door stood open and he paused for a moment as his eyes swept the interior of the little room. A desk, upon which reposed a battered typewriter and a half dozen calf-bound volumes, stood against one wall. A couple of chairs and a tin spittoon completed the furnishings. The rough board walls were hung with plats and maps evidently of various mining locations.

"Step right in, brother," invited a voice at his side, and Bill turned to glance into the sallow face of a flabby-jowled man with a bulbous nose upon which showed a criss-cross pattern of tiny red and blue veins. A pair of bright round eyes which their owner seemed to have some difficulty in focusing stared from under the brim of a derby hat, as the man continued: "You were looking for me—Josephus B. Creech? Step right inside. What's your trouble, brother—got a contest on? Overlapping claims? Water rights? Base line location? I'm your man. Take the matter right up with the Commissioner himself. He and I are one, two, three. Save you time and trouble. Have your matter all cleared up before the court gets organized."

Bill grinned. "I ain't needin' any legal advice," he said. "I'm a stranger here, an' the fact is I've got a pain in my belly. I was huntin' a doctor. It might be appendicitis."

The other thrust out a pudgy hand.

"Good-by, brother, if it is," he said. "Old Doc Pettus is the only doctor in camp. If it was me I'd let nature take her course, appendicitis or no appendicitis. Got any property to dispose of? Just step inside and I'll draw your will. Never had a will busted yet. I'll attend to notifying your folks, too. And see to it that your estate don't get gouged for the funeral. Couple of ounces'll take care of the whole thing, and you can rest easy, even if you die hard."

The man seemed about half seas over, and Bill wondered whether a few more drinks wouldn't further loosen his tongue. Surely, a man who talked as much as this one did must eventually drop something that would be of value to him.

"I guess the will can wait," he laughed. "I haven't got any property worth mentionin'. An' my belly feels better already. Guess all I need's a couple of drinks."

"You an' me both! We'll step over to the Klondike Palace. Cuter'll have something that's good for what ails us. Plenty good looking girls over there, too. Like to look at pretty girls when I'm drinking—even if I can't go any further. I've got too heavy on my feet for dancing."

FOR THE next couple of hours the two drank at Cuter Malone's bar, but although Bill adroitly turned the conversation to wills, and the notification of relatives, and kindred subjects, not once did Creech drop a word that even hinted of Sam Hartley, although it seemed to Bill that the man mentioned everyone else he had ever known or heard of in the course of his voluminous outpourings. Several times Bill was on the point of mentioning his uncle's name, hoping that the man would let slip something of value. But each time he thought better of it and as the minutes passed his respect for the lawyer's drinking ability grew apace. Apparently the man was no drunker than when he started. For a while, Bill suspected that he was adroitly ditching his drinks, but close observation disproved the thought. There was no doubt that Creech was drinking drink for drink with him—and out of the same bottle. No mean drinker, himself, Bill was forced to admit when he made his way back to his tent, that any fair minded jury would have pronounced him the drunker of the two.

## IV

**FOR DAYS THEREAFTER** Bill hung about Dawson drinking by the hour with Creech in Cuter Malone's Klondike Palace, the rococo saloon, dance hall, and gambling house frequented by the tin horns and crooks who preyed upon the chechakos attracted to the place by blazing lights and bizarre entertainment. The Palace was the hell-hole of Dawson.

Always he hoped that, in his cups, Creech would let slip some word regarding his uncle—and always he was disappointed. But for all his loose lipped babble, Creech was a canny drinker, and never a word escaped him that would indicate he had ever even heard of Sam Hartley. Bill played a waiting game. He knew that sooner or later, the short man of the shifty eyes would show up in Dawson, and that when he did he would report directly to Creech. And when that time came, Bill resolved that somehow he would be a party to the meeting. To that end, he had, by means of a word here, and a hint there, put it across to Creech that he, himself, was not too particular in the matter of ethics—that his past was, in fact, rather shady in spots. He had more than once voiced the opinion that in a new country like this, a smart man should be able to line his pockets without resorting to the grueling labor of shoveling gravel. To which thesis Creech had heartily subscribed, even going so far as to hint, with a knowing wink, that if Bill stuck around he, Creech, might be able to throw something his way that would redound greatly to the profit of both. With this vague promise Bill's spirits rose, for he realized that with the passing of Slim, Creech had lost an important henchman, and he devoutly hoped that he would be selected to fill the vacancy in whatever nefarious scheme the lawyer had on foot.

Despite his habitual drinking, it was evident that no inconsiderable volume of business came Creech's way. On numerous occasions Bill had seen the little office jammed with clients, and at such times he would pass on to the Tivoli, a saloon frequented by the sourdoughs, there to mingle inconspicuously with the mighty men of the North.

**ONE DAY** invited to drink with three or four of the old timers, he asked indifferently: "Did any of you know a fella by the name of Sam Hartley?"

"Sam Hartley!" exclaimed Camillo Bill. "I'll tell the world we know'd him! Everyone around Forty Mile know'd Sam. He was some man! Why? Did you know him?"

"I used to," answered Bill, aware that the eyes of the sourdoughs were upon him. "He came from the same part of the country I did—back in Montana. He pulled out for the North a long time ago—when I was jest a kid. I thought, maybe, if I could run acrost him he might kind of put me onto somethin' where I could do myself some good."

Old Bettles nodded. "He prob'ly would of, seein' you come from his country. Sam never went back on a friend. He took out plenty of dust, hisself, too. But yer too late, feller—Sam's dead."

"Dead!"

"Yeah—Corporal Downey told us a couple of months ago. He didn't have no particulars. Sam he'd located him a good claim on a crick that runs into Halfaday—up in the White River country. Use' to come down here about onct in so often an' kind of hit the high spots along with us old Forty Milers. Things shore use' to liven up when Sam hit camp."

"I'll say they did!" seconded Swiftwater Bill. "Remember the time he throw'd all them girls from the Palace in the river to see if they could swim?"

"Yeah," laughed Moosehide Charlie, "an' then bought 'em all new dresses."

"That's right," agreed Old Bettles, "an' what a hell of a time we had draggin' them ones out that couldn't. An' was they mad! Gawd, we use' to have good times 'fore the damn chechakos come in!"

"Downey ain't quite satisfied about Sam's death. He's goin' up an' investigate it as quick as he gits time. The police has be'n rushed to death this spring—what with the damn chechakos, an' all. It was Creech reported it. He claims that Slim O'Leary an' Shorty Crump found Sam dead on his claim when they come through there moose huntin'. He claims that he draw'd Sam's will an' he's notified his heir, which he's a nephew or somethin'—an' he's sent down to Montana fer affidavits from the judge there that Sam was a single man, an' didn't have no other heirs."

"Creech is hell fer wills," said Moosehide.

"Well," said Camillo Bill, "wills is all right. I had him draw me one. You can't never tell what'll happen."

"Yeah, he draw'd mine, too," said Bettles. "Only charged an ounce. What I claim—wills at an ounce apiece is cheap enough."

"I wouldn't do no business with Creech," opined Swiftwater Bill. "He's crooked as a dog's hind leg."

"But hell—he can't be crooked about a will," argued Camillo. "All you do is tell him who you want to leave yer property to, an' he writes it down on the typewriter jest like you say—only in legal language, which there can't nobody but a judge make out—an' then you read it, an' sign it, an' have a couple of more sign it fer witnesses—an' there you be. Then when yer dead, you know the ones you wanted to has got yer property."

"But who gives a damn who's got his property after he's dead?" contended Swiftwater. "You bet, I'll damn well spend mine while I'm livin'!"

"Yeah, a man will if he kin," agreed Bettles. "But s'pose he don't live long enough to? S'pose you was to kick out right now? What then?"

"Then," laughed Swiftwater, "you old sand hogs kin play a showdown fer what I've got. I'd sooner it was that way than have that damn Creech git holt of it. You know what he does— he stirs up rows, an' contests, an' water right trouble amongst the chechakos jest to git to settle 'em. Then he charges both sides all he figgers they'll pay—even cuts hisself in on a percentage of the dust they take out—when he thinks he kin git away with it. An' the hell of it is, when we git strung out so we've got a regular judge here, them settlements he's made won't be worth the paper they're wrote on. He makes some of the damndest decisions."

"Well," said Bettles complacently, "it's only amongst the chechakos. No one that had any sense would go to him. Hell, the police straighten them matters out fer nothin'. That's what they're here fer."

"Shore," agreed Moosehide. "Let him clean up while he kin, as long as it's only chechakos. When we git a reg'lar judge here, I'll bet the damn shyster'll git throw'd out of court. I don't believe he's even got a license to be a lawyer."

"What did Downey say ailed Sam?" asked Camillo.

"Creech didn't know. He jest told Downey that them two found him dead, an' Downey told him that he'd have to furnish proof of death before he put any will through. The police handles them will cases till we git a public administrator."

"If it was me," said Bettles, "he couldn't prove nothin' by them two damn skunks that found him. I wouldn't trust either one of 'em around a corner. What was they doin' up there, anyhow? They don't have to go that far after moose."

"Maybe some of that Halfaday Crick bunch knocked him off," hazarded Moosehide.

BETTLES SHOOK his head. "I don't believe it. Sam was a damn good friend of Black John Smith's—an' even if he wasn't, Black John don't stand fer no murderin' around Halfaday. He keeps 'em good as hell up there, so the police won't come in."

"That's right," agreed Camillo. "A man might better do his murderin' somewheres else. Black John's too damn handy with a rope. I'd ruther murder a man right in front of police detachment, than up on Halfaday. A man would stand a better chanct of gettin' turned loose by a judge, er a lawyer, er a jury."

"Black John's got a hard bunch to handle up there. They're hard-boiled eggs, all right. Damn near every one of 'em's wanted somewheres."

"Yeah," grinned Bettles, "incloodin' Black John. He don't make no bones about braggin' that he stuck up the army fer a payroll over to Fort Gibbon."

"Shore—but Black John never done nothin' mean," said Swiftwater. "You got to hand it to a man that'll hold up an' army an' git away with it—an' then own right up to it. Tellin' you about me, I'd trust Black John with anything I've got—an' he could go 'round the world with it, too. He never hung no one without callin' a miners' meetin' an' doin' it as legal as it kin be done without no police er judge. An' he never hung no one that didn't need hangin'—an' that he know'd damn well needed hangin' before he called the meetin'. What with the riff-raff that's up on Halfaday, he does a damn good job. Ask Downey—he knows."

"Thanks fer the vote of confidence, as they'd say in Parliament," boomed a deep voice, as a huge man whose teeth showed ivory white behind a jet black beard stepped smiling to the bar.

"Er, in other words—speak of the devil, an' up he pops."

"Black John, hisself!" exclaimed Moosehide.

"In person—an' buyin' a drink," admitted the big man.

"What's the news from Halfaday?" asked Bettles, as the glasses were filled.

"Best in the world—there ain't none," grinned Black John.

"We heard Sam Hartley was dead," ventured Swiftwater Bill.

"Hell, that ain't news—it's hist'ry! It happened a couple of months ago."

"What did he die of?"

"Of a Tuesday," answered Black John, "er mebbe, a Saturday night." He tossed off his whiskey and turned toward the door. "See you later," he called over his shoulder. "I want a word with Corporal Downey."

"Meanin'," said Camillo Bill, nodding sagely, as the man passed from the room, "that Sam Hartley was murdered, an' he's goin' to give Downey the facts in the case."

Old Bettles shook his head. "If Black John had the facts he wouldn't never bother Downey with 'em. He'd cut him a len'th of rope—an' call a miners' meetin'."

V

CORPORAL DOWNEY GLANCED up from his desk as a figure darkened the doorway of the little office at detachment. "Hello, John!" he greeted. "Come in. What brought you down to Dawson?"

"A canoe. How's things in the ranks of the sinful?"

Downey grinned. "The chechakos are so busy filin' claims that they haven't had time to think up no sins to speak of. They're sure swarmin' in on us."

"Yeah, I thought I recognized several thousan' new faces as I come down the street. When they begin goin' broke, yer goin' to have yer hands full."

Downey nodded. "You're lucky to be way up there on Half-aday."

Black John returned the grin. "Yeah, that's what we figger—what with bein' right handy to the line, an' all."

"How's everything on the crick?"

"Oh, about like always. I come down to file a batch of claims fer the boys."

"By the way—didn't Sam Hartley have a claim up there, somewheres?"

"Yeah. Not right on Halfaday. On a crick that runs into it."

"Creech reported that he was dead. Claims he drew up a will for Hartley a while back. He's got it in his safe, an' he's notified the heir—a nephew, I believe. He also sent to Montana for affidavits that Hartley had no other legal heirs. I told him that we wouldn't turn over Hartley's property to anyone until we had proof of death. He says that Slim O'Leary an' Shorty Crump found the body while they was moose huntin'. But I won't turn over the property on their say-so, without further investigation. How do I know he's dead?"

"He was shot," announced Black John gravely, "in the head. I found him myself layin' near his cabin, on his claim."

"Did you bury him?"

"Well, you can't leave a man layin' around on the snow fer the wolves to eat, kin you? What do you s'pose I done? Hung him up in a tree?"

"H-u-m-m—that establishes the fact of the death, all right. Did he leave any property?"

"Yeah. All he had."

Downey chuckled. "An' what was that?"

"Couple of good claims, an' somewheres around six thousan' ounces in Cush's safe."

"Six thousan' ounces!" exclaimed Downey. "Close to a hundred thousan' dollars!"

"Yeah—some such item."

"Why the devil didn't you report the matter to me? A shootin' like that looks like murder!"

"Well, me an' Cush talked it over. We was kind of waitin' developments, as a fella would say."

"What kind of developments?"

"How the hell do I know? If I did, I wouldn't be waitin' fer 'em. Figger it out fer yerself—Sam Hartley was shot. He didn't shoot hisself; then someone else shot him. If so, it was done accidental; er on purpose. If accidental, there won't be no developments. If not accidental, it was done fer a purpose. The purpose would nach'elly be his dust an' his claim. That's logical, ain't it? Well, that's what I mean. Someone's goin' to claim Sam's gold, an' when they do there's liable to be developments. That's what me an' Cush is waitin' fer."

Corporal Downey sat for some time, his brow wrinkled in thought. "It looks like a murder, all right," he said.

"Yeah," agreed Black John dryly. "It has some of the ear marks."

"If I could see how there was anyway they could benefit, I wouldn't put it beyond O'Leary an' Crump."

"Why leave Creech out?"

"Well, for the same reason. I don't see how Hartley's death could benefit him. He might collect a small fee from the heir, but you bet I'll make it plain when I give him an order for the property that he's under no obligation to pay Creech an unreasonable amount. He got his fee when he drew up the will."

"If he draw'd the will, he might of cut hisself in fer a big slice of Sam's property. If he done that Sam's death would benefit him plenty."

DOWNEY SHOOK his head. "He didn't. Creech showed me the will. It leaves everything he had to this nephew, William G. Hartley. No strings on it, an' no other bequests."

"There didn't no one sneak up there an' knock Sam off jest to see him kick," reminded Black John.

"That's so—an' the devil of it is, we're short-handed here an' so damn busy with the chechakos boilin' in on us, that it might be quite a while before I can get up there. Now that I know Hartley's dead, I'll have to turn over the property to the heir if he shows up. You tell Cush to hang onto that dust, an' not pay it out to anyone without he presents an order from me. In the meantime, you keep your eyes open an' see what you can find out."

"Yeah, I'll keep my eyes open. I don't hardly believe anyone on Halfaday done it. We've got the local boys discouraged on murder. Well—so long."

"So long. When you goin' back?"

"Jest as soon as I kin transact my business. I'm goin' down to the Tivoli first an' git thirty, forty drinks, an' then I'm goin' down to the recorder's. When I come by his office, a few minutes ago there was a line of chechakos waitin' a half a mile long. By the way, Downey, what's the fine fer jostlin' chechakos? I might as well pay it now. Er—better make me a price by the dozen."

## VI

ONE DAY, A week after the departure of Black John from Dawson, Bill Hartley stood in the doorway of the Tivoli and idly watched the chechakos passing to and fro upon the street.

"The damn fools," he muttered, "there won't one in a hundred of 'em get their ante back." He drew back hurriedly at sight of a familiar face—the face of the short man he had encountered twice upon the trail. "Got here, at last," he breathed. "Well—it's now or never, if I'm going to find out what happened to Uncle Sam."

The man passed the door, paused to peer into Creech's empty office, and continued on to the Klondike Palace.

Bill hurried after him, slipped into the saloon, and saw him join the lawyer, who stood near the end of the bar. Lurching drunkenly through the crowd, he maneuvered into position directly behind Creech, who was speaking, evidently in answer to a question asked by the short man.

"No, he hasn't showed up! And where in hell have you been all this time?"

The man started to answer, when Creech interrupted him. "And, you didn't find young Hartley?"

Before the other had time to answer Bill clapped a heavy hand on the lawyer's shoulder: "Hello, Creechie, ol' top! Come on—have a li'l drink! Be'n down to the Tivoli drinkin' wish the shourdosh. Hell of a plash. Like the Palish better."

Creech scowled, shook the hand from his shoulder, and turned to the other. "Come on over to the office," he said abruptly.

"Hell wish the offich," grinned Bill, pawing in maudlin good nature at the lawyer's sleeve. "Can't get noshin' to drink in the offich." He straightened up and blinked owlishly into the face of the short man. "Hell—I know you! Put 'er there!" He extended a hand. "Sure—sheen you down on Dyea Beach. You an' that damn big long geared crane that wash whis you. He won't never pull a gun on anyone elsh. Called me Bill Hartley, the damn liar! An' Bill Hartley won't never shteal no one's—" he paused abruptly and laughed. "Don't pay no 'tenshun to me. I'm li'l tight—thash all. Run off at the head too mush when I'm tight."

SWIFT GLANCES passed between the short man and Creech, who clapped Bill heartily upon the shoulder. "You're right— there's nothing to drink in the office. Come on, I'll buy one— we'll drink up and then we'll all go down to the office. Or better yet, we'll just slip into Cuter's back room where we can sit and talk without all these damn chechakos butting in on us."

"Sure—sure," agreed Bill, "we'll take a bottle 'long. Can't talk when yer dry. I'll buy a bottle, an' we'll take it 'long. Git shome glashish. Can't drink out of bottle—one fella gits it all. An' you might introdoosh me to yer frien', Creechie!"

"Sure—this is Shorty Crump. Shorty, this is Mr.—" he glanced inquiringly at Bill. "You know, I don't believe you ever told me your name."

"Thash right," grinned Bill. "An' I ain' goin' to tell you now— sho how do you like that? I never tell my name to no one. Let 'em guesh what it ish. Man might git in lot of trouble—tell hish name. Call me Jesse James—damn shame the way they shot poor ol' Jesse!"

"All right, Jesse—here's your bottle. Come on."

Bill stripped a bill from a roll he drew from his pocket, paid for the bottle, and lurched after Creech who led the way to a door that opened into a little room behind the back bar. Shorty brought up the rear, pausing to close and lock the door behind him. Seating themselves at the single table, the three filled their glasses.

"Here's how," said Creech, raising his glass. "It's a lot better in here—just us three friends together. We can say what we damn please, and it won't get any further."

"Shore," agreed Shorty. "Them damn chechakos might talk."

"Thash right," seconded Bill. "Well—heresh mud in yer eye!"

They drank, and Creech smiled at Bill. "I'm glad to hear you say that damn Slim won't pull a gun on any one else. He pulled one on me once—and he'd shoot a man as quick as he'd look at one, too. He's a dangerous character."

"He ain't now," said Bill. "Lishen—you're a lawyer, ain' you?"

"Sure. Whatever you've got to say will never get any farther."

"Thish is Canadian territory—an' they can't do nothin' to a man for what he done in Sheep Camp, can they?"

"No, of course not."

"Couldn't do nothin' to a man that shot another one in shelf defench, anyhow, could they?"

"No."

"Well thash what I done. He pulled a gun on me, an' shaid I wash that damn Bill Hartley, an' I plugged him right through

255

the middle. Can't no one call me Bill Hartley!"

"Do you know Bill Hartley?" asked Creech in ill disguised eagerness.

"Do I know him! I'll tell the world I know him—damn him! But he won't—"

"Yes? He won't—what?" encouraged Creech, with a smile.

"He won't do nothin'."

"Say," cut in Shorty, eyeing Bill narrowly, "you told me an' Slim down on Dyea Beach that you didn't know him! Slim asked you if you'd met up with him on the boat."

"Sure," chuckled Bill. "You don't s'pose I'd do that damn Bill Hartley a good turn, do you? You two said you was pals of his, an' you wanted to let him in on a good thing." He paused and winked knowingly. "I wanted to let him in on a good thing, too. An' believe me, I did! He'll never steal no one else's girl!"

"Where did he steal your girl?" asked Creech.

"In Montana—where the hell do you s'pose?" answered Bill, and fixed his wavering eyes on the lawyer. "They said you was a pal of Bill Hartley's, too. I think yer all lyin'—unless you was pals in Minneapolis. 'Cause I know every damn pal he had in Montana—an' you wasn't none of you there."

CREECH POURED himself a drink, and winked knowingly at Bill. "You're smart, all right. They did lie about us being pals of Bill Hartley. In fact we—er—we're damn glad to hear he's put out of the way."

"So'm I," said Bill. "The damn pup—he can't steal my girl, an' git away with it!"

"So you knew him, eh? Live around his part of the country? Know all his folks?"

"Sure—know 'em all. Know'd Bill Hartley since we was kids together. Went to school with him. Ol' John Hartley, his dad, owned the Heart Bar. It was a big outfit, once. Ol' John an' Ol' Sam owned it together. They was brothers. When the nesters first begun to come in, Ol' Sam claimed the country was goin' to hell, an' he sold out to Ol' John, an' went away. Some said he went north to hunt gold—but hell—that was long before anyone know'd there was any gold up north. But Ol' Sam was right about the range goin' to hell. The nesters kep' movin' in on 'em, fencin' the water an' the range, an' every year the Heart Bar branded fewer calves. Then Ol' John died, an' Bill put a foreman on the ranch, an' went off to Minneapolis winters to learn to be a doctor. My folks was nesters an' the Hartleys hated us—an' we hated back, you bet! Hell—I was raised on Heart Bar beef, and none of it was paid for, neither. Me an' Bill got to courtin' the same girl—an' it was an even break till that damn Bill quit the range an' went to learn him a white collar job. After that I wasn't good 'nough for her no more. She couldn't see nothin' but Bill Hartley. But she won't see him no more!"

"How did you know Hartley was coming here to Dawson?"

"Hell—I didn't know it! Seen him on the boat. Thought he was in Minneapolis learnin' to be a doctor. I heard all the talk about gold up here, an' I come. I figgered that if I could come up here an' grab off a lot of gold so I was rich, I could go back an' Rosie would marry me, instead of him. Doctors don't git rich so quick. I figgered I could beat him to it. An' I guess he had the same hunch—to git rich quick—'cause there he was on the boat. I kep' out of sight, an' when we landed, Shorty an' the tall guy come along an' said did I meet up with a guy named Bill Hartley on the boat, an' I asks 'em what they wanted of him, an' they said they was pals of his, an' wanted to let him in on a good thing. I didn't want him in on no good thing, so I told 'em I didn't know him. Then on the trail I watched my chance an' got him. An' as quick as I find a lot of gold, I'm goin' back an' marry Rosie."

"Did Bill Hartley have any brothers or sisters?"

"No, he was the only one. His ma died when he was born."

"Then, Sam Hartley had no other heirs? He had no children of his own?"

"If he did, he'd shut up about it," grinned Bill. "Ol' Sam never married. He was too ornery."

"What sort of a looking fellow was this Bill Hartley?"

"Oh—'bout like any cow-puncher. till he begun dressin' up like a damn dude."

"Was he tall? Or short? Or fat? Or slim?"

"'Bout like me. Rosie use' to say she couldn't tell which one of us was comin' till we'd got out of the lane. Then Bill got a pinto an' she could tell him by that."

**THERE WAS** a silence during which Creech filled the three glasses. "Here's luck!" he said. "A hell of a lot of luck for all three of us!"

"Yeah," said Bill. "I'm goin' to hit out tomorrow an' dig me some gold. I thought there might be some easy money here in Dawson, but I ain't seen none."

Creech laughed. "It's a lucky thing for you you ran onto me. Didn't I tell you that if you stuck around I'd put you next to something good?"

"Yeah—but I ain't seen nothin' yet."

"Listen; do you want to get hold of a lot of gold—quick?"

"Sure, who wouldn't?"

"All right, then—you're Bill Hartley, William G. Hartley, to be exact, of Bear Paw, Montana."

"Not by a damn sight! I wouldn't be—"

"Hold on," Creech interrupted. "You let me do the talking for a minute or two. It's like this—Sam Hartley is dead, an' he left a will bequeathing all of his property to his nephew, William G. Hartley. I drew the will, and I notified this nephew at Minneapolis. Sam gave me his address in case anything should happen. That's why he was on the boat. He didn't come to dig gold, like all the rest—he came to claim Sam Hartley's estate."

"Did Ol' Sam leave much?"

"Plenty. There's somewhere around a hundred thousand in

dust, besides a couple of good claims. He was in here early and struck it lucky."

"An' you want I should tell 'em I'm Bill Hartley, an' claim the gold an' the claims?"

"Exactly. And then we split it three ways. A third for you, a third for Shorty, and a third for me."

**BILL PONDERED** the proposition, and shook his head doubtfully. "How do you know Ol' Sam's dead?" he asked. "If he caught me passin' myself off fer Bill, it would be good night! I know Ol' Sam—he's hard. What did he die of?"

"Never mind what he died of," replied Creech. "He's dead, all right. Slim an' Shorty, here, found him. That's why we're cuttin' Shorty in for a third."

"Oh, they found him, eh? Well, tellin' you about me, I think a third of a hundred thousan' dollars an' two claims is a hell of a price to pay fer jest findin' a dead man."

"Is that so," flared Shorty. "Well—"

Creech held up his hand. "That'll do. No quarreling. Let me do the talking. Under ordinary circumstances, Jesse—or Hartley, as we will call you now—your point would be well taken. But when we consider that they found the body on an isolated crick more than two hundred miles from here, and that if they had not found it, it would in all probability have been devoured by wolves so that no proof of death could have been established, it throws a different light on the matter. In that case, none of us would have received a penny."

"I see," said Bill. "An' your cut?"

"My cut," repeated Creech, his voice sounding a trifle hard, "comes because I engineered the whole deal."

"What deal?"

"Why—ringing you in for young Hartley. There will be certain legal formalities to be gone through, and it takes a lawyer to put it over. See here, Jesse. I'm giving you the chance to ring in on a damn good piece of money. It's as good as in our hands, already—and no risks run. You better take what we're offering you, or you don't get a cent."

"Guess that's right," grinned Bill. "No hard feelin's. Where's this hundred thousan' in dust at? Let's go."

"Hold on," advised Creech. "There's more to it than that. In the first place, we've got to figure some way of identifying you as William G. Hartley."

"You mean, so the judge'll think I'm Bill, an' fork over the gold."

"Exactly. Only it's the police, and not a judge. They're handling all cases of this kind until a public administrator is appointed."

BILL LAUGHED. "It won't be hard to put that over. When I knocked Bill off, I went through his pockets an' took every damn thing he had on him. I figgered if anyone found the body, an' they couldn't find out who it was, they'd bury it an' let it go at that. But if they found out it was Bill, there might be a hell of a stink. He's got a lot of friends in Montana. Then, besides, I figgered that if someone got worried about not hearin' from him, or somethin', an' started an investigation, I could plant his stuff in some cabin, somewheres, an' throw 'em way off the scent. You see, I come through the customs under Bill's name, so they won't be huntin' him on the American side."

Creech nodded. "Pretty damn smart, at that. What did he carry in the way of identification?"

Bill drew a watch and a wallet from his pocket. "Here's his watch. It's got his name on it—where it was give to him by his dad on his birthday when he was eighteen. An' here's his pocket book, which it's got his pass book in the Minneapolis bank, an' some papers about the college where he's goin'. Then there's the paper the police give me when I passed customs."

Creech examined the watch, and went through the papers in the wallet. "No letters?" he asked.

Bill shook his head. "No—no letters."

The lawyer looked relieved, as he handed back the evidence.

"That's all we need," he said. "We're all set. Corporal Downey told me a couple of days ago that when I could produce the heir, he'd turn over the property. It seems that Black John Smith found the body and buried it."

"I thought you said that Shorty an' Slim found the body?"

"To be sure—they found it. But they didn't do anything about it except report it to me. Black John found it later. To tell you the truth, I'm glad he did. I was a little worried for fear the police wouldn't accept the word of Shorty and Slim as proof of death."

Bill grinned at the scowling Shorty. "Well, you couldn't blame 'em much, at that. Who's Black John Smith?"

"Oh, he's king of the outlaws up on Halfaday. I don't know him personally, but I've heard a lot about him. It seems he was in Dawson a few days ago, and reported the matter."

"Does he come in fer a cut, too? Looks like if many more folks found the body there won't be enough of Ol' Sam's dust to go around."

"No! No! He probably reported it as a matter of policy. He's foxy, all right. You see, living up there near Halfaday like he did, Sam Hartley probably knew too much to suit the gang, so they knocked him off. Then, Black John reports finding the body to throw suspicion off the gang. With Hartley's gold waiting right there in Cushing's safe for the legal claimants, the police wouldn't suspect any of the Halfaday Crickers."

"Who's Cushing?"

"He runs Cushing's Fort, a trading post and saloon on Half-aday."

"But will the gold be there?"

"You bet it will! They got what they wanted when they shut Sam Hartley's mouth. They aren't fools enough to make a play for the gold. They want it right in the safe when the police go up to investigate the murder."

"So Ol' Sam was murdered, eh?"

"Well, Downey told me that Black John reported he'd been shot. Slim an' Shorty didn't examine the body close. They just saw that he was dead, and came away. The police will investigate as soon as they can get around to it."

"If they're all outlaws up there, what's to prevent their knockin' us off before we can get back with the gold?"

"They won't. They'll know the police sent us up after that dust, and Black John's too foxy to let anything happen to us. He brags that there's no crime on Halfaday. The last thing they want is the police nosing around up there."

"When do we go?"

"Tomorrow, we'll establish your identity. I've already turned the will over to Downey. Then, he'll give us an order for the dust and make the proper transfer of the claims. We could do it today—but it'll be better if you're stone cold sober. He may ask a lot of questions, an' you don't want to be fuzzy in the head."

"That's right," agreed Bill. "Guess I'll go home an' lay down. I don't want to be feelin' tough in the mornin'."

WHEN THE door closed behind Bill, Creech filled his glass and drained it at a gulp. "I'll tell the world we're lucky—to have things work out like they did. God—that fellow just tumbled into our lap out of a clear sky! Knowing the whole Hartley tribe like he does, there won't be any questions he can't answer if the police should happen to know more about Hartley than we think they do. Even with young Hartley's identification papers we might have had some trouble in putting a fake heir over on Downey."

Shorty scowled and filled his own glass. "Yeah, but mebbe he's too damn smart fer us. D'you notice he was so damn drunk he couldn't talk straight when he first braced us, an' he kep' gittin' soberer an' soberer till at last he wasn't hardly drunk at all."

"Well, what of it? He's a damn good drinking man. I've been drinking with him for two, three weeks, off and on. He can hold his liquor well. He just got too much down in the Tivoli, and the effects of it gradually wore off. He only took one drink in here. Then, too, talking over our proposition sobered him. He pulled himself together. And just remember this—there's no damn chechako that's too smart for Josephus B. Creech!"

"He didn't want to let me in on the cut," growled Shorty. "He even kicked about you comin' in. Wants to hog it all, hisself. An' besides, he knocked off Slim. I got a notion to blow his guts out fer that. Slim was my pal. He was a good guy."

"Listen to me, sap," said Creech, his eyes narrowing. "I'm running this show. You lay off that bird till after we collect Sam Hartley's dust. Then, coming back down the White River, we'll watch our chance and you can let him have it. We can sink him in the river, split the dust two ways, and beat it out of the country. If we're missed, the Halfaday Crick gang'll get credit for doing away with all three of us."

"Yeah! Well, what's the matter with you lettin' him have it? Always I got to do the dirty work—an' if anything goes wrong, it'll be me that'll stretch rope."

"Nothing can go wrong if you do as I say. Hell's fire, man! Everything's working out even better than we could have expected. I'm furnishing the brains to put this deal across—and, by God, you've got to do something for your cut! You hustle around now, an' get an outfit together—one good canoe ought to do it—and grub enough to take the three of us to Halfaday."

Later, as he poked about among the craft on the water front, hunting for a canoe, Shorty grinned evilly. "Yeah," he muttered, pondering Creech's words, "but brains ain't no good in a dead man. Creech won't never be missed none, nohow. It looks like Old Sam's dust'll only cut one way, after all."

## VII

**AT DETACHMENT NEXT** day formalities were quickly complied with, Bill's credentials having established his right to the property of Sam Hartley under the terms of the will. And two weeks after Corporal Downey handed over an order for the dust in Cushing's safe, Bill, accompanied by Creech and Shorty, pushed open the door of Cushing's saloon and entered to be greeted by a huge black bearded man who stood drinking at the bar with the proprietor.

"Howdy, gents! Jest step right up an' wet yer whistle. The house is buyin' one. Smith's the name—Black John, fer reasons of identification. An' this here's Old Cush. If no handy alias occurs to you, jest reach in the name can an' help yerself—the name of Smith, in all its various phases, bein' barred."

"Bill Hartley's my name—William G. Hartley, to be exact. This is Josephus B. Creech, an attorney, of Dawson. And this other is Shorty Crump."

"Hartley," repeated Black John. "Any kin to Sam Hartley?"

"I'm his nephew. I came up to take over his property under a will he had drawn, naming me as sole heir. Here's the order from Corporal Downey of the Mounted Police."

Old Cush pushed the steel rimmed spectacles from his forehead to the bridge of his nose and spreading the paper on the bar, perused it carefully, while Black John, craning his neck, read it also.

"An' what," he asked, "has these two got to do with it?"

"Creech is my attorney in the matter," answered Bill. "And Shorty is one of two men who claimed to have found the body."

Black John eyed Shorty, who shifted uncomfortably. "Was it hard to find?" he asked dryly.

"No," mumbled Shorty.

"You didn't say nothin' to the police?"

"No. Creech is a lawyer. We figgered he'd know more about tellin' the police."

"Ain't it customary, where you come from," asked Black John, "to bury folks you find layin' around dead? Or at least take 'em to where someone else kin bury 'em?"

"The ground was froze, an' we was in too much of a hurry to

take him along."

"An' the other one that found him—the one that was with you—where's he?"

"I shot him," answered Bill. "In Sheep Camp."

**BLACK JOHN** eyed the young man with interest. "That's a straightforward admission," he said approvingly, "an' stated concise." His glance strayed from Bill's face and came to rest on Shorty. "What was the matter?" he asked. "Didn't you have but the one shell?"

"Let's get this over with," cut in Creech, glancing uneasily at Bill. He turned to Old Cush. "I assume that you have Sam Hartley's dust in your safe—about a hundred thousand dollars' worth, I believe."

Cush swung open the door of the huge iron safe and consulted a memorandum. "Six thousan' an' sixty-two ounces," he announced.

"Well," replied Creech, "there you have the order for it. We demand the dust."

"Just a moment," interrupted Bill. "That dust is heavy. It will weigh up nearly four hundred pounds. I think I'll just leave it where it is."

"Leave it where it is!" cried Creech. "What do you mean?"

"Just what I said," answered Bill. "I guess if that safe was good enough for Uncle Sam, who knew the country, to deposit his dust in; it's good enough for me, who don't. And now, Creech, if you'll just make out a bill for legal service rendered, I'll pay it here and now."

"Legal service!" The lawyer's face had gone a brick red. "What the hell are you talking about?"

"About Uncle Sam's dust. I'm leaving it where it is—at least, for the present."

"Like hell you be!" cried Shorty. "An' where the hell do we git off at? Don't try pullin' that 'Uncle Sam' stuff on us!"

"Shut up, you fool!" yelled Creech.

"Like hell I'll shut up!" screamed Shorty, gone suddenly beside himself with rage. "When it was us knocked off old Sam Hartley an' put him in the way of claimin' to be his heir!"

"I am Bill Hartley. Sam Hartley was my uncle. I know you damned thugs knocked him off—and now I can prove it."

"You kin, eh—you dirty, doublecrossin' skunk—take that!"

A six-gun was in Shorty's hand as he raised his arm. There was a loud report, the acrid smell of powder smoke, and Shorty slumped to the floor and lay beside the brass rail, gently twitching, as Bill Hartley returned a blue-black revolver to the front of his shirt.

"Two for Uncle Sam," he remarked grimly.

"That was mighty competent shootin'," said Black John admiringly eyeing the body. "I kind of wondered, when you told about shootin' the other one, why you hadn't finished yer job."

"Don't let him kill me! Don't let him shoot! I'm not armed!" cried Creech, elevating his hands high above his head.

From some recess beneath the bar Old Cush produced a long black six-shooter and solemnly tendered it to the terrified lawyer.

"No! No!" cried Creech. "He'd kill me before I could cock it! Disarm him! Don't let him shoot me down in cold blood!"

"You kin take yer hands down," advised Black John. "The gent don't show no signs of goin' on with his manslaughter. But jest to ease yer mind, I'm askin' him to lay his gun on the bar."

BILL READILY complied with the request, and Black John took a step nearer, resting his elbow on the bar within easy reach of the pistol. "The case," he said, "seems to call fer further enlightenment."

"It's like this," began Creech, with a knowing leer that included both Black John and Old Cush. "While I never had the pleasure of meeting either of you boys personally, I know all about you—that is, I know that up here on Halfaday everything goes—just so the police don't get wind of it. There's no use beating the devil around the stump—Shorty told the truth about that Hartley job. When I drew Sam Hartley's will, I started to figure how I could get my hands on his dust—and it wasn't long before I had it all doped out. I sent Slim and Shorty up here to knock him off, and then I notified his only heir. After that, I sent the two down to Dyea Beach to watch the boats and get rid of young Hartley somewhere on the trail to Dawson, figuring on substituting some chechako for the heir in claiming the estate. Something went wrong somewhere, and this bird shot Slim at Sheep Camp—he claims Slim mistook him for young Hartley and pulled a gun on him."

"Well, ain't he Hartley?" asked Black John.

"Hell, no! He's an enemy of Hartley's—and he knocked him off somewhere between Dyea Beach and Sheep Camp, stole Hartley's watch and his wallet with his identification papers in it, and came on through to Dawson. There, by accident, I ran across him, and when Shorty showed up without Slim, we rang this bird in as Sam Hartley's heir. It was a cinch—with young Hartley's watch and papers in his possession. The police never even questioned his identity. Everything was working fine, till the damn crook starts in to doublecross us by refusing to draw the dust from the safe. He isn't so dumb, at that. He figures that, having established his identity with the police, we wouldn't dare to repudiate it. And we wouldn't either—with the police! But up here it's different. Where he made his mistake was in not realizing that everything goes up here." The man paused, and Black John nodded thoughtfully.

"An' havin' established that fact to the best of yer knowledge an' belief," he said dryly. "What's yer next step in this here orgy of crime?"

"Well," answered Creech, pouring a drink and downing it, "we'd figured on splitting Sam Hartley's dust three ways. We can still split it three ways."

"Yeah? Between who, an' who, an' who?"

"Why—between you an' me an' the proprietor, here, of course."

"An' how about him?" asked Black John, indicating Bill with a jerk of the head.

"Hell—he can go the same road Sam Hartley went. He's nothing but a damned impostor, anyhow. If there's any inquiry about him later we can say he took his dust and went downriver. Shorty and I had decided he'd never get back to the Yukon with it, anyway."

"Knockin' folks off seems to be right down your alley—when you kin git someone else to do it, don't it, Creech?"

"Well, if I furnish the brains it's no more than right that someone else should do the rough work. So let's get the job over with. I've gone ahead and laid all my cards on the table. You see, up here, I feel that I'm among friends."

"It must be a comfortin' feelin'," replied Black John, "an' if I was in your shoes, I'd make the most of it while it lasts."

"What do you mean?"

"Meanin' that you've be'n misinformed about Halfaday bein' a place where everything goes. I'll admit that we're lib'ral in regards to minor infringements—like spittin' on the floor, an' pourin' yer coffee into yer saucer. But such items as murder an' obtainin' money under false pretences ain't neither permitted nor condoned. You've admitted one murder, an' planned another—showin' that yer more onscrupulous than even a lawyer is supposed to be. The case calls fer a miners' meetin' to try you fer murder, an' yer friend here fer skullduggery in attemptin' to obtain money under false pretences."

Sudden panic seized Creech. Rumor had reached the Yukon of the swift and sure punishment that invariably followed conviction by miners' meeting on Halfaday. "But—hell!" he cried. "We're all crooks together up here! I know two or three men who—"

Black John silenced the man with a gesture. "Don't say nothin' that might injure any of our citizens, some of whom packs reputations that even a slight injury might prove fatal to."

**CREECH POINTED** a shaking finger at Bill. "If you try me for murder, you've got to try him, too," he cried. "He killed two men on the trail between Dyea and the Chilkoot!"

Black John shook his head. "Such acts was ondoubless reprehensible," he said. "But they ain't tryable on Halfaday. What a man done before he come to Halfaday, ain't none of our business. After he gits here he's got his choice between stayin' moral; or gittin' hung."

Creech heaved a sigh of vast, relief. "All right then—you can't try me either. Sam Hartley wasn't killed on Halfaday. His claims were on another crick altogether."

"The p'int is well taken; but don't amount to nothin'," replied Black John. "Hartley's Crick runs into Halfaday, an' we've repeatedly held, in previous cases, that our jurisdiction extends, not only to Halfaday proper, but also to every crick, rill, feeder, pup, gulch an' dry wash that runs into it, as well as to the surroundin' hills. Such bein' the case, it looks from here, Creech, like a successful hangin' is about all you kin look forward to. At that, yer future ain't so black—the boys has got so they don't bungle more'n about one hangin' in six."

**THE BLOOD** had receded from Creech's face, leaving it blotched and mottled. "You—you can't prove I had a damn thing to do with Sam Hartley's death," he mouthed hurriedly.

"We don't have to prove it. You admitted it—even bragged about it."

"I repudiate every word! I lied! That statement wasn't made under oath. You can't use it against me!"

"It'll be up to the boys whether to believe it, or not," replied Black John. "We've got three witnesses here, that heard you admit the killin'."

"But it isn't evidence! It can't be used!"

"You might bring that p'int up," said Black John, "but I'm doubtin' if you kin put it acrost to the boys. They ain't none of 'em lawyers, an' most of 'em's kind of dense about the finer p'ints of pleadin' an' practice. We realize that we ain't no reg'lar court, an' we don't pretend to do no more than arrive at a sort of rough an' ready justice—like if a man's guilty we hang him; an' if he ain't, we don't."

"You mean, you're actually going to hang me—Josephus B. Creech—like any common murderer!" cried the man, his eyes wide with horror.

"Well—onlest there's some special way you'd like to be hung. We ain't never gone in fer no fancy hangin's, but if you've got any suggestions that wouldn't interfere with the general result, we might try 'em. We aim to please."

"It's murder—that's what it is!"

"Have it yer own way," replied Black John indifferently. "One good murder deserves another, is the way I look at it. Turnabout's fair play, as the sayin' goes."

Creech suddenly went all to pieces. His knees sagged and he fell grovelling to the floor, as words poured from his lips in a shrill quavering falsetto. "Mercy! Oh—don't hang me! I'll do anything you say! Oh—think of my poor wife and children!" The blotched cheeks were wet with tears as the man raised his face in a frenzy of terror.

**BLACK JOHN** scowled down upon the grovelling figure in disgust. "Git up!" he growled, administering a hearty kick. "You ain't got no more wife an' children than what I have! You ain't got the guts of a worm! Yer nothin' but a low-lived ornery damn skunk that hires folks to kill others fer profit! You ain't got the guts to stand up an' take yer medicine like a man! There wouldn't hardly be no pleasure at all in hangin' you! The boys would be disgusted with yer whinin' an' cryin' an' beggin' an' bellerin'! It would be a shame to submit 'em to the ordeal! You claim you'll do anything I say. I'm givin' you one chanct!" Grasping the lawyer by the collar, the huge man spun him around, headed him for the door, and propelled him across the floor with a series of well directed kicks. "Up that gulch, yonder, lays Alasky! You kin git there in fifteen minutes if you pick 'em up an' lay 'em down as fast as God'll let you! When you come to the line you keep on goin'. Don't never show up in the Yukon agin. From now on it's open season fer you the year around. If we don't shoot you on Halfaday, the police'll hang you on the river!" With a parting kick he propelled the man from the doorway, and stood watching the terrified fleeing figure till it disappeared into the gulch. Then he returned to the bar, and eyed Bill Hartley.

"An' now," he said, "we'll look into your case."

Bill cleared his throat, and met the scrutiny of the hard blue eyes. "I killed the man, Slim, in Sheep Camp, after he'd pulled a gun on me," he said. "And I killed this man—"

Black John interrupted with a gesture of impatience. "Yer killin's before you come to Halfaday is yer own business." He paused and prodded the body of Shorty with the toe of his pac. "An', this one was not only justified as a matter of self defense, but praise-worthy in regard to its promptitude. I don't never remember to have seen a prettier killin'. But an' however, layin' all killin's aside, you stand accused of conspirin' along with this here late lamented, an' that damn ornery skunk of a Creech, to obtain Sam Hartley's dust an' claims under false pretences. Such act comes under the headin' of skullduggery, an' as such, con-stitutes a hangable crime on Halfaday—providin' yer convicted by a duly app'inted miners' meetin'." The man paused and glanced toward the door which opened to admit a half dozen men who halted midway of the floor to glance interrogatively from the corpse on the floor to the face of Black John.

"A self defence killin'," explained that worthy. "You kin see for yerselves the corpse's gun is in his hand. He made the fatal mistake of bein' a mite slow fer the job he picked. He can't be regarded as no loss, bein' one of the two damn bushwhackers that shot Sam Hartley. The other, accordin' to reports, met up with similar luck at Sheep Camp. Drag him over to one side, pendin' interment, as a undertaker would say, an' Cush'll buy a drink while I call a miners' meetin'."

"No use callin' a meetin' if it was self defence," opined one.

"This ain't a meetin' to set on the killin'," explained Black John. "It's to try this here party—which he's either Sam Hartley's nephew, er he ain't—fer conspirin' with a couple of other damn crooks, one of which is the corpse, here, an' the other's headin' out into Alasky with such speed as he kin muster, fer to obtain Sam Hartley's dust an' his claims under false pretences. I declare a quorum present an' hereby call the meetin' to order, pausin' only to take a drink, an' remind you not to shirk yer duty—no convicted skulldug has ever left Halfaday in person. I'll state the facts so fer as I know 'em, an' then the prisoner will be give a chanct to try an' git out of it. Meanwhile one of you boys might cut a len'th of rope an' be tyin' the knot, in case the verdick goes contrary to the prisoner's interests."

ONE OF the men stepped into the back room, and returned presently with a rope. All drank and assumed attitudes of decorous attention as Black John took his place at the end of the bar.

"You recollect," he began, "that along in February Sam Hartley was shot in the head on his claim by some party onknown. Well, today a lawyer from Dawson, named Creech, an' the deceased yonder, an' this here defendant come in here, an' the defendant, to wit, either Bill Hartley, or alias Bill Hartley, presents to Cush an order from Corporal Downey fer to turn over to said defendant all, or any part of Sam Hartley's dust which the said Cush is holdin' in his safe.

"The defendant stated in the hearin' of me an' Cush, an' Creech, an' the corpse, that he was Bill Hartley, an' instead of drawin' out the dust, he decided to leave it in the safe, statin' that if Cush's safe was a good enough place fer his Uncle Sam to leave it; it was good enough fer him. Which statement riled

Creech an' the corpse to the extent that the corpse pulled a gun on the defendant with words that signified he meant business. The defendant bein' empty handed at the time, draw'd an' fired with fatal results to the corpse. Whereupon Creech throws up his hands an' begs an' whines not to be shot, until I requests the defendant to lay his gun on the bar, which he done.

"Then, Creech, wrongfully assumin' that we was plumb lawless up here on Halfaday, an' that anything a man might do would be all right, up an' tells how it was him that planned the murder of Sam Hartley, an' that the corpse an' his pardner which defendant claims he killed at Sheep Camp, done the shootin', an' was sent down to knock off Sam Hartley's heir which Creech had notified to come up an' claim Sam's property under a will that Creech had drawed fer Sam. With the heir out of the way, Creech was goin' to run in some chechako fer the heir. But it seems that the defendant, bein' what you might call a confirmed killer, had slew young Hartley on the trail an' stole his watch an' identifyin' papers. So Creech rings him in as the Hartley heir, gettin' an order from the police fer the dust, which it lays there on the bar, an' is Exhibit A. Everything was okay till the defendant refused to draw out the dust, which gummed Creech's game, an' caused the corpse to make his unsuccessful gun play.

"Then Creech proposes to me an' Cush that we do away with the defendant, an' split Sam's dust three ways, statin' that him an' Shorty had planned to knock him off anyhow, before they got back to the big river, an' divide the dust between 'em.

"**THE PROPOSITION** savored of doubtful ethics, an' of course we turned it down, an' I explains to Creech that he's due fer a hangin' as soon as we could git a quorum together. He interposed several objections which was immaterial an' irreverent, an' when I overruled 'em, he got down on his knees an' whined an' begged, an' blubbered. I seen how we wouldn't take no comfort in hangin' such a yellow mongrel, so I kicked his pants out the door an' headed him fer Alasky with a hint that he couldn't show up in the Yukon agin with no safety whatever.

"So with the other two disposed of, that leaves the defendant to face charges of conspirin' to obtain dust under false pretences." The man paused and turned to Bill, who had been listening intently. "You've heard the charges, an' will now be give a chanct to refute 'em, if you kin, or to think up some mitigatin' circumstances. Jest as a matter of form we'll put you under oath, knowin', however, that if a serviceable lie occurred to a man he'd be a damn fool not to use it to save hisself a hangin'. Do you swear to tell the hull truth, er any part of it, s'elp'e God?"

"I do," answered Bill. "The only defense I've got is that I am, in fact, William G. Hartley, nephew of Sam Hartley, and sole heir under his will. Such being the case I am not attempting to obtain Uncle Sam's dust under false pretences."

"Important, if true," admitted Black John, combing at his thick beard with his fingers. "But how you goin' to prove it?"

"The only way I can, is to show you just what I showed Corporal Downey—my customs receipt, watch, bank book, and some tuition receipts from the university."

"Creech claimed you told him they was stole off young Hartley when you knocked him off on the trail from Dyea."

"I told Creech that, so he would make me a party to his scheme. I wanted to get the goods on him—to get evidence that would convict him of the murder of my uncle. I have here two letters that I didn't show to Creech—one from my uncle, and the other from Creech himself, notifying me of my uncle's death." Bill produced the letters, and Black John passed them around, and laid them on the bar.

"They could have be'n stole when you stole his watch an' other papers—an' ondoubtless was. There ain't nothin' conclusive about such evidence. Nevertheless, we don't like to hang a man onless he's guilty. We know'd Sam Hartley, an' liked him. He was a man that minded his own business, an' let other folks mind theirn. If you could describe Sam to us in a convincin' manner, it would go a long ways toward establishin' yer iden-tity."

Bill shook his head. "I haven't seen Uncle Sam since I was fourteen years old. I don't know what he looked like at the time of his death."

"That's pretty thin," growled a man. "Put it to a vote, John, an' let's git it over with."

"You got anything further to say?" asked Black John, turning to Bill.

"Nothing—except to repeat that I am Sam Hartley's heir. If you choose to disregard my only means of identification, I have no way of proving it. If you hang me it'll be murder—that's all."

"Yer p'int ain't well taken," replied Black John. "A miners' meetin', bein' a quasi-legal institution, an' execution in accordance with its verdick, couldn't be deemed a murder. It would only be a quasi-murder, at most. In our efforts to keep Halfaday moral, we figger that it's better to hang a few innocent men ruther than let one guilty one escape. Such hangin's is regrettable, but, in certain cases, onavoidable. We aim to give a prisoner all the breaks he's got comin'. Jest bear in mind that if the verdick happens to go agin you, there ain't nothin' personal in this hangin'. It's a matter of policy."

He turned and addressed the assembled miners: "All right, boys. All in favor of hangin' the said defendant fer skullduggery, signify by holdin' up yer hand an' sayin' 'Aye'."

Several hands went up, and a scattering of 'Aye's were heard.

"Contrary—'No'."

Again several hands went up, and several 'No's were voiced.

"H-u-m," said Black John. "It calls fer a count. Mostly our verdicks is unamerous. Keep them 'No' hands up while I count 'em—one, two, three, four, five. Five fer acquittal. Now, the 'Aye's. Six fer conviction," he announced, after a careful tally. "Clostest verdick we ever had!" He turned to Bill. "Congratulations!" he said. "You damn near won!"

"Go ahead, you damned murderers, and get it over with," retorted Bill, tightlipped.

IGNORING THE retort, Black John addressed the others. "You kin fix the rope an' git all ready—but don't do no hangin' till I git back." Turning abruptly, he left the room and ascended the stairs from whence a few moments later, sounded a shuffling of feet. Then in the doorway to the storeroom a gaunt, bearded form appeared, side by side with Black John, whose supporting arm was about the man's waist.

Slowly the gaunt one's glance swept the assembled faces and came to rest upon the body upon the floor. Suddenly the eyes narrowed and a lean forefinger pointed to the body. "That's one of 'em, damn 'em! One of them two damn coyotes that dry-gulched me!"

"Uncle Sam!" There was a swift movement at the bar, and out from the group that had surrounded him leaped a stalwart young man with a length of rope knotted about his neck.

"Billy!" The gaunt form broke from Black John's arm and lurched toward the younger man. "I know'd you'd come, boy! An', by God, you come a shootin'!" Then as if for the first time noticing the rope, he whirled upon the others. "By God, you don't hang him fer that! Not without—"

A huge arm, half restraining, half supporting was about his shoulders, and he glanced into the face of Black John whose blue eyes were twinkling above his black beard. "We wasn't hangin' him fer that, Sam. You kin see fer yerself the corpse had a gun in his hand. It was fer obtainin' dust under false pretences; but since you've identified him, the hangin's cancelled—the dust not havin' be'n obtained, nor the pretences false. It's a case of trial an' error."

"But," cried the bewildered Bill, "I don't understand! Uncle Sam—"

"Yeah," interrupted Black John, "he was supposed to be dead.

Them two damn assassins left him fer such—but I happened along an' fetched him to my cabin an' nursed him along, an' later we moved him upstairs here in Cush's. Me an' Cush give it out that he was dead—not even another soul on Halfaday know'd he wasn't. We know'd that whoever done it would show up sometime fer Sam's dust, an' when they done so we figgered on settin' in on the game."

"It's a hell of a rough game, I'll say," replied Bill, a smile twisting the corners of his mouth.

"Yeah," admitted Black John, "but not half so rough as it would of be'n if you'd turned out to be someone else than who you are."

"You might as well hang a man as scare him to death," persisted Bill. "You could have brought Uncle Sam in to identify me long ago. Why did you go on with the trial?"

"Two, three reasons. In the first place, if you had be'n an impositor, we'd saved quite a bit of time in havin' the case disposed of. In the second place, I seen that it was a good chanct to warn the boys agin jumpin' at hasty conclusions. An' in the third place, after that pulin', drivlin', exhibition that Creech give, I wanted to take the bad taste out of my mouth by seein' a man with real guts preform under sim'lar circumstances."

"Creech!" exclaimed Sam Hartley. "Where is that damn scoundrel? I know'd he was at the bottom of this, somehow. It was when I suspected him that I sent fer you, Billy!"

"By this time," answered Black John, "Creech should be well into Alasky."

"You mean, you had that damn murderer here an' let him go? Let him git plumb away! Hell's bells, man—he should have be'n turned over to the police!"

"Yeah—an' what fer?" queried Black John. "There ain't a damn thing on him that you kin prove, except that he acted as attorney fer yer nephew here—an' that ain't no crime. He'd of gone scot free—a menace to other folks. I know he's a murderer at heart—that it wasn't his fault he ain't one in fact—an' I debated with myself about tryin' him an' hangin' him as such. It would of served him right. He had it comin'. But I recollected that with you bein' still alive, Downey or some of the police might of questioned the ethics of such hangin'—an' we don't want no dispute with them. So I give him a break. I headed him out into Alasky, with the fear of God in his heart—an' no grub. The nearest settlement bein' on the far side of a hundred miles er more of mountains, what might happen to him out there would be food fer thought. My personal guess is that society at large won't never be hampered by his reappearance."

# Leelanau Historical Society

**Celebrating 150 Years of Leelanau History**

Leelanau County was officially established in 1863 when the State of Michigan was a young 26 years old. People were attracted to the natural resources from the beginning—first as a way to earn a living and build a home, and later to enjoy recreation away from the cities. Early settlers arrived on the islands beginning in 1839, while Native Americans populated the Leelanau peninsula until pioneers began exploring the area in 1847. For the next 45 years, the villages known today—and some that are abandoned—were settled. North and South Manitou Islands and the Fox Islands officially joined the county in 1895.

The Leelanau Historical Society was launched in 1957 by a group of residents dedicated to collecting and preserving Leelanau's history. Leland, first established in 1853 and later the county seat, seemed the natural location for the Society. When the old county jail became available in 1959, the museum found its first home. Through generous donations and grants, a new museum was built in 1985 and later expanded.

Today, the collections and archives contain more than 11,000 items. Visitors to the museum learn about Leelanau life and maritime history from exhibits, educational programs and publications. The Society continues to collect, document and preserve items relating to Leelanau history.

203 East Cedar Street, Leland, MI 49654

Tel. (231) 256-7475

info@LeelanauHistory.org

http://www.leelanauhistory.org/

# THE
# HALFADAY CREEK
## LIBRARY

# JAMES B. HENDRYX

James B. Hendryx's classic series returns to print! The author of more than 50 novels and anthologies, he's best known for his characters set around the outlaw community of Halfaday Creek in the Yukon. Set during the Gold Rush of the late 1890s, Hendryx penned over a hundred stories featuring these characters over the span of 25 years for a variety of pulp magazines.

Now, Altus Press has committed to return these to print. Using the original pulp magazines as the source material, along with the illustrations from their original pulp magazine appearances, these uniform edition books will be augmented with rare material taken from the James B. Hendryx archives held by the Leelanau Historical Society in Leland, MI.

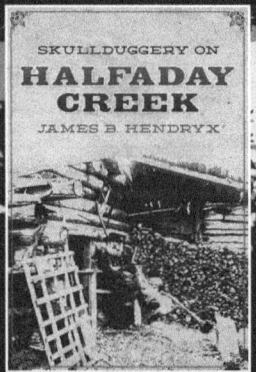